600

Masterpieces

OF

Mystery

Masterpieces

OF

Mystery

The Golden Age: Part One

Selected by ELLERY QUEEN

C O N T E N T S

INTRODUCTION

DEAR READER:

Let us recapitulate the major trends and developments leading up to the writers whose work designated the years between 1920 and 1940 as The Golden Age of the Detective Story.

(1) Edgar Allan Poe is the acknowledged Father of the Detective Story. His first tale of ratiocination, "The Murders in the Rue Morgue," about C. Auguste Dupin, appeared in the April 1841 issue of *Graham's Magazine,* published in Philadelphia. Poe wrote only three more detective stories: "The Mystery of Marie Rogêt," about Dupin, in Snowden's *The Ladies' Companion,* New York, November and December 1842, and February 1843; "The Purloined Letter," about Dupin, in *The Gift: 1845,* Philadelphia, published before October 1844; and "Thou Art the Man," about the first anonymous detective, in *Godey's Lady's Book,* Philadelphia, November 1844. In these four stories Poe created the basic and classic principles of detective-story technique as we know it today.

In the Poe Period, primary emphasis was placed on the intellectual branch of development (analysis and deduction), and secondary emphasis on the sensational branch (the "thriller"). But bear in mind that all periods after Poe inevitably overlap and intermingle.

(2) 1856 to 1894: the Pseudo-Real Life Period in England and the Dime Novel Period, beginning in 1872, in America. "Realism" in England assumed the guise of "reminiscences," "memoirs," etc., and there was a shift in emphasis, both in England and America, to the melodramatic type of detective story, with a strong element of adventure added to the plot structure.

(3) 1866: the first detective novel—Emile Gaboriau's *L'Affair Lerouge.*

(4) 1887: the birth of Sherlock Holmes ("a bombshell") and the beginning of the Doyle Period, with a reversion of emphasis to the analytical and deductive school.

(5) 1894: the beginning of the "medical mystery," culminating in

(6) 1907: the rise of the scientific detective story, reaching its first peak in R. Austin Freeman's stories about Dr. Thorndyke. This represents a major change in trend—from the

whodunit to the *howdunit*. Simultaneously, between 1897 and 1907, the fictional criminal became the protagonist (Grant Allen's Colonel Clay, E. W. Hornung's A. J. Raffles, Maurice Leblanc's Arsène Lupin, etc.).

(7) 1908: the birth of the Had-I-But-Known school, usually credited to Mary Roberts Rinehart.

(8) 1910: the first stage of the Psychological Period—the scientific phase pioneered by William MacHarg's and Edwin Balmer's stories about Luther Trant.

(9) 1912: the birth of the "inverted" detective story, invented by R. Austin Freeman.

(10) 1913: the beginning of naturalism in the detective story, especially in characterization, starting with E. C. Bentley's *Trent's Last Case*.

(11) the 1920's: the reaction from "naturalism," resulting in the birth of the hardboiled school, attributed to Dashiell Hammett, and the beginning of The Golden Age of English and American detective writers.

(12) 1929: the first psychoanalytical detective—Harvey J. O'Higgins's Detective Duff.

(13) the 1930's: The Golden Age in full flower. Simultaneously, the emerging of the "suspense story" and the "crime novel," ushering in the second stage of the Psychological Period, representing another major change in detective development—from the *whodunit* and *howdunit* to the *whydunit*.

The detective stories, particularly the novels, of The Golden Age were characterized by

ingenuity and complexity of plot

originality of concept, including the "locked room," the "miracle problem," and the "impossible crime"

subtle and legitimate misdirection of clues—poetic license—but always with complete fairness to the reader

and often a stunning surprise solution

in a phrase (R. Austin Freeman's), "an exhibition of mental gymnastics"

The 12 stories in this volume—*The Golden Age: Part*

One—offer the work of Earl Derr Biggers (creator of Charlie Chan) and A. A. Milne, and stories about Agatha Christie's Hercule Poirot, Freeman Wills Crofts's Inspector Joseph French, H. C. Bailey's Dr. Reginald (Reggie) Fortune, G. D. H. and M. I. Cole's Superintendent Wilson, Dorothy L. Sayers's Lord Peter Wimsey, Philip MacDonald's Colonel Anthony Gethryn, Edgar Wallace's The Three Just Men, Leslie Charteris's Simon Templar (The Saint), Dashiell Hammett's The Continental Op, and Ellery Queen's E.Q.

The next volume of MASTERPIECES OF MYSTERY *(The Golden Age: Part Two)* will contain 16 stories—about Ellery Queen's E.Q. (one of the bridges from the first decade of The Golden Age to the second), Carter Dickson's (John Dickson Carr's) Colonel March, Anthony Berkeley's Roger Sheringham, David Frome's (Leslie Ford's) Evan Pinkerton, Stuart Palmer's Hildegarde Withers, Patrick Quentin's (Q. Patrick's) Peter and Iris Duluth, Erle Stanley Gardner's Sidney Zoom, Margery Allingham's Albert Campion, Irvin S. Cobb's Judge William Priest, Helen Reilly's Inspector McKee, Rex Stout's Nero Wolfe, Nicholas Blake's Nigel Strangeways, Michael Innes's Inspector John Appleby, Clayton Rawson's The Great Merlini, Ngaio Marsh's Inspector Roderick Alleyn, and Georges Simenon's Inspector Maigret.

Happy detecting!

ELLERY QUEEN

DEAD MAN'S MIRROR

BY AGATHA CHRISTIE

Agatha Christie was born in Devon, England, on September 15, 1890, the daughter of a New Yorker, Frederick Miller, who died when she was a child. She was raised by her mother, who along with their neighbor Eden Phillpotts encouraged her to write. Her first published novel, *The Mysterious Affair at Styles,* introducing Hercule Poirot, was published in 1920. She was divorced from her first husband, Col. Archibald Christie, in 1928 and married archeologist Max E. L. Mallowan in 1930. When she died on January 12, 1976, the Ambassador Theatre dimmed its lights before raising the curtain on her play *The Mousetrap's* 9,612th performance.

THE FLAT WAS A modern one. The furnishings of the room were modern, too. The armchairs were squarely built, the upright chairs angular. A modern writing-table was set squarely in front of the window, and at it sat a small, elderly man. His head was practically the only thing in the room that was not square. It was egg-shaped.

M. Hercule Poirot was reading a letter:

M. Hercule Poirot.

Dear Sir,—A matter has arisen which requires handling with great delicacy and discretion. I have heard good accounts of you, and have decided to entrust the matter to you. I have reason to believe that I am the victim of fraud, but for family reasons I do not wish to call in the police.

I am taking certain measures of my own to deal with the business, but you must be prepared to come down here immediately on receipt of a telegram. I should be obliged if you will not answer this letter.

Yours faithfully,

Gervase Chevenix-Gore

The eyebrows of M. Hercule Poirot climbed slowly up his forehead until they nearly approached the point of disappearing into his hair.

"And who, then," he demanded of space, "is this Gervase Chevenix-Gore?'

He crossed to a bookcase, took out a large fat book, and found what he wanted.

Chevenix-Gore, Sir Gervase Francis Xavier, 10th Bt. cr. 1694; formerly Captain 17th Lancers; b, 18th May, 1879; e.s. of Sir Guy Chevenix-Gore, 9th Bt., and Lady Claudia Bretherton, 2nd d. of 8th Earl of Wallingford. S. father, 1911; m. 1912, Vanda Elizabeth, e.d. of Colonel Frederick Arbuthnot, q.v.; educ. Eton. Served European War, 1914-18. Recreations; traveling, big-game hunting. Address: Hamborough St. Mary, Westshire, and 218 Lowndes Square, S.W.I. Clubs: Cavalry. Travellers.

Poirot shook his head in a slightly dissatisfied manner. For a moment or two he remained lost in thought, then he went to the desk, pulled open a drawer, and took out a little pile of invitation cards.

His face brightened.

"*A la bonne heure!* Exactly my affair! He will certainly be there."

A duchess greeted M. Hercule Poirot in fulsome tones. "So you could manage to come after all, M. Poirot! Why, that's splendid."

"The pleasure is mine, Madame," murmured Poirot, bowing.

He escaped from several important and splendid beings— a famous diplomat, an equally famous actress, a well-known sporting peer—and found at last the person he had come to seek, that invariably "also present" guest, Mr. Satterthwaite.

Mr. Satterthwaite twittered amiably.

"The dear Duchess—I always enjoy her parties. Such a *personality*, if you know what I mean. I saw a lot of her in Corsica some years ago."

Mr. Satterthwaite's conversation was apt to be unduly burdened by mentions of his titled acquaintances. It is possible that he *may* sometimes have found pleasure in the company of Messrs. Jones, Brown, and Robinson, but, if so, he did not mention the fact. And yet, to describe Mr. Satterthwaite as a mere snob and leave it at that would have been to do him an injustice. He was a keen observer of human nature, and if it is true that the looker-on knows most of the game, Mr. Satterthwaite knew a good deal.

"You know, my dear fellow, it is really ages since I saw you. I always feel myself privileged to have seen you work at close quarters in the Crow's Nest business. I feel since then that I am in the know, so to speak. I saw Lady Mary only last week, by the way. A charming creature!"

After passing lightly on one or two scandals of the moment —the indiscretions of an Earl's daughter, and the lamentable conduct of a Viscount—Poirot succeeded in introducing the name of Gervase Chevenix-Gore.

Mr. Satterthwaite responded immediately.

"Ah, now, there *is* a character, if you like! The last of the Baronets—that's his nickname."

"*Pardon*, I do not quite comprehend."

Mr. Satterthwaite unbent indulgently to the lower comprehension of a foreigner.

11

"It's a joke, you know—a *joke*. Naturally, he's not *really* the last Baronet in England—but he *does* represent the end of an era. The Bold Bad Baronet—the mad harum-scarum Baronet so popular in the novels of the last century—the kind of fellow who laid impossible wagers and won 'em."

He went on to expound what he meant. In his younger years Gervase Chevenix-Gore had sailed round the world in a windjammer. He had been on an expedition to the South Pole. He had challenged a peer to a duel. For a wager he had ridden his favorite mare up the staircase of a ducal house. He had once leaped from a box to the stage, and carried off a well-known actress in the middle of her role.

The anecdotes of him were innumerable.

"It's an old family," went on Mr. Satterthwaite. "Sir Guy de Chevenix went on the First Crusade. Now, alas, the line looks as if it is coming to an end. Old Gervase is the last Chevenix-Gore."

"The estate, it is impoverished?"

"Not a bit of it. Gervase is fabulously wealthy. Owns valuable property and in addition he staked out a claim to some mine in Peru or somewhere in South America, when he was a young man, which has yielded him a fortune. An amazing man. Always lucky in everything he's undertaken."

"He is now an elderly man, of course?"

"Yes, poor old Gervase." Mr. Satterthwaite sighed. "Most people would describe him to you as mad as a hatter. It's true, in a way. He *is* mad—not in the sense of being certifiable or having delusions—but mad in the sense of being abnormal. He's always been a man of great originality of character."

"And originality becomes eccentricity as the years go by?" suggested Poirot.

"Very true. That's exactly what's happened to poor old Gervase."

"He has, perhaps, a swollen idea of his own importance?"

"Absolutely. I should imagine that, in Gervase's mind, the world has always been divided into two parts—the Chevenix-Gores and the other people."

"An exaggerated sense of family?"

"Yes. The Chevenix-Gores are all arrogant as the devil—a law unto themselves. Gervase, being the last of them, has got it badly. He is—well, really, you know, to hear him talk, you might imagine him to be—er, the Almighty!"

Poirot nodded thoughtfully.

"Yes, I imagined that. I have had, you see, a letter from him. It was an unusual letter. It did not demand. It summoned!"

"A royal command," said Mr. Satterthwaite.

"Precisely. It did not seem to occur to this Sir Gervase that I, Hercule Poirot, am a man of importance, a man of infinite affairs! That it was extremely unlikely that I should be able to fling everything aside and come hastening like an obedient dog—like a mere . nobody, gratified to receive a commission!"

Mr. Satterthwaite bit his lip in an effort to suppress a smile. It may have occurred to him that where egoism was concerned, there was not much to choose between Hercule Poirot and Gervase Chevenix-Gore.

He murmured, "Of course, if the cause of the summons were urgent—?"

"It was not!" Poirot's hands rose in the air in an emphatic gesture. "I was to hold myself at his disposition, that was all, *in case* he should require me!"

Again the hands rose eloquently, expressing better than words M. Hercule Poirot's sense of utter outrage.

"I take it," said Mr. Satterthwaite, "that you refused?"

"I have not yet had the opportunity," said Poirot slowly.

"But you will refuse?"

A new expression passed over the little man's face. His brow furrowed itself perplexedly.

He said, "How can I express myself? To refuse—yes, that was my first instinct. But I do not know . . . One has, sometimes, a feeling. Faintly, I seem to smell the fish."

Mr. Satterthwaite received this last statement without any sign of amusement.

"Oh?" he said. "That is interesting."

"It seems to me," went on Hercule Poirot, "that a man such as you have described might be very vulnerable—"

"Vulnerable?" queried Mr. Satterthwaite. For the moment he was surprised. The word was not one that he would naturally have associated with Gervase Chevenix-Gore. But he was a man of perception, quick in observation. "I think I see what you mean."

"Such a one is encased, is he not, in an armor—such an armor! The armor of the crusaders was nothing to it—an armor of arrogance, of pride, of complete self-esteem. This armor, it is in some ways a protection—the arrows, the

13

everyday arrows of life glance off it. But there is this danger: Sometimes a man in armor might not even know he was being attacked. He will be slow to see, slow to hear—slower still to feel."

He paused, then asked with a change of manner, "Of what does the family of this Sir Gervase consist?"

"There's Vanda—his wife. She was an Arbuthnot—very handsome girl. She's still quite a handsome woman. Frightfully vague, though. Devoted to Gervase. She's got a leaning toward the occult, I believe. Wears amulets and scarabs and gives out that she's the reincarnation of an Egyptian queen.

"Then there's Ruth—she's their adopted daughter. They've no children of their own. Very attractive girl in the modern style. That's all the family. Except, of course, for Hugo Trent. He's Gervase's nephew.

"Pamela Chevenix-Gore married Reggie Trent and Hugo was their only child. He's an orphan. He can't inherit the title, of course, but I imagine he'll come in for most of Gervase's money in the end. Good-looking lad, he's in the Blues."

Poirot nodded. "It is a grief to Sir Gervase that he has no son to inherit his name?"

"I should imagine it cuts pretty deep."

"The family name, it is a passion with him?"

"Yes."

Mr. Satterthwaite was silent a moment or two. Finally he ventured, "You see a definite reason for going down to Hamborough Close?"

Poirot shook his head.

"No," he said. "As far as I can see, there is no reason at all. But, all the same, I fancy I shall go."

Hercule Poirot sat in the corner of a first-class carriage speeding through the English countryside. Meditatively he took from his pocket a neatly folded telegram, which he opened and reread:

TAKE FOUR THIRTY FROM ST. PANCRAS INSTRUCT GUARD HAVE EXPRESS STOPPED AT WHIMPERLEY.

CHEVENIX-GORE

He folded up the telegram again and put it back in his pocket.

14

The guard on the train had been obsequious. The gentleman was going to Hamborough Close? Oh, yes, Sir Gervase Chevenix-Gore's guests always had the express stopped at Whimperley. "A special kind of prerogative, I think it is, sir."

Since then the guard had paid two visits to the carriage—the first in order to assure the traveler that everything would be done to keep the carriage for himself, the second to announce that the express was running ten minutes late.

The train was due to arrive at 7:50, but it was exactly two minutes past eight when Hercule Poirot descended onto the platform of the little country station and pressed the expected half crown into the attentive guard's hand.

There was a whistle from the engine, and the Northern Express began to move once more. A tall chauffeur in dark green uniform stepped up to Poirot.

"Mr. Poirot? For Hamborough Close?"

He picked up the detective's neat valise and led the way out of the station. A big Rolls was waiting. The chauffeur held the door open for Poirot to get in, arranged a fur rug over his knees, and they drove off.

After ten minutes of cross-country driving, round sharp corners and down country lanes, the car turned in at a wide gateway flanked with huge stone griffins.

They drove through a park and up to the house. The door of it was opened as they drew up, and a butler showed himself on the front step.

"Mr. Poirot? This way, sir."

He led the way down the hall and threw open a door half-way along it on the right.

"Mr. Hercule Poirot," he announced.

The room contained a number of people in evening dress, and as Poirot walked in, his quick eyes perceived at once that his appearance was not expected. The eyes of all present rested on him in unfeigned surprise.

Then a tall woman, whose dark hair was threaded with gray, made an uncertain advance toward him.

Poirot bowed over her hand.

"My apologies, Madame," he said. "I fear that my train was late."

"Not at all," said Lady Chevenix-Gore vaguely. Her eyes still stared at him in a puzzled fashion. "Not at all, Mr.—er—I didn't quite hear—"

"Hercule Poirot."

15

He said the name clearly and distinctly.

Somewhere behind him he heard a sudden sharp intake of breath. At the same time he realized that clearly his host could not be in the room.

He murmured gently, "You knew I was coming, Madame?"

"Oh—oh, yes." Her manner was not conviving. "I think—I mean I suppose so, but I am so terribly impractical, M. Poirot. I forget everything." Her tone held a melancholy pleasure in the fact. "I am told things. I appear to take them in—but they just pass through my brain and are gone! Vanished! As though they had never been."

Then, with a slight air of performing a duty long overdue, she glanced round her vaguely and murmured, "I expect you know everybody."

Though this was patently not the case, the phrase was clearly a well-worn formula by means of which Lady Chevenix-Gore spared herself the trouble of introduction and the strain of remembering people's right names.

Making a supreme effort to meet the difficulties of this particular case, she added, "My daughter—Ruth."

The girl who stood before him was also tall and dark, but she was of a very different type. Instead of the flattish, indeterminate features of Lady Chevenix-Gore, she had a well-chiseled nose, slightly aquiline, and a clear sharp line of jaw. Her black hair swept back from her face into a mass of little tight curls. Her coloring was of carnation clearness and brilliance, and owed little to make-up. She was, Hercule Poirot thought, very easily one of the loveliest girls he had ever seen.

He recognized, too, that she had brains as well as beauty, and guessed at certain qualities of pride and temper. Her voice, when she spoke, came with a slight drawl that struck him as deliberately put on.

"How exciting," she said, "to entertain M. Hercule Poirot! The Old Man arranged a little surprise for us, I suppose."

"So you did not know I was coming, Mademoiselle?" he said quickly.

"I had no idea of it. As it is, I must postpone getting my autograph book until after dinner."

The notes of a gong sounded from the hall, then the butler opened the door and announced, "Dinner is served."

And then, almost before the last word, "served," had been uttered, something very curious happened. The pontifical do-

16

mestic figure became, just for one moment, a highly astonished human being.

The metamorphosis was so quick, and the mask of the well-trained servant was back again so soon, that anyone who had not happened to be looking would have failed to see the change. Poirot, however, *had* been looking. He wondered.

The butler hesitated in the doorway. Though his face was again correctly expressionless, an air of tension hung about his figure.

Lady Chevenix-Gore said uncertainly, "Oh, dear—this is most extraordinary. Really, I—one hardly knows what to do."

Ruth said to Poirot, "This singular consternation, M. Poirot, is occasioned by the fact that my father, for the first time for at least twenty years, is late for dinner."

"It is most extraordinary—" wailed Lady Chevenix-Gore. "Gervase never—"

An elderly man of upright soldierly carriage came to her side. He laughed genially.

"Good old Gervase! Late at last! Upon my word, we'll rag him over this. Elusive collar stud, d'you think? Or is Gervase immune from our common weaknesses?"

Lady Chevenix-Gore said in a low, puzzled voice, "But Gervase is *never* late."

It was almost ludicrous, the consternation caused by this simple *contretemps*. And yet, to Hercule Poirot, it was *not* ludicrous.

Behind the consternation he felt uneasiness—perhaps even apprehension. And he, too, found it strange that Gervase Chevenix-Gore should not appear to greet the guest he had summoned in such a mysterious manner.

In the meantime, it was clear that nobody knew quite what to do. An unprecedented situation had arisen.

Lady Chevenix-Gore at last took the initiative, if initiative it could be called.

"Snell," she said, "is your master—?"

She did not finish the sentence, merely looked at the butler expectantly.

Snell, who was clearly used to his mistress's methods of seeking information, replied promptly to the unspecified question.

"Sir Gervase came downstairs at five minutes to eight, m'lady, and went straight to the study."

"Oh, I see—" Her mouth remained open, her eyes seemed

17

far away. "You don't think—I mean—he heard the gong?"

"I think he must have done so, m'lady, the gong being immediately outside the study door. I did not, of course, know that Sir Gervase was still in the study, otherwise I should have announced to him that dinner was ready. Shall I do so now, m'lady?"

Lady Chevenix-Gore seized on the suggestion with manifest relief.

"Oh, thank you, Snell. Yes, please do."

She said, as the butler left the room, "Snell is such a treasure. I rely on him absolutely. I really don't know what I should *do* without Snell."

Somebody murmured a sympathetic assent, but nobody spoke. Hercule Poirot, watching that room full of people with suddenly sharpened attention, had an idea that all were in a state of tension.

His eyes ran quickly over them, tabulating them roughly. Two elderly men—the soldierly one who had spoken just now, and a thin, spare, gray-haired man with closely pinched legal lips.

Two youngish men—very different in type from each other. One with a mustache and an air of modest arrogance, he guessed to be Sir Gervase's nephew, the one in the Blues. The other, with sleek brushed-back hair and a rather obvious style of good looks, he put down as of a definitely inferior social class.

There were also a small middle-aged woman with pince-nez and intelligent eyes and a girl with flaming red hair.

Snell appeared at the door. His manner was perfect, but once again the veneer of the impersonal butler showed signs of the perturbed human being.

"Excuse me, m'lady, the study door is locked."

"Locked?"

It was a man's voice—young, alert, with a ring of excitement in it. It was the good-looking young man with the slicked-back hair who had spoken. "Shall I go and see—?"

But very quietly Hercule Poirot took command. He did it so naturally that no one thought it odd that this stranger, who had just arrived, should suddenly assume charge of the situation.

"Come," he said. "Let us go to the study." He continued, speaking to Snell, "Lead the way, if you please."

Snell obeyed. Poirot followed close behind him, and, like

a flock of sheep, the others followed behind Poirot.

Snell led the way through the big hall, past the great branching curve of the staircase, past an enormous grandfather clock and a recess in which stood a gong, then along a narrow passage which ended in a door.

Here Poirot passed Snell and gently tried the handle. It turned, but the door did not open. Poirot rapped gently with his knuckles on the panel of the door. He rapped louder. Then, suddenly desisting, he dropped to his knees and applied his eye to the keyhole.

Slowly he rose and looked around. His face was stern.

"Gentlemen," he said, "this door must be broken open immediately!"

Under his direction the two young men, who were both tall and powerfully built, attacked the door. It was no easy matter. The doors of Hamborough Close were solidly built.

At last, however, the lock gave, and the door swung inward with a noise of splintering wood.

And then, for a moment, everyone stood still, huddled in the doorway looking at the scene inside. The lights were on. Along the left-hand wall was a big writing-table, a massive affair of solid mahogany. Sitting, not at the table, but sideways to it, so that his back was directly toward them, was a big man slouched down in a chair. His head and the upper part of his body hung down over the right side of the chair, and his right hand and arm hung limply down.

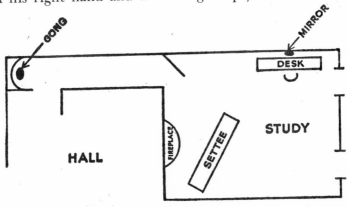

Just below it on the carpet was a small, gleaming pistol.

There was no need of speculation. The picture was clear. Sir Gervase Chevenix-Gore had shot himself.

For a moment or two the group in the doorway stood motionless, staring at the scene. Then Poirot strode forward.

At the same moment Hugo Trent said crisply, "My God, the Old Man's shot himself!"

And there was a long, shuddering moan from Lady Chevenix-Gore.

"Oh, Gervase—Gervase!"

Over his shoulder Poirot said sharply, "Take Lady Chevenix-Gore away."

The soldierly man said, "Come, Vanda, my dear. You can do nothing. Ruth, come and look after your mother."

But Ruth Chevenix-Gore had pressed into the room and stood close by Poirot's side as he bent over the sprawled figure in the chair—the figure of a man of Herculean build with a Viking beard.

She said in a low, tense voice, curiously restrained and muffled, "You're quite sure he's—dead?"

Poirot looked up.

The girl's face was alive with some emotion—an emotion sternly checked and repressed—that he did not quite understand. It was not grief—it seemed more like a kind of half-fearful excitement.

The little woman in the pince-nez murmured, "Your mother, my dear—don't you think—?"

In a high, hysterical voice the girl with the red hair cried out, "Then it *wasn't* a backfire or a champagne cork! It was a *shot* we heard . . ."

Poirot turned and faced them. "Somebody must communicate with the police."

Ruth Chevenix-Gore cried out violently, "No!"

The elderly man with the legal face said, "Unavoidable, I am afraid. Will you see to that, Burrows? Hugo—"

Poirot said, "You are Mr. Hugo Trent?" to the tall young man with the mustache. "It would be well, I think, if everyone except you and I were to leave this room."

Again his authority was not questioned. The lawyer shepherded the others away. Poirot and Hugo Trent were left alone.

The latter said, staring, "Look here—who *are* you? I mean, I haven't the foggiest idea. What are you doing here?"

Poirot took a card case from his pocket and selected a card.

Hugo Trent said, "Private detective—eh? But I still don't see what you are doing *here.*"

"You did not know that your uncle—he was your uncle, was he not—?"

Hugo's eyes dropped for a fleeting moment to the dead man. "The Old Man? Yes, he was my uncle."

"You did not know that he had sent for me?"

Hugo shook his head. "I'd no idea of it."

There was an emotion in his voice that was rather hard to classify. His face looked wooden and stupid—the kind of expression, Poirot thought, that made a useful mask in times of stress.

Poirot said quietly, "We are in Westshire, are we not? I know your Chief Constable, Major Riddle, very well."

Hugo said, "Riddle lives about half a mile away. He'll probably come over himself."

"That," said Poirot, "will be very convenient."

He began prowling round the room. He twitched aside the window curtains and examined the French windows, trying them gently. They were closed.

On the wall behind the desk hung a round mirror. The mirror was splintered. Poirot bent and picked up a small object.

"What's that?" asked Hugo Trent.

"The bullet."

"It passed straight through his head and struck the mirror?"

"It seems so."

Poirot replaced the bullet meticulously where he had found it. He came up to the desk. Some papers were arranged neatly. On the blotting pad itself there was a loose sheet of paper with the word *SORRY* printed across it in large, shaky handwriting.

Hugo said, "He must have written that just before he— did it."

Poirot nodded thoughtfully.

He looked again at the smashed mirror, then at the dead man. His brow creased itself a little as though in perplexity. He went over to the door, where it hung crookedly with its splintered lock.

There was no key in the door, as he knew—otherwise he would not have been able to see through the keyhole. There was no sign of it on the floor. Poirot leaned over the dead man and ran his fingers over him.

"Yes," he said. "The key is in his pocket."

Hugo drew out a cigarette case and lighted a cigarette. He spoke rather hoarsely.

"It seems all quite clear," he said. "My uncle shut himself up in here, scrawled that message on a piece of paper, and then shot himself."

Poirot nodded meditatively as Hugo went on, "But I don't understand why he sent for you."

"That is rather more difficult to explain. While we are waiting, Mr. Trent, for the authorities to take charge, perhaps you will tell me exactly who all the people are whom I saw tonight."

"Who they are?" Hugo spoke almost absently. "Oh, yes, of course. Sorry. Shall we sit down?" He indicated a settee in the farthest corner of the room from the body. He went on, speaking jerkily, "Well, there's Vanda—my aunt, you know. And Ruth, my cousin. Then the other girl is Susan Cardwell. She's just staying here. And there's Colonel Bury. He's an old friend of the family. And Mr. Oswald Forbes. He's an old friend, too, besides being the family lawyer.

"Both the old boys had a passion for Vanda when she was young, and they still hang round in a faithful, devoted sort of way. Ridiculous, but rather touching. Then there's Godfrey Burrows, the Old Man's—I mean my uncle's—secretary, and Miss Lingard, who's here to help him write a history of the Chevenix-Gores. She does research work for writers. That's the lot, I think."

Poirot nodded. "And I understand you actually heard the shot that killed your uncle?"

"Yes, we did. Thought it was a champagne cork—at least, I did. Susan and Miss Lingard thought it was a car backfiring outside—the road runs quite near, you know."

"When was this?"

"Oh, about ten past eight. Snell had just sounded the first gong."

"And where were you when you heard it?"

"In the hall. We were laughing about it—arguing, you know, as to where the sound came from. I said it came from the dining room, and Susan said it came from the direction of the drawing room, and Miss Lingard said it sounded like upstairs, and Snell said it came from the road outside, only it came through the upstairs windows. And Susan said, 'Any more theories?' And I laughed and said there was always murder! Seems pretty rotten to think of now."

"It did not occur to anyone that Sir Gervase might have shot himself?"

Hugo said slowly, "Oh, well, I shouldn't say tnat—"

"You *have* an idea?"

"Yes—well—it's difficult to explain. Naturally I didn't expect him to commit suicide, but all the same I'm not frightfully surprised. The truth is, my uncle was as mad as a hatter, M. Poirot. Everyone knew that."

"That strikes you as a sufficient explanation?"

"Well, people do shoot themselves when they're a bit balmy."

"An explanation of an admirable simplicity."

Hugo stared.

Poirot wandered aimlessly round the room. It was comfortably furnished, mainly in a heavy Victorian style. There were massive bookcases, huge armchairs, and upright chairs of genuine Chippendale. There were not many ornaments, but some bronzes on the mantelpiece attracted Poirot's attention and apparently stirred his admiration.

He picked them up one by one, carefully examining them before replacing them with care. From the one on the extreme left he detached something with a fingernail.

"What's that?" asked Hugo.

"Nothing very much. A tiny sliver of the looking glass, I should say."

Hugo said, "Funny the wa, that mirror was smashed by the shot. A broken mirror means bad luck. Poor old Gervase . . . I suppose his luck had held a bit too long."

"Your uncle was a lucky man?"

Hugo gave a short laugh.

"Why, his luck was proverbial! Everything he touched turned to gold! If he backed an outsider, it romped home. If he invested in a doubtful mine, they struck a vein of ore. He's had the most amazing escapes from tight places. His life's been saved by a kind of miracle more than once. He was rather a fine old boy, in his way, you know. He'd certainly 'been places and seen things'—more than most of his generation."

Poirot murmured in a conversational tone, "You were attached to your uncle, Mr. Trent?"

Hugo Trent seemed a little startled by the question.

"Oh—er—yes, of course," he said rather vaguely. "You know, he was a bit difficult at times. Frightful strain to live with, and all that. Fortunately I didn't have to see much of him."

"*He* was fond of *you?*"

"Not so that you'd notice it! As a matter of fact, he rather resented my existence, so to speak."

"How was that, Mr. Trent?"

"Well, you see, he had no son of his own. He was mad about family and all that sort of thing. I believe it cut him to the quick to know that when he died the Chevenix-Gores would cease to exist. They've been going ever since the Norman Conquest, you know. The Old Man was the last of them. I suppose it *was* rather rotten from his point of view."

"You yourself do not share that sentiment?"

Hugo shrugged. "All that sort of thing seems to me rather out of date."

"What will happen to the estate?"

"Don't really know. I might get it. Or he may have left it to Ruth. Probably Vanda has it for her lifetime."

"Your uncle did not definitely declare his intentions?"

"Well, he had his pet idea."

"And what was that?"

"His idea was that Ruth and I should make a match of it."

"That would doubtless have been very suitable."

"Eminently suitable. But Ruth—well, Ruth has very decided views of her own about life. Mind you, she's an extremely attractive young woman, and she knows it. She's in no hurry to marry and settle down."

Poirot leaned forward. "But you yourself would have been willing, M. Trent?"

Hugo said in a bored tone of voice, "I really can't see it makes a ha'p'orth of difference who you marry nowadays. Divorce is so easy. If you're not hitting it off, nothing is easier than to cut the tangle and start again."

The door opened and Forbes, the family lawyer, entered with a tall, spruce-looking man.

The latter nodded to Trent.

"Hallo, Hugo. I'm extremely sorry about this. Very rough on all of you."

Hercule Poirot came forward. "How do you do, Major Riddle? You remember me?"

"Yes, indeed," The Chief Constable shook hands. "So *you're* down here?"

There was a meditative note in his voice. He glanced curiously at Hercule Poirot.

24

"Well?" said Major Riddle.

It was twenty minutes later. The Chief Constable's interrogative "Well?" was addressed to the police surgeon, a lank man with grizzled hair.

The latter shrugged. "He's been dead over half an hour—but not more than an hour. You don't want technicalities, I know, so I'll spare you them. The man was shot through the head, the pistol being held only a few inches from the right temple. Bullet passed right through the brain and out again."

"Compatible with suicide?"

"Oh, perfectly. The body then slumped down in the chair, and the pistol dropped from his hand."

"You've got the bullet?"

"Yes." The doctor held it up.

"Good," said Major Riddle. "We'll keep it for comparison with the pistol. Glad it's a clear case with no difficulties."

Hercule Poirot asked gently, "You are sure there *are* no difficulties, Doctor?"

The doctor replied slowly, "Well, I suppose you might call one thing a little odd. When he shot himself he must have been leaning slightly over to the right. Otherwise the bullet would have hit the wall *below* the mirror, instead of in the middle."

"An uncomfortable position in which to commit suicide," said Poirot.

The doctor shrugged again. "Oh, well—comfort—if you're going to end it all—" He left the sentence unfinished.

Major Riddle said, "The body can be moved now?"

"Oh, yes. I've done with it until the P.M."

"What about you, Inspector?" Major Riddle spoke to a tall impassive-faced man in plain clothes.

"Okay, sir. We've got all we want. Only the deceased's fingerprints are on the pistol."

The mortal remains of Gervase Chevenix-Gore were removed. The Chief Constable and Poirot were left together.

"Well," said Riddle, "everything seems quite clear and aboveboard. Door locked on the inside, windows fastened, key of door in dead man's pocket. Everything according to Hoyle—but for one circumstance."

"And what is that, my friend?" inquired Poirot.

"*You!*" said Riddle bluntly. "What are *you* doing down here?"

By way of reply, Poirot handed to him the letter he had

received from the dead man a week ago, and the telegram which had finally brought him there.

"Humph," said the Chief Constable. "Interesting. We'll have to get to the bottom of this. I should say it had a direct bearing on his suicide."

"I agree."

"We must check up on who is in the house."

"I can tell you their names. I have just been making inquiries of Mr. Trent."

He repeated the list of names.

"Perhaps you, Major Riddle, know something about these people?"

"I know something of them, naturally. Lady Chevenix-Gore is quite as mad in her own way as old Sir Gervase. They were devoted to each other—and both quite mad. She's the vaguest creature that ever lived, with an occasional uncanny shrewdness that strikes the nail on the head in the most surprising fashion. People laugh at her a good deal. I think she knows it, but she doesn't care. She has absolutely no sense of humor."

"Miss Chevenix-Gore is only their adopted daughter, I understand?"

"Yes."

"A very handsome young lady."

"She's a devilishly attractive girl. Has played havoc with most of the young fellows round here. Leads them all on and then turns round and laughs at them. Good seat on a horse, and wonderful hands."

"That, for the moment, does not concern us."

"Er—no, perhaps not. Well, about the other people. I know old Bury, of course. He's here most of the time. Almost a tame cat about the house. Kind of A.D.C. to Lady Chevenix-Gore. He's a very old friend. They've known him all their lives. I think he and Sir Gervase were both interested in some company of which Bury is a director."

"Forbes, do you know anything of him?"

"I believe I've met him once."

"Miss Lingard?"

"Never heard of her."

"Miss Susan Cardwell?"

"The good-looking girl with red hair? I've seen her about with Ruth Chevenix-Gore the last few days."

"Burrows?"

"Yes, I know him. Chevenix-Gore's secretary. Between you and me, I don't take to him much. He's good-looking, and knows it. Not quite out of the top drawer."

"Had he been with Sir Gervase long?"

"About two years, I fancy."

"And there is no one else—?"

Poirot broke off as a tall, fair-haired man came hurrying in. He was out of breath and looked disturbed.

"Good evening, Major Riddle. I heard a rumor that Sir Gervase had shot himself, and I hurried up here. Snell tells me it's true. It's incredible! I can't believe it!"

"It's true enough, Lake. Let me introduce you. This is Captain Lake, Sir Gervase's agent for the estate. M. Hercule Poirot, of whom you may have heard."

Lake's face lit up with what seemed a kind of delighted incredulity. "M. Hercule Poirot? I'm pleased to meet you. At least—" He broke off, the quick charming smile vanished; he now looked disturbed and upset. "There isn't anything—fishy—about this suicide, is there, sir?"

"Why should there be anything 'fishy,' as you call it?" asked the Chief Constable sharply.

"I mean, because M. Poirot is here. Oh, and because the whole business seems so incredible!"

"No, no," said Poirot quickly. "I am not here on account of the death of Sir Gervase. I was already in the house—as a guest."

"Oh, I see. Funny, he never told me you were coming when I was going over accounts with him this afternoon."

Poirot said quietly, "You have twice used the word 'incredible,' Captain Lake. Are you, then, so surprised to hear of Sir Gervase committing suicide?"

"Indeed I am. Of course, he was mad as a hatter—everyone would agree about that. But all the same, I simply can't imagine his thinking the world would be able to get along without him."

"Yes," said Poirot. "It is a point, that." And he looked with appreciation at the frank, intelligent countenance of the young man.

Major Riddle cleared his throat.

"Since you are here, Captain Lake, perhaps you will answer a few questions."

"Certainly, sir."

Lake took a chair opposite to the other two.

27

"When did you last see Sir Gervase?"

"This afternoon, just before three o'clock. There were some accounts to be checked, and the question of a new tenant for one of the farms."

"How long were you with him?"

"Perhaps half an hour."

"Think carefully, and tell me whether you noticed anything unusual in his manner."

The young man considered. "No, I hardly think so. He was, perhaps, a trifle excited—but that wasn't unusual with him."

"He was not depressed in any way?"

"Oh, no, he seemed in good spirits. He was enjoying himself very much just now, writing up a history of the family."

"How long had he been doing this?"

"He began it about six months ago."

"Is that when Miss Lingard came here?"

"No. She arrived about two months ago, when he had discovered that he could not manage the necessary research work by himself."

"And you consider he was enjoying himself?"

"Oh, enormously! He really didn't think that anything else mattered in the world except his family."

There was a momentary bitterness in the young man's tone.

"Then, as far as you know, Sir Gervase had no worries of any kind?"

There was a slight—a very slight—pause before Captain Lake answered.

"No."

Poirot suddenly interposed a question. "Sir Gervase was not, you think, worried about his daughter in any way?"

"His daughter?"

"That is what I said."

"Not as far as I know," said the young man stiffly.

Poirot said nothing further.

Major Riddle said, "Well, thank you, Lake. Perhaps you'd better stay around."

"Certainly, sir." He rose. "Anything I can do?"

"Yes, you might send the butler here. And perhaps you'd find out for me how Lady Chevenix-Gore is, and if I could have a few words with her presently, or if she's too upset."

The young man nodded and left the room with a quick, decisive step.

"An attractive personality," said Hercule Poirot.

"Yes, nice fellow, and good at his job. Everyone likes him."

"Sit down, Snell," said Major Riddle in a friendly tone. "I've a good many questions to ask you, and I expect this has been a shock to you."

"Oh, it has indeed, sir. Thank you, sir." Snell sat down with such a discreet air that it was practically the same as though he had remained on his feet.

"Been here a good long time, haven't you?"

"Sixteen years, sir, ever since Sir Gervase—er—settled down, so to speak."

"Ah, yes, of course, your master was a great traveler in his day."

"Yes, sir. He went on an expedition to the South Pole and many other interesting places."

"Now, Snell, can you tell me when you last saw your master this evening?"

"I was in the dining room, sir, seeing that the table arrangements were all complete. The door into the hall was open, and I saw Sir Gervase come down the stairs, cross the hall, and go along the passage to the study."

"That was at what time?"

"Just before eight o'clock. It might have been as much as five minutes before eight."

"And that was the last you saw of him?"

"Yes, sir."

"Did you hear a shot?"

"Oh, yes, indeed, sir; but of course I had no idea at the time—how could I have had?"

"What did you think it was?"

"I thought it was a car, sir. The road runs quite near the park wall. Or it might have been a shot in the woods—a poacher, perhaps. I never dreamed—"

Major Riddle cut him short. "What time was that?"

"It was exactly eight minutes past eight, sir."

The Chief Constable said sharply, "How is it you can fix the time to a minute?"

"That's easy, sir. I had just sounded the first gong."

"The first gong?"

"Yes, sir. By Sir Gervase's orders, a gong was always to be sounded seven minutes before the actual dinner gong. Very particular he was, sir, that everyone should be assembled in the drawing room when the second gong went. As soon as I had sounded the second gong, I went to the drawing room and announced dinner."

"I begin to understand," said Hercule Poirot, "Why you looked so surprised when you announced dinner this evening. It was usual for Sir Gervase to be in the drawing room?"

"I'd never known him not be there before, sir. It was quite a shock. I little thought—"

Again Major Riddle interrupted. "And were the others also usually there?" Snell coughed. "Anyone late for dinner, sir, was never asked to the house again."

"H'm, very drastic."

"Sir Gervase, sir, employed a chef who was formerly with the Emperor of Moravia. He used to say, sir, that dinner was as important as a religious ritual."

"And what about his own family?"

"Lady Chevenix-Gore was always very particular not to upset him, sir, and even Miss Ruth dared not be late for dinner."

"Interesting," murmured Hercule Poirot.

"I see," said Riddle. "So, dinner being at a quarter past eight, you sounded the first gong at eight minutes past as usual?"

"That is so, sir—but it wasn't as usual. Dinner was usually at eight. Sir Gervase gave orders that dinner was to be a quarter of an hour later this evening, as he was expecting a gentleman by the late train."

Snell made a little bow toward Poirot as he spoke.

"When your master went to the study did he look worried in any way?"

"I could not say, sir. It was too far for me to judge of his expression."

"Was he alone when he went to the study?"

"Yes, sir."

"Did anyone go to the study after that?"

"I could not say, sir. I went to the butler's pantry after that, and was there until I sounded the first gong at eight minutes past eight."

"That was when you heard the shot?"

"Yes, sir."

Poirot gently interposed a question. "There were others, I think, who also heard the shot?"

"Yes, sir. Mr. Hugo and Miss Cardwell. And Miss Lingard."

30

"These people were also in the hall?"

"Miss Lingard came out from the drawing room, and Miss Cardwell and Mr. Hugo were just coming down the stairs."

Poirot asked, "Was there any conversation about the matter?"

"Well, sir, Mr. Hugo asked if there was champagne for dinner. I told him that sherry, hock, and burgundy were being served."

"He thought it was a champagne cork?"

"Yes, sir."

"But nobody took it seriously?"

"Oh, no, sir. They all went into the drawing room talking and laughing."

"Where were the other members of the household?"

"I could not say, sir."

Major Riddle said, "Do you know anything about this pistol?" He held it out as he spoke.

"Oh, yes, sir. That belonged to Sir Gervase. He always kept it in the drawer of his desk in here."

"Was it usually loaded?"

"I couldn't say, sir."

Major Riddle laid down the pistol and cleared his throat. "Now, Snell, I'm going to ask you a rather important question. I hope you will answer it as truthfully as you can. Do you know of any reason which might lead your master to commit suicide?"

"No, sir. I know of nothing."

"Sir Gervase had not been odd in his manner of late?"

Snell coughed apologetically. "You'll excuse my saying it, sir, but Sir Gervase was always what might have seemed to strangers a little odd in his manner. He was a highly original gentleman, sir."

"Yes, yes, I am quite aware of that."

"Outsiders, sir, did not always understand Sir Gervase."

Snell gave the word the definite value of a capital letter.

"I know. But there was nothing that *you* would have called unusual?"

The butler hesitated. "I think, sir, that Sir Gervase was worried about something," he said at last.

"Worried and depressed?"

"I shouldn't say depressed, sir. But worried, yes."

"Have you any idea of the cause of that worry?"

"No, sir."

31

"Was it connected with any particular person?"

"I could not say, sir. In any case, it is only an impression of mine."

Poirot spoke again. "You were surprised at his suicide?"

"Very surprised, sir. It has been a terrible shock to me. I never dreamed of such a thing."

Riddle glanced at him, then said, "Well, Snell, I think that is all we want to ask you."

"Thank you, sir."

Moving toward the doorway, Snell drew back and stood aside. Lady Chevenix-Gore floated into the room.

She was wearing an Oriental-looking garment of purple and orange silk wound tightly round her body. Her face was serene.

"Lady Chevenix-Gore." Major Riddle sprang to his feet.

She said, "They told me you would like to talk to me, so I came."

"Shall we go into another room? This must be painful for you in the extreme."

Lady Chevenix-Gore shook her head and sat down on one of the Chippendale chairs. She murmured, "Oh, no, what does it matter?"

"It is very good of you, Lady Chevenix-Gore, to put your feelings aside. I know what a frightful shock this must have been and—"

She interrupted him. "It was rather a shock at first," she admitted. Her tone was easy and conversational. "But there is no such thing as Death, really, you know, only Change."

She added, "As a matter of fact, Gervase is standing just behind your left shoulder now. I can see him distinctly."

Major Riddle's left shoulder twitched. He looked at Lady Chevenix-Gore rather doubtfully.

She smiled at him, a vague, happy smile.

"You don't believe, of course! So few people do. To me, the spirit world is quite as real as this one. But please ask me anything you like, and don't worry about distressing me. I'm not in the least distressed. Everything, you see, is Fate. One cannot escape one's Karma. It all fits in—the mirror—everything."

"The mirror, Madame?" asked Poirot.

She nodded her head toward it vaguely.

"Yes. It's splintered, you see. A symbol! You know Tennyson's poem? I used to read it as a girl—though, of course, I didn't realize then the esoteric side of it. 'The mirror crack'd

32

from side to side. "The curse is come upon me!" cried the Lady of Shalott.' That's what happened to Gervase. The Curse came upon him suddenly. I think, you know, most very old families have a curse . . . The mirror cracked. He knew that he was doomed! The Curse had come!"

"But, Madame, it was not a curse that cracked the mirror—it was a bullet!"

Lady Chevenix-Gore said, still in the same sweet, vague manner. "It's all the same thing, really. It was Fate."

"But your husband shot himself."

Lady Chevenix-Gore smiled indulgently.

"He shouldn't have done that, of course. But Gervase was always impatient. He could never wait. His hour had come—he went forward to meet it. It's all so simple, really."

Major Riddle, clearing his throat in exasperation, said sharply, "Then you weren't surprised at your husband's taking his own life? Had you been expecting such a thing to happen?"

"Oh, no." Her eyes opened wide. "One can't always foresee the future. Gervase, of course, was a very strange man, a very unusual man. He was quite unlike anyone else. He was one of the Great Ones born again. I've known that for some time. I think he knew it himself. He found it very hard to conform to the silly little standards of the everyday world."

She added, looking over Major Riddle's shoulder, "He's smiling now. He's thinking how foolish we all are. So we are really. Just like children. Pretending that life is real and that it matters. Life is only one of the Great Illusions."

Feeling that he was fighting a losing battle, Major Riddle asked desperately, "You can't help us at all as to *why* your husband should have taken his life?"

She shrugged her thin shoulders. "Forces move us—you cannot understand. You move only on the material plane."

Poirot coughed. "Talking of the material plane, have you any idea, Madame, as to how your husband has left his money?"

"Money?" she stared at him. "I never think of money." Her tone was disdainful.

Poirot switched to another point. "At what time did you come downstairs to dinner tonight?"

"Time? What is Time? Infinite, that is the answer. Time is infinite."

Poirot murmured, "But your husband, Madame, was rather

particular about time—especially, so I have been told, as to the dinner hour."

"Dear Gervase." She smiled indulgently. "He was very foolish about that. But it made him happy. So we were never late."

"Were you in the drawing room, Madame, when the first gong went?"

"No, I was in my room then."

"Do you remember who was in the drawing room when you did come down?"

"Nearly everybody, I think," said Lady Chevenix-Gore vaguely. "Does it matter?"

"Possibly not," admitted Poirot. "Then there is something else. Did your husband ever tell you that he suspected he was being robbed?"

Lady Chevenix-Gore did not seem much interested in the question. "Robbed? No, I don't think so."

"Robbed, swindled—victimized in some way?"

"No—no—I don't think so. Gervase would have been very angry if anybody had dared to do anything like that."

"At any rate, he said nothing about it to you?"

"No—no." Lady Chevenix-Gore shook her head, still without much interest. "I should have remembered."

"When did you last see your husband alive?"

"He looked in, as usual, on his way downstairs before dinner. My maid was there. He just said that he was going down."

"What has he talked about most in the last few weeks?"

"Oh, the family history. He was getting on so well with it. He found that funny old thing, Miss Lingard, quite invaluable. She looked up things for him in the British Museum—all that sort of thing. She worked with Lord Mulcaster on his book, you know. And she was tactful—I mean, she didn't look up the wrong things. After all, there are ancestors one doesn't want raked up. Gervase was very sensitive. She helped me, too. She got a lot of information for me about Hatshepsut. I am a reincarnation of Hatshepsut, you know."

Lady Chevenix-Gore made this announcement in a calm voice. "Before that," she went on, "I was a Priestess in Atlantis."

Major Riddle shifted a little in his chair.

"Er—er—very interesting," he said. "Well, really, Lady Chevenix-Gore, I think that will be all. Very kind of you."

34

Lady Chevenix-Gore rose, clasping her Oriental robes about her.

"Good night," she said. And then, her eyes shifting to a point behind Major Riddle, "Good night, Gervase dear. I wish you could come, but I know you have to stay here." She added in an explanatory fashion, "You have to stay in the place where you've passed over for at least twenty-four hours. It's some time before you can move about freely and communicate."

She trailed out of the room.

Major Riddle wiped his brow.

"Phew," he murmured. "She's a great deal madder than I thought. Does she really believe all that nonsense?"

"It is possible that she finds it helpful," Poirot said. "She needs, at this moment, to create for herself a world of illusion so she can escape the reality of her husband's death."

"She seems almost certifiable to me," said Major Riddle. "A long farrago of nonsense without one word of sense in it."

"No, no, my friend. The interesting thing is, as Mr. Hugo Trent casually remarked to me, that amid all the vaporing there is an occasional shrewd thrust. She showed it by her remark about Miss Lingard's tact in not stressing undesirable ancestors. Believe me, Lady Chevenix-Gore is no fool."

He paced up and down.

"There are things in this affair that I do not like. No, I do not like them at all."

Riddle looked at him curiously.

"You mean the motive for his suicide?"

"Suicide—suicide! It is all wrong, I tell you. It is wrong psychologically. How did Chevenix-Gore think of himself? As a Colossus, as an immensely important person, as the center of the universe! Does such a man destroy himself? Surely not. He is far more likely to destroy someone else—some miserable, crawling ant of a human being who has dared to cause him annoyance. Such an act he might regard as necessary. But self-destruction? The destruction of such a Self?"

"It's all very well, Poirot. But the evidence is clear enough. Door locked, key in his own pocket, windows closed and fastened. Anything else needed?"

"Yes, there is something else." Poirot sat down in the chair. "Here I am. I am Chevenix-Gore. I am sitting at my desk. I am determined to kill myself because—because, let us say, I have made a discovery concerning some terrific dishonor to

35

the family name. It is not very convincing, that, but it must suffice.

"*Eh bien,* what do I do? I scrawl on a piece of paper the word SORRY. Yes, that is quite possible. Then I open the drawer of the desk, take out the pistol which I keep there, load it, if it is not loaded, and then—do I proceed to shoot myself? No, I first turn my chair round—so, and I lean over a little to the right—so—and then—*then* I put the pistol to my temple and fire!"

Poirot sprang from his chair, and wheeling round, demanded, "I ask you, does that make sense? *Why* turn the chair round? If, for instance, there had been a picture on the wall there, then, yes, there might be an explanation. Some portrait which a man about to die might wish to be the last thing on earth his eyes would see. But a window curtain—*ah non,* that does not make sense."

"He might have wished to look out of the window. Last view of the estate."

"My dear friend, you know that is nonsense. At eight minutes past eight it was dark—no, there must be some other explanation."

"There's only one as far as I can see. Gervase Chevenix-Gore was mad."

Poirot shook his head in a dissatisfied manner.

Major Riddle rose.

"Come," he said. "Let us go and interview the rest of the party. We may get at something that way."

After the difficulties of getting a direct statement from Lady Chevenix-Gore, Major Riddle found considerable relief in dealing with a shrewd lawyer like Oswald Forbes.

Forbes was, in the best legal style, extremely guarded and cautious in his statements, but his replies were all directly to the point.

He admitted that Sir Gervase's suicide had been a great shock to him. He should never have considered Sir Gervase the kind of man who would take his own life. He knew of no possible motive for such an act.

"Sir Gervase was not only my client, he was a very old friend. I have known him since boyhood. I should say that he had always enjoyed life."

"In the circumstances, Mr. Forbes, I must ask you to speak quite candidly. You did not know of any secret anxiety or sorrow in Sir Gervase's life?"

"No. He had minor worries, like most men, but there was nothing of a serious nature."

"No illness? No trouble between him and his wife?"

"No. Sir Gervase and Lady Chevenix-Gore were devoted to each other."

Major Riddle said cautiously, "Lady Chevenix-Gore appears to hold somewhat curious views."

Mr. Forbes smiled. "Ladies,", he said, "must be allowed their fancies."

The Chief Constable went on, "You managed all Sir Gervase's legal affairs?"

"Yes, my firm, Forbes, Ogilvie and Spence, have acted for the Chevenix-Gore family for well over a hundred years."

"Were there ever any scandals in the family?"

Mr. Forbes's eyebrows rose. "Really, I fail to understand you."

"Mr. Poirot, will you show Mr. Forbes the letter you showed me."

In silence Poirot handed the letter to Forbes with a little bow.

Mr. Forbes read it and his eyebrows rose still more.

"A most remarkable letter," he said. "I appreciate your question now. No, so far as my knowledge went, there was nothing to justify the writing of such a letter."

"He was accustomed to confide in you?"

"I think he relied on my judgment."

"And you have no idea as to what this letter refers?"

"I should not like to make any rash speculations."

Major Riddle appreciated the subtlety of this reply. "Now, Mr. Forbes, perhaps you can tell us how Sir Gervase has left his property."

"Certainly. To his wife, Sir Gervase left an annual income of six thousand pounds chargeable to the estate, and the choice of the Dower House or the town house in Lowndes Square, whichever she should prefer. There were, of course, several legacies and bequests, but nothing of an outstanding nature. The residue of his property was left to his adopted daughter, Ruth, on condition that, if she married, her husband should take the name of Chevenix-Gore."

"Was nothing left to his nephew, Mr. Hugo Trent?"

"Yes. A legacy of five thousand pounds."

"And I take it that Sir Gervase was a rich man?"

"He was extremely wealthy. He had a vast private fortune

apart from the estate. Of course, he was not quite so well-off as in the past. Practically all invested incomes have felt the strain. Also, Sir Gervase had dropped a good deal of money over a certain company—the Paragon Synthetic Rubber Substitute, in which Colonel Bury persuaded him to invest a good deal of money."

"Not very wise advice?"

Mr. Forbes sighed. "Retired soldiers are the worst sufferers when they engage in financial operations. I have found that their credulity far exceeds that of widows—and that is saying a good deal."

"But these unfortunate investments did not seriously affect Sir Gervase's income?"

"Oh, no, not seriously. He was still a very rich man."

"When was this will made?"

"Two years ago."

Poirot murmured, "This arrangement, was it not possibly a little unfair to Mr. Hugo Trent, Sir Gervase's nephew? He is, after all, Sir Gervase's nearest blood relation."

Mr. Forbes shrugged. "One has to take a certain amount of family history into account."

"Such as—?"

Mr. Forbes seemed slightly unwilling to proceed.

Major Riddle said, "You mustn't think we're unduly concerned with raking up old scandals or anything of that sort. But this letter of Sir Gervase's to M. Poirot has got to be explained."

"There is certainly nothing scandalous in the explanation of Sir Gervase's attitude to his nephew," said Mr. Forbes quickly. "It was simply that Sir Gervase always took his position as head of the family very seriously. He had a younger brother and sister. The brother, Anthony Chevenix-Gore, was killed in the war. The sister, Pamela, married, and Sir Gervase disapproved of the marriage. That is to say, he considered that she ought to have obtained his consent and approval before marrying. He thought that Captain Trent's family was not of sufficient prominence to be allied with a Chevenix-Gore. His sister was merely amused by his attitude. As a result, Sir Gervase has always been inclined to dislike his nephew. I think that dislike may have influenced him in deciding to adopt a child."

"There was no hope of his having children of his own?"

"No. There was a still-born child about a year after his

marriage. The doctors told Lady Chevenix-Gore that she would never be able to have another child. About two years later he adopted Ruth."

Poirot asked, "And who *was* Mademoiselle Ruth? How did they come to settle upon her?"

"She was, I believe, the child of a distant connection."

"That I had guessed," said Poirot. He look up at the wall which was hung with family portraits. "One can see that she was of the same blood—the nose, the line of the chin. It repeats itself on these walls many times."

"She inherits the temper, too," said Mr. Forbes dryly.

"So I should imagine. How did she and her adopted father get on?"

"Much as you might imagine. There was a fierce clash of wills more than once. But in spite of these quarrels I believe there was also an underlying harmony."

"Nevertheless, might it be said that she caused him a good deal of anxiety?"

"Incessant anxiety. But, I can assure you, not to the point of causing him to take his own life."

"Ah, that, no," agreed Poirot. "One does not blow one's brains out because one has a headstrong daughter! And so Mademoiselle inherits. Sir Gervase, he never thought of altering his will?"

"Ahem!" Mr. Forbes coughed to hide a little discomposure. "As a matter of fact, I took instructions from Sir Gervase on my arrival here—two days ago, that is to say—as to the drafting of a new will."

"What's this?" Major Riddle hitched his chair a little closer. "You didn't tell us this."

Mr. Forbes said quickly, "You merely asked me what the terms of Sir Gervase's will were. I gave you the information for which you asked. The new will was not even properly drawn up, much less signed."

"What were its provisions? They may be some guide to Sir Gervase's state of mind."

"In the main, they were the same as before, but Miss Chevenix-Gore was only to inherit on condition that she married Mr. Hugo Trent."

"Aha," said Poirot. "A very decided difference there."

"I did not approve of the clause," said Mr. Forbes. "And I felt bound to point out that it was quite possible it might be contested successfully. The Court does not look upon such conditional bequests with approval. Sir Gervase, however, was quite decided."

"And if Miss Chevenix-Gore—or, incidentally, Mr. Trent—refused to comply?"

"If Mr. Trent was not willing to marry Miss Chevenix-Gore, then the money went to her unconditionally. But if *he* was willing and *she* refused, then the money went to him instead."

"Odd business," said Major Riddle.

Poirot leaned forward. He tapped the lawyer on the knee. "But what is behind it? What was in the mind of Sir Gervase when he made that stipulation? There must have been something very definite. There must, I think, have been the image of another man—a man of whom he disapproved. I think, Mr. Forbes, that *you* must know who that man was?"

"Really, M. Poirot, I have no information."

"But you could make a guess."

"I never guess," said Mr. Forbes, and his tone was scandalized.

Removing his pince-nez, he wiped them with a silk handkerchief. "Is there anything else that you desire to know?"

"At the moment, no," said the Chief Constable. "Thank you, Mr. Forbes. I should like, if I may, to speak to Miss Chevenix-Gore."

"Certainly. I think she is upstairs with Lady Chevenix-Gore."

"Oh, well, perhaps I'll have a word with—what's his name? —Burrows, first, and the family-history woman."

"They're both in the library. I will tell them."

"Hard work, that," said Major Riddle, as the lawyer left the room. "Extracting information from these old-fashioned legal wallahs takes a bit of doing. The whole business seems to me to center about the girl."

"It would seem so—yes."

"Ah, here comes Burrows."

Godfrey Burrows, the dead man's secretary, came in with a pleasant eagerness to be of use. His smile was discreetly tempered with gloom and showed only a fraction too much teeth. It seemed more mechanical than spontaneous.

"Now, Mr. Burrows, we want to ask you a few questions."

"Certainly, Major Riddle."

"Well, first and foremost, to put it quite simply, have you any ideas of your own about Sir Gervase's suicide?"

"Absolutely none. It was the greatest shock to me."

"You heard the shot?"

"No, I must have been in the library at the time, as far as I can make out. I came down rather early to look up a reference I wanted. The library's right the other side of the house from the study, so I shouldn't hear anything."

"Was anyone with you in the library?" asked Poirot.

"No one."

"You've no idea where the other members of the household were at that time?"

"Mostly upstairs dressing, I should imagine."

"When did you come to the drawing room?"

"Just before M. Poirot arrived. Everybody was there then —except Sir Gervase, of course."

"Did it strike you as strange that he wasn't there?"

"Yes, it did, as a matter of fact. As a rule he was always in the drawing room before the first gong sounded."

"Have you noticed any difference in Sir Gervase's manner lately? Has he been worried? Depressed?"

Godfrey Burrows considered. "No—I don't think so. A little —well, preoccupied, perhaps."

"No financial worries of any kind?"

"He was rather perturbed about the affairs of one particular company—the Synthetic Paragon Rubber Company, to be exact."

"What did he actually say about it?"

Again Godfrey Burrows' mechanical smile flashed, and again it seemed slightly unreal.

"Well, as a matter of fact, what he said was, 'Old Bury's either a fool or a knave. A fool, I suppose. I must go easy with him for Vanda's sake.' "

"And why did he say that—for Vanda's sake?" inquired Poirot.

"Well, you see, Lady Chevenix-Gore was very fond of Colonel Bury, and he worshipped her. Followed her about like a dog."

"Sir Gervase was not jealous at all?"

"Jealous?" Burrows stared and then laughed. "Sir Gervase jealous? He wouldn't know how to go about it. Why, it would never have entered his head that anyone could ever prefer another man to him. Such a thing just couldn't be!"

Poirot said gently, "You did not, I think, like Sir Gervase Chevenix-Gore very much?"

41

Burrows flushed. "Oh, yes, I did. At least—well, all that sort of thing strikes one as rather ridiculous nowadays."

"All what sort of thing?" asked Poirot.

"Well, the feudal motif, if you like. This worship of ancestry, this personal arrogance. Sir Gervase was a very able man in many ways, and had led an interesting life, but he would have been more interesting if he hadn't been so entirely wrapped up in his own egoism."

"Did his daughter agree with you there?"

Burrows flushed again, this time a deep purple. "I should imagine Miss Chevenix-Gore is quite one of the moderns! Naturally, I shouldn't discuss her father with her."

"But the moderns *do* discuss their fathers a good deal," said Poirot.

Major Riddle asked, "And there was nothing else—no other financial anxiety? Sir Gervase never spoke of having been *victimized?*"

"Victimized?" Burrows sounded astonished. "Oh, no."

"And you yourself were on good terms with him?"

"Certainly I was. Why not?"

"I am asking you, Mr. Burrows."

The young man looked sulky.

"Did you know that Sir Gervase had written to M. Poirot asking him to come down here?"

"No."

"Did Sir Gervase usually write his own letters?"

"No, he nearly always dictated them to me."

"You can suggest no reason why he should have written this particular letter himself?"

"No, I can't."

"Ah!" said Major Riddle, adding smoothly, "Rather curious. When did you last see Sir Gervase?"

"Just before I went to dress for dinner. I took some letters to him for his signature."

"What was his manner then?"

"Quite normal. In fact, I should say he was feeling rather pleased with himself."

Poirot stirred a little in his chair.

"Ah?" he said. "So that was your impression, was it? That he was pleased about something. And yet, not so very long afterwards, he shoots himself. It is odd, that!"

Godfrey Burrows shrugged. "I'm only telling you my impression."

42

"Yes, yes, very valuable. After all, you are probably one of the last people who saw Sir Gervase alive."

"Snell was the last person to see him."

"To see him, yes, but not to speak to him."

Burrows did not reply.

Major Riddle said, "What time was it when you went up to dress for dinner?"

"About five minutes past seven."

"What did Sir Gervase do?"

"I left him in the study."

"How long did he usually take to change?"

"He usually gave himself a full three-quarters of an hour, I should say."

"Then, if dinner was at a quarter past eight, he would probably have gone up at half-past seven at the latest?"

"Very likely."

"You yourself went to change early?"

"Yes, I thought I would change and then go to the library and look up the references I wanted."

Poirot nodded thoughtfully.

Major Riddle said, "Well, I think that's all for the moment. Will you send Miss What's-her-name in?"

Little Miss Lingard tripped in almost immediately. She was wearing several bracelets which tinkled a little as she sat down.

"This is all very—er—sad, Miss Lingard," began Major Riddle.

"Very sad indeed," said Miss Lingard decorously.

"You came to this house—when?"

"About two months ago. Sir Gervase wrote to a friend of his in the Museum—Colonel Fotheringay, it was—and Colonel Fotheringay recommended me. I have done a good deal of historical research work."

"Did you find Sir Gervase difficult to work for?"

"Oh, not really. One had to humor him a little, of course. But then I always find one has to do that with men."

With an uneasy feeling that Miss Lingard was probably humoring him at this moment, Major Riddle went on, "Your work here was to help Sir Gervase with the book he was writing?"

"Yes."

"What did that involve?"

For a moment Miss Lingard looked quite human. Her eyes

twinkled as she replied, "Well actually, you know, it involved writing the book! I looked up all the information and made notes, and arranged the material. And then, later, I revised what Sir Gervase had written."

"You must have had to exercise a good deal of tact, Mademoiselle," said Poirot.

"Tact and firmness. One needs them both," said Miss Lingard.

"Sir Gervase did not resent your—er—firmness?"

"Oh, not at all. Of course, I put it to him that he mustn't be bothered with all the petty details."

"Oh, yes, I see."

"It was quite simple, really," said Miss Lingard. "Sir Gervase was perfectly easy to manage if one took him the right way."

"Now, Miss Lingard, I wonder if you know anything that can throw light on this tragedy?"

Miss Lingard shook her head.

"I'm afraid I don't. You see, naturally he wouldn't confide in me at all. I was practically a stranger. In any case, I think he was far too proud to speak to anyone of family troubles."

"But you think it *was* family troubles that caused him to take his life?"

Miss Lingard looked rather surprised.

"But of course! Is there any other suggestion?"

"You feel sure family troubles were worrying him?"

"I know that he was in great distress of mind."

"Oh, you know that?"

"Why, of course."

"Tell me, Mademoiselle, did he speak to you of the matter?"

"Not explicitly."

"What did he say?"

"Let me see. I found that he didn't seem to be taking in what I was saying—"

"One moment. *Pardon.* When was this?"

"This afternoon. We usually worked from three to five."

"Pray go on."

"As I say, Sir Gervase seemed to be finding it hard to concentrate—in fact, he said as much, adding that he had several grave matters on his mind. And he said—let me see—something like this—of course, I can't be sure of the exact words: 'It's a terrible thing, Miss Lingard, when a family has been

44

one of the proudest in the land, that dishonor should be brought on it.' "

"And what did you say to that?"

"Oh, just something soothing. I think I said that every generation had its weaklings—that was one of the penalties of greatness—but their failings were seldom remembered by posterity."

"And did that have the soothing effect you hoped?"

"More or less. We got back to Sir Roger Chevenix-Gore. I had found a most interesting mention of him in a contemporary manuscript. But Sir Gervase's attention wandered again. In the end he said he would not do any more work this afternoon. He said he had had a shock."

"A shock?"

"That is what he said. Of course, I didn't ask any questions. I just said, 'I am sorry to hear it, Sir Gervase.' And then he asked me to tell Snell that M. Poirot would be arriving and to put off dinner until eight fifteen, and send the car to meet the seven-fifty train."

"Did he usually ask you to make these arrangements?"

"Well—no—that was really Mr. Burrows' business. I did nothing but my own literary work. I wasn't a secretary in any sense of the word."

Poirot asked, "Do you think Sir Gervase had a definite reason for asking you to make these arrangements, instead of asking Mr. Burrows to do so?"

Miss Lingard considered.

"Well, he may have had, although I did not think of it at the time. I thought it was just a matter of convenience. Still, it's true now I come to think of it, that he *did* ask me not to tell anyone that M. Poirot was coming. It was to be a surprise, he said."

"Ah, he said that, did he? Very curious, very interesting. And *did* you tell anyone?"

"Certainly not, M. Poirot. I told Snell about dinner and to send the chauffeur to meet the seven-fifty."

"Did Sir Gervase say anything else that may have had a bearing on the situation?"

"No, I don't think so—he was very much strung-up. I do remember that just as I was leaving the room, he said, 'Not that it's any good his coming now. It's too late.' "

"And you have no idea at all what he meant by that?"

"N—no."

45

There was just the faintest suspicion of indecision about the simple negative. Poirot repeated with a frown, " *Too late.* "

Major Riddle said, "You can give us no idea, Miss Lingard, as to the nature of the circumstance that so distressed Sir Gervase?"

Miss Lingard said slowly, "I have an idea that it was in some way connected with Mr. Hugo Trent."

"Why do you think that?"

"Well, it was nothing definite, but yesterday afternoon we were just touching on Sir Hugo de Chevenix—who, I'm afraid, didn't bear too good a character in the Wars of the Roses—and Sir Gervase said, 'My sister *would* choose the family name of Hugo for her son! It's always been an unsatisfactory name in our family. She might have known no Hugo would ever turn out well.' "

"What you tell us is suggestive," said Poirot. "Mademoiselle, you, a stranger, have been here for two months. It would be, I think, very valuable if you were to tell us quite frankly your impressions of the family and household."

Miss Lingard took off her pince-nez and blinked reflectively.

"Well, at first, quite frankly, I felt as though I'd walked straight into a madhouse! What with Lady Chevenix-Gore continually seeing things that weren't there, and Sir Gervase behaving like—like a king—and dramatizing himself in the most extraordinary way—well, I really did think they were the oddest people I had ever come across. Of course, Miss Chevenix-Gore is perfectly normal, and I soon found that Lady Chevenix-Gore is really an extremely kind, nice woman. Nobody could be kinder and nicer to me than she has been. Sir Gervase—well, I really think he *was* mad. His egomania—isn't that what you call it?—was getting worse and worse every day."

"And the others?"

"Mr. Burrows had rather a difficult time with Sir Gervase, I should imagine. I think he was glad that our work on the book gave him a little more breathing space. Colonel Bury was always charming. He was devoted to Lady Chevenix-Gore and he managed Sir Gervase quite well. Mr. Trent, Mr. Forbes, and Miss Cardwell have only been here a few days, so of course I don't know much about them."

"Thank you, Mademoiselle. And what about Captain Lake, the agent?"

"Oh, he's very nice. Everybody liked him."

46

"Including Sir Gervase?"

"Oh, yes, I've heard him say Lake was much the best agent he'd ever had. Of course, Captain Lake had his difficulties with Sir Gervase, too—but he managed pretty well on the whole. It wasn't easy."

Poirot nodded thoughtfully. He murmured, "There was something—something—that I had in mind to ask you—some little thing . . . What was it now?"

Miss Lingard turned a patient face toward him.

Poirot shook his head vexedly. "Tchah! It is on the tip of my tongue."

Major Riddle waited a minute, then as Poirot continued to frown perplexedly, he took up the interrogation once more.

"When was the last time you saw Sir Gervase?"

"At tea-time, in this room.

"What was his manner then? Normal?"

"As normal as it ever was."

"Where did Sir Gervase go after tea?"

"He took Mr. Burrows with him into the study, as usual."

"That was the last time you saw him?"

"Yes. I went to the small morning-room where I worked, and typed a chapter of the book from the notes I had gone over with Sir Gervase, until seven o'clock, when I went upstairs to rest and dress for dinner."

"You actually heard the shot, I understand?"

"Yes, I heard what sounded like a shot and I went out into the hall. Mr. Trent was there, and Miss Cardwell. Mr. Trent asked Snell if there was champagne for dinner, and made rather a joke of it. It never entered our heads to take the matter seriously, I'm afraid."

Poirot said, "Did you hear Mr. Trent say, 'There's always murder'?"

"I believe he did say something like that—joking, of course."

"What happened next?"

"We all came in here."

"Can you remember the order in which the others came down to dinner?"

"Miss Chevenix-Gore was the first, I think, and then Mr. Forbes. Then Colonel Bury and Lady Chevenix-Gore together, and Mr. Burrows immediately after them. I think that was the order, but I can't be quite sure because they more or less came in all together."

"Gathered by the sound of the first gong?"

"Yes. Everyone always hustled when they heard that first gong. Sir Gervase was a terrible stickler for punctuality in the evening."

"What time did he himself usually come down?"

"He was nearly always in the room before the first gong sounded."

"Did it surprise you that he was not down on this occasion?"

"Very much."

"Ah, I have it!" cried Poirot.

As the other two looked inquiringly at him, he went on, "I have remembered what I wanted to ask. This evening, Mademoiselle, as we all went along to the study on Snell's reporting it to be locked, you stooped and picked something up from the floor."

"I did?" Miss Lingard seemed very surprised.

"Yes, just as we turned into the straight passage to the study. Something small and bright."

"How extraordinary—I don't remember. Wait a minute—yes, I do. Only I wasn't thinking. Let me see—it must be in here."

Opening her black satin bag, she poured the contents on a table.

Poirot and Major Riddle surveyed the collection with interest. There were two handkerchiefs, a powder compact, a small bunch of keys, a spectacle case, and one other object on which Poirot pounced eagerly.

"A bullet, by Jove!" said Major Riddle.

The thing was indeed shaped like a bullet, but it proved to be a small pencil.

"That's what I picked up," said Miss Lingard. "I'd forgotten all about it."

"Do you know who this belongs to, Miss Lingard?"

"Oh, yes, it's Colonel Bury's. He had it made out of a bullet that hit him—or rather, didn't hit him, if you know what I mean—in the South African War."

"Do you know when he had it last?"

"Well, he had it this afternoon because I noticed him writing with it on the score pad when I came in to tea."

"Who was playing bridge?"

"Colonel Bury, Lady Chevenix-Gore, Mr. Trent, and Miss Cardwell."

"I think," said Poirot gently, "we will keep this and return it to the Colonel ourselves."

"Oh, please do. I am so forgetful, I might not remember."

"Perhaps, Mademoiselle, you would be so good as to ask Colonel Bury to come here now?"

"Certainly. I will go and find him at once."

She hurried away. Poirot got up and began walking aimlessly round the room.

"We begin," he said, "to reconstruct the afternoon. It is interesting. At half-past two Sir Gervase goes over accounts with Captain Lake. *He is slightly preoccupied.* At three, he discusses the book he is writing with Miss Lingard. *He is in great distress of mind.* Miss Lingard associates that distress of mind with Hugo Trent on the strength of a chance remark. At tea-time *his behavior is normal.* After tea, Godfrey Burrows tells us *he was in good spirits over something.* At five minutes to eight he comes downstairs, goes to his study, scrawls 'Sorry' on a sheet of paper, and shoots himself!"

Riddle said slowly, "I see what you mean. It isn't consistent."

"Strange alternations of moods in Sir Gervase Chevenix-Gore! He is preoccupied—he is seriously upset—he is normal——he is in high spirits! There is something very curious here. And then that phrase he used, '*Too late.*' That I should get here 'Too late.' Well, it is true, that. I *did* get here too late—*to see him alive.*"

"I see. You really think—?"

"I shall never know now why Sir Gervase sent for me."

Poirot was still wandering round the room. He straightened one or two objects on the mantelpiece; he examined a card table that stood against a wall; he opened the drawer of it and took out the bridge score pad.

Then he wandered over to the writing table and peered into the wastepaper basket. There was nothing in it but a paper bag. Poirot took it out, smelled it, murmured, "Oranges," and flattened it out, reading the name on it. "Carpenter and Sons, Fruiterers, Hamborough St. Mary."

Colonel Bury dropped into a chair, shook his head, sighed and said, "Terrible business, this, Riddle. Lady Chevenix-Gore is being wonderful—wonderful. Grand woman! Full of courage!"

Coming softly back to his chair, Poirot said, "You have known her many years?"

"Yes, indeed, I was at her coming-out dance. Wore rosebuds in her hair, I remember. And a white, fluffy dress. . . ."

His voice was full of enthusiasm. Poirot held out the pencil to him.

"This is yours, I think?"

"Eh? What? Oh, thank you. Had it this afternoon when we were playing bridge. Amazing, you know, I held a hundred honors in spades three times running. Never done such a thing before."

"You were playing bridge before tea, I understand?" said Poirot. "What was Sir Gervase's frame of mind when he came in to tea?"

"Usual—quite usual. Never dreamed he was thinking of making away with himself. Perhaps he was a little more excitable than usual, now I come to think of it."

"When was the last time you saw him?"

"Why, then! Tea-time. Never saw the poor chap alive again."

"You didn't go to the study at all after tea?"

"No, never saw him again."

"What time did you come down to dinner?"

"After the first gong."

"You and Lady Chevenix-Gore came down together?"

"No, we—er—met in the hall. I think she'd been into the dining room to see to the flowers—something like that."

Major Riddle said, "I hope you won't mind, Colonel Bury, if I ask you a somewhat personal question. Was there any trouble between you and Sir Gervase over the question of the Synthetic Paragon Rubber Company?"

Colonel Bury's face became suddenly purple. He spluttered a little. "Not at all. Not at all! Old Gervase was an unreasonable sort of fellow. You've got to remember that. He always expected everything he touched to turn out trumps!"

"So there *was* trouble between you?"

"No trouble. Just damned unreasonable of Gervase!"

"He blamed you for certain losses he had sustained?"

"Gervase wasn't normal! Vanda knew that. But she could always handle him. I was content to leave it all in her hands."

Poirot coughed and Major Riddle, after glancing at him, changed the subject.

"You are a very old friend of the family, I know, Colonel Bury. Had you any knowledge as to how Sir Gervase left his money?"

50

"Well, I should imagine the bulk of it would go to Ruth. That's what I gathered from what Gervase let fall."

"You don't think that was at all unfair to Hugo Trent?"

"Gervase didn't like Hugo. Never could stick him."

"But he had a great sense of family. Miss Chevenix-Gore was, after all, only his adopted daughter."

Colonel Bury hesitated, then after humming and hawing a moment, he said, "Look here, I think I'd better tell you something. Strict confidence, and all that."

"Of course."

"Ruth's illegitimate, but she's a Chevenix-Gore all right. Daughter of Gervase's brother, Anthony, who was killed in the War. Seemed he'd had an affair with a typist. When he was killed, the girl wrote to Vanda. Vanda went to see her —girl was expecting a baby. Vanda took it up with Gervase— she'd just been told that she herself could never have another child. Result was, they took over the child when it was born, adopted it legally. The mother renounced all rights in it. They've brought Ruth up as their own daughter and to all intents and purposes, she *is* their own daughter, and you've only got to look at her to realize she's a Chevenix-Gore all right."

"Aha," said Poirot. "I see. That makes Sir Gervase's attitude much clearer. But if he did not like Mr. Hugo Trent, why was he so anxious to arrange a marriage between him and Mademoiselle Ruth?"

"To regularize the family position. It pleased his sense of fitness."

"Even though he did not like or trust the young man?"

Colonel Bury snorted. "You don't understand old Gervase. He couldn't regard people as human beings. He arranged alliances as though the parties were royal personages! He considered it fitting that Ruth and Hugo should marry, Hugo taking the name of Chevenix-Gore. What Hugo and Ruth thought about it didn't matter."

"And was Mademoiselle Ruth willing to fall in with this arrangement?"

Colonel Bury chuckled. "Not she! She's a tartar!"

"Did you know that shortly before his death Sir Gervase was drafting a new will by which Miss Chevenix-Gore would inherit only on condition that she marry Mr. Trent?"

Colonel Bury whistled. "Then he really *had* got the wind up about her and Burrows—"

51

As soon as he had spoken, he bit the words off, but it was too late. Poirot had pounced on the admission.

"There was something between Mademoiselle Ruth and young Monsieur Burrows?"

"Probably nothing in it—nothing at all."

Major Riddle coughed and said, "I think, Colonel Bury, that you must tell us all you know. It might have a direct bearing on Sir Gervase's state of mind."

"I suppose it might," said Colonel Bury doubtfully. "Well, the truth of it is, young Burrows is not a bad-looking chap— at least, women seem to think so. He and Ruth seem to have got as thick as thieves lately, and Gervase didn't like it— didn't like it at all. Didn't like to sack Burrows for fear of precipitating matters. He knows what Ruth's like. She won't be dictated to in any way. So I suppose he hit on this scheme. Ruth's not the sort of girl to sacrifice everything for love. She likes money."

"Do you yourself approve of Mr. Burrows?"

The Colonel delivered himself of the opinion that Godfrey Burrows was slightly hairy at the heel, a pronouncement which baffled Poirot completely, but made Major Riddle smile into his mustache.

A few more questions were asked and answered, and then Colonel Bury departed.

Riddle glanced over at Poirot who was sitting absorbed in thought.

"What do you make of it all, M. Poirot?"

The little man raised his hands.

"I seem to see a purposeful design."

Riddle said, "It's difficult."

"Yes, it is difficult. But more and more one phrase, lightly uttered, strikes me as significant."

"What was that?"

"That laughing sentence spoken by Hugo Trent: 'There's always murder.' "

Riddle said sharply, "Yes, I can see that you've been leaning that way all along."

"Do you not agree, my friend, that the more we learn, the less and less motive we find for suicide? But for murder, we begin to have a surprising collection of motives!"

"Still, you've got to remember the facts—door locked, key in dead man's pocket. Oh, I know there are ways and means. Bent pins, strings—all sorts of devices. It would, I suppose, be *possible*. But do you think those things really work?"

"At all events, let us examine the position from the point of view of murder, not of suicide."

"Oh, all right. As *you* are on the scene, it probably *would* be murder!"

For a moment Poirot smiled.

"I hardly like that remark."

Then he became grave once more. "Yes, let us examine the case from the standpoint of murder. The shot is heard, four people are in the hall—Miss Lingard, Hugo Trent, Miss Cardwell, and Snell. Where are all the others?"

"Burrows was in the library, according to his own story. No one to check that statement. The others were presumably in their rooms, but who is to know if they were really there? Everybody seems to have come down separately. Even Lady Chevenix-Gore and Bury met in the hall. Lady Chevenix-Gore came from the dining room. Where did Bury come from? Isn't it possible that he came, not from upstairs, but *from the study?* There's that pencil."

"Yes, the pencil is interesting. He showed no emotion when I produced it, but that might be because he did not know where I found it and was unaware himself of having dropped it. Let us see, who else was playing bridge when the pencil was in use? Hugo Trent and Miss Cardwell. They're out of it. Miss Lingard and the butler can vouch for their alibis. The fourth was Lady Chevenix-Gore."

"You can't seriously suspect her."

"Why not, my friend? I tell you, me, I can suspect everybody! Supposing that, in spite of her apparent devotion to her husband, it is the faithful Bury she really loves?"

"H'm," said Riddle. "In a way it has been a kind of *ménage à trois* for years."

"And there is some trouble between Sir Gervase and Colonel Bury about this company."

"It's true that Sir Gervase might have been meaning to turn really nasty. We don't know the ins-and-outs of it. It might fit in with that summons to you. Say Sir Gervase suspects that Bury has deliberately fleeced him, but he doesn't want publicity because of a suspicion that his wife may be mixed up in it. Yes, that's possible. That gives either of those two a possible motive. And it *is* a bit odd that Lady Chevenix-Gore should take her husband's death so calmly. All this spirit business may be pure acting!"

"Then there is the other complication," said Poirot. "Miss Chevenix-Gore and Burrows. It is very much to their interest that Sir Gervase should not sign the new will. As it is, she gets everything on condition that her husband takes the family name—"

"Yes, and Burrows' account of Sir Gervase's attitude this evening is a bit fishy. High spirits, pleased about something! That doesn't fit with anything else we've been told."

"There is, too, Mr. Oswald Forbes. Most correct, most severe, of an old and well-established firm. But lawyers, even the most respectable, have been known to embezzle their clients' money when they themselves are in a hole."

"You're getting a bit too sensational, I think, Poirot."

"You think what I suggest is too like the motion pictures? But life, Major Riddle, I find to be often amazingly like the cinema."

"It hasn't been, so far, in Westshire," said the Chief Constable. "We'd better finish interviewing the rest of them, don't you think? It's getting late. We haven't seen Ruth Chevenix-Gore yet, and she's probably the most important of the lot."

"I agree. There is Miss Cardwell, too. Perhaps we might see her first, since that will not take long, and interview Miss Chevenix-Gore last."

"Quite a good idea."

That evening Poirot had given Susan Cardwell only a fleeting glance. He examined her now more attentively. An intelligent face, he thought, not strictly good-looking but possessing an attraction that a merely pretty girl might envy. Her hair was magnificent, her face skillfully made-up. Her eyes, he thought, were watchful.

After a few preliminary questions, Major Riddle said, "I don't know how close a friend you are of the family, Miss Cardwell."

"I don't know them at all. Hugo arranged that I should be asked down here."

"You are a friend of Hugo Trent's?"

"Yes, Hugo's girl friend." Susan Cardwell smiled as she drawled out the words.

"You have known him a long time?"

"Oh, no, just a month or so." She paused and then added, "I'm by way of being engaged to him."

54

"And he brought you down here to introduce you to his people?"

"Oh, dear no, nothing like that. We were keeping it very hush-hush. I just came down to spy out the land. Hugo told me the place was just like a madhouse. I thought I'd better come and see for myself. Hugo, poor sweet, is a perfect pet, but he's got absolutely no brains. The position, you see, was rather critical. Neither Hugo nor I have any money, and old Sir Gervase, who was Hugo's main hope, had set his heart on Hugo making a match of it with Ruth. Hugo's a bit weak, you know. He might agree to this marriage and count on being able to get out of it later."

"That idea did not commend itself to you, Mademoiselle?" inquired Poirot gently.

"Definitely not. Ruth might have refused to divorce him or something. I put my foot down. No trotting off to St. Paul's, Knightsbridge, until I could be there dithering with a sheaf of lilies."

"And you therefore came down to study the situation for yourself?"

"Yes. And, of course, Hugo was right—the whole family was bughouse! Except Ruth, who seems perfectly sensible. She's got her own boy friend and wasn't any keener on the marriage idea than I was."

"You refer to M. Burrows?"

"Burrows? Of course not. Ruth wouldn't fall for a bogus person like that."

"Then who was the object of her affection?"

Susan Cardwell paused, stretched for a cigarette, lit it, and remarked, "You'd better ask *her* that. After all, it isn't my business."

"When was the last time you saw Sir Gervase?"

"At tea."

"Did his manner strike you as peculiar in any way?"

"Not more than usual."

"What did you do after tea?"

"Played billiards with Hugo."

"What about the shot?"

"That was rather odd. You see, I thought the first gong had gone, so I hurried up with my dressing, came dashing out of my room, heard; as I thought, the second gong, and fairly raced down the stairs. I'd been one minute late for dinner the first night I was here and Hugo told me it had

55

just about wrecked our chances with the old man, so I fairly hared down.

"Hugo was just ahead of me and then there was a queer kind of pop-bang and Hugo said it was a champagne cork, but Snell said, 'No,' and besides, I didn't think it had come from the dining room. Miss Lingard thought it came from upstairs, but anyway we agreed it was a backfire, trooped into the drawing room, and forgot about it."

"It did not occur to you that Sir Gervase might have shot himself?" asked Poirot.

"I ask you, should I be likely to think of such a thing? The Old Man seemed to enjoy himself throwing his weight about. I never imagined he'd do such a thing. I can't think why he did it."

"An unfortunate occurrence."

"Very—for Hugo and me. I gather he's left Hugo nothing at all, or practically nothing."

"Who told you that?"

"Hugo got it out of old Forbes."

"Well, Miss Cardwell—" Major Riddle paused a moment. "I think that's all. Do you think Miss Chevenix-Gore is feeling well enough to come down and talk to us?"

"Oh, I should think so. I'll tell her."

Poirot intervened.

"A little moment, Mademoiselle. Have you seen this before?" He held out the bullet pencil.

"Oh, yes, at bridge this afternoon. Belongs to Colonel Bury, I think."

"Did he take it when the rubber was over?"

"I haven't the faintest idea."

"Thank you, Mademoiselle. That is all."

"Right, I'll tell Ruth."

Ruth Chevenix-Gore came into the room like a queen. Her color was vivid, her head held high. But her eyes, like the eyes of Susan Cardwell, were watchful.

She wore the same frock she had on when Poirot arrived. It was a pale shade of apricot. On her shoulder was pinned a salmon-pink rose. It had been fresh and blooming an hour earlier, but now it drooped.

"Well?" said Ruth.

"I'm extremely sorry to bother you," began Major Riddle.

She interrupted him.

"Of course you have to bother me. You have to bother

everyone. I can save you time, though. I haven't the faintest idea why the Old Man killed himself. All I can tell you is that it wasn't a bit like him."

"Did you notice anything amiss in his manner today? Was there anything at all abnormal?"

"I don't think so. I wasn't noticing—"

"When did you see him last?"

"Tea-time."

Poirot spoke, "You did not go to the study—later?"

"No. The last I saw of him was in this room. Sitting there." She indicated a chair.

"I see. Do you know this pencil, Mademoiselle?"

"It's Colonel Bury's."

"Have you seen it lately?"

"I don't really remember."

"Do you know anything of a disagreement between Sir Gervase and Colonel Bury?"

"Over the Paragon Rubber Company, you mean?"

"Yes."

"I should think so. The Old Man was rabid about it!"

"He considered, perhaps, that he had been swindled?"

"He didn't understand the first thing about finance."

Poirot said, "May I ask you a question, Mademoiselle—a somewhat impertinent question?"

"Certainly, if you like."

"It is this—are you sorry that your father is dead?"

She stared at him.

"Of course I'm sorry. I don't indulge in sob stuff. But I shall miss him. I was fond of the Old Man. That's what we called him, Hugo and I, always. The 'Old Man'—you know—something of the primitive-anthropoid-original-Patriach-of-the-tribe business. It sounds disrespectful, but there's really a lot of affection behind it. Of course, he was really the most completely muddle-headed old ass that ever lived!"

"You interest me, Mademoiselle."

"The Old Man had the brains of a bunny! Sorry to have to say it, but it's true. He was incapable of any kind of head-work. Mind you, he was a character—fantastically brave and all that. Could go careering off to the Pole, or fighting duels. I always think that he blustered such a lot because he really knew that his brains weren't up to much. Anyone could have got the better of him."

Poirot took the letter from his pocket.

57

"Read this, Mademoiselle."

She read it through and handed it back to him.

"So that's what brought you here!"

"Does it suggest anything to you, that letter?"

She shook her head.

"No. It's probably quite true. Anyone could have robbed the poor old pet. John says the last agent before him swindled him right and left. You see, the Old Man was so grand and so pompous that he never really condescended to look into details. He was an open invitation to crooks."

"You paint a different picture of him, Mademoiselle, from the accepted one."

"Oh, well—he put up a pretty good camouflage. Vanda backed him for all she was worth. He was so happy stalking round pretending he was God Almighty. That's why, in a way, I'm glad he's dead. It's the best thing for him."

"I do not quite follow you, Mademoiselle."

Ruth said broodingly, "It was growing on him. One of these days he would have had to be locked up."

"Did you know, Mademoiselle, that he was contemplating a will whereby you could inherit his money only if you married Mr. Trent?"

She cried, "How absurd! Anyway, I'm sure that could be set aside by law. I'm sure you can't dictate to people about whom they shall marry."

"If he had actually signed such a will, would you have complied with its provisions, Mademoiselle?"

She stared.

"I—I—"

She broke off. For two or three minutes she sat irresolute, looking down at her dangling slipper. A little piece of earth detached itself from the heel and fell on the carpet.

Suddenly Ruth Chevenix-Gore said, "Wait!"

She got up and ran out of the room. She returned almost immediately with Captain Lake by her side.

"It's got to come out," she said rather breathlessly. "You might as well know now. John and I were married in London three weeks ago."

Of the two of them, Captain Lake looked far more embarrassed.

"This is a great surprise, Miss Chevenix-Gore—Mrs. Lake, I should say," said Major Riddle. "Did no one know of this marriage of yours?"

58

"No, we kept it quite dark. John didn't like that part of it much."

Lake said, stammering a little, "I—I know that it seems rather a rotten way to set about things. I ought to have gone straight to Sir Gervase—"

Ruth interrupted, "And told him you wanted to marry his daughter, and been kicked out on your head and he'd probably have disinherited me, raised hell generally in the house, and we could have told each other how nobly we'd behaved! Believe me, my way was better. If a thing's done, it's done. There would still have been a row—but he'd have come round."

Lake still looked unhappy.

Poirot asked, "When did you intend to break the news to Sir Gervase?"

Ruth answered. "I was preparing the ground. He'd been rather suspicious about me and John, so I pretended to turn my attentions to Godfrey. Naturally, he was ready to go quite off the deep end about *that*. I figured that the news I was married to John would come almost as a relief!"

"Did anybody at all know of this marriage?"

"Yes, I told Vanda. I wanted her on my side."

"And you succeeded?"

"Yes. You see, she wasn't very keen about my marrying Hugo—because he was a cousin, I think. She seemed to think the family was so batty already that we'd probably have completely batty children. That was probably rather absurd, because I'm only adopted, you know. I believe I'm some quite distant cousin's child."

"You are sure Sir Gervase had no suspicion of the truth?"

"Oh, no."

Poirot said, "Is that true, Captain Lake? In your interview with Sir Gervase this afternoon, are you quite sure the matter was not mentioned?"

"No, sir, it was not."

"Because, you see, Captain Lake, there is certain evidence to show that Sir Gervase was in a highly excitable condition after the time he spent with you, and that he spoke once or twice of family dishonor."

"The matter was not mentioned," Lake repeated thinly.

"Where were you at eight minutes past eight this evening?"

"Where was I? In my house. At the end of the village, about half a mile away."

"You did not come up to Hamborough Close about that time?"

"No."

Poirot turned to the girl. "Where were you, Mademoiselle, when your father shot himself?"

"In the garden."

"In the garden? You heard the shot?"

"Oh, yes. But I didn't think about it particularly. I thought it was someone out shooting rabbits, although now I remember I did think it sounded quite close at hand."

"You returned to the house—which way?"

"I came in through this window."

Ruth indicated with a turn of her head the window behind her.

"Was anyone in here?"

"No. But Hugo and Susan and Miss Lingard came in from the hall almost immediately. They were talking about shooting and murders and things."

"I see," said Poirot. "Yes, I think I see now."

Major Riddle said rather doubtfully, "Well—er—thank you. I think that's all for the moment."

Ruth and her husband turned and left the room, hurrying as they neared the door.

"What the devil—" began Major Riddle, and ended rather hopelessly, "It gets more and more difficult to keep track of this business."

Poirot nodded. He had picked up the little piece of earth that had fallen from Ruth's shoe and was holding it thoughtfully in his hand.

"It is like the mirror smashed on the wall," he said. "The dead man's mirror. Every new fact we come across shows us some different angle of the dead man. He is reflected from every conceivable point of view. We shall soon have a complete picture."

He rose and put the little piece of earth tidily in the wastepaper basket.

"I will tell you one thing, my friend. The clue to the whole mystery is the mirror. Go into the study and look for yourself, if you do not believe me."

Major Riddle said decisively, "If it's murder, it's up to you to prove it. If you ask me, I say it's definitely suicide. Did you notice what the girl said about a former agent having swindled old Gervase? I bet Lake told that tale for his own

60

purposes. He was probably helping himself a bit, Sir Gervase suspected it, and sent for you because he didn't know how far things had gone between Lake and Ruth.

"Then this afternoon Lake told him they were married. That broke Gervase up. It was 'too late' now for anything to be done. He determined to get out of it all. In fact, his brain—never very well balanced at the best of times—gave way. In my opinion that's what happened. What have you got to say against it?"

Poirot stood still in the middle of the room.

"What have I to say? This: I have nothing to say against your theory—but it does not go far enough. There are certain things it does not take into account."

"Such as?"

"The discrepancies in Sir Gervase's moods today; the finding of Colonel Bury's pencil; the evidence of Miss Cardwell —which is very important; the evidence of Miss Lingard as to the order in which people came down to dinner; the position of Sir Gervase's chair when he was found; the paper bag which had held oranges; and, finally, the all-important clue of the broken mirror."

Major Riddle stared.

"Are you going to tell me that rigmarole makes *sense?*" he asked.

Hercule Poirot replied softly, "I hope to make it do so—tomorrow."

It was just after dawn when Hercule Poirot awoke the following morning. He had been given a bedroom on the east side of the house.

Getting out of bed. he drew aside the window blind and satisfied himself that the sun had risen, and that it was a fine morning.

He began to dress with his usual meticulous care. Having finished, he wrapped himself in a thick overcoat, a muffler round his neck.

Then he tiptoed out of his room and through the silent house down to the drawing room. He opened the French windows noiselessly, went out into the garden, and followed the terraced walk round the side of the house until he came to the windows of Sir Gervase's study. Here he stopped and surveyed the scene.

Immediately outside the windows was a strip of grass that

ran parallel with the house. In front of that was a wide herbaceous border. The Michaelmas daisies still made a fine show.

In front of the border was the flagged walk where Poirot was standing. A strip of grass ran from the grass walk behind the border to the terrace. Poirot examined it carefully, then shook his head. He turned his attention to the border on either side of it.

Very slowly he nodded his head. In the right-hand bed, distinct in the soft mold, there were footprints.

As he stared down at them, frowning, a sound caught his ears and he lifted his head sharply.

Above him a window had been pushed up. He saw a head of red hair and the intelligent face of Susan Cardwell.

"What on earth are you doing at this hour, M. Poirot? A spot of sleuthing?"

Poirot bowed with utmost correctitude.

"Good morning, Mademoiselle. Yes, it is as you say. You now behold a detective—a great detective, I may say—in the act of detecting!"

"I must remember this in my memoirs," Susan remarked. "Shall I come down and help?"

"I should be enchanted."

"I thought you were a burglar at first. Which way did you get out?"

"Through the drawing-room window."

"Just a minute and I'll be with you."

She was as good as her word. To all appearances Poirot was exactly in the same position as when she had first seen him.

"You are awake very early, Mademoiselle?"

"I haven't been to sleep really. I was just getting that desperate feeling one gets at five in the morning."

"It is not quite so early as that!"

"It feels like it. Now then, my supersleuth, what are we looking for?"

"Observe, Mademoiselle, footprints."

"So they are."

"Four of them," continued Poirot. "See, I will point them out. Two going towards the window, two coming from it."

"Whose are they? The gardener's?"

"Mademoiselle, Mademoiselle! Those footmarks are made by the small dainty high-heeled shoes of a woman. See, convince yourself. Step, I beg of you, in the earth here beside them."

62

Susan hesitated, then placed a foot gingerly onto the mold in the place indicated by Poirot. She was wearing small high-heeled slippers of dark brown leather.

"You see, yours are nearly the same size. Nearly, but not quite. These others are made by a longer foot than yours. Perhaps Miss Chevenix-Gore's—or Miss Lingard's—or even Lady Chevenix-Gore's."

"Not Lady Chevenix-Gore—she's got tiny feet. People did in those days—manage to have small feet, I mean. And Miss Lingard wears queer, flat-heeled things."

"Then they are the marks of Miss Chevenix-Gore's shoes. Ah, yes, I remember she mentioned having been out in the garden yesterday evening."

He led the way back round the house.

"Are we still sleuthing?" asked Susan.

"But certainly. We will go now to Sir Gervase's study."

He led the way, Susan Cardwell following.

The door still hung in a melancholy fashion. Inside, the room was as it had been last night. Poirot pulled the curtains and admitted the daylight.

He stood looking out at the border a minute or two, then he said, "You have not, I presume, Mademoiselle, much acquaintance with burglars?"

Susan Cardwell shook her red head regretfully.

"I'm afraid not, M. Poirot."

"The Chief Constable, he, too, has not had the advantages of a friendly relationship with them. His connection with the criminal classes has always been strictly official. With me that is not so. I had a very pleasant chat with a burglar once. He told me an interesting thing about French windows—a trick that could sometimes be employed if the fastening was sufficiently loose."

He turned the handle of the left-hand window as he spoke; the middle shaft came up out of the hole in the ground, and Poirot was able to pull the two doors of the window toward him. Having opened them wide, he closed them again—closed them without turning the handle, so as not to send the shaft down into its socket.

He let go of the handle, waited a moment, then struck a quick jarring blow high up on the center of the shaft. The jar of the blow sent the shaft down into the socket in the ground—and the handle turned of its own accord.

He turned to Susan in triumph.

63

"You see, Mademoiselle?"

"I think I do."

"The window is now closed. It is impossible to *enter* a room when the window is closed, but it *is* possible to *leave* a room, pull the doors to from outside, then hit it as I did, and the bolt goes down into the ground, turning the handle. The window then is firmly closed, and anyone looking at it would say it had been closed from the *inside*."

"Is that"—Susan's voice shook a little—"is that what happened last night?"

"I think so, Mademoiselle."

Susan said violently, "I don't believe a word of it."

Poirot did not answer. He walked over to the mantelpiece, then wheeled sharply round.

"Mademoiselle, I have need of you as a witness. I have already one witness—Mr. Trent. He saw me find this tiny sliver of looking glass last night. I spoke of it to him. I left it where it was for the police. I even told the Chief Constable that a valuable clue was the broken mirror. But he did not avail himself of my hint. Now you are a witness that I place this sliver of looking glass—to which, remember, I have already called Mr. Trent's attention—into a little envelope— so. And I write on it—so—and seal it up. You are a witness, Mademoiselle?"

"Yes—but—but I don't know what it means."

Poirot walked over to the other side of the room. He stood in front of the desk and stared at the shattered mirror on the wall in front of him.

"I will tell you what it means, Mademoiselle. If you had been standing here last night, looking into this mirror, you could have seen in it *murder being committed . . .*"

For once in her life Ruth Chevenix-Gore—now Ruth Lake —came down to breakfast in good time. Hercule Poirot was in the hall and drew her aside before she went into the dining room.

"I have a question to ask you, Madame."

"Yes?"

"You were in the garden last night. Did you at any time step in the flowerbed outside Sir Gervase's study window?"

Ruth stared at him.

"Yes, twice."

"Ah! *Twice.* How twice?"

64

"The first time I was picking Michaelmas daisies. That was about seven o'clock."

"Was it not rather an odd time of day to pick flowers?"

"Yes, it was, as a matter of fact. I'd fixed the flowers yesterday morning, but Vanda said after tea that the flowers on the dinner table weren't good enough. I had thought they would be all right, so I hadn't done them fresh."

"But then your mother requested you to do them? Is that right?"

"Yes. So I went out just before seven. I took them from that part of the border because hardly anyone goes round there, and so it didn't matter spoiling the effect."

"Yes, but you went there a *second* time, you said?"

"That was just before dinner. I had dropped a spot of brilliantine on my dress—just by the shoulder. I didn't want to bother to change, and none of my artificial flowers went with the yellow of that dress. I remembered I'd seen a late rose when I was picking the Michaelmas daisies, so I hurried out and got it and pinned it on my shoulder."

Poirot nodded his head slowly.

"Yes, I remember that you wore a rose last night. What time was it when you picked that rose?"

"I don't really know."

"But it is *essential,* Madame. Consider—reflect—"

Ruth frowned. She looked swiftly at Poirot and then away again.

"I can't say exactly," she said at last. "It must have been—oh, of course—it must have been about five minutes past eight. It was when I was on my way back round the house that I heard the gong go, and then that funny bang. I was hurrying because I thought it was the second gong and not the first."

"Ah, so you thought that—and did you not try the study window when you stood there in the flowerbed?"

"As a matter of fact, I did. I thought it might be open, and it would be quicker to come in that way. But it was fastened."

"So everything is explained. I congratulate you, Madame."

"What do you mean?"

"That you have an explanation for everything—for the mold on your shoes, for your footprints in the flowerbed, for your fingerprints on the outside of the window. It is very convenient, that."

Before Ruth could answer, Miss Lingard came hurrying down the stairs. There was a queer purple flush on her cheeks, and she looked a little startled at seeing Poirot and Ruth standing together.

"I beg your pardon," she said. "Is anything the matter?"

Ruth said angrily, "I think M. Poirot has gone mad!"

She swept by them and into the dining room. Miss Lingard turned an astonished face on Poirot.

He shook his head.

"After breakfast," he said, "I will explain. I should like everyone to assemble in Sir Gervase's study at ten o'clock."

He repeated this request on entering the dining room.

Susan Cardwell gave him a quick glance, then transferred her gaze to Ruth. When Hugo said "Eh? What's the idea?" she gave him a sharp nudge in the side, and he shut up obediently.

When he had finished his breakfast, Poirot rose and walked to the door. He turned and drew out a large old-fashioned watch.

"It is five minutes to ten. In five minutes—in the study."

Poirot looked round him. A circle of interested faces stared back at him. Everyone was there, he noted, with one exception, and at that very moment the exception swept into the room. Lady Chevenix-Gore came in with a soft, gliding step. She looked haggard and ill.

Poirot drew forward a big chair for her, and she sat down.

She looked up at the broken mirror, shivered, and pulled her chair a little way round.

"Gervase is still here," she remarked in a matter-of-fact tone. "Poor Gervase. He will soon be free now."

Poirot cleared his throat and announced, "I have asked you all to come here so that you may hear the true facts of Sir Gervase's suicide."

"It was Fate," said Lady Chevenix-Gore. "Gervase was strong, but his Fate was stronger."

Colonel Bury moved forward a little.

"Vanda—my dear."

She smiled up at him, then put up her hand. He took it in his. She said softly, "You are such a comfort, Ned."

Ruth said sharply, "Are we to understand, M. Poirot, that you have definitely ascertained the cause of my father's suicide?"

Poirot shook his head, saying, "No, Madame."

"Then what is all this rigmarole about?"

Poirot said quietly, "I do not know the cause of Sir Gervase Chevenix-Gore's suicide, *because Sir Gervase Chevenix-Gore did not commit suicide.* He did not kill himself. *He was killed.*"

"Killed?" Several voices echoed the word. Startled faces were turned in Poirot's direction. Lady Chevenix-Gore looked up, said, "Killed? Oh, no!" and gently shook her head.

"Killed, did you say?" It was Hugo who spoke now. "Impossible. There was no one in the room when we broke in. The windows were fastened. The door was locked on the inside, and the key was in my uncle's pocket. How could he have been killed?"

"Nevertheless, he was killed."

"And the murderer escaped through the keyhole, I suppose?" said Colonel Bury skeptically. "Or flew up the chimney?"

"The murderer," said Poirot, "went out through a window. I will show you how."

He repeated his maneuvers with the window.

"You see?" he said. "That was how it was done! From the first I could not consider it likely that Sir Gervase had committed suicide. He had pronounced egomania, and such a man does not kill himself.

"And there were other things. Apparently, just before his death, Sir Gervase sat down at his desk, scrawled the word *SORRY* on a sheet of notepaper, and then shot himself. But before this last action he had, for some reason or other, altered the position of his chair, turning it so that it was sideways to the desk. Why? There must be some reason. I began to see light when I found, sticking to the base of a heavy bronze statuette, a tiny sliver of looking glass.

"I asked myself, how does a sliver of broken looking glass come to be there?—and an answer suggested itself to me. The mirror had been broken, not by a bullet, *but by being struck with the heavy bronze figure.* That mirror had been broken *deliberately.*

"But why? I returned to the desk and looked down at the chair. Yes, I saw now. It was all wrong. No suicide would turn his chair round, lean over the edge of it, and then shoot himself. The whole thing was arranged. The suicide was a fake!

"And now I come to something very important—the evidence of Miss Cardwell. Miss Cardwell said that she hurried downstairs last night because she thought that the *second* gong had sounded. That is to say, she thought that she had already heard the *first* gong.

"Now observe, *if* Sir Gervase *was* sitting at his desk in the normal fashion when he was shot, where would the bullet go? Traveling in a straight line, it would pass through the door, if the door were open, and *hit the gong!*

"You see now the importance of Miss Cardwell's statement? No one else heard that first gong, but, then, her room is situated immediately above this one, and she was in the best position to hear it. It would consist of only one single note, remember.

"There could be no question of Sir Gervase's shooting himself. A dead man cannot get up, shut the door, lock it, and arrange himself in a convenient position! Somebody else was concerned, and therefore it was not suicide, but murder. Someone whose presence was accepted by Sir Gervase, who stood by his side talking to him.

"Sir Gervase was busy writing, perhaps. The murderer brings the pistol up to the right side of his head and fires. The deed is done! Then quick, to work!

"The murderer slips on gloves. The door is locked, the key put in Sir Gervase's pocket. But supposing that one loud note of the gong has been heard? Then it will be realized that the door was *open,* not *shut,* when the shot was fired. So the chair is turned, the body rearranged, the dead man's fingers pressed on the pistol, the mirror deliberately smashed.

"Then the murderer goes out through the window, jars it shut, steps, not on the grass, but in the flowerbed where footprints can be smoothed out afterwards; then round the side of the house and into the drawing room."

He paused and said, *"There was only one person who was out in the garden when the shot was fired.* That person left her footprints in the flowerbed and her fingerprints on the outside of the window."

He came toward Ruth.

"And there was a motive, wasn't there? Your father had learned of your secret marriage. He was preparing to disinherit you."

"It's a lie!" Ruth's voice came scornful and clear. "There's not a word of truth in your story from start to finish!"

"The proofs against you are very strong, Madame. A jury *may* believe you—or may *not!*"

68

"She won't have to face a jury."

The others turned—startled. Miss Lingard was on her feet. Her face had altered. She was trembling all over.

"*I* shot him. I admit it! I had my reasons. I—I've been waiting for some time. M. Poirot is quite right. I followed him in here. I had taken the pistol out of the drawer earlier. I stood beside him talking about the book—and I shot him. That was just after eight.

"The bullet struck the gong. I never dreamt it would pass right through his head like that. There wasn't time to go out and look for it. I locked the door and put the key in his pocket. Then I swung the chair round, smashed the mirror, and, after scrawling 'Sorry' on a piece of paper, I went out through the window and shut it the way M. Poirot showed you.

"I stepped in the flowerbed, but I smoothed out the foot-prints with a little rake I had put there earlier. Then I went round to the drawing room.

"I had left the window open. I didn't know Ruth had gone out through it. She must have come round the front of the house while I went round the back. I had to put the rake away, you see, in a shed. I waited in the drawing room till I heard someone coming downstairs and Snell going to the gong, and then—"

She looked at Poirot.

"You don't know what I did then?"

"Oh, yes, I do. I found the bag in the wastepaper basket. It was very clever, that idea of yours. You did what children love to do. You blew up the paper bag and then hit it. It made a satisfactory big bang. You threw the bag into the wastepaper basket and rushed out into the hall. You had established the time of the suicide—and also an alibi for yourself.

"But there was still one thing that worried you. You had not had time to pick up the bullet. It must be somewhere near the gong. It was essential that the bullet should be found in the study somewhere near the mirror. I don't know when you had the idea of taking Colonel Bury's pencil—"

"It was just then," said Miss Lingard. "When we all came in from the hall. I was surprised to see Ruth in the room. I realized she must have come from the garden through the window. Then I noticed Colonel Bury's pencil lying on the bridge table. I slipped it into my bag. If, later, anyone saw me pick up the bullet, I could pretend it was the pencil. As a matter of fact, I didn't think anyone saw me pick up the bullet. I dropped it by the mirror while you were looking at the body. When you questioned me, I was very glad I had thought of the pencil."

"Yes, that was clever. It confused me completely."

"I was afraid someone must have heard the real shot, but I knew everyone was dressing for dinner, and would be shut away in their rooms. The servants were in their quarters. Miss Cardwell was the only one at all likely to hear it, and she would probably think it was a backfire. What she did hear was the gong. I thought—I thought everything had gone without a hitch. . . ."

Mr. Forbes said slowly in his precise tones, "This is a most extraordinary story. There seems no motive—"

Miss Lingard said clearly, "There *was* a motive." She added fiercely, "Go on, ring up the police! What are you waiting for?"

Poirot said gently, "Will you all please leave the room? Mr. Forbes, ring up Major Riddle. I will stay here till he comes."

Slowly, one by one, the others filed out of the room. Puzzled, uncomprehending, shocked, they cast abashed glances at the trim, upright figure with its neatly parted gray hair.

Ruth was the last to go. She stood, hesitating in the doorway.

"I don't understand." She spoke angrily, defiantly, accusing Poirot. "Just now, you thought *I* had done it."

"No, no," Poirot shook his head. "No, I never thought that."

Ruth went out slowly.

Poirot was left with the little middle-aged prim woman who had just confessed to a cleverly planned, cold-blooded murder.

"No," said Miss Lingard. "You didn't think she had done it. You accused *her* to make *me* speak. That's right, isn't it?"

Poirot bowed his head.

"While we're waiting," said Miss Lingard in a conversational tone, "you might tell me what made you suspect *me*."

"Several things. To begin with, your account of Sir Gervase. A proud man like Sir Gervase would never speak disparagingly of his nephew to an outsider, especially someone in your position. You wanted to strengthen the theory of suicide. You

70

also went out of your way to suggest that the cause of the suicide was some dishonorable trouble connected with Hugo Trent. That, again, was a thing Sir Gervase would never have admitted to a stranger.

"Then there was the object you picked up in the hall, and the very significant fact that you did not mention that Ruth, when she entered the drawing room, did so *from the garden*. And then I found the paper bag—a most unlikely object to find in the wastepaper basket in the drawing room of a house like Hamborough Close!

"You were the only person who had been in the drawing room when the 'shot' was heard. The paper-bag trick was one that would suggest itself to a woman—an ingenious home-made device. So everything fitted in. The endeavor to throw suspicion on Hugo, and to keep it away from Ruth. The mechanism of crime—and its motive."

The little gray-haired woman stirred.

"You know the motive?' '

"I think so. Ruth's happiness—that was the motive. I fancy that you had seen her with John Lake—you knew how it was with them. And then with your access to Sir Gervase's papers, you came across the draft of his new will—Ruth disinherited unless she married Hugo Trent. That decided you to take the law into your own hands, using the fact that Sir Gervase had previously written to me. You probably saw a copy of that letter. What muddled feeling of suspicion and fear caused him to write originally, I do not know. He must have suspected either Burrows or Lake of systematically robbing him.

"His uncertainty regarding Ruth's feelings made him seek a private investigation. You used that fact and deliberately set the stage for suicide, backing it up by your account of his being very distressed over something connected with Hugo Trent. You sent a telegram to me and reported Sir Gervase as having said I would arrive 'too late.' "

Miss Lingard said fiercely, "Gervase Chevenix-Gore was a bully, a snob, and a windbag! I wasn't going to have him ruin Ruth's happiness."

Poirot said gently, "Ruth is your daughter?"

"Yes—she is my daughter. I've—often—thought about her. When I heard Sir Gervase Chevenix-Gore wanted someone to help him with a family history, I jumped at the chance. I was curious to see my—my girl. I knew Lady Chevenix-Gore wouldn't recognize me. It was years ago—I was young and

71

pretty then, and I had changed my name. Besides, Lady
Chevenix-Gore is too vague to know anything definitely. I
liked her, but I hated the Chevenix-Gore family. They treated
me like dirt. And here was Gervase going to ruin Ruth's life
with his pride and snobbery. But I determined that she should
be happy. And she *will* be happy—*if she never knows about
me!*"

It was a plea—not a question.

Poirot bent his head gently. "No one shall know from me."

Miss Lingard said quietly, "Thank you."

Later, when the police had come and gone, Poirot found
Ruth Lake with her husband in the garden.

She said challengingly, "Did you really think that I had
done it, M. Poirot?"

"I knew, Madame, that you could *not* have done it—because
of the Michaelmas daisies."

"The Michaelmas daisies? I don't understand."

"Madame, there were four footprints and four footprints
only in the border. But if you had been picking flowers there
would have been many more. That meant that between your
first visit and your second, *someone had smoothed all your first
footsteps away.* That could only have been done by the guilty
person, and since your second footprints had *not* been removed, you were *not* the guilty person. You were automati-
cally cleared."

Ruth's face lightened.

"Oh, I see. You know—I suppose it's dreadful, but I feel
sorry for that poor woman. After all, she did confess rather
than let me be arrested—or at any rate, that is what she
thought. That was rather noble in a way. I hate to think of
her going through a trial for murder."

Poirot said gently, "Do not distress yourself. It will not
come to that. The doctor, he tells me that she has serious
heart trouble. She will not live many weeks."

"I'm glad of that." Ruth picked an autumn crocus and
pressed it idly against her cheek. "Poor woman. I wonder why
she did it."

THE HUNT BALL

BY FREEMAN WILLS CROFTS

Freeman Wills Crofts was born in June 1879. He was educated in Belfast. At seventeen he began to study civil engineering and for some years he worked in that capacity for the Irish railways. In 1912 he married Mary Bellas Canning. During a long illness he began to write, and his first book, *The Cask*, published in 1920, is considered a classic in the genre. In 1929 he abandoned engineering and moved to London, where he devoted himself to writing until he died on April 11, 1957. Many of his ingeniously constructed stories featured Inspector Joseph French of Scotland Yard.

HOWARD SKEFFINGTON had reached the end of his tether. He sat, hunched forward and staring unseeingly into the fire, as he faced the terrible conclusion to which inexorably he was being impelled: that his only escape from ruin lay in the death of his former friend, Justin Holt.

He, Howard Skeffington, must murder Holt! If he didn't, this pleasant life he was living, this fortune which seemed almost within his grasp, would be irretrievably lost. He would have to leave the country and everything he valued and look somewhere abroad for a job. And what sort of job could he get?

To a certain extent Skeffington was an adventurer. Possessed of a good appearance, charming manners and an admirable seat on a horse, he had made friends at Cambridge with some of the young men from this Seldon Sorby country, this center of the hunting life in England. At their homes he had spent vacations, riding their horses with skill, if not distinction. Alone in the world and not drawn to any career which involved hard work, he had conceived the idea of settling down at Seldon Sorby, and if possible marrying money.

The first part of this scheme he had carried out successfully. He had taken rooms in the district and been accepted as a member of the hunt. He had joined an associated and very select club and his social prospects seemed flourishing.

But he was up against one difficulty—money. His capital, he had estimated, would last him for four years, and on these four years he had staked his all. If before the end of that period he was unable to bring off the second part of his program, he would be finished: down and out.

His chances in this respect, however, he considered rosy. Elaine Goff-Powell, Sir Richard Goff-Powell's only daughter, would have enough for any husband. Moreover, he was sure she admired him, and he had made himself very agreeable to her father. Elaine was neither a beauty nor a wit: in fact, in moments of depression he realized she was, as he put it, damned plain and damned dull, too. But this gave him all the more hope. It wiped out the most dangerous of his potential competitors. As yet he had not risked a proposal, but he felt the time would soon be ripe and he had little fear of the result.

Unhappily, while the affair was moving, it was not moving quickly enough. Unless an engagement could be achieved soon, his resources would not stand the strain. Another five or six hundred would undoubtedly enable him to pull it off. As it was, the thing would be touch and go.

He had done what he could to borrow, but with indifferent success. Professional money-lenders would not touch him. Friends who might with luck be good for a tenner certainly would not stretch to anything more: and it would take a good many tenners to be of use to Skeffington.

In this difficulty he had embarked on a course which normally he would have avoided like the plague. He had taken to cheating at cards. He realized very fully the risk he ran, but he did not see that any other way was open to him.

For some weeks he had managed successfully, and he had determined to put his fortunes to the test at the Christmas Hunt Ball, which was to take place in a few days. With reasonable luck he would be accepted, and then this dreadfully wearing period of his life would be over.

But now, five days before the ball, disaster had overtaken him. His cheating had been discovered.

And yet not wholly discovered. What happened was this.

During a game at the club one of the men, this Justin Holt, suddenly ceased playing. His face took on an expression of agony, and after swaying about for a moment, his head pitched forward on the table, the cards dropping from his nerveless fingers. The others jumped to their feet, but before they could do anything Holt raised himself. He was covered with confusion and apologized profusely. He had, he explained, got a severe pain and giddiness. It had come so suddenly that for the moment it had bowled him over, but already it was better. Infinitely he regretted breaking up the party, but with the others' consent he would go home and lie down. When they wanted to help he hesitated, then asked Skeffington, who lived in his direction, if he would mind seeing him to his quarters.

The affair puzzled Skeffington, who had never before seen such a seizure. But for him the mystery was soon cleared up. When they were alone Holt suddenly found himself able to walk normally and the expression of pain vanished from his face.

He remained, however, looking extremely worried. "I did that little bit of play-acting for a reason, Skeffington," he said. "The truth is, I saw what you were doing. I've been suspicious for some time, and so, I may tell you, have been a number of the others. But tonight I watched you, and I saw the whole thing. Skeffington, you're finished at Seldon Sorby."

To Skeffington it sounded like a sentence of death, but he quickly pulled himself together. Staring at Holt as coolly as he could, he said: "Perhaps you'll kindly explain what you're talking about?"

Holt shook his head irritably. "Don't be a complete fool," he begged. "I tell you I saw it. There's no use in your pretending. I know."

"You can't know anything," Skeffington returned doggedly. "If you had seen anything at that table, you'd have said so at the time. You didn't."

"I didn't," Holt explained, "for an obvious reason. I have some thought for the hunt, if you haven't. I didn't want to make a scandal. If we had been by ourselves I would have spoken. But with outsiders present naturally I didn't."

"Very thoughtful," Skeffington sneered. "It hasn't occurred to you that your consideration has rendered your story useless? Even if you had seen anything, which I deny, you can't prove it."

"I can tell what I saw."

"That's not proof. I shall deny it and then where will you be? You will have made a libelous statement which you can't prove. I think, my dear Holt, you, and not I, will be the one to retire."

Again Holt shook his head. "That sounds all right, Skeffington, but you know as well as I do that I would be believed. You know, or you ought to, that several of the men suspect you as it is. If I describe what I saw you do, they will believe me."

"You just try it on," Skeffington said as contemptuously as he could. "It doesn't matter what anybody believes or doesn't believe privately. You can prove nothing, and you'll be the one who will suffer."

"That may be," Holt admitted, "but I'll tell you what I shall do. I'll give you three days to think it over. If by then you have sent in your resignation from the hunt, I will never refer to the matter again. If you have not resigned, I shall tell the committee. You do what you like."

76

Though Skeffington had attempted a mild bluff, he knew that Holt had the whip hand. It was true what the man said: he would be believed rather than Skeffington. Holt's transparent honesty was universally recognized, whereas Skeffington was aware that his own reputation was by no means too secure. His phenomenal luck had been remarked on jokingly —or was it jokingly?—by several members, and the somewhat spectacular wins which had produced these remarks would be remembered—if Holt told what he had seen.

Skeffington rapidly considered the matter. He must somehow get Holt to keep his silence. There must be no scandal, for scandal would mean complete ruin. The least breath and all chance of marrying Elaine Goff-Powell would be at an end. Indeed, if he didn't pull off an engagement at the ball next Tuesday, this last hope would be gone. He could not propose again for some weeks, and his money would not stretch to that.

But what could he do to restrain Holt? Nothing! Holt was one of those men who believed in doing what they considered was their duty. No, he could not hope to influence Holt.

Then first occurred to Skeffington the terrible idea that there was a way in which he could silence his enemy. One way: and only one.

Skeffington felt that he was at the most dreadful crisis of his life. To give up his present position, and practically penniless, to begin looking for a job—for which he had no training—would mean destitution, misery and death. And he could look forward to nothing else—if Holt were to live. But could he face the alternative; if Holt were to die? . . . Drops of sweat formed on his forehead.

He realized of course that his future did not depend solely on Holt. If Elaine turned him down he would equally be ruined. Therefore if Elaine turned him down there was no need to consider Holt any more. He was down and out in any case.

But if Elaine accepted him? Then Holt's actions would become vital. In this case . . .

All Skeffington's instincts were now prompting him to gain time. At all costs he must close Holt's mouth till after the ball. Then he, Skeffington, would either disappear and go under, or he would somehow deal with Holt. He turned to the man and spoke quietly and with more hesitation.

"Don't be in a hurry, Holt, I must think this over. Without admitting anything, I see you can do me a lot of harm. You have given me an ultimatum: resign or take the consequences. I want you to compromise."

"Compromise?" Holt was shocked. "How can I compromise on a thing of that sort? Why, it's fundamental! You're not a fool, Skeffington: you must see that."

Skeffington shrugged. "I suppose you're right," he admitted presently. "Well, I'll tell you. I'll agree to your conditions provided you give me six days instead of three to make my arrangements. And what's more: during these six days I promise not to enter the card room. At the end of the six days, if I haven't resigned, you can go to the committee. Hang it all, Holt, that's not too much to ask. I must fix up some reason for the resignation. I'll have an uncle die in America and leave me money, or something of that kind. Then I'll go abroad and that will be the end of me so far as you're concerned."

Holt hesitated.

"Look here," went on Skeffington, "I'll not ask six days. Give me till the ball. We'll meet there and I'll let you have every satisfaction."

"But damn it, Skeffington, you mustn't come to the ball."

This was what Skeffington had feared. He shrugged, then turned away. "Oh well," he said coldly, "if you're going to be unreasonable I withdraw my offer. You tell the committee now, and when I am approached I shall deny everything and ask for your proof. And if you don't give it I shall press for your expulsion, and if you don't leave I shall start proceedings against you for defamation of character. A worse scandal, that, than my going to the ball!" He paused, then continued in a pleasanter tone. "But I don't want to do that. If you will wait till the ball it'll give me a chance to explain my departure. That's all I ask." He suddenly changed his tone. "I'm not attempting any extenuation, Holt, but try and imagine the ruin this means for me. It's not like you to kick a man when he's down."

There had been some further argument and Skeffington had triumphed. Holt had agreed to say nothing provided that at or before the ball Skeffington resigned.

Left alone, Skeffington hardened his heart and began to work out the solution of his terrible problem. First, if Elaine refused him. By borrowing from his friends and selling some

78

of his stuff he could raise, he thought, a couple of hundred pounds. He had better do this at once and buy tickets to the Argentine, where he thought his knowledge of horses might stand him in good stead. No doubt before leaving he could borrow a little more. Enough to get past the immigration laws at all events. It would be hell after what he was accustomed to: but it would be at least a chance for life.

But if Elaine accepted him?

Then he was set up for life with all the money he could want: his future absolutely assured—if only Holt were dealt with.

Skeffington took care to speak to various members of the committee and others to whom Holt might have told his story, and in every case he was satisfied from their manner that they had heard nothing. Holt therefore was the only danger. If he were silenced, Skeffington would be safe.

For three days Skeffington thought over the problem and then at last he saw how the man might be eliminated, and with absolute secrecy. Admittedly there would be a little risk at one point, but that point once passed, no further hitch could arise. Carefully Skeffington made his preparations. He avoided the club on the excuse of private business and kept rigorously out of Holt's way.

At last the fateful night arrived, a dark and bitter evening with the ground like iron and a frosty fog in the air. The Christmas Hunt Ball was *the* social event of the year, when the local four hundred thronged the Seldon Sorby Town Hall and everyone who was anyone felt he must be present. The somewhat drab building was transformed out of all recognition with bunting and greenery, and the hunt colors made the gathering what the local paper invariably called a spectacle of sparkling brilliance.

The first two essentials of Skeffington's plan were to drive some people to the ball and to park his car in a secluded place near the back entrance of the hall. The former he managed by inviting a young married couple called Hatherley and a bachelor friend named Scarlett to accompany him, the second by a careful timing of his arrival, coupled with his knowledge of how the park filled. The market at the back of the hall was used as a park, and there he succeeded in placing the car in the corner he desired. He knew that before long it would be completely surrounded and that no one was likely to remain near it.

In the car, hooked up under the dash, was a heavy spanner round which he had wrapped a soft cloth. It was so fixed that he could lift it out by simply opening the door and putting in his hand.

He had taken just enough whisky to steady his nerves, and in spite of the terrible deed which was in front of him, he felt confident and in his best form.

To his delight Elaine had greeted him with more than her usual warmth. For half the evening he had danced exclusively with her, and now he led her to a deserted corner and with trepidation put the vital question. A thrill of overwhelming satisfaction shot through him when he heard the answer. Elaine would marry him, and further would agree to the engagement being announced at once.

But that thrill was accompanied by a pang of something not far removed from actual horror. To preserve what he had won he must now pass through the most hideous ten minutes of his life. Now also he realized that here would be more danger in the affair than he had anticipated. However, there was no alternative. The thing must be faced.

When he judged the time propitious—when the chauffeurs were at supper—he told Elaine that he wished to ask her father's blessing on the engagement. She suggested accompanying him, and he had to use all his tact to prevent her. However, by assuring her that he could speak more movingly of her goodness and charm if she were not present, he was able to leave her dancing with Scarlett.

Instead of seeking out Sir Richard Goff-Powell, Skeffington found Holt. Waiting till he had handed on his partner, he passed him, and without stopping, murmured: "Come to the cloak room. I've something to show you."

Skeffington hung about the passages till Holt hove in sight. "I've decided to resign," he said in a low voice, "but I've got a strange letter which I wish to show you. We can't talk here in private. Come out to my car and let me explain what has arisen."

Holt was unwilling, but Skeffington persuaded him by the argument that if they were seen discussing confidential matters, it might connect him with the resignation.

Skeffington passed out to the park, followed by his victim. Though the tops of the cars were faintly illuminated by distant lights, the spaces between them were dark as pitch. As they walked Skeffington removed his immaculate gloves, fearing tell-tale stains or even smears of blood. He was satisfied that they reached the car unobserved.

"Here's the letter," he said, opening the forward door and taking a paper from a cubby-hole. "My inside light has failed, but the letter's very short and you can read it by the side light. I'll switch it on. Then we can get in out of the cold and discuss it."

Holt, grumbling about being brought out of the warm hall, moved forward to the front of the wing to bring the paper to the lamp. In doing so he momentarily turned his back to Skeffington.

To produce this movement had been Skeffington's aim. Instead of switching on the light, his fingers grasped the spanner, and as Holt made that slight turn he brought the heavy tool down with all his force on the man's head. Holt dropped like a log.

With a tiny pocket torch Skeffington glanced at his victim's head. It was all right. There was no blood, but there was deformation of the bone. There could be no doubt that Holt was dead.

Hastily Skeffington completed his program. Opening the rear door of his car, he tried to lift the body in. This he found more difficult than he had expected. He had to leave it sitting on the floor propped up against the seat and go to the other side of the car and draw it in after him, returning to lift in the feet, one by one. He left it on the floor covered with a rug, then hastened back to the hall. This time also he was sure he was unobserved. A wash, a brush and a stiff glass of whisky, and he was once more in the ballroom.

He would have given anything to have slipped off to his rooms, but he daren't do so. Instead he found Sir Richard, and taking his courage in both hands, he went up to him.

"I have something to tell you, sir," he began, "and I most sincerely hope you will be pleased. Elaine has done me the honor to say she will marry me," and he expatiated on his news.

Sir Richard did not appear particularly pleased, but neither did he raise any objection. He shrugged and said the matter was one for Elaine. As soon as Skeffington could, he returned to the young woman.

How he endured to the end of the proceedings Skeffington scarcely knew. But at long last Elaine departed with her family and he went in search of his friends.

"I'll bring the car to the steps," he told the Hatherleys, then adding to Scarlett: "You might come and help me if you don't mind. It's a job to get out of such a jam."

Reaching the car, Skeffington opened the near forward door for Scarlett, then went round to the driver's side and got in himself. He thus had a witness of all his proceedings, while Scarlett had not seen the body.

As Skeffington pulled in to the steps a commissionaire opened the rear door for Mrs. Hatherley. He lifted away the rug, then swore hoarsely while Mrs. Hatherley gave a shrill scream.

What happened then seemed a confused muddle to Skeffington. He got out and tried to edge round to the door through the dense crowd which had instantly formed.

"What is it?" he heard himself shouting. "What's wrong?"

He heard murmurs all about him. "A man!" "Seems to be dead!" "There in the back of the car!"—then an authoritative voice which he recognized as that of the Chief Constable of the county: "Keep back everyone, please, and let Dr. Hackett pass. Doctor, will you please have a look here."

Everyone but Skeffington and Scarlett moved back. For a moment time seemed to stand still, then the doctor said slowly: "It's Holt and I'm afraid he's dead. A blow on the head. Must have been instantaneous."

Time began to move once more, in fact it now raced so quickly that Skeffington could hardly keep up with it.

As if by magic police appeared. The guests were politely herded back into the ballrooms. Skeffington was asked by a sharp-looking young inspector if he could give any explanation of the affair, and when he replied that he could not, he was told not so politely to wait where he was for a further interrogation.

The whole place buzzed as if a swarm of colossal bees had invaded it. Then gradually people began to leave, their names and addresses taken and a few questions put and answered. At long last the police returned to Skeffington.

He had taken a little more whisky, enough to subdue his fear and steady his hands, but not enough to make him stupid.

"Will you tell me what you know of this affair, Mr. Skeffington?" asked the local superintendent, who had now arrived and taken charge of the proceedings.

Skeffington replied without hesitation. He had driven Mr.

and Mrs. Hatherley and Mr. Scarlett to the ball. He had parked in the corner of the market. All had then got out and gone into the hall. When Mrs. Hatherley was ready to go home he and Scarlett had gone for the car. He had driven it to the steps and when the rear door had been opened the body had been found. The affair was just as great a mystery to him as to the super.

It was a simple story and Skeffington told it well. Superintendent Redfern asked many questions, but he could not in any way shake the tale, and at last he thanked Skeffington and said that would be all.

Rather shakily Skeffington drove home.*

During the next couple of days events moved quickly at police headquarters at Seldon Sorby. The place had been shaken to the core. Such a murder, taking place at the most fashionable event in the town's year, and involving the death of a relative of Lord Bonniton, the master of the most famous hunt in the country, seemed almost a national disaster. The Chief Constable was frantic and without delay had wired to Scotland Yard for help. A couple of hours later Chief Inspector French and Sergeant Carter had arrived to assist in the inquiry. French had heard all that had been done, had studied the various statements made, and had examined the Town Hall and market. As he had not thereupon laid his hand on the guilty party, the Chief Constable had asked querulous and suggestive questions.

"Silly fool," French grumbled to Carter that night at their hotel. "Does he think we're thought readers? If he was in all that hurry, why didn't he do the job himself?"

Later that evening French sat smoking over the lounge fire and imbibing cup after cup of strong coffee, as he puzzled his brains in the attempt to find some line of investigation which would give him his solution. He had put in train all the obvious inquiries: about Holt's career and recent activities, who had seen him at the ball, who had been in the market while the cars were parked, and such like, but he wanted to find some short-cut, some royal road almost, to the criminal. Sir Mortimer Ellison, the Assistant Commissioner at the Yard, had given him a hint before he started. "It's a society place," he had said, "and the big bugs are society people. You'll find

*Note to Reader—Where had Skeffington given himself away?

them touchy down there because this case will get them on the raw. Hence the quicker you pull it off, the better for all concerned." And now he had been down for two days and he was no further on than when he arrived.

For three hours he considered the matter and then a point struck him, a very simple point. It might not lead to anything, but, on the other hand, it might. The following day he would try a reconstruction.

Accordingly next morning he demanded a man of the approximate build of the deceased and a car like Skeffington's. These he took to a secluded corner of the police yard.

The dummy was a young constable named Arthurs. He grinned when French explained that he wanted to smash in his head.

"Right, sir," he agreed. "I hope you'll remember the wife and kiddies when I'm gone."

"No one, I'm afraid, will know how it was done," French assured him. "Now, Arthurs, just where you're standing I hit you a bat on the head and stove in your skull. See?"

"Yes, sir."

"Well, go ahead. You don't want me to do it in reality, I suppose?"

"I'm afraid, sir, if my skull . . ."

French jerked round. "Good heavens, man, use your brains! Collapse!"

With a sudden look of comprehension Arthurs sank quietly on to the ground beside the car, while French adjured him to relax completely.

"Now, Carter, lift him into the position the dead man occupied."

Carter opened the rear door, and lifting the grinning Arthurs beneath the arms, tried to get him into the car. But, like Skeffington, he found he couldn't do it from where he was standing. He also had to go round to the other side and draw him in.

"Can't you pull in the legs?" French prompted.

Carter tried. "No, sir," he returned, "I'll have to go back and lift them in."

French watched him, a smile of satisfaction playing on his lips. "I rather thought that might happen," he declared. "Come along to the mortuary." He looked into the car. "Thank you, Arthurs, we've done with you. You made a good corpse."

84

On reaching the room where Holt's clothes lay, French took out his powdering apparatus and dusted the deceased's patent leather shoes. Several fingerprints showed up. French blew away the surplus, then photographed the prints.

"Now the deceased's fingers," he went on.

Soon the ten impressions were taken and photographed in their turn. A proper comparison would require enlargements and detailed observation, but a certain amount could be learned from mere casual inspection. French quickly satisfied himself. Most of the prints belonged to the deceased himself, but certain others were not his. From their position they might well have been caused by lifting the feet into a car.

Two hours later the club started a new waiter in the bar. Gradually a row of used glasses accumulated, each neatly labeled with name of the drinker. At intervals French tested and compared the fingerprints. Suddenly the affair clicked. Skeffington had lifted Holt's shoes.

The correct line of investigation was now indicated. Judicious inquiries brought to light Skeffington's financial position and mysterious luck at cards, Holt's strange illness, and the fact that Holt had asked Skeffington to accompany him to his rooms. The fact of the latter's engagement also became known. Here, French saw, was the motive.

"He thought putting the corpse in his own car would absolve him from suspicion, but the prints on the shoes are proof positive that he did it," he concluded to the Chief Constable. "We're ready for an arrest, I think?"

"Tonight," nodded the Chief Constable.

THE YELLOW SLUGS

BY H. C. BAILEY

H. C. Bailey, creator of Dr. Reggie Fortune, was born
on February 1, 1878, in London. He attended University
College, Oxford, and won First Class Classical Honours
at Corpus Christi College, Oxford, where he was also
coxswain of the college crew. His first novel, *My Lady
of Orange,* was published in England and the U.S. while
he was still an undergraduate. This was followed by
more historical novels until during the war, when he
was war correspondent for the *London Daily Telegraph,*
he turned to the detective story. He and his wife Lydia,
whom he married in 1908, had two daughters. He died
in Wales in 1961.

THE BIG CAR closed up behind a florid funeral procession which held the middle of the road. On either side was a noisy congestion of lorries. Mr. Fortune sighed and closed his eyes.

When he looked out again he was passing the first carriage of another funeral, and saw beneath the driver's seat the white coffin of a baby. For the road served the popular cemetery of Blaney.

Two slow miles of dingy tall houses and cheap shops slid by, with vistas of meaner streets opening on either side. The car gathered speed across Blaney Common, an expanse of yellow turf and bare sand, turbid pond and scrubwood, and stopped at the brown pile of an old hospital.

Entering its carbolic odor, Mr. Fortune was met by Superintendent Bell. "Here I am," he moaned. "Why am I?"

"Well, she's still alive, sir," said Bell. "They both are."

Mr. Fortune was taken to a ward in which, secluded by a screen, a little girl lay asleep.

Her face had a babyish fatness, but in its pallor looked bloated and unhealthy. Though the close July air was oppressive and she was covered with heavy bedclothes, her skin showed no sign of heat and she slept still as death.

Reggie sat down beside her. His hands moved gently within the bed. . . . He listened . . . he looked . . .

A nurse followed him to the door. "How old, do you think?" he murmured.

"That was puzzling me, sir. She's big enough for seven or eight, but all flabby. And when she came to she was talking almost baby talk. I suppose she may be only about five."

Reggie nodded. "Quite good, yes."

From the ward he passed to a small room where a nurse and a doctor stood together watching the one bed.

A boy lay in it, restless and making noises—inarticulate words mixed with moaning and whimpering.

The doctor lifted his eyebrows at Reggie. "Get that?" he whispered. "Still talking about hell. He came absolutely unstuck. I had to risk a shot of morphia. I——" He broke off in apprehension as Reggie's round face hardened to a cold severity. But Reggie nodded and moved to the bed.

The boy tossed in stertorous sleep, one thin arm flung up above a tousled head. His sunken cheeks were flushed, and drops of sweat stood on the upper lip and the brow. Not a bad brow—not an uncomely face but for its look of hungry misery—not the face of a child—a face which had been the prey of emotions and thwarted desires.

Reggie's careful hands worked over him . . . bits of the frail body were laid bare. . . . Reggie stood up, and still his face was set in ruthless, passionless determination.

Outside the door the doctor spoke nervously. "I hope you don't——"

"Morphia's all right," Reggie interrupted. "What do you make of him?"

"Well, Mr. Fortune, I wish you'd seen him at first." The doctor was uncomfortable beneath the cold insistence of a questioning stare. "He was right out of hand—a sort of hysterical fury. I should say he's quite abnormal. Neurotic lad, badly nourished—you can't tell what they won't do, that type."

"I can't. No. What age do you give him?"

"Now you've got me. To hear him raving, you'd think he was grown up, such a flow of language. Bible phrases and preaching. I'd say he was a twelve-year-old, but he might only be eight or ten. His development is all out of balance. He's unhealthy right through."

"Yes, that is so," Reggie murmured. "However. You ought to save him."

In a bare, grim waiting-room Reggie sat down with Superintendent Bell. "Well, sir?"

"Possible. Probable," Reggie told him. "On the evidence."

"Ah. Cruel, isn't it? I hate these child cases."

"Any more evidence?"

Bell stared at his hard calm gloominess. "I have. Plenty."

The story began with a small boy on the bank of one of the ponds on Blaney Common. That was some time ago. That was the first time anybody in authority had been aware of the existence of Eddie Hill. One of the keepers of the common made the discovery. The pond was one which children used for the sailing of toy boats. Eddie Hill had no boat, but he loitered round all the morning, watching the boats of other children. There was little wind, and one boat lay becalmed in the middle of the pond when the children had to go home to dinner.

88

An hour later the keeper saw Eddie Hill wade into the pond and run away. When the children came back from dinner there was no boat to be seen. Its small owner made weeping complaint to the keeper, who promised to keep his eyes open, and some days later found Eddie Hill and his little sister Bessie lurking among the gorse of the common with the stolen boat.

It was taken from them and their sin reported to their mother, who promised vengeance.

Their mother kept a little general shop. She had been there a dozen years—ever since she married her first husband. She was well liked and looked up to; a religious woman, regular chapel-goer, and all that. Her second husband, Brightman, was the same sort—hard-working, respectable man; been at the chapel longer than she had.

The day-school teachers had nothing against Eddie or the little girl. Eddie was rather more than usually bright, but dreamy and careless; the girl a bit stodgy. Both of 'em rather less naughty than most.

"Know a lot, don't you?" Reggie murmured. "Got all this today?"

"No, this was all on record," Bell said. "Worked out for another business."

"Oh. Small boy and small girl already old offenders. Go on."

The other business was at the chapel Sunday school. Eddie Hill, as the most regular of its pupils, was allowed the privilege of tidying up at the end of the afternoon. On a Sunday in the spring the superintendent came in unexpectedly upon the process and found Eddie holding the money-box in which had been collected the contributions of the school to the chapel missionary society.

Eddie had no need nor right to handle the money-box. Moreover, on the bench beside him were pennies and a sixpence. Such wealth could not be his own. Only the teachers ever put in silver. Moreover, he confessed that he had extracted the money by rattling the box upside down, and his small sister wept for the sin.

The superintendent took him to the police station and charged him with theft.

"Virtuous man," Reggie murmured.

"It does seem a bit harsh," Bell said. "But they'd had suspicions about the money-box before. They'd been watching for something like this. Well, the boy's mother came and tried to beg him off, but of course the case had to go on. The boy came up in the Juvenile Court—you know the way, Mr. Fortune; no sort of criminal atmosphere, magistrate talking like a father. He let the kid off with a lecture."

"Oh, yes. What did he say? Bringin' down mother's gray hairs in sorrow to the grave—wicked boy—goin' to the bad in this world and the next—anything about hell?"

"I couldn't tell you." Bell was shocked. "I heard he gave the boy a rare old talking to. I don't wonder. Pretty bad, wasn't it, the Sunday-school money-box? What makes you bring hell into it?"

"I didn't. The boy did. He was raving about hell today. Part of the evidence. I was only tracin' the origin."

"Ah. I don't like these children's cases," Bell said gloomily. "They don't seem really human sometimes. You get a twisted kind of child and he'll talk the most frightful stuff—and do it too. We can only go by acts, can we?"

"Yes. That's the way I'm goin'. Get on."

The sharp impatience of the tone made Bell look at him with some reproach. "All right, sir. The next thing is this morning's business. I gave you the outline of that on the phone. I've got the full details now. This is what it comes to. Eddie and his little sister were seen on the common; the keepers have got to keep an eye on him. He wandered about with her—he has a casual, drifting sort of way, like some of these queer kids do have—and they came to the big pond. That's not a children's place at all; it's too deep; only dog bathing and fishing. There was nobody near; it was pretty early. Eddie and Bessie went along the bank, and a laborer who was scything thistles says the little girl was crying, and Eddie seemed to be scolding her, and then he fair chucked her in and went in with her. That's what it looked like to the keeper who was watchin' 'em. Him and the other chap, they nipped down and chucked the lifebuoy; got it right near, but Eddie didn't take hold of it; he was clutching the girl and sinking and coming up again. So the keeper went in to 'em and had trouble getting 'em out. The little girl was unconscious, and Eddie sort of fought him." Bell stopped and gave a look of inquiry, but Reggie said nothing, and his face showed neither opinion nor feeling. "Well, you know how it is with these rescues from the water," Bell went on. "People often seem to be fighting to drown themselves and it don't mean anything except fright. And about the boy throwing

90

the girl in—that might have been just a bit of a row or play—it's happened often—not meant vicious at all; and then he'd panic, likely enough." Again Bell looked an anxious question at the cold, passionless face. "I mean to say, I wouldn't have bothered you with it, Mr. Fortune, but for the way the boy carried on when they got him out. There he was with his little sister unconscious, and the keeper doing artificial respiration, and he called out, 'Don't do it. Bessie's dead. She must be dead.' And the keeper asked him, 'Do you want her dead, you little devil?' And he said, 'Yes, I do. I had to.' Then the laborer chap came back with help and they got hold of Eddie; he was raving, flinging himself about and screaming if she lived she'd only get like him and go to hell, so she must be dead. While they brought him along here he was sort of preaching to 'em bits of the Bible, and mad stuff about the wicked being sent to hell and tortures for 'em."

"Curious and interestin'," Reggie drawled. "Any particular torture?"

"I don't know. The whole thing pretty well gave these chaps the horrors. They didn't get all the boy's talk. I don't wonder. There was something about worms not dying, they told me. That almost turned 'em up. What do you make of it?"

"I should say it happened," Reggie said. "All of it. As stated."

"You feel sure he could have thrown that fat little girl in? He seemed to me such a weed."

"Yes. Quite a sound point. I took that point. Development of both children unhealthy. Girl wrongly nourished. Boy inadequately nourished. Boy's physique frail. However. He could have done it. Lots of nervous energy."

Bell drew in his breath. "You take it cool."

"Only way to take it," Reggie murmured, and Bell shifted uncomfortably. He has remarked since that he had seen Mr. Fortune look like that once or twice before—sort of inhuman, heartless, and inquisitive; but there it seemed all wrong, it didn't seem his way at all.

Reggie settled himself in his chair and spoke—so Bell has reported, and this is the only criticism which annoys Mr. Fortune—like a lecture. "Several possibilities to be considered. The boy may be merely a precocious rascal. Having committed some iniquity which the little girl knew about, he tried to drown her to stop her giving him away. Common type of crime, committed by children as well as their elders."

91

"I know it is," Bell admitted. "But what could he have done that was worth murdering his sister?"

"I haven't the slightest idea. However. He did steal. Proved twice by independent evidence. Don't blame if you don't want. 'There, but for the grace of God, go I.' I agree. Quite rational to admit that consideration. We shall certainly want it. But he knew he was a thief; he knew it got him into trouble—that's fundamental."

"All right," said Bell gloomily. "We have to take it like that."

"Yes. No help. Attempt to murder sister may be connected with consciousness of sin. I should say it was. However. Other possibilities. He's a poor little mess of nerves; he's unsound, physically, mentally, spiritually. He may not have meant to murder her at all; may have got in a passion and not known what he was doing."

"Ah. That's more likely."

"You think so? Then why did he tell everybody he did mean to murder her?"

"Well, he was off his head, as you were saying. That's the best explanation of the whole thing. It's really the only explanation. Look at your first idea: he wanted to kill her so she couldn't tell about some crime he'd done. You get just the same question, why did he say he meant murder? He must know killing is worse than stealing. However you take the thing, you work back to his being off his head."

Reggie's eyelids drooped. "I was brought here to say he's mad. Yes. I gather that. You're a merciful man, Bell. Sorry not to satisfy your gentle nature. I could swear he's mentally abnormal. If that would do any good. I couldn't say he's mad. I don't know. I can find you mental experts who would give evidence either way."

"I know which a jury would believe," Bell grunted.

"Yes. So do I. Merciful people, juries. Like you. Not my job. I'm lookin' for the truth. One more possibility. The boy's motive was just what he said it was—to kill his little sister so she shouldn't get wicked and go to hell. That fits the other facts. He'd got into the way of stealing; it had been rubbed into him that he was doomed to hell. So, if he found her goin' the same way, he might think it best she should die while she was still clean."

"Well, if that isn't mad!" Bell exclaimed.

"Abnormal, yes. Mad—I wonder," Reggie murmured.

"But it's sheer crazy, sir. If he believed he was so wicked, the thing for him to do was to pull up and go straight, and see that she did too."

"Yes. That's common sense, isn't it?" A small, contemptuous smile lingered a moment on Reggie's stern face. "What's the use of common sense here? If he was like this—sure he was going to hell; sure she was bein' driven there too—kind of virtuous for him to kill her to save her. Kind of rational. Desperately rational. Ever know any children, Bell? Some of 'em do believe what they're taught. Some of 'em take it seriously. Abnormal, as you say. Eddie Hill is abnormal." He turned and looked full at Bell, his blue eyes dark in the failing light. "Aged twelve or so—too bad to live—or too good. Pleasant case."

Bell moved uneasily. "These things do make you feel queer," he grunted. "What it all comes to though—we mean much the same—the boy ought to be in a home."

"A home!" Reggie's voice went up, and he laughed. "Yes. Official home for mentally defective. Yes. We can do that. I daresay we shall." He stood up and walked to the window and looked out at the dusk. "These children had a home of their own. And a mother. What's she doing about 'em?"

"She's been here, half off her head, poor thing," said Bell. "She wouldn't believe the boy meant any harm. She told me he couldn't, he was so fond of his sister. She said it must have been accident."

"Quite natural and motherly. Yes. But not adequate. Because it wasn't accident, whatever it was. We'd better go and see mother."

"If you like," Bell grunted.

"I don't like," Reggie mumbled. "I don't like anything. I'm not here to do what I like." And they went.

Shutters were up at the little shop which was the home of Eddie Hill, and still bore in faded paint his father's name. No light showed in the windows above. Bell rapped on the door, and they waited in vain. He moved to a house door close beside the shop. "Try this. This may be theirs too," he said, and knocked.

After a minute it was opened by a woman who said nothing, but stared at them. From somewhere inside came the sound of a man's voice, talking fervently.

The light of the street lamp showed her of full figure, in neat black, and a face which was still pretty but distressed.

"You remember me, Mrs. Brightman," said Bell. "I'm Superintendent Bell."

"I know." She was breathless. "What's the matter? Are they —is Eddie—what's happened?"

"They're doing all right. I just want a little talk with you."

"Oh, they're all right. Praise God!" She turned; she called out: "Matthew, Matthew dear, they're all right."

The man's voice went on talking with the same fervor.

"I'll come in, please," said Bell.

"Yes, do. Thank you kindly. Mr. Brightman would like to see you. We were just asking mercy."

She led the way along a passage, shining clean, to a room behind the shop. There a man was on his knees praying, and most of the prayer was texts: "And we shall sing of mercy in the morning. Amen. Amen."

He stood up before them, tall and gaunt, a bearded man with melancholy eyes. He turned to his wife. "What is it, my dear?"

"It's about the children, Matthew." His wife came and took his arm. "It's the police superintendent, I told you."

The man sucked in his breath. "Ay, ay. Please sit down. They must sit down, Florrie." There was a fluster of setting chairs. "This is kind, sir. What can you tell us tonight?"

"Doin' well. Both of 'em," Reggie said.

"There's our answer, Florrie," the man said, and smiled, and his somber eyes glowed. "There's our prayers answered."

"Yes. I think they're going to live," said Reggie. "But that's not the only thing that matters. We have to ask how it was they were nearly drowned."

"It was an accident. It must have been," the woman cried. "I'm sure Eddie wouldn't—he never would, would he, Matthew?"

"I won't believe it," Brightman answered quickly.

"Quite natural you should feel like that," Reggie nodded. "However. We have to deal with the facts."

"You must do what you think right, sir." Brightman bent his head.

"Yes, I will. Yes. Been rather a naughty boy, hasn't he?"

Brightman looked at his wife's miserable face and turned to them again. "The police know," he said. "He has been a thief—twice he has been a thief—but little things. There is mercy, surely there is mercy for repentance. If his life is spared, he should not be lost; we must believe that."

"I do," Reggie murmured. "Any special reason why he should have been a thief?"

Brightman shook his head. "He's always had a good home, I'm sure," the woman moaned. She looked round her room, which was ugly and shabby, but all in the cleanest order.

"What can I say?" Brightman shook his head. "We've always done our best for him. There's no telling how temptation comes, sir, and it's strong and the little ones are weak."

"That is so. Yes. How much pocket money did they have?"

"Eddie has had his twopence a week since he was ten," Brightman answered proudly. "And Bessie has her penny."

"I see. And did anything happen this morning which upset Bessie or Eddie?"

"Nothing at all, sir. Nothing that I know." Brightman turned to his wife. "They went off quite happy, didn't they?"

"Yes, of course they did," she said eagerly. "They always loved to have a day on the common. They took their lunch, and they went running as happy as happy—and then this."

"Well, well." Reggie stood up. "Oh. By the way. Has Eddie —or Bessie—ever stolen anything at home here?"

Brightman started and stared at him. "That's not fair, sir. That's not a right thing to ask. There isn't stealing between little ones and their mother and father."

"No. As you say. No," Reggie murmured. "Good night. You'll hear how they get on. Good night."

"Thank you, sir. We shall be anxious to hear. Good night, sir," said Brightman, and Mrs. Brightman showed them out with tearful gratitude. As the door was opened, Brightman called: "Florrie! Don't bolt it. Mrs. Wiven hasn't come back."

"I know. I know," she answered, and bade them good night.

A few paces away, Reggie stopped and looked back at the shuttered shop and the dark windows. "Well, well. What does the professional mind make of all that?"

"Just what you'd expect, wasn't it?" Bell grunted.

"Yes. Absolutely. Poor struggling shopkeepers, earnestly religious, keeping the old house like a new pin. All in accordance with the evidence." He sniffed the air. "Dank old house."

"General shop smell. All sorts of things mixed up."

"As you say. There were. And there would be. Nothing you couldn't have guessed before we went. Except that Mrs. Wiven is expected—whoever Mrs. Wiven is."

"I don't know. Sounds like a lodger."

"Yes, that is so. Which would make another resident in the home of Eddie and Bessie. However. She's not come back yet. So we can go home. The end of a beastly day. And to-morrow's another one. I'll be out to see the children in the morning. Oh, my Lord! Those children." His hand gripped Bell's arm.

By eight o'clock in the morning he was at the bedside of Bessie Hill—an achievement of stupendous but useless energy, for she did not wake till half-past.

Then he took charge. A responsible position, which he interpreted as administering cups of warm milk and bread and butter. She consumed them eagerly.

"Good girl." Reggie wiped her mouth. "Feelin' better?"

She sighed and snuggled down, and gazed at him with large eyes. "Umm. Who are you?"

"They call me Mr. Fortune. Is it nice here?"

"Umm. Comfy." The big eyes were puzzled. "Where is it?"

"Blaney Hospital. People brought you here after you were in the pond. Do you remember?"

She shook her head. "Is Eddie here?"

"Oh, yes. Eddie's asleep. He's all right. Were you cross with Eddie?"

Tears came into the brown eyes. "Eddie was cross wiv me," the child whimpered. "I wasn't. Eddie said must go into ve water. I didn't want. But Eddie was so cross. Love Eddie."

"Yes. Little girl." Reggie stroked her hair. "Eddie shouldn't have been cross. Just a little girl. But Eddie isn't often cross, is he?"

"No. Love Eddie. Eddie's dear."

"Why was he cross yesterday?"

The brown eyes opened wider. "I was naughty. It was Mrs. Wiven. Old Mrs. Wiven. I did go up to her room. I didn't fink she was there. Sometimes is sweeties. But she was vere. She scolded me. She said I was little fief. We was all fiefs. And Eddie took me away and oh, he was so cross; he said I would be wicked and must not be. I aren't. I aren't. Eddie was all funny and angry, and said not to be like him and go to hell, and then he did take me into pond wiv him. I didn't want. I didn't want!"

"No. Of course not. No. Poor little girl. Eddie didn't understand."

"Is Eddie still cross wiv me?"

"Oh, no. No. Eddie won't be cross any more. Nobody's cross, little girl." Reggie bent over her. "Everybody's going to be kind now. You only have to be quiet and happy. That's all."

"Oooh." She gazed up at him. "Tell Eddie I'm sorry."

"Yes. I'll tell him." Reggie kissed her hand and turned away.

The nurse met him at the door. "Did she wake in the night?" he whispered.

"Yes, sir, asking for Eddie. She's a darling, isn't she? She makes me cry, talking like that of him."

"That won't do any harm," Reggie said, and his face hardened. "But you mustn't talk about him."

He went to the room where Eddie lay. The doctor was there, and turned from the bedside to confer with him. "Not too bad. He's put in a long sleep. Quite quiet since he waked. Very thirsty. Taken milk with a dash of coffee nicely. But he's rather flat."

Reggie sat down by his bed. The boy lay very still. His thin face was white. Only his eyes moved to look at Reggie, so little open, their pupils so small that they seemed all greenish-gray. He gave no sign of recognition, or feeling, or intelligence. Reggie put a hand under the clothes and found him cold and damp.

"Well, young man, does anything hurt you now?"

"I'm awful tired," the boy said.

"Yes. I know. But that's going away."

"No, it isn't; it's worse. I didn't ought to have waked up." The faint voice was drearily peevish. "I didn't want to. It's no good. I thought I was dead. And it was good being dead."

"Was it?" Reggie said sharply.

The boy gave a quivering cry. "Yes, it was!" His face was distorted with fear and wonder. "I thought it would be so dreadful and it was all quiet and nice, and then I wasn't dead, I was alive and everything's awful again. I've got to go on still."

"What's awful in going on?" said Reggie. "Bessie wants you. Bessie sent you her love. She's gettin' well quick."

"Bessie? Bessie's here in bed like I am?"

"Of course she is. Only much happier than you are."

The boy began to sob.

"Why do you cry about that?" Reggie said. "She's got to

be happy. Boys and girls have to be happy. That's what they're for. You didn't want Bessie to die."

"I did. You know I did," the boy sobbed.

"I know you jumped in the pond with her. That was silly. But you'd got rather excited, hadn't you? What was it all about?"

"They'll tell you," the boy muttered.

"Who will?"

"The keepers, the p'lice, the m-magistrate, everybody. I'm wicked. I'm a thief. I can't help it. And I didn't want Bessie to be wicked too."

"Of course you didn't. And she isn't. What ever made you think she was?"

"But she was." The boy's voice was shrill. "She went to Mrs. Wiven's room. She was looking for pennies. I know she was. She'd seen me. And Mrs. Wiven said we were all thieves. So I had to."

"Oh, no, you hadn't. And you didn't. You see? Things don't happen like that."

"Yes, they do. There's hell. Where their worms don't die."

The doctor made a muttered exclamation.

Reggie's hand held firm at the boy's as he moved and writhed. "There's God too," he murmured. "God's kind. Bessie's not going to be wicked. You don't have to be wicked. That's what's come of it all. Somebody's holding you up now." His hand pressed. "Feel?" The boy's lips parted; he looked up in awe. "Yes. Like that. You'll see me again and again. Now goodbye. Think about me. I'm thinking about you."

Outside, in the corridor, the doctor spoke: "I say, Mr. Fortune, you got him then. That was the stuff. I thought you were driving hard before. Sorry I spoke."

"I was." Reggie frowned. His round face was again of a ruthless severity. " 'Difficult matter to play with souls,' " he mumbled. "We've got to." He looked under drooping eyelids. "Know the name of the keeper who saw the attempted drowning? Fawkes? Thanks."

He left the hospital and walked across the common.

The turf was parched and yellow, worn away on either side. Reggie descried the brown coat of a keeper, made for him, and was directed to Fawkes.

Fawkes was a slow-speaking, slow-thinking old soldier, but he knew his own mind.

There was no doubt in it that Eddie had tried to kill Bessie, no indignation, no surprise. Chewing his words, he gave judgment. He had known Eddie's sort, lots of 'em. 'Igh-strung, wanting the earth, kicking up behind and before 'cause they couldn't get it. He didn't mind 'em. Rather 'ave 'em than young 'uns like sheep. But you 'ad to dress 'em down proper.

That business of the boat? Yes, Eddie pinched that all right. Smart kid; you'd got to 'and him that. And yet not so smart. Silly, lying up with it on the common; just the way to get nabbed. Ought to 'ave took it 'ome and sailed it over at Wymond Park. Never been spotted then. But 'im and 'is sister, they made a reg'lar den up in the gorse. Always knew where to look for 'em. Silly. Why, they was up there yesterday, loafing round, before 'e did 'is drowning act.

"Take you there? I can, if you like."

Reggie did like. They went up the brown slope of the common to a tangle of gorse and bramble over small sand-hills.

"There you are." The keeper pointed his stick to a patch of loose sand in a hollow. "That's young Eddie's funk-'ole."

Reggie came to the place. The sand had been scooped up by small hands into a low wall round a space which was decked out with pebbles, yellow petals of gorse, and white petals of bramble.

"Ain't that just like 'em!" The keeper was angrily triumphant. "They know they didn't ought to pick the flowers."

Reggie did not answer. He surveyed the pretense of a garden and looked beyond. "Oh, my Lord!" he muttered. On the ground lay a woman's bag.

" 'Allo, 'allo." The keeper snorted. "They've pinched something else."

Reggie took out his handkerchief, put his hand in it, and thus picked up the bag. He looked about him; he wandered to and fro, going delicately, examining the confusion of small footmarks, farther and farther away.

"Been all round, ain't they?" the keeper greeted him on his return.

"That is so. Yes," Reggie mumbled and looked at him with searching eyes. "Had any notice of a bag lost or stolen?"

"Not as I've 'eard. Better ask the 'ead keeper. 'E'll be up at the top wood about now."

The wood was a thicket of birch and crab-apple and thorn.

As they came near, they saw on its verge the head keeper and two other men who were not in the brown coats of authority. One of these was Superintendent Bell.

"I tried to catch you at the hospital, Mr. Fortune," he said. "But I suppose you've heard about Mrs. Wiven?"

"Oh. The Mrs. Wiven who hadn't come back," Reggie said slowly. "No. I haven't heard anything."

"I thought you must have, by your being out here on the common. Well, she didn't come back at all. This morning Brightman turned up at the station very rattled to ask if they had any news of his lodger, Mrs. Wiven. She never came in last night, and he thought she must have had an accident or something. She'd been lodging with them for years. Old lady, fixed in her habits. Never went anywhere, that he knew of, except to chapel and for a cup o' tea with some of her chapel friends, and none of them had seen her. These fine summer days she'd take her food out and sit on the common here all day long. She went off yesterday morning with sandwiches and a vacuum flask of tea and her knitting. Often she wouldn't come home till it was getting dark. They didn't think much of her being late; sometimes she went in and had a bit o' supper with a friend. She had her key, and they left the door unbolted, like we heard, and went to bed, being worn out with the worry of the kids. But when Mrs. Brightman took up her cup of tea this morning and found she wasn't in her room, Brightman came running round to the station. Queer business, eh?"

"Yes. Nasty business. Further you go the nastier."

Bell looked at him curiously and walked him away from the keeper. "You feel it that way? So do I. Could you tell me what you were looking for out here—as you didn't know she was missing?"

"Oh, yes. I came to verify the reports of Eddie's performances."

"Ah! Have you found any error?"

"No. I should say everything happened as stated."

"The boy's going to get well?"

"It could be. If he gets the chance."

"Poor little beggar," Bell grunted. "What do you really think about him?"

"Clever child, ambitious child, imaginative child. What children ought to be—twisted askew."

"Kind of perverted, you mean."

"That is so. Yes. However. Question now is, not what I think of the chances of Eddie's soul, but what's been happening. Evidence inadequate, curious, and nasty. I went up to the private lair of Eddie and Bessie. Same where he was caught with the stolen boat. I found this." He showed Bell the woman's bag.

"My oath!" Bell muttered, and took it from him gingerly. "You wrapped it up! Thinkin' there might be fingerprints."

"Yes. Probably are. They might even be useful."

"And you went looking for this—not knowing the woman was missing?"

"Wasn't lookin' for it," Reggie snapped. "I was lookin' for anything there might be. Found a little pretense of a garden they'd played at—and this."

"Ah, but you heard last night about Mrs. Wiven, and this morning you go up where Eddie hides what he's stolen. Don't that mean you made sure there was something fishy? You see when we're blind, Mr. Fortune."

"Oh, no. I don't see. I knew more than you did. Little Bessie told me this morning she was in Mrs. Wiven's room yesterday, privily and by stealth, and Mrs. Wiven caught her and called her a thief, and said they were all thieves. I should think little Bessie may have meant to be a thief. Which would agree with Eddie's effort to drown her so she should die good and honest. But I don't see my way."

"All crazy, isn't it?" Bell grunted.

"Yes. The effort of Eddie is an incalculable factor. However. You'd better look at the bag."

Bell opened it with cautious fingers. A smell of peppermint came out. Within was a paper bag of peppermint lozenges, two unclean handkerchiefs marked E. W., an empty envelope addressed to Mrs. Wiven, a bottle of soda-mint tablets, and some keys.

"Evidence that it is the bag of the missing Mrs. Wiven strong," Reggie murmured. He peered into it. "But no money. Not a penny." He looked up at Bell with that cold, ruthless curiosity which Bell always talks about in discussing the case. "Stealin' is the recurrin' motive. You notice that?"

"I do." Bell stared at him. "You take it cool, Mr. Fortune."

"No use feelin' feelings," Reggie drawled. "We have to go on. We want the truth, whatever it is."

"Well, all right, I know," Bell said gloomily. "They're searching the common for her. That's why I came out here.

They knew her. She did sit about here in summer." He went back to the head keeper and conferred again.

Reggie purveyed himself a deck-chair, and therein sat extended and lit a pipe and closed his eyes.

"Mr. Fortune!" Bell stood over him. His lips emitted a stream of smoke. No other part of him moved. "They've found her. I suppose you expected that."

"Yes. Obvious possibility. Probable possibility." It has been remarked that Mr. Fortune has a singular capacity for becoming erect from a supine position. A professor of animal morphology once delivered a lecture upon him—after a hospital dinner—as the highest type of the invertebrates. He stood up from the deck-chair in one undulating motion. "Well, well. Where is the new fact?"

Bell took him into the wood. No grass grew in it. Where the sandy soil was not bare, dead leaves made a carpet. Under the crab-apple trees, between the thornbrakes, were nooks obviously much used by pairs of lovers. By one of these, not far from the whale-back edge of rising ground which was the wood's end, some men stood together.

On the gray sand there lay a woman's body. She was small; she was dressed in a coat and skirt of dark gray cloth and a black and white blouse. The hat on her gray hair was pulled to one side, giving her a look of absurd frivolity in ghastly contrast to the distortion of her pallid face. Her lips were closely compressed and almost white. The dead eyes stared up at the trees with dilated pupils.

Reggie walked round the body, going delicately.

Beside the body was a raffia bag which held some knitting, a vacuum flask, and an opened packet of sandwiches.

Reggie's discursive eyes looked at them and looked again at the dead face, but not for long. He was more interested in the woman's skirt. He bent over that, examined it from side to side, and turned away and went on prowling farther and farther away, and as he went he scraped at the dry sand here and there.

When he came back to the body, his lips were curved in a grim, mirthless smile. He looked at Bell. "Photographer," he mumbled.

"Sent a man to phone, sir."

Reggie continued to look at him. "Have you? Why have you?"

102

"Just routine." Bell was startled.

"Oh. Only that. Well, well." Reggie knelt down by the body. His hands went to the woman's mouth. . . . He took something from his pocket and forced the mouth open and looked in. . . . He closed the mouth again, and sat down on his heels and contemplated the dead woman with dreamy curiosity. . . . He opened her blouse. Upon the underclothes was a dark stain. He bent over that and smelt it; he drew the clothes from her chest.

"No wound, is there?" Bell muttered.

"Oh, no. No." Reggie put back the clothes and stood up and went to the flask and the sandwiches. He pulled the bread of an unfinished sandwich apart, looked at it, and put it down. He took the flask and shook it. It was not full. He poured some of the contents into its cup.

"Tea, eh?" said Bell. "Strong tea."

"Yes. It would be," Reggie murmured. He tasted it and spat, and poured what was in the cup back into the flask and corked it again.

"There you are. Cause of death, poisoning by oxalic acid or binoxalate of potassium—probably the latter—commonly called salts of lemon. And we shall find some in that awful tea. We shall also find it in the body. Tongue and mouth, white, contracted, eroded. Time of death, probably round about twenty-four hours ago. No certainty."

"My oath! It's too near certainty for my liking," Bell muttered.

"Is it?" Reggie's eyelids drooped. "Wasn't thinkin' about what you'd like. Other interestin' facts converge."

"They do!" Bell glowered at him. "One of the commonest kinds of poisoning, isn't it?"

"Oh, yes. Salts of lemon very popular."

"Anybody can get it."

"As you say. Removes stains, cleans brass and whatnot. Also quickly fatal."

"This boy Eddie could have got some easy."

"That is so. Yes. Lethal dose for a penny or two anywhere."

"Well, then—look at it!"

"I have," Reggie murmured. "Weird case. Ghastly case."

"Gives me the horrors," said Bell. "The old lady comes out here to spend the day as usual, and somebody's put a spot of poison in her drop o' tea and she dies; and her bag's stolen, and found without a farthing where the boy Eddie hides his loot. And about the time the old lady's dying, Eddie tries to drown his sister. What are you going to make of it? What can you make of it? It was a poison any kid could get hold of. One of 'em must have poisoned her to steal her little bit o' money. But the girl's not much more than a baby. It must have been Eddie that did it—and that goes with the rest of his doings. He's got the habit of stealing. But his little sister saw something of it, knew too much, so he put up this drowning to stop her tongue—and then, when she was saved, made up this tale about killing her to keep her honest. Devilish, isn't it? And when you find a child playing the devil— my oath! But it is devilish clever—his tale would put the stealing and all the rest on the baby. And we can't prove anything else. She's too little to be able to get it clear, and he's made himself out driven wild by her goings-on. If a child's really wicked, he beats you."

"Yes, that is so," Reggie drawled. "Rather excited, aren't you? Emotions are not useful in investigation. Prejudice the mind into exaggeratin' facts and ignorin' other facts. Both fallacies exhibited in your argument. You mustn't ignore what Bessie did say—that she went into Mrs. Wiven's room yesterday morning and Mrs. Wiven caught her. I shouldn't wonder if you found Bessie's fingerprints on that bag."

"My Lord!" Bell stared at him. "It's the nastiest case I ever had."

"Not nice, no. Discoverin' the possibilities of corruption of the soul. However. We haven't finished yet. Other interestin' facts have been ignored by Superintendent Bell. Hallo!" Several men were approaching briskly. "Is this your photographer and other experts?"

"That's right."

"Very swift and efficient." Reggie went to meet them. "Now then. Give your attention to the lady's skirt. Look." He indicated a shining streak across the dark stuff. "Bring that out."

"Can do, sir," the photographer said, and fell to work.

Reggie turned to Bell. "They'll go over the whole of her for fingerprints, what? Then she can be taken to the mortuary."

"Very good," Bell said, and turned away to give the orders, but, having given them, stood still to stare at the thin glistening streak on the skirt.

Reggie came quietly to his elbow. "You do notice that?

Well, well." Bell looked at him with a puzzled frown and was met for the first time in this case by a small, satisfied smile which further bewildered him. He bent over again to pore over the streak.

"It's all right." Reggie's voice was soothing. "That's on record now. Come on." Linking arms, he drew Bell away from the photographers and the fingerprint men. "Well? What does the higher intelligence make of the line on the skirt?"

"I don't know. I can't make out why you think so much of it."

"My dear chap! Oh, my dear chap!" Reggie moaned. "Crucial fact. Decisive fact." He led Bell on out of the wood and across the common, and at a respectful distance Bell's two personal satellites followed.

"Decisive, eh?" Bell frowned. "It was just a smear of something to me. You mean salts of lemon would leave a shiny stain?"

"Oh, no. Wouldn't shine at all."

"Has she been sick on her skirt?"

"Not there. No. Smear wasn't human material."

"Well, I thought it wasn't. What are you thinking of?"

"I did think of what Eddie said—where their worm dieth not."

"My God!" Bell muttered. "Worms?" He gave a shudder. "I don't get you at all, sir. It sounds mad."

"No. Connection is sort of desperate rational. I told you Eddie was like that. However. Speakin' scientifically, not a worm, but a slug. That streak was a slug's trail."

"Oh. I see." Bell was much relieved. "Now that you say so, it did look like that. The sort o' slime a slug leaves behind. It does dry shiny, of course."

"You have noticed that?" Reggie admired him. "Splendid!"

Bell was not pleased. "I have seen slugs before," he grunted. "But what is there to make a fuss about? I grant you, it's nasty to think of a slug crawling over the woman as she lay there dead. That don't mean anything, though. Just what you'd expect, with the body being all night in the wood."

"My dear chap! Oh, my dear chap!" Reggie moaned. "You mustn't talk like that. Shakes confidence in the police force. Distressin' mixture of inadequate observation and fallacious reasonin'."

"Thank you. I don't know what's wrong with it." Bell was irritated.

"Oh, my Bell! You shock me. Think again. Your general principle's all right. Slugs do come out at night. Slugs like the dark. That's a general truth which has its particular application. But you fail to observe the conditions. The body was in a wood with no herbage on the ground: and the ground was a light dry sand. These are not conditions which attract the slug. I should have been much surprised if I'd found any slugs there, or their tracks. But I looked for 'em—which you didn't, Bell. I'm always careful. And there wasn't a trace. No. I can't let you off. A slug had crawled over her skirt, leavin' his slime from side to side. And yet his slime didn't go beyond her skirt on to the ground anywhere. How do you suppose he managed that? Miracle—by a slug. I don't believe in miracles if I can help it."

"You go beyond me," said Bell uneasily. "You grasp the whole thing while I'm only getting bits. What do you make of it all?"

"Oh, my Bell!" Reggie reproached him. "Quite clear. When the slug walked over her, she wasn't lying where she was found."

"Is that all?" Bell grunted. "I daresay. She might have had her dose, and felt queer and lay down, and then moved on to die where we found her. Nothing queer in that, is there?"

"Yes. Several things very queer. It could be. Oxalic poisoning might lay her out and still let her drag herself somewhere else to die. Not likely she'd take care to bring her flask and her sandwiches with her. Still less likely she'd lie long enough for a slug to walk over her and then recover enough to move somewhere else—and choose to move into the wood, where she wouldn't be seen. Why should she? She'd try for help if she could try for anything. And, finally, most unlikely she'd find any place here with slugs about. Look at it; it's all arid and sandy and burnt up by the summer. No. Quite unconvincin' explanation. The useful slug got onto her somewhere else."

"Then you mean to say she was poisoned some other place, and brought here dead?" Bell frowned. "It's all very well. You make it sound reasonable. But would you like to try this slug argument on a jury? They'd never stand for it, if you ask me. It's all too clever."

"You think so?" Reggie murmured. "Well, well. Then it does give variety to the case. We haven't been very clever so far. However. Study to improve. There is further evidence. She'd been sick. Common symptom of oxalic poisoning. But she'd been sick on her underclothes and not on her outside clothes. That's very difficult. Think about it. Even juries can be made to think sometimes. Even coroners, which is very hard. Even judges. I've done it in my time, simple as I am. I might do it again. Yes, I might. With the aid of the active and intelligent police force. Come on."

"What do you want to do?"

"Oh, my Bell! I want to call on Mr. and Mrs. Brightman. We need their collaboration."

"All right. I don't mind trying 'em," Bell agreed gloomily. "We've got to find out all about the old woman somehow. We don't really know anything yet."

"I wouldn't say that. No," Reggie mumbled. "However. One moment."

They had come to the edge of the common by the hospital, where his car waited. He went across to it and spoke to his chauffeur.

"Just calmin' Sam," he apologized on his return. "He gets peevish when forgotten. Come on."

They arrived again at the little general shop. Its unshuttered window now enticed the public with a meager array of canned goods and cartons which had been there for some time. The door was shut but not fastened. Opening it rang a bell. They went in, and found the shop empty.

Mrs. Brightman came from the room behind, wiping red arms and hands on her apron. Her plump face, which was tired and sweating, quivered alarm at the sight of them. "Oh, it's you!" she cried. "What is it?"

"Your children are doing well," said Reggie. "Thought I'd better let you know that."

She stared at him, and tears came into her eyes. "Praise God!" she gasped. "Thank you, sir."

"No. You don't have to thank me. I'm just doin' my job."

But again she thanked him, and went on nervously: "Have you heard anything of Mrs. Wiven?"

"I want to have a little talk about her. Is Mr. Brightman in?"

"No, he isn't, not just now. Have you got any news of her, sir?"

"Yes. There is some news. Sorry Mr. Brightman's out. Where's he gone?"

"Down to the yard, sir."

"Out at the back here?"

"No. No. Down at his own yard."

"Oh. He has a business of his own?"

"Yes, sir, a little business. Furniture dealing. Second-hand furniture."

"I see. Well, well. We could get one of the neighbors to run down and fetch him, what?"

"That's the way," Bell nodded. "What's the address, ma'am?"

She swallowed. "It's just round the corner. Smith's Buildings. Anybody would tell you. But he might be out on a job, you know; I couldn't say."

Bell strode out, and the messenger he sent was one of his satellites.

"Well, while we're waitin', we might come into your nice little room," Reggie suggested. "There's one or two things you can tell me."

"Yes, sir, I'm sure, anything as I can, I'll be glad. Will you come through, please?" She lifted the flap of the counter for him, she opened the curtained glass door of the room behind. It was still in exact order, but she had to apologize for it. "I'm sorry we're all in a mess. I'm behindhand with my cleaning, having this dreadful trouble with the children and being so worried I can't get on. I don't half know what I'm doing, and then poor Mrs. Wiven being lost—" She stopped, breathless. "What is it about Mrs. Wiven, sir?"

"Not good news," Reggie said. "Nobody will see Mrs. Wiven alive again."

The full face grew pale beneath its sweat, the eyes stood out. "She's dead! Oh, the poor soul! But how do you know? How was it?"

"She's been found dead on the common."

Mrs. Brightman stared at him: her mouth came open and shook; she flung her apron over her head and bent and was convulsed with sobbing.

"Fond of her, were you?" Reggie sympathized.

A muffled voice informed him that she was a dear old lady.

"Was she? Yes. But I wanted to ask you about the children. What time did they go out yesterday?" Still sobbing under her apron, Mrs. Brightman seemed not to hear. "Yesterday morning," Reggie insisted. "You must remember. What time was it when Eddie and Bessie went out?"

After a moment the apron was pulled down from a swollen, tearful face. "What time?" she repeated, looking at her lap and wiping her eyes. "I don't know exactly, sir. Just after breakfast. Might be somewheres about nine o'clock."

"Yes, it might be," Reggie murmured. "They were pulled out of the pond about ten."

"I suppose so," she whimpered. "What's it got to do with Mrs. Wiven?"

"You don't see any connection?"

She stared at him. "How could there be?"

The shop-door bell rang, and she started up to answer it. She found Bell in the shop. "Oh, have you found Mr. Brightman?" she cried.

"No, not yet. Where's Mr. Fortune?"

Reggie called to him, "Come on, Bell," and she brought him into the back room and stood looking from one to the other. "So Mr. Brightman wasn't in his yard?"

"No sir. Nobody there."

"Well, well," Reggie murmured.

"But I told you he might have gone off on a job."

"You did say so. Yes," Reggie murmured. "However. I was asking about the children. Before they went out yesterday—Bessie got into trouble with Mrs. Wiven, didn't she?"

The woman looked down.

"You didn't tell us that last night," Reggie said.

"I didn't want to. I didn't see as it mattered. And I didn't want to say anything against Bessie. She's my baby." Her eyes were streaming.

"Bessie told me," said Reggie.

"Bessie confessed! Oh, it's all too dreadful. The baby! I don't know why this was to come on us. I brought 'em up to be good. I have. And she was such a darling baby. But it's God's will."

"Yes. What did happen?"

"Mrs. Wiven was always hard on the children. She never had a child herself, poor thing. Bessie got into her room, and Mrs. Wiven caught her and said she was prying and stealing like Eddie. I don't know what Bessie was doing there. Children will do such, whatever you do. And there was Bessie crying and Eddie all wild. He does get so out of himself. I packed 'em off, and I told Mrs. Wiven it wasn't nothing to be so cross about, and she got quite nice again. She was a dear with me and Brightman."

"And when did Mrs. Wiven go out?" said Reggie.

"It must have been soon after. She liked her days on the common."

"Oh, yes. That's clear." Reggie stood up and looked out at the yard, where some washing was hung out to dry. "What was Mrs. Wiven wearing yesterday?"

"Let me see—" Mrs. Brightman was surprised by the turn in the conversation. "I don't rightly remember—she had on her dark coat and skirt. She always liked to be nicely dressed when she went." Under the frown of this mental effort swollen eyes blinked at him. "But you said she'd been found. You know what she had on."

"Yes. When she was on the common. Before she got there —what was she wearing?"

Mrs. Brightman's mouth opened and shut.

"I mean, when she caught Bessie in her room. What was she wearing then?"

"The same—she wouldn't have her coat on—I don't know as I remember—but the same—she knew she was going out— she'd dress for it—she wouldn't ever dress twice in the same morning."

"Wouldn't she? She didn't have that overall on?" Reggie pointed to a dark garment hanging on the line in the yard which stretched from house to shed.

"No, she didn't, I'm sure. That was in the dirty clothes."

"But you had to wash it today. Well, well. Now we want to have a look at Mrs. Wiven's room."

"If you like. Of course, nothing's been done. It's all untidy."

But Mrs. Wiven's room was primly neat and as clean as the shining passage and stairs. The paint had been worn thin by much washing, the paper was so faded that its rosebud pattern merged into a uniform pinkish gray. An old fur rug by the bedside, a square of threadbare carpet under the rickety round table in the middle of the room, were the only coverings of the scoured floor. The table had one cane chair beside it, and there was a small basket chair by the empty grate— nothing else in the room but the iron bedstead and a combination of chest of drawers, dressing-table, and washstand.

"Is this her own furniture?" Reggie asked.

"No, sir, she hadn't anything. We had to furnish it for her."

"Quite poor, was she?"

"I don't really know how she managed. And, of course, we

didn't ever press her; you couldn't. She had her savings, I suppose."

"No relations?"

"No, sir. She was left quite alone. That was really why she came to us, she was that lonely. She'd say to me she did so want a home, till we took her. When she was feeling down, she used to cry and tell me she didn't know what would become of her. Of course, we wouldn't ever have let her want, poor dear. But I think her bit of money was running out."

Reggie gazed about the room. On the walls were many cards with texts.

"Mr. Brightman put up the good words for her," Mrs. Brightman explained.

" 'In my Father's house are many mansions.' " Reggie read one out slowly.

Mrs. Brightman sobbed, "Ah, she's gone there now. She's happy."

Bell was moving from one to the other of the cupboards beside the grate. Nothing was in them but clothes. He went on to the dressing-table. "She don't seem to have any papers. Only this." He lifted a cash-box, and money rattled in it.

"I couldn't say, I'm sure," Mrs. Brightman whimpered.

Reggie stood by the table. "Did she have her meals up here?" he asked.

Mrs. Brightman thought about that. "Mostly she didn't. She liked to sit down with us."

Reggie fingered the table-cloth, pulled it off, and looked at the cracked veneer beneath. He stooped, felt the strip of old carpet under the table, drew it back. On the boards beneath was a patch of damp.

Mrs. Brightman came nearer. "Well there!" she said. "That comes of my not doing out the room. She must have had an accident with her slops and never told me."

Reggie did not answer. He wandered round the room, stopped by the window a moment, and turned to the door.

"I'm taking this cash-box, ma'am," said Bell.

"If you think right—" Mrs. Brightman drew back. "It's not for me to say—I don't mind, myself." She looked from one to the other. "Will that be all, then?"

"Nothing more here." Reggie opened the door.

As they went downstairs, the shop bell rang again, and she hurried on to answer it. The two men returned to the room behind the shop.

"Poor old woman," Bell grunted. "You can see what sort of a life she was having—that dingy room and her money running out—I wouldn't wonder if she committed suicide."

"Wouldn't be wonderful. No," Reggie murmured. "Shut up."

From the shop came a man's voice, lazy and genial. "Good afternoon, mum. I want a bit o' salts o' lemon. About two penn'orth would do me."

There was a mutter from Mrs. Brightman. "We don't keep it."

"What? They told me I'd be sure to get it 'ere. Run out of it, 'ave you?"

"We never did keep it," Mrs. Brightman said. "Whoever told you we did?"

"All right, all right. Keep your hair on, missus. Where can I get it?"

"How should I know? I don't rightly know what it is."

"Don't you? Sorry I spoke. Used for cleaning, you know."

Bell glowered at Reggie, for the humorous cockney voice was the voice of his chauffeur. But the cold severity of Reggie's round face gave no sign.

"We don't use it, nor we don't keep it, nor any chemist's stuff," Mrs. Brightman was answering.

"Oh, good day!" The bell rang again as the shop door closed.

Mrs. Brightman came back. "Running in and out of the shop all day with silly people," she panted. She looked from one to the other, questioning, afraid.

"I was wonderin'," Reggie murmured. "Did Mrs. Wiven have her meals with you yesterday—or in her room?"

"Down here." The swollen eyes looked at him and looked away. "She did usual, I told you. She liked to."

"And which was the last meal she ever had?"

Mrs. Brightman suppressed a cry. "You do say things! Breakfast was the last she had here. She took out a bit o' lunch and tea."

"Yes. When was that put ready?"

"I had it done first thing, knowing she meant to get out— and she always liked to start early. It was there on the sideboard waiting at breakfast."

"Then it was ready before the children went out? Before she had her quarrel with Bessie?"

Mrs. Brightman swallowed. "So it was."

112

"Oh. Thank you. Rather strong, the tea in her flask," Reggie mumbled.

"She always had it fairly strong. I'm just the same myself."

"Convenient," Reggie said. "Now you'll take me down into the cellar, Mrs. Brightman."

"What?" She drew back so hastily that she was brought up by the wall. "The cellar?" Her eyes seemed to stand out more than ever, so they stared at him, the whites of them more widely bloodshot. With an unsteady hand she thrust back the hair from her sweating brow. "The cellar? There's nothing in the cellar."

"You think not?" Reggie smiled. "Come down and see."

She gave a moaning cry; she stumbled away to the door at the back, and opened it, and stood holding by the door-post, looking out to the paved yard.

From the shed in it appeared Brightman's bearded face. "Were you looking for me, dearie?" he asked, and brought his lank shape into sight.

She made a gesture to him; she went to meet him and muttered: "Matthew! They're asking me to take 'em down to the cellar."

"Well, to be sure!" Brightman gave Reggie and Bell a glance of melancholy, pitying surprise. "I don't see any reason in that." He held her up, he stroked her and gently remonstrated. "But there's no reason they shouldn't go to the cellar if they want to, Florrie. We ain't to stand in the way of anything as the police think right. We ain't got anything to hide."

An inarticulate quavering sound came from her.

"That's all right, my dearie, that's all right," Brightman soothed her.

"Is it?" Bell growled. "So you've been here all the time, Mr. Brightman. While she sent us to look for you down at your own place. Why didn't you show up before?"

"I've only just come in, sir," Brightman said quietly. "I came in by the back. I was just putting things to rights in the wash-house. The wife's been so pushed. I didn't know you gentlemen were here. You're searching all the premises, are you? I'm agreeable. I'm sure it's in order, if you say so. But I don't know what you're looking for."

"Mrs. Brightman will show us," said Reggie, and grasped her arm.

"Don't, don't," she wailed.

"You mustn't be foolish, dearie," said Brightman. "You know there's nothing in the cellar. Show the gentlemen if they want. I'll go with you."

"Got a torch, Bell?" said Reggie.

"I have." Bell went back into the room. "And here's a lamp, too." He lit it.

Reggie drew the shaking woman through the room into the passage. "That's the door to your cellar. Open it. Come on."

Bell held the lamp overhead behind them. Reggie led her stumbling down the stairs, and Brightman followed.

A musty, dank smell came about them. The lamplight showed a large cellar of brick walls and an earth floor. There was in it a small heap of coal, some sacks and packing-cases and barrels, but most of the dim space was empty. The light glistened on damp.

"Clay soil," Reggie murmured, and smiled at Brightman. "Yes. That was indicated."

"I don't understand you, sir," said Brightman.

"No. You don't. Torch, Bell." He took it and flashed its beam about the cellar. "Oh, yes." He turned to Bell. With a finger he indicated the shining tracks of slugs. "You see?"

"I do," Bell muttered.

Reggie moved to and fro. He stooped. He took out his pocketbook and from it a piece of paper, and with that scraped something from a barrel side, something from the clay floor.

Standing up, he moved the ray of the torch from place to place, held it steady at last to make a circle of light on the ground beneath the steps. "There," he said, and Mrs. Brightman screamed. "Yes. I know. That's where you put her. Look, Bell." His finger pointed to a slug's trail which came into the circle of light, stopped, and went on again at another part of the circle. "It didn't jump. They don't."

He swung round upon Mrs. Brightman. He held out to her the piece of paper cupped in his hand. On it lay two yellow slugs.

She flung herself back, crying loathing and fear.

"Really, gentlemen, really now," Brightman stammered. "This isn't right. This isn't proper. You've no call to frighten a poor woman so. Come away now, Florrie, dearie."

"Where are you going?" Reggie murmured. She did not go. Her eyes were set on the two yellow slugs. " 'Where their

114

worm dieth not,' " Reggie said slowly.

She broke out in screams of hysterical laughter; she tore herself from Brightman, and reeled and fell down writhing and yelling.

"So that is it, Mr. Brightman." Reggie turned to him.

"You're a wicked soul!" Brightman whined. "My poor dearie!" He fell on his knees by her; he began to pray forgiveness for her sins.

"My oath!" Bell muttered, and ran up the steps shouting to his men.

Some time afterwards Reggie left. On the other side of the street, aloof from the gaping, gossiping crowd, superior and placid, his chauffeur smoked a cigarette. It was thrown away; the chauffeur followed him, fell into step beside him. "Did I manage all right, sir?"

"You did. Very neat. Very effective. We are good at destruction. Efficient incinerators. Humble function. Other justification for existence, doubtful. However. Study to improve. What we want now is a toy shop."

"Sir?" Sam was puzzled.

"I said a toy shop," Reggie complained. "A good toy shop. Quick."

The last of the sunlight was shining into the little room at the hospital where Eddie Hill lay. Upon his bed stood part of a bridge built of strips of metal bolted together, a bridge of grand design. He and Reggie were working on the central span.

There was a tap at the door, a murmur from Reggie, and the nurse brought in Bell. He stood looking at Reggie with reproachful surprise. "So that's what you're doing."

"Yes. Something useful at last." Reggie sighed. "Well, well. We'll have to call this a day, young man. Mustn't get yourself tired."

"I'm not tired," the boy protested eagerly. "I'm not, really."

"No. Of course not. Ever so much better. But there's another day tomorrow. And you have a big job. Must keep fit to go on with it."

"All right." The boy lay back, looked at his bridge, looked wistfully at Reggie. "I can keep this here, can I, sir?"

"Rather. On the table by the bed. So it'll be there when you wake. Nice, making things, isn't it? Yes. You're going to make a lot now. Goodbye. Jolly, tomorrow, what? Good-bye." He went out with Bell. "Now what's the matter with you?" he complained.

"Well, I had to have a word with you, sir. This isn't going to be so easy. I thought I'd get you at the mortuary doing the post-mortem."

"Minor matter. Simple matter. Only the dead buryin' their dead. The boy was urgent."

"I'm not saying you're not right," said Bell wearily. "But it is a tangle of a case. The divisional surgeon reports Mrs. Brightman's mad."

"Yes. I agree. What about it?"

"Seemed to me you pretty well drove her to it. Those slugs— oh, my Lord."

"Got you, did it? It rather got me. I'd heard Eddie talk of 'the worm that dieth not.' I should say he'd seen that cellar. Dreamed of it. However. I didn't drive the woman mad. She'd been mad some time. Not medically mad. Not legally mad. But morally. That was the work of our Mr. Brightman. I only clarified the situation. He almost sent the boy the same way. That's been stopped. That isn't going to happen now. That's the main issue. And we win on it. Not too bad. But rather a grim day. Virtue has gone out of me. My dear chap!" He took Bell's arm affectionately. "You're tucked up too."

"I don't mind owning I've had enough," said Bell. "This sort of thing tells me I'm not as young as I was. And it's all a tangle yet."

"My dear chap! Oh, my dear chap!" Reggie murmured. "Empty, aren't we? Come on. Come home with me."

While Sam drove them back, he declined to talk. He stretched in the corner of the car and closed his eyes, and bade Bell do the same. While they ate deviled sole and an entre-côte Elsie, he discussed the qualities of his cook, and of the Romanée which they drank, and argued bitterly (though he shared it) that the cheese offered in deference to Bell's taste, a bland Stilton, was an insult to the raspberries, the dish of which he emptied.

But when they were established in big chairs in his library, with brandy for Bell and seltzer for himself, and both pipes were lit, "Did you say a tangle?" he murmured. "Oh, no. Not now. The rest is only routine for your young men and the lawyers. It'll work out quite easy. You can see it all. When

Mrs. Brightman was left a widow with her little shop, the pious Brightman pounced on her and mastered her. The little shop was only a little living. Brightman wanted more. Children were kept very short—they might fade out, they might go to the bad—either way the devout Brightman would be relieved of their keep; and meanwhile it was pleasant making 'em believe they were wicked. Old Mrs. Wiven was brought in as a lodger—not out of charity as the wretched Mrs. Brightman was trained to say; she must have had a bit of money. Your young men will be able to trace that. And they'll find Brightman got it out of her and used it to set up his second-hand furniture business. Heard of that sort of thing before, what?"

"I should say I have," Bell grunted. "My Lord, how often! The widow that falls for a pious brute—the old woman lodger with a bit of money."

"Oh, yes. Dreary old game. And then the abnormal variations began. Pious bullyin' and starvin' didn't turn the boy into a criminal idiot. He has a mind. He has an imagination, poor child. Mrs. Wiven didn't give herself up to Brightman like his miserable wife. She had a temper. So the old game went wrong. Mrs. Wiven took to fussin' about her money. As indicated by Bessie. Mrs. Wiven was going to be very awkward. Your young men will have to look about and get evidence she'd been grumbling. Quite easy. Lots of gossip will be goin'. Some of it true. Most of it useful at the trial."

Bell frowned. "Fighting with the gloves off, aren't you?"

"Oh, no. No. Quite fair. We have to fight the case without the children. I'm not going to have Eddie put in the witness-box, to be tortured about his mad mother helpin' murder. That might break him up forever. And he's been tortured enough. The brute Brightman isn't going to hurt him any more. The children won't be givin' evidence. I'll get half the College of Physicians to certify they're not fit, if they're asked for. But that's not goin' to leave Mr. Brightman any way out. Now then. Things bein' thus, Brightman had his motive to murder Mrs. Wiven. If he didn't stop her mouth she'd have him in jail. Being a clever fellow, he saw that Eddie's record of stealin' would be very useful. By the way— notice that queer little incident, Bessie bein' caught pilferin' by Mrs. Wiven yesterday morning? Brightman may have fixed that up for another black mark against the children. I wonder. But it didn't go right. He must have had a jolt when

Mrs. Wiven called out they were all thieves. Kind of compellin' immediate action. His plan would have been all ready, of course—salts of lemon in her favorite strong tea; a man don't think of an efficient way of poisonin' all of a sudden. And then the incalculable Eddie intervened. Reaction of Mrs. Wiven's explosion on him, a sort of divine command to save his sister from hell by seeing she died innocent. When Brightman had the news of that effort at drowning, he took it as a godsend. Hear him thanking heaven? Boy who was wicked enough for anything. Mr. Brightman read his title clear to mansions in the skies. And Mrs. Wiven was promptly given her cup o' tea. She was sick in her room, sick on her overall and on her underclothes. Evidence for all that conclusive. Remember the damp floor. I should say Mrs. Brightman had another swab at that today. She has a craze about cleaning. We saw that. Feels she never can get clean, poor wretch. Well. Mrs. Wiven died. Oxalic poisoning generally kills quick. I hope it did. They hid the body in the cellar. Plan was clever. Take the body out in the quiet of the night and dump it on the common with a flask of poisoned tea—put her bag in Eddie's den. All clear for the intelligent police. Devil of a boy poisoned the old lady to steal her money, and was drownin' his little sister so she shouldn't tell on him. That's what you thought, wasn't it? Yes. Well-made plan. It stood up against us last night."

"You did think there was something queer," Bell said.

"I did," Reggie sighed. "Physical smell. Damp musty smell. Probably the cellar. And the Brightmans didn't smell nice spiritually. However. Lack of confidence in myself. And I have no imagination. I ought to have waited and watched. My error. My grave error. Well. It was a clever plan. But Brightman was rather bustled. That may account for his errors. Fatal errors. Omission to remove the soiled underclothes when the messed-up overall was taken off. Failure to allow for the habits of *limax flavus*."

"What's that?" said Bell.

"Official name of yellow slug—cellar slug. The final, damning evidence. I never found any reason for the existence of slugs before. However. To round it off—when you look into Mr. Brightman's furniture business, you'll find that he has a van, or the use of one. You must prove it was used last night. That's all. Quite simple now. But a wearin' case." He gazed at Bell with large solemn eyes, "His wife! He'd

118

schooled her thorough. Ever hear anything more miserably appealing than her or her dear babies and poor old Mrs. Wiven? No. Took a lot of breakin' down."

"Ah. You were fierce."

"Oh, no. No." Reggie sighed. "I was bein' merciful. She couldn't be saved. My job was to save the children. And she— if that brute hadn't twisted her, she'd have done anything to save 'em, too. She'd been a decent soul once. No. She won't be giving evidence against me."

"Why, how should she?" Bell gaped.

"I was thinkin' of the day of judgment," Reggie murmured. "Well, well. Post-mortem in the morning. Simple straight job. Then I'll be at the hospital if you want me. Have to finish Eddie's bridge. And then we're going to build a ship. He's keen on ships."

A PERFECTLY ORDINARY CASE
OF BLACKMAIL

BY A. A. MILNE

A. A. Milne was born on January 18, 1882, in London. At Trinity College he edited the *Granta*. After graduation in 1903 he returned to London to become a journalist, with little success until 1906, when he was offered the assistant editorship of *Punch*. He married Dorothy de Sélincourt and in 1915 joined the Royal Warwickshire Regiment. By the time he was demobilized he was sufficiently recognized as a writer so that he could turn to writing full-time. Although best known for his Winnie-the-Pooh stories, his detective fiction is noteworthy. Alexander Woollcott called *The Red House Mystery* one of the three best mystery stories of all time.

A STOUT, OLD-YOUNG man of forty, Mr. Cedric Watherston of Watherston & Reeves, Solicitors, sat at his office table, knitting. He was not a good knitter, but he was proud of the fact that he could knit at all. He had learned when a prisoner of war in 1917, having walked straight into a German trench on his first journey up the line; and with the passage of years the circumstance of his capture had also become, in some odd way, a matter for pride. He liked sentences which began, "I remember when I was a prisoner in Holzminden." When a client was announced, he put the ball of wool, the needles, and the unfinished sock in the top left-hand drawer, smoothed his hair with both hands, and waited for the visitor to be shown in.

"Sir Vernon Filmer."

Mr. Watherston rose to shake hands with one of his most distinguished clients. "Glad to see you, Sir Vernon. You don't often give us the pleasure. On no unpleasant business, I trust?"

Sir Vernon did not look as if he were glad to see Mr. Watherston. He was a tall, fair, cold man, with pale-blue eyes, a prominent nose, and a small prim mouth. He was one of those natural politicians who are always conveniently there when ministerial posts are being given out. If there were to be ten knighthoods on New Year's Day for what could only be described as "public services," and nine had been decided upon, his name would come irresistibly to the mind for the tenth place.

"Cigarette?"

Sir Vernon waved it away. Mr. Watherston lighted one for himself, leaned back in his chair, remembered to put his fingertips together.

"I am being blackmailed," Sir Vernon said.

"Dear, dear, we must do something about that," said Mr. Watherston with an exaggerated calm which hid most of his emotions. Surprise was the least of these, for he had a dislike of politicians.

"That is naturally what I am expecting."

Mr. Watherston tried over a few sentences in his mind until he got the right opening. "Blackmail," he said deli-

121

cately, "implies the previous commission, or alleged commission, of some offense. Offenses can be classified as offenses against the law, offenses against morality, and offenses against the social code. Perhaps, in this case, one should add political offenses. Which class or classes of offense, Sir Vernon, does the threatened exposure allege?"

"Legal," said Sir Vernon, adding primly, "I have nothing whatever on my conscience."

Yes, yes, thought Mr. Watherston, but your conscience must be in pretty good training by now.

"To put it frankly, then, Sir Vernon, the blackmailer is threatening to reveal some action of yours which is punishable by law?"

"Yes. To put it with greater accuracy, if the truth had come out at the time, I might have been prosecuted, but need not necessarily have been convicted. I should think that today there was no possibility of conviction."

"When did this happen?"

"Nearly thirty years ago—1909, to be exact."

"Ah! So it is the social and political consequences which really matter today?"

"Obviously. As they did, to an overwhelming extent, at the time. Do you not think it would be illuminating if I told you about it?"

Mr. Watherston held up a hasty hand. He had had no experience of blackmail, and he disliked the idea of being accessory after the fact to an apparently undiscovered crime. His mind wandered vaguely back to 1909, trying to think of the sort of contemporary illegalities in which Sir Vernon, then a young man of twenty-two, might have been mixed up. Having himself been a boy of twelve at the time, he came to no conclusion.

"Sir Vernon," he said. "It will be distressing for you to confide this story to anyone. Let us consider the matter on general lines for the moment. There are three ways of dealing with a blackmailer. The first is to submit to his demands."

Sir Vernon indicated what he thought of that.

"The second is to prosecute him. As you know, this can be done anonymously, under the disarming name of Mr. X."

Sir Vernon gave a short, unpleasant laugh.

"The only remaining method is to settle with the blackmailer out of court. I could pay his demands for you; I could instruct the prosecution for you. But frankly, Sir Vernon, I am

122

not competent to get the better of a scoundrel whether by negotiation, threat, or personal violence." He let this sink in for a moment and then added, "Fortunately I know the man who is."

"Private detective or shady solicitor?"

"Solicitor. A shady solicitor in the sense that he usually acts for the submerged classes, but entirely loyal to his clients, whether prostitutes or Prime Ministers. And a very able man."

"You know him personally?"

"Oh, yes. The fortunes of war threw us together at Holzminden, where we happened to be prisoners."

"H'm," said Sir Vernon doubtfully

"I understand your dislike of confiding in a stranger. Perhaps I should have added that he has very strong feelings about the detestable crime of blackmail. It is the one charge which he has always refused to defend in court—which is more than can be said for the whole of the bar. To get the better of a blackmailer he would go to the extreme length of his purse, his time, and—the law."

"Very well," said Sir Vernon. "I agree to accept your advice. I had better see this fellow in my own house at, say nine o'clock this evening. Will you arrange that?"

Mr. Watherston made a note, saying, "His name is Scroope." He got up and held out his hand. "Perhaps you will let me know how the matter goes on. And if there is anything else I can do, Sir Vernon—"

They shook hands and went to the door together.

"Cold fish," thought Mr. Watherston, as he returned to his table. "One can't help disliking him. I wonder what he did."

He picked up the telephone. Afterward, there being nothing else to do, he went back to his knitting.

Being asked by an interviewer to what he attributed his success in life Mr. Scroope replied, "My eyebrows." These had a natural quirk which seemed to express a good-tempered amusement with the world, and to admit his companion of the moment to an equal share in that amusement. "You and I," they seemed to say, "*we* know." It is doubtful if anybody had ever had a private joke with Sir Vernon, nor was he the man to wish to be on confidential terms with anyone less important than himself, least of all a shady solicitor; but even he recognized the eyebrows as evidence of a knowledge of the world. Mr. Scroope obviously knew his way about.

"A cigar, thanks," said Mr. Scroope. "Nothing to drink.

Now then, Sir Vernon, Watherston tells me that you are being blackmailed. Who told *you*?"

"I don't understand," said Sir Vernon coldly.

"Dammit, one doesn't wake up in the morning and say, 'I've a sort of feeling that there are blackmailers about.' Something must have given you the idea."

"Naturally I had a letter," Sir Vernon said.

"Why 'naturally'? You might have had a telephone message. Is that the letter?"

Sir Vernon released it. "It came this morning through the post."

"H'm. Typed. Signed, 'Well-Wisher.' Humorous. D'you know who wrote it?"

"Not with any certainty."

"Five hundred in pound notes on Saturday as a guarantee of good faith, followed by five hundred every six weeks. Sounds as if he wanted to get married. Well, that gives us six weeks before the second payment. Six weeks in which to think of something."

"You suggest I should pay the five hundred?"

"Oh, certainly. At least, *you* won't, I will. We'll keep you out of it."

"Read the rest of the letter."

"I have. You are given till Saturday to get the money; you are to communicate with nobody; you are to have your car waiting outside your door on Saturday morning, ready to drive yourself to a rendezvous which will be given you by letter before you start."

"Perhaps you are not aware that I am lunching at Chequers on Saturday?"

"Nobody tells me anything," said Mr. Scroope sadly. "But then, why shouldn't you? The food's quite good, I hear. And who could give you a better alibi than the Prime Minister?"

"You propose to keep the rendezvous yourself?"

"As Sir Vernon Filmer? Do I look like it? But I daresay I can find somebody who will pass for you at a distance. All you'll be asked to do, I fancy, is to leave the money in a certain spot, where the blackmailer will pick it up afterward. He's giving nothing away. Now then, he says, 'I have a letter written on board the *Ladybird* on September 15, 1909. Don't tell me you've forgotten it.'" He looked up. "Have you forgotten it?"

"No."

"Right. Then you'd better tell me."

"There were three of us on the *Ladybird* that summer afternoon: Robert Hayforth, the owner, myself, and a local hand called Towers. We had been fishing close inshore. Hayforth, a powerful and devoted swimmer, had suggested a swim. The wind was freshening, the sea uninviting, and I stayed on board. Hayforth, whose idea of a swim was half a mile out and half a mile back, had been gone about ten minutes, when suddenly Towers came sidling up to me, his right hand behind his back. I'd never liked him, nobody in the place did, but he was a useful man in a boat, and Hayforth often took him on. He had a bottle in his hand, and he was holding it like a club. He—he accused me of"—Sir Vernon's face could still show disgust at the idea—" 'messing about with his wife.' "

"Were you?"

Sir Vernon looked at Scroope contemptuously, and went on: "I asked him what the devil he was talking about. I thought he was drunk. He said that when he had finished with me I'd have the sort of face that nobody's girl would want to mess about with. It was horrible. Such a foul weapon, and he was much more powerful than I. Hayforth was out of sight and hailing distance. I was at the man's mercy. It was his life or mine. I saw red."

He poured himself out a brandy and swallowed it quickly. In another moment, thought Scroope, all his past life will flash before his eyes. Why must politicians always talk in clichés?

"And you killed him," Scroope said. "How?"

"I don't know to this day how I did it. I seemed to be endowed with superhuman strength. Fear, I suppose, and furious indignation at that loathsome weapon."

"You killed him, and you went on killing him. Is that right?"

"Yes."

"And when you had finished, it didn't look like self-defense, it looked like deliberate, premeditated, brutal murder. Is that right?"

"Yes, but it wasn't."

"It's what things look like which matter to the law. Well, and then Hayforth yelled, 'Ship ahoy!' and you helped him on board, and he saw the body and said, 'Lawks a mussy, what's all this?' And you told him. And he agreed to help you. Is that right?"

"Agreed on conditions."

"Ah, yes, now I'm seeing it. That letter was to him. Exonerating him and admitting sole responsibility. Why a letter? Couldn't he trust you?"

"If anything had happened to me, if the body had been washed up—"

"It would have been awkward for him. Because—stop me if I'm wrong—*he* was the man who had been messing about."

"Yes. I had no idea of it, but I suppose there were other people who had guessed."

"So, when he had got the letter safely in his pocket, you put out to sea—the wind was freshening, you said—and it sounded sufficiently plausible to say that Towers had been washed overboard. No attempts to save him?"

"It blew up into a gale, and we didn't pick up our moorings until three o'clock next morning; we put the accident at just after midnight. In the dark, in that weather, with only two of us to work the boat, what could we have done? We nearly followed him as it was. I never expected to see land again."

"Convincing. And no suspicions by anybody?"

"None that I heard of. Towers was a thoroughgoing rascal. Nobody missed him."

"Not even his wife?"

"She least of all." Sir Vernon cleared his throat and added, "I should explain that my whole career was in the balance at this time, and that I had no other course open to me. I had just left Oxford with unusually brilliant prospects—"

Scroope picked up the letter. "D'you think this is Hayforth, Sir Vernon?" he asked.

"It might be, of course. Equally, I suppose, he might be dead, and somebody might have found my letter among his papers. I lost sight of him in the war, and haven't heard of him since."

"That sort of man?"

"Obviously not in those days," said Sir Vernon somewhat stiffly, "or he wouldn't have been my friend. But he was always a reckless fellow, and might have been knocked about by the war, have fallen on hard times, and slowly sunk to— this. The war," said Sir Vernon, who had fortunately missed it, "did not improve people's characters."

"Is there anything in this letter which indicates knowledge not contained in your letter to Hayforth?"

"I don't think so."

"For instance, why should it be taken for granted that you can drive your own car? Lots of people can't."

For the first time that evening Sir Vernon looked at Scroope with respect. "That's true," he said thoughtfully.

"Were you driving a car at that time?"

"My wife gave me a Rolls as a wedding present a few months later."

"I congratulate you. Driven Hayforth in it?"

"Probably. I saw something of him up until the war began."

Scroope got up and threw the end of his cigar into the fire. "Obviously we must find the man first. I shall sleep here on Friday night, so as to be with you when your instructions come." He took a notebook and pencil from his pocket. "Turn your head to one side, I want the profile." He began to draw. "About five feet eleven inches, aren't you? I think I've got just the man. Muffled and goggled, of course, which is what anyone would be who was keeping a date with a blackmailer. My man—Dean is his name—will come in the back way at eight o'clock on Saturday morning. With a false mustache. This is going to be fun. There, that's not bad." He had the drawing up and admired it. "Thank God, it's money he wants."

"What else are blackmailers ever after?" asked Sir Vernon contemptuously.

"Seats in the Cabinet," said Mr. Scroope. "The way I'm going to work, that would have made it more difficult."

On Saturday morning at 8:30, Sir Vernon stepped nervously from his front door and walked across to his garage. It was a chilly February morning, and even for that short distance he thought it well to wear a thick fawn traveling coat and a checked cap. He brought his car round to the front door and left it there. Mr. Scroope and breakfast were waiting for him in the morning room.

"Now then, Sir Vernon," Mr. Scroope said, his mouth full of omelette, "let's get down to it. You are to be at the fifth milestone between Wellborough and Chiselton at twelve-thirty. You say you know the road. How?"

"It was near Chiselton that Hayforth kept his boat."

"Good. How long would it take you to get there?"

"Three hours."

"Then Dean must take three hours. He's just arrived; we'll

have him in directly, and you can show him tne place on the map. What's the country like?"

"Quite flat. No houses, no trees, no possibility of concealment, as I remember. A long, almost straight road."

"Dean will hide the money behind the milestone—nothing elaborate, just enough not to catch the eye of a passer-by. Then he'll drive on, turning off at Chiselton and coming back to London another way. Obviously, the blackmailer will be a little way behind him up to the milestone. He may be outside the house now—he was in London last night to post the letter—in which case he'll follow your car down. Dean, in your coat and cap, will be good enough for him."

Sir Vernon had picked up the letter again, and was studying it. "You talk of 'him' all the time," he said. "Does it not occur to you that it is more likely to be the work of a gang?"

"With a mastermind at the center of the spider's web?" said Mr. Scroope hopefully.

"I gather," said Sir Vernon coldly, "that you think otherwise."

Scroope pushed the toast away, and spoke seriously. "I'll tell you what I think," he said, "and then I'll tell you my plans. You're paying for this treat, and you're entitled to know. I think that if two young men go out in a boat for a summer afternoon's offshore fishing and bathing, they will not be wearing oilskins. I think that if one of them has just had a desperate fight for his life, any letter which he writes immediately after, with a shaking hand and under the stress of great emotion, will be uncharacteristic and only just legible. I think that if a small boat, manned by two people in flannels, is fighting a gale for eight hours, the occupants will not merely be wet, but soaked literally to the skin. And I think that after it's all over, and now that the unexpected storm has removed all possibility of suspicion, Mr. Robert Hayforth will find a piece of sodden paper in his pocket with not a single decipherable word on it, will wonder what the devil it is, and then throw it away with a laugh at the ridiculous caution which inspired it. What that piece of paper would have looked like thirty years later baffles the imagination. In short, you may be certain that the blackmailer is Hayforth himself, and that it is only his word against yours."

Sir Vernon permitted himself a little enthusiasm. "But that is most satisfactory, Mr. Scroope. You relieve my mind considerably."

128

"Yes, but even so, he can be extremely mischievous. So, since blackmailers are better out of action, I propose, with your financial assistance, to put him out of action."

"Now that we know who he is—"

"We don't. We only know who he was: a face and a name of thirty years ago. That doesn't help. But this letter shows that he is sticking to familiar ground. It is probable that he is living in the district, and almost certain that he has a car. Ever studied history?"

"I got a first in history in my finals at Oxford," said Sir Vernon.

"Pooh, I don't mean that sort of dead-alive history. Real history. Criminal history. Ever studied the Lindbergh case?"

There was no need to wait for an answer; Sir Vernon's delicate shrug had given it.

"What it came to in the end was that they knew all about the man except who he was. However, he had the ransom notes—numbers taken, of course—and one day he would use them. That was their only hope of getting him. But how? Every gasoline station in the neighborhod was given a list of the notes, and told to write down secretly on the back of any ten-dollar bill paid in exchange for gas the number of the car which was filled. Then the list of ransom notes could be consulted at leisure in the evening."

"Most ingenious. And now you have taken the numbers of the notes?"

"Of course. And I shall go down to Wellborough this afternoon, and make arrangements. Not being official, it will cost money. But by the time we've made the second payment to Hayforth, I shall know what he's calling himself and where he lives. I'll tell you something else. He says that he will give you the second rendezvous on March twenty-fifth, and that it will be in an entirely different part of the country. It won't. If his plan works successfully today, as I mean it to do, he will repeat it exactly. It leaves you just as uncertain until the last moment, and saves him the trouble of looking for an equally convenient place."

"And when you've found him?"

"Then," said Mr. Scroope with happy smile, "the real fun begins."

When a man calling himself Mr. Richard Hastings was arrested for possessing and passing forged notes, he did what all intelligent prisoners do. He sent for Mr. Scroope.

"Well," said Mr. Scroope, twinkling at him, "what's the story, Mr. Hastings?" He looked at the man with interest, summed him up as a gentleman gone to the bad, and offered him a cigarette.

"Thanks. I've been arrested, the Lord only knows why, for—"

"Yes, I know the police story, now I want to know yours."

"I swear to you that I am—"

"—absolutely innocent. Naturally. But we still need a story to explain why a quantity of forged notes was found in your safe, and why several others which had been passed in the neighborhood were traced to you. What is that story?"

"They were planted on me."

"By whom?"

"Some enemy, I suppose."

"I see. What about the notes in circulation which have been through your hands?"

"They must have gone through many hands. Why pick on me?"

"Obviously because you had such a large store of them in your safe. We want a better story than you're giving me, Mr. Hastings."

"I can't tell you anything better."

"Then," said Mr. Scroope politely, "I will wish you good morning." He got up. "Just one word of advice, if I may. The story which you will be telling to some other solicitor need not be true; but it must sound sufficiently like the truth to allow him a temporary hallucination that it was possible." He held out his hand with a smile.

Richard Hastings waved the hand away. "Wait," he said. "You'd better have it. I found the damned things."

"That's better. Where?"

"Oh, hidden under a stone."

"You know, I don't think that that will quite carry convic-tion—using the word 'conviction' in its less technical sense, of course. It must have been rather a moment in your life when you found such a large packet of notes. You would be ex-pected to remember the historic spot."

"Oh, well, if you want the exact place, it was behind the fifth milestone on the Wellborough-Chiselton road."

"You counted—and remembered?"

Richard Hastings looked up angrily. "What the devil do you mean? It said, 'Wellborough, five miles,' didn't it?"

"You were looking behind milestones for something?"

"I happened to sit down there. Convenient to lean against for a few minutes. I noticed that the ground was disturbed, and investigated."

"And said 'Hallo, what's this?' "

"Exactly."

"And what was it?"

"A parcel of one-pound notes. Damned odd, I thought."

"And so you decided to steal them?"

"What's that?"

"You wish to plead guilty to an alternative charge of stealing by finding. Is that right?"

"Right!" Hastings said suddenly. "I stole them. That's not very serious, is it? Well, now you've got the truth."

"It's odd," Mr. Scroope said, "that a man, driving along the Wellborough-Chiselton road on a cold and frosty morning, should stop at precisely the fifth milestone, lean against it rather than against the cushions of his car."

Richard Hastings jumped to his feet, and said angrily, "What's all this? You trying to trap me?"

"I'm trying to do," said Scroope mildly, "what counsel for the prosecution will do much more thoroughly."

"Sorry. I see the point; but naturally"—he gave an awkward little laugh—"I'm a bit upset about the whole thing. But I do absolutely swear, and it's gospel truth, that I didn't know that the notes were forged, and that I found them precisely where I said I did."

"Oh, come, we must tell them a little more. When you happened to find them."

"I can't remember the exact date."

"Which date can't you remember?"

Mr. Richard Hastings wiped his forehead with the back of his hand and said, "I haven't the vaguest idea what you're talking about."

"I want the date which you can't exactly remember, when you got out of your car, leaned against the fifth milestone, and accidentally found a packet of notes. Just venture a rough guess."

"The first week in February."

"About seven weeks ago. The first forged note which came to hand was paid to the Lion Garage at Chiselton on February eighteenth. So that fits nicely. Now what about the second date? When you again got out of your car, leaned against the fifth milestone, and accidentally found a second packet of notes."

Mr. Richard Hastings licked his lips. "What makes you think I did that?"

"Two parcels were found in your safe. One, opened, contained about four hundred fifty forged notes. The other, unopened—or, possibly, opened, examined and tied up again—contained five hundred."

"I can explain that. It's all coming back to me. The parcel which I found—"

"In the first week in February?"

"Yes. It was really two parcels, done up together. I counted the top one and it was five hundred. I was forgetting for the moment about the other parcel, which I didn't open. Obviously there was another five hundred in that. Making the thousand, as you were saying. Silly of me."

"Not at all. Very natural. Then all that we have left to explain," said Mr. Scroope cheerfully, "is why the inner wrapper of the second parcel was a sheet of *The Western Morning News* dated March twenty-fourth—six weeks later."

Robert Hayforth banged the table with his hand, and cried, "Blast him, he's framed me! The sniveling devil!"

"Sniveling—? Who is he?"

"The Right Honorable Sir Vernon Filmer." He dragged the words out sneeringly. "All right, you've got it. It was hush money. He killed a man, murdered him; that's your smug, hypocritical Right Honorable. You want me to tell the truth in court. Right, I'll tell it—and we'll go down together."

Mr. Scroope got up. "I've chosen never to defend blackmail cases. Everything which you have told me is, of course, in the strictest confidence, and I now fade out of the case. I warn you, the penalty for blackmail is, next to that for murder, the severest known to the law. Any written evidence which you may have had against Sir Vernon Filmer will be in possession of the police, and you will not be permitted to use it. An unsupported accusation made in your defense would only make your case worse and your punishment more severe. If you take my unprofessional advice, you will plead 'Not Guilty' to the present charge, give no evidence, and leave it to your counsel to suggest that in some way you are the innocent victim of a conspiracy."

He picked up his hat and went to the door. "Oh, by the way," he added, "if it gets about, though I don't see why it should, that I declined this case, it will not prejudice the court against you." The eyebrows went up in that humorous quirk of his. "It may even do you good. There is an absurd legend in legal circles that I defend only the guilty."

Mr. Cedric Watherston picked up the telephone and said, "Watherston here."

"Busy?"

"Just turning the heel."

"Anyone listening in?" the voice said.

"My dear fellow!"

"Right. Then I thought you would like to know that your honorable friend is relieved of all anxiety for five years."

"Fancy! I do congratulate you. I was reading an interesting case this morning, forging and passing and all that sort of thing, and oddly enough—but, of course, it's only a coincidence."

"I expect so. A respectable family lawyer really shouldn't read criminal cases."

"It just caught the eye. Ah, what do you think will happen at the end of the five years?"

"I think that you will lose a distinguished client, and the country a distinguished servant. Quite suddenly."

"Ah! I was fearing the same thing myself." Mr. Watherston chuckled. "You know, you're a very naughty man. Here was a perfectly ordinary case of blackmail and there is hardly a crime in the calendar which you have not committed in order to bring the blackmailer to justice. If," he added, "you know what I mean by justice."

"Well, you see," the voice said apologetically, "I don't *like* blackmailers."

"Neither do I."

"Comes to that, I don't like Sir Vernon Filmer."

"How right you are," said Mr. Watherston cheerfully.

A LESSON IN CRIME

BY G. D. H. AND M. I. COLE

Economists George D. and M. I. (Margaret Isabel) Cole, who were married in 1918, were for many years among the leaders of socialist thought in England and an important mystery-writing team. He was educated at Oxford, where he later became a fellow and reader of economics; Mrs. Cole, sister of mystery writer Raymond Postgate, was educated at Cambridge and lectured at London University for a number of years. Both were officers of the Fabian Society. They had three children. Mr. Cole died in 1959. Critics have especially acclaimed their *Death in the Quarry*, *The Murder at Crome House*, and the short-story collection, *Superintendent Wilson's Holiday*.

(No photograph available of Mrs. Cole)

JOSEPH NEWTON SETTLED himself comfortably in his corner of a first-class compartment on the Cornish Riviera express. So far, he had the compartment to himself; and if, by strewing rugs, bags, books and papers about he could make himself look numerous enough to drive fellow-travellers away, there was hope he might remain undisturbed—for the long train was far from full. Let us take a look at him, and learn a little about him before his adventures begin—and end.

Age? Forty-five would not be a bad guess, though, in fact, he is rather less. As for his physical condition, "well-nourished" is a polite description; and we, who desire to have no illusions, can safely call him paunchy, and, without positive grossness, flabby with good living. His face is puffy; his mouth is loose, and inclined to leer.

His fair hair, which is rapidly growing thin, is immaculately brushed, and his clothes are admirably cut and well-tended, though he has not the art of wearing them well. Altogether he looks a prosperous, thoroughly self-satisfied, and somewhat self-indulgent member of the British middle class; and that is precisely what he is.

His walk in life? You would put him down as a business man, possibly a merchant or a middle-sized employer, not a professional man. There you would be both right and wrong. He is a professional man, in a sense; and he is certainly in business.

In fact, he is Joseph Newton, the best-seller, whose crime stories and shockers were plastered all over the bookstall he has just left with his burden of newspapers under his arm. He has sold—heaven knows how many million copies of his stories, and his serial rights, first, second, and third, cost fabulous sums to secure.

But why describe him further? All the world knows him. And now he is on his way to Cornwall, where he has a pleasant little seaside cottage with no less than twenty-seven bedrooms.

The train starts, and Newton's carriage still remains empty save for himself. He heaves a fat sigh of relief and picks up a magazine, in which he turns instinctively to a story by himself. For the moment he cannot remember who wrote it. Poor stuff, he thinks. He must find out which "ghost" was responsible, and sack him.

Joseph Newton was interrupted in his reflections at this point by the consciousness that someone was looking at him. He glanced up and saw the figure of a man who was standing in the corridor and staring fixedly at him, with a curious air of abstraction. Newton stared back, trying to look as unwelcoming as possible. It would be really bad luck, he felt, if someone were to invade his compartment now.

The newcomer, after a moment more of staring, pushed back the door and came in, flinging down on top of one of Newton's bags a rug and a pillow done up in a strap. He seemed to have no other luggage. Newton unwillingly got up and cleared a corner of his belongings, and the stranger sat down and began to unbuckle his strap. Then he settled himself comfortably with the pillow behind his head, and closed his eyes. "I hope to goodness he doesn't snore," Newton thought.

While our second traveller is thus peacefully settling himself for a doze, we may as well take a good look at him also; for it may be important to know him later on. He is a scraggy little man, probably of sixty or more, with a completely bald pink head and a straggling grey beard which emerges from an incredibly folded and puckered yellow chin. His height is hardly more than five foot six, and his proportions are puny; but there is a wiriness about his spare person that contrasts strongly with Newton's fleshy bulk.

He is dressed, not so much ill as with a carelessness amounting to eccentricity. His clothes, certainly cut by a good tailor, hang in bags all over him. His pockets bulge. His waistcoat is buttoned up wrong, and sets awry, and his shirt has come apart at the neck, so that a disconsolate shirt-stud is hanging out on one side, while his red tie is leaning towards the other. Moreover, the sole of one of his boots has come loose, and flaps helplessly as his crossed leg swings slowly to the rhythm of the train.

Yet, despite these appearances, the newcomer is certainly a gentleman, and one is inclined to deem him eccentric rather than poor. He might be an exceptionally absent-minded professor; though, as a matter of fact, he is not. But who he is Joseph Newton has no idea.

For some time there was silence in the compartment, as the Cornish Riviera sped westward past the long, spreading ribbon of London. Newton's fellow-traveller did not snore. His eyes were closed whenever Newton glanced at him; and yet between whiles the novelist had still a queer feeling of being stared at. He told himself it was nonsense, and tried to bury himself in a Wild West story; but the sensation remained with him. Suddenly, as the train passed Maidenhead Station, his companion spoke, in a quiet positive voice, as of one used to telling idiots what idiots they were. A professional voice, with a touch of Scots accent.

"Talking of murders," it said, "you have really no right to be so careless."

"Eh?" said Newton, so startled that his magazine dropped from his hand to the floor. "Eh, what's that?"

"I said you had no right to be so careless," repeated the other.

Newton retrieved his magazine, and looked his fellow-traveller contemptuously up and down. "I am not aware," he said, "that we were talking of murders, or of anything else, for that matter."

"There, you see," said the other, "you did hear what I said the first time. What I mean to say is that, if you expect intelligent people to read your stories, you might at least trouble to make them plausible."

Newton suppressed the rejoinder that rose instantly to his lips. It was that he had far too large a circulation among fools to bother about what intelligent people thought. He only said, "I doubt, sir, if you are likely to find my conversation any more satisfactory than my books," and resumed his magazine.

"Probably not," said the stranger. "I expect success has spoiled you. But you had some brains to begin with. . . . Those Indian stories of yours—"

Perhaps no other phrase would have induced Joseph Newton to embark upon a conversation with the stranger. But nobody nowadays ever read or bothered about his Indian stories, though he was very well aware that they were the best things he had ever done.

"—had glimmerings of quality," the other was saying, "and you might have accomplished something had you not taken to writing for money."

"Are you aware, sir," Newton said, "that you are being excessively rude?"

"Quite," said the other with calm satisfaction. "I always

am. It is so good for people. And really, in your last book, you have exceeded the limit."

"Which of my last books are you talking about?" asked Newton, hovering between annoyance and amusement.

"It is called *The Big Noise*."

"Oh, that," said Newton.

"Now, in that book," the stranger went on, "you call the heroine Elinor and Gertrude on different pages. You cannot make up your mind whether her name was Robbins with two *b*'s or with one. You have killed the corpse in one place on Sunday and in another on Monday evening. That corpse was discovered twelve hours after the murder still wallowing in a pool of wet blood. The coroner committed no fewer than seventeen irregularities in conducting the inquest; and, finally, you have introduced three gangs, a mysterious Chinaman, an unknown poison that leaves no trace, and a secret society high up in the political world."

The little old man held up his hands in horror as he ended the grisly recital.

"Well," Newton asked, "any more?"

"Alas, yes," said the other. "The volume includes, besides many misprints, fifteen glaring inconsistencies, nine cases of gross ignorance, and enough grammatical mistakes to—to stretch from Paddington to Penzance."

This time Newton laughed outright. "You seem to be a very earnest student of my writings," he said.

The stranger picked up the rug from his knees and folded it neatly beside him. He removed the pillow, and laid that down too. He then moved across to the corner seat opposite Newton and, taking a jewelled cigarette case from his pocket, selected a cigarette, returned the case to his pocket, found a match, lighted up, and began to smoke. Then he again drew out the case and offered it to Newton. "Lavery's," he said. "I know your favorite brand."

As a matter of fact, Newton never smoked Lavery's; but for a handsome sum he allowed his face, and a glowing testimonial to their virtues, to appear on their advertisements. Well, he might as well find out what the things were like. He took the proffered cigarette, and the stranger obligingly gave him a light. Newton puffed. Yes, they were good stuff— better than might be expected, though rather heavy.

"Now, in my view," the stranger was saying, "the essence of a really good murder is simplicity. All your books—all most people's books—have far too much paraphernalia about them. A really competent murderer would need no special appliances, and practically no preparations. Ergo, he would be in far less danger of leaving any clues behind him. Why, oh why, Mr. Newton, do you not write a murder story on those lines?"

Again, Newton laughed. He was disposed to humour the old gentlemen. "It wouldn't make much of a story," he said, "if the murderer really left no clues."

"Oh, but there you are wrong," said the other. "What is needed is a perfectly simple murder, followed by a perfectly simple solution—so simple that only a great mind could think of it, by penetrating to the utter simplicity of the mind of the murderer."

"I can't abide those psychological detectives," Newton said. "You'd better go and read Mr. Van Dine." ("Or some of those fellows who would give their ears for a tenth of my sales," his expression added.)

"Dear me, you quite misunderstand me. That wasn't what I meant at all. There would be no psychology in the story I have in mind. It would be more like William Blake's poetry."

"Mad, you mean," said Newton.

"Crystal sane," replied the other. "Perhaps it will help you if I illustrate my point. Shall I outline the sort of murder I have in mind?"

"If you like," said Newton, who found himself growing suddenly very sleepy.

"Very well," said the stranger. "Then I'll just draw down the blinds."

He jumped up and lowered the blinds on the corridor side of the compartment.

"That's better," he said. "Now we shall be undisturbed. Now supposing—only supposing, of course—that there were two men in a railway carriage just like us, and they were perfect strangers, but one of them did not really care for the other's face—Are you listening, Mr. Newton?"

"Yes," said Newton, very sleepily. He was now having real difficulty in keeping his eyes open.

"And, further, supposing neither of them had brought any special paraphernalia with him, except what any innocent traveller might be carrying—say, a rug, a pillow, and a rug-strap—"

As he spoke, the stranger picked up the rug-strap from the seat beside him.

"Hey, what's that about a rug-strap?" said Newton, roused for a moment by a connection of ideas he was too sleepy to sort out.

"Except, of course, just one doped cigarette, containing an opiate—strong, but in no wise fatal," the other went on blandly.

"What the—?" murmured Newton, struggling now vainly against an absolutely stupefying drowsiness.

"There would really be nothing to prevent him from committing a nice, neat murder, would there?" the old man continued, rising as he spoke with startling agility and flinging the loop of the rug-strap over Newton's head. "Now, would there?" he repeated, as he drew it tight around his victim's neck, and neatly fastened it. Newton's mouth came wide open; his tongue protruded, and he began to gurgle horribly; his eyes stuck out from his head.

"And then," said the stranger, "the pillow would come in so handy to finish him off." He dragged Newton down on the seat, placed the pillow firmly on his upturned face, and sat on it, smiling delightedly. The gurgling slowly ceased.

"The rug," the cheerful voice went on, "has proved to be superfluous. Really, Mr. Newton, murder is even easier than I supposed—though it is not often, I imagine, that a lucky chance enables one to do a service to the literary craft at the same time."

Newton said nothing; for he was dead.

The stranger retained his position a little longer, still smiling gently to himself. Then he rose, removed the pillow from Newton's face, and, after a careful survey of the body, undid the strap. Next, he picked up a half-smoked cigarette and threw it out of the window, folded his rug neatly, did it and the pillow up in the strap, and, opening the door into the corridor, walked quietly away down the train.

"What a pity!" he murmured to himself as he went. "It would make such a good story; and I am afraid the poor fellow will never have the sense to write it."

The body of Joseph Newton was actually discovered by a restaurant-car attendant who was going round to collect orders for the first lunch. Opening the door of a first-class compartment, which had all its blinds drawn down, he found New-

140

ton, no pleasant sight and indubitably dead, stretched out upon the seat where his companion had left him.

Without waiting to do more than make sure the man was dead, he scuttled along to fetch the guard. A brief colloquy of train-officials then took place in the fatal compartment, and it was decided to stop the train short of Newbury Station, and send for the police before anyone had a chance of leaving it. It seemed clear, as there had· been no stop since they left Paddington, that the murderer must still be on it, unless he had leaped from an express travelling at full speed.

The police duly arrived, inspected the body, hunted the compartment in vain for traces of another passenger—for the murderer had taken the precaution of wearing gloves through-out his demonstration—took the name and address of every person on the train, to the number of some hundreds, had the carriage in which the murder had occurred detached, with much shunting and grunting, from the rest of the train, and finally allowed the delayed express to proceed.

Only those travellers who had been actually in the carriage of which Newton's compartment had formed a part were kept back for further inquiries. But Newton's companion was not among them. Having given his correct name and address to the police, he proceeeded quietly upon his journey in the empty first-class compartment two carriages farther back to which he had moved after his successful experiment.

There were four hundred and ninety-eight passengers on the Cornish Riviera express whose names were taken by the police at Newbury; or, if you count Newton, four hundred and ninety-nine. Add guards and attendants, restaurant-car staff, and the occupants of a travelling Post Office van—total five hundred and nineteen.

Of these one hundred and twenty-six were women, one hundred and fifty-three children, and the rest men. That allowed for quite enough possible suspects for the police to follow up. They were followed up, exhaustively. But it did not appear that any single person among them had any acquaintance with Joseph Newton, or any connection with him save as readers of his books. Nor did a meticulous ex-amination of Newton's past suggest the shadow of a reason why he should have been murdered.

The police tried their hardest, and the public and the Press did their best to assist, for the murder of a best-seller, by a criminal who left no clue, was enough to excite anybody's imagination. Several individuals, in their enthusiasm, went so far as to confess to the crime, and gave Scotland Yard several days' work in disproving their statements. But nothing helpful was forthcoming, and at long last the excitement died down.

It was more than three months later that the young Marquis of Queensferry called upon Henry Wilson, formerly the chief official of Scotland Yard, and now the foremost private detective in England. His modest request was that Wilson should solve for him the mystery of Joseph Newton's murder.

When Wilson asked him why he wanted it solved, the Marquis explained that it was for a bet. It appeared that his old uncle, the Honorable Roderick Dominic Acres-Noel, had bet him fifty thousand pounds to a penny he could not solve the problem, and he, who had the title but not the money, would be very willing to lay his hands on fifty thousand pounds which his uncle, who had the money but not the title, would never miss. Asked the reason for so unusual a bet, he replied that the reason was Uncle Roderick, who was always betting on something, the sillier the better.

"Our family's like that, you know," the Marquis added. "We're all mad. And my uncle was quite excited about the case, because he was on the train when it happened. He even wrote to *The Times* about it."

Wilson rejected the idea that he could solve a case which had utterly baffled Scotland Yard when the trail was fresh, now that it was stone cold, and all clues, presumably, vanished into limbo. Even the most lavish promises of shares in the fifty thousand pounds did not tempt him, and he sent the young Marquis away with a flea in his ear.

But, after the Marquis had gone, he found that he could not get the case out of his head. In common with everybody else, he had puzzled his brains over it at the time; but it was weeks since he had given it a thought. But now—here it was again—bothering his mind.

Hang it all, it wasn't reasonable—it was against nature—that a man should be able to murder another man and get away without leaving any clue at all. So, at any rate, the Marquis's crazy old uncle seemed to think, unless, indeed, he was merely crazy. Most likely he was.

Wilson rang up his old colleague, Inspector Blaikie, as to have one more shot at this impossible mystery. Perhaps it was when he recollected that, according to the Marquis, Mr.

Acres-Noel had himself travelled on that train to Cornwall. It might be that Mr. Acres-Noel had noticed something that the police had missed; he was just the sort of old gentleman who would enjoy keeping a tit-bit of information to himself. At any rate, it was one thing one could try.

Wilson rang up his old colleague, Insepctor Blaikie, at Scotland Yard, and Blaikie guffawed at him.

"Solve it, by all means," he said. "We'll be delighted. We're sick of the sound of Newton's name....Yes, old Acres-Noel was on the train—I don't know anything more about him.... Oh, mad as a hatter. Completely...Yes, he wrote to *The Times,* and they printed it ... Three days afterwards, I think. Shall I have it looked up for you? ...Right you are. Let us know when you catch the murderer, won't you?"

Wilson sent for his own file of *The Times,* and looked up the letter of Mr. Acres-Noel. *The Times* had not thought it worth the honor of the middle page, but fortunately had not degraded it into the "Points" column.

"Sir," it ran.

"The methods of the police in dealing with the so-called Newton Mystery appear to show more than the usual official incompetence. As one of the passengers on the train on which Mr. Newton died, I have been subjected to considerable annoyance—and I may add compensated in part by some amusement—at the fruitless and irrelevant inquiries made by the police.

"It is plain the police have no notion of the motives which prompted the murder. Their inquiries show that. If they would devote more attention to *thinking* what the motive was, and less to the accumulation of useless information, the apparent complexity of the case would disappear. The truth is usually simple—too simple for idiots to see. *Why* was Newton murdered? Answer that, and it will appear plainly that only one person could have murdered him. Motive is essentially individual.

"I am, yours, etc.,
"R. D. ACRES-NOEL."

"Upon my word," said Wilson to himself, "that's a very odd letter."

He read it over several times, staring at it as if the name of the murderer was written between the lines.

Suddenly he leaped to his feet, and with an excitement he seldom showed, dashed down Whitehall to Inspector Blaikie's office. Within ten minutes he was making a proposition to that official which left him starkly incredulous.

"I know," Wilson persisted, "it isn't a certainty, it's a thousand to one chance. But it *is* a chance, and I want to try it. I'm not asking the Department to commit itself in any way, only to let me have a couple of men standing by. Don't you see, the whole point about this extraordinary letter is the way it stresses the question of motive? And, more than that, it suggests that the writer knows what the motive was. Now, how could he do that unless—"

"But, if that's so, the man's mad!" Blaikie protested. "Whoever heard of anybody murdering a complete stranger just to *show* him?"

"Well, he certainly is mad, isn't he? You said so yourself, and his family's notoriously crazy."

"He'll have to be pretty well off his rocker," Blaikie remarked, "if he's to be kind enough to come and shove his neck in a noose for you."

"One can but try," Wilson said. "If you won't help me I'm going to try alone. I must have one shot at getting to the bottom of it." And eventually Blaikie agreed.

The upshot was that Wilson, immediately after his interview, arranged for the posting of the following letter, forged with extreme care so as to imitate the handwriting of the supposed author. It was dispatched from the pillar-box nearest to Joseph Newton's Cornish cottage.

"Dear Mr. Acres-Noel," it said.

"Ever since our chance meeting a few months ago, I have been thinking over the very interesting demonstration you were kind enough to give me on that occasion. May I confess, however, that I am still not quite satisfied; and I should be even more deeply obliged if I could induce you to repeat it. As it happens, I shall be returning to London this weekend, and travelling down again to Cornwall on the Riviera express next Wednesday. If you too should chance to be travelling that way, perhaps we may meet again.

"Yours very truly,
"Joseph Newton."

Someone remarkably like the late Joseph Newton settled

144

himself comfortably in the corner of a first-class compartment in the Cornish Riviera express. He had the compartment to himself, and, although the train had begun to fill up, no other traveller had entered when the train drew out of the station. Very discreetly, passengers who came near it had been warned away by the station officials.

The train had not yet gathered its full speed when the solitary traveller became conscious that someone was standing outside the compartment, and staring in at him. He raised his eyes from the magazine he was reading, and looked back. Slowly, the newcomer pushed back the sliding door, entered the compartment, and sat down in the far corner.

He was a little old man, with a straggling beard, wearing very shabby clothes. He flung down on the seat beside him a rug and a pillow tied up in a strap. Undoing his bundle, he settled himself with the pillow behind his head, the rug over his knees, and the strap beside him.

Wilson said nothing. It was nervous work, waiting for his cue. But by this time he knew he was right. The millionth chance had come off.

The train flashed at length through Maidenhead Station. Suddenly the old man spoke.

"Talking of murders," he said, "it is my turn to apologize. I am afraid I bungled it last time."

"Not at all," said Wilson, hoping that his voice would not give him away; "but if you would just show me again how—"

"With pleasure," said the old man.

He moved with alacrity to the corner opposite Wilson, took from his pocket a jewelled cigarette-case, and proffered it. Wilson took a cigarette, and did a second's rapid thinking before the match was produced. A cigarette was something he had not allowed for, and it might even turn out to be poisoned. However, no use to hesitate now. He suffered Mr. Acres-Noel to light it, and the heavy sweetish taste confirmed his fears.

Fortunately, however, it was hardly alight before the other rose and went to the window.

"You won't mind my pulling down the blinds, will you?" he said; and Wilson took advantage of his movement to effect a lightning exchange of the suspicious cigarette for one of his own. This was a relief, but clearly he must show some signs of being affected. Sleepiness seemed the most likely cue. He yawned.

145

"You follow me so far, I trust," said the other.

"Perfectly," said Wilson slowly. "Please—go—" Slowly his eyes closed, and his head began to wag.

The old man seized the rug strap.

"This is the next step," he said, attempting to cast it over Wilson's head. But Wilson sprang to his feet, warded off the strap, and pressed a button beside him which had been fixed to communicate with the adjoining compartment.

Almost as he grappled with his now frenzied antagonist, two stalwart policemen in plain clothes rushed in to his aid. Mr. Acres-Noel, alternately protesting his innocence and shrieking with wild laughter, was soon safely secured.

Mr. Acres-Noel, safe in Broadmoor, has only one complaint. The authorities will not supply him with Joseph Newton's new books. He wants to see whether that popular writer has benefited by his lesson in practical criminology.

THE HAUNTED POLICEMAN

BY DOROTHY L. SAYERS

Dorothy Leigh Sayers was born on June 13, 1893, the only child of the headmaster of the Christchurch Choir School, Oxford. She grew up in the East Anglian fen country familiar to readers of *The Nine Tailors* and was one of the first women to obtain a degree from Oxford. She was editor of *Oxford Poetry* and wrote advertising copy before writing her first mystery, featuring Lord Peter Wimsey—*Whose Body?* (1923). She secretly gave birth to a son in 1924 and later married journalist Oswold Atherton Fleming. She wrote 11 novels and 44 stories and is highly regarded as an anthologist. She died on December 17, 1957.

"GOOD GOD!" said his lordship. "Did I do that?"

"All the evidence points that way," replied his wife.

"Then I can only say that I never knew so convincing a body of evidence produce such an inadequate result."

The nurse appeared to take this reflection personally. She said in a tone of rebuke: "He's a *beautiful* boy."

"H'm," said Peter. He adjusted his eyeglass carefully. "Well, you're the expert witness. Hand him over."

The nurse did so, with a dubious air. She was relieved to see that this disconcerting parent handled the child competently; as, in a man who was an experienced uncle, was not, after all, so very surprising. Lord Peter sat down gingerly on the bed.

"Do you feel it's up to standard?" he inquired with some anxiety. "Of course, *your* workmanship's always sound—but you never know with these collaborate efforts."

"I think it'll do," said Harriet.

"Good." He turned abruptly to the nurse. "All right; we'll keep it. Take it and put it away, and tell 'em to invoice it to me. It's a very interesting addition to you, Harriet; but it would have been a hell of a rotten substitute." His voice wavered a little, for in the last twenty-four hours he had had the fright of his life.

The doctor, who had been doing something in the other room, entered in time to catch the last words.

"There was never any likelihood of that, you goop," he said, cheerfully. "Now, you've seen all there is to be seen, and you'd beter run away and play." He led his charge firmly to the door. "Go to bed," he advised him in kindly accents; "you look all in."

" I'm all right," said Peter. "I haven't been doing anything. And look here—" He stabbed a belligerent finger in the direction of the adjoining room. "Tell those nurses of yours, if I want to pick my son up, I'll pick him up. If his mother wants to kiss him, she can kiss him. I'll have none of your infernal hygiene in *my* house."

"Very well," said the doctor, "just as you like. Anything for a quiet life. I rather believe in a few healthy germs myself. Builds up resistance. No, thanks, I won't have a drink. I've got to go to another one, and an alcoholic breath impairs confidence."

"Another one?" said Peter, aghast.

"One of my hospital mothers. You're not the only fish in the sea by a long chalk. One born every minute."

"God! what a world." They passed down the great curved stair. In the hall a sleepy footman clung, yawning, to his post of duty.

"All right, William," said Peter. "Buzz off now; I'll lock up." He let the doctor out. "Good night—and thanks very much, old man. I'm sorry I swore at you."

"They mostly do," replied the doctor philosophically. "Well, bung-ho, Flim. I'll look in again later, just to earn my fee, but I shan't be wanted. You've married into a good tough family, and I congratulate you."

The car, spluttering and protesting a little after its long wait in the cold, drove off, leaving Peter alone on the doorstep. Now that it was all over and he could go to bed, he felt extraordinarily wakeful. He would have liked to go to a party. He leaned back against the wrought-iron railings and lit a cigarette, staring vaguely into the lamp-lit dusk of the square. It was thus that he saw the policeman.

The blue-uniformed figure came up from the direction of South Audley Street. He too was smoking, and he walked, not with the firm tramp of a constable on his beat, but with the hesitating step of a man who has lost his bearings. When he came in sight he had pushed back his helmet and was rubbing his head in a puzzled manner. Official habit made him look sharply at the bare-headed gentleman in evening dress, abandoned on a doorstep at three in the morning, but since the gentleman appeared to be sober and bore no signs of being about to commit a felony, he averted his gaze and prepared to pass on.

" 'Morning officer," said the gentleman, as he came abreast with him.

" 'Morning sir," said the policeman.

"You're off duty early," pursued Peter, who wanted somebody to talk to. "Come in and have a drink."

This offer reawakened all the official suspicion.

"Not just now, sir, thank you," replied the policeman guardedly.

"Yes, now. That's the point." Peter tossed away his cigarette. It described a fiery arc in the air and shot out a little train of sparks as it struck the pavement. "I've got a son."

"Oh, ah!" said the policeman, relieved by this innocent confidence. "Your first, eh?"

"And last, if I know anything about it."

"That's what my brother says, every time," said the policeman. "Never no more, he says. He's got eleven. Well, sir, good luck to it. I see how you're situtated, and thank you kindly, but after what the sergeant said I dunno as I better. Though if I was to die this moment, not a drop 'as passed me lips since me supper beer."

Peter put his head on one side and considered this.

"The sergeant said you were drunk?"

"He did, sir."

"And you were not?"

"No, sir. I saw everything just the same as I told him, though what's become of it now is more than I can say. But drunk I was not, sir."

"Then," said Peter, "as Mr. Joseph Surface remarked to Lady Teazle, what is troubling you is the consciousness of your own innocence. He insinuated that you had looked on the wine when it was red—you'd better come in and make it so. You'll feel better."

The policeman hesitated.

"Well, sir, I dunno. Fact is, I've had a bit of a shock."

"So've I," said Peter. "Come in for God's sake and keep me company."

"Well, sir—" said the policeman again. He mounted the steps.

The logs in the hall-chimney were glowing a deep red through their ashes. Peter raked them apart, so that the young flame shot up between them. "Sit down," he said; "I'll be back in a moment."

The policeman sat down, removed his helmet, and stared about him, trying to remember who occupied the big house at the corner of the Square. The engraved coat-of-arms upon the great silver bowl on the chimney-piece told him nothing, even though it was repeated in color upon the backs of two tapestried chairs: three white mice skipping upon a black ground. Peter, returning from the shadows beneath the stair, caught him as he traced the outlines with a thick finger.

"A student of heraldry?" he said. "Seventeenth-century work and not very graceful. You're new to this beat, aren't you? My name's Wimsey."

150

He put down a tray on the table.

"If you'd rather have beer or whisky, say so. These bottles are only a concession to my mood."

The policeman eyed the long necks and bulging silver-wrapped corks with curiosity. "Champagne?" he said. "Never tasted it, sir. But I'd like to try the stuff."

"You'll find it thin," said Peter, "but if you drink enough of it, you'll tell me the story of your life." The cork popped, and the wine frothed out into the wide glasses, glinting as it caught the firelight.

"Well!" said the policeman. "Here's to your good lady, sir, and the new young gentleman. Long life and all the best. A bit in the nature of cider, ain't it, sir?"

"Just a trifle. Give me your opinion after the third glass, if you can put up with it so long. And thanks for your good wishes. You a married man?"

"Not yet, sir. Hoping to be when I get promotion. If only the sergeant—but that's neither here nor there. You been married long, sir, if I may ask?"

"Just over a year."

"Ah! and do you find it comfortable, sir?"

Peter laughed.

"I've spent the past twenty-four hours wondering why, when I'd had the blazing luck to get onto a perfectly good thing, I should be fool enough to risk the whole show on a silly experiment."

The policeman nodded sympathetically.

"I see what you mean, sir. Seems to me, life's like that. If you don't take risks, you get nowhere. If you do, they may go wrong, and then where are you? And 'alf the time, when things happen, they happen first, before you can even think about 'em."

"Quite right," said Peter, and filled the glasses again. He found the policeman soothing. True to his class and training, he turned naturally in moments of emotion to the company of the common man. Indeed, when the recent domestic crisis had threatened to destroy his nerve, he had headed for the butler's pantry with the swift instinct of the homing pigeon. There, they had treated him with great humanity, and allowed him to clean the silver.

With a mind oddly clarified by champagne and lack of sleep, he watched the constable's reaction to Pol Roger 1926. The first glass had produced a philosophy of life; the second

151

produced a name—Alfred Burt—and further hints of some mysterious grievance against the station sergeant; the third glass, as prophesied, produced the story.

"You were right, sir" (said the policeman) "when you spotted I was new to the beat. I only come on it at the beginning of the week, and that acounts for me not being acquainted with you, sir, nor with most of the residents about here. Jessop, now, he knows everybody, and so did Pinker— but he's been took off to another division. You'd remember Pinker—big chap, make two o' me, with a sandy mustache. Yes, I thought you would.

"Well, sir, as I was saying, me knowing the district in a general way, but not, so to speak, like the palm o' me 'and, might account for me making a bit of a fool of myself, but it don't account for me seeing what I did see. See it I did, and not drunk nor nothing like it. And as for making a mistake in the number, well, that might happen to anybody. All the same, sir, thirteen was the number I see, plain as the nose on your face."

"You can't put it stronger than that," said Peter, whose nose was of a kind difficult to overlook.

"You know Merriman's End, sir?"

"I think I do. Isn't it a long cul-de-sac running somewhere at the back of South Audley Street, with a row of houses on one side and a high wall on the other?"

"That's right, sir. Tall, narrow houses they are, all alike, with deep porches and pillars to them."

"Yes. Like an escape from the worst square in Pimlico. Horrible. Fortunately, I believe the street was never finished, or we should have had another row of the monstrosities on the opposite side. This house is pure eighteenth century. How does it strike you?"

P. C. Burt contemplated the wide hall—the Adam fireplace and paneling with their graceful shallow moldings, the pedimented doorways, the high roundheaded window lighting hall and gallery, the noble proportions of the stair. He sought for a phrase.

"It's a gentleman's house," he pronounced at length. "Room to breathe, if you see what I mean. Seems like you couldn't act vulgar in it." He shook his head. "Mind you, I wouldn't call it cosy. It ain't the place I'd choose to sit down to a kipper in me shirtsleeves. But it's got class. I never thought about it before, but now you mention it I see what's wrong with them other houses in Merriman's End. They're sort of squeezed-like. I been into more'n one o' them tonight, and that's what they are; they're squeezed. But I was going to tell you about that.

"Just upon midnight it was" (pursued the policeman) "when I turns into Merriman's End in the ordinary course of my dooties. I'd got pretty near down towards the far end, when I see a fellow lurking about in a suspicious way under the wall. There's back gates there, you know, sir, leading into some gardens, and this chap was hanging about inside one of the gateways. A rough-looking fellow, in a baggy old coat—might a-been a tramp off the Embankment. I turned my light on him—that street's not very well lit, and it's a dark night—but I couldn't see much of his face, because he had on a ragged old hat and a big scarf round his neck. I thought he was up to no good, and I was about to ask him what he was doing there, when I hear a most awful yell come out o' one o' them houses opposite. Ghastly it was, sir. 'Help!' it said. 'Murder! help!' fit to freeze your marrow."

"Man's voice or woman's?"

"Man's, sir, I think. More of a roaring kind of yell, if you take my meaning. I says, 'Hullo! What's up there? Which house is it?' The chap says nothing, but he points, and him and me runs across together. Just as we gets to the house, there's a noise like as if someone was being strangled just inside, and a thump, as it might be something falling against the door."

"Good God!" said Peter.

"I gives a shout and rings the bell. 'Hoy!' I says. 'What's up here?' and then I knocks on the door. There's no answer, so I rings and knocks again. Then the chap who was with me, he pushes open the letter-flap and squints through it."

"Was there a light in the house?"

"It was all dark, sir, except the fanlight over the door. That was lit up bright, and when I looks up, I see the number of the house—Number Thirteen, painted plain as you like on the transom. Well, this chap peers in, and all of a sudden he gives a kind of gurgle and falls back. 'Here!' I says, 'what's amiss? Let me have a look.' So I puts me eye to the flap and I looks in."

P. C. Burt paused and drew a long breath. Peter cut the wire of the second bottle.

"Now, sir," said the policeman. "believe me or believe me

153

not, I was as sober at that moment as I am now. I can tell you everything I see in that house, same as if it was wrote up there on that wall. Not as it was a great lot, because the flap wasn't all that wide, but by squinnying a bit, I could make shift to see right across the hall and a piece on both sides and part way up the stairs. And here's what I see, and you take notice of every word, on account of what came after."

He took another gulp of the Pol Roger to loosen his tongue and continued:

"There was the floor of the hall. I could see that very plain. All black and white squares it was, like marble, and it stretched back a good long way. About halfway along, on the left, was the staircase, with a red carpet, and the statue of a white naked woman at the foot, carrying a big pot full of blue and yellow flowers. In the wall next the stairs there was an open door, and a room all lit up. I could just see the end of a table, with a lot of glass and silver on it. Between that door and the front door there was a big black cabinet, shiny with gold figures painted on it, like them things they had at the Exhibition. Right at the back of the hall there was a place like a conservatory, but I couldn't see what was in it, only it looked very gay. There was a door on the right, and that was open, too. A very pretty drawing-room, by what I could see of it, with pale-blue paper and pictures on the walls. There were pictures in the hall, too, and a table on the right with a copper bowl, like as it might be for visitors' cards to be put in. Now, I see all that, sir, and I put it to you, if it hadn't a' been there, how could I describe it so plain?"

"I have known people describe what wasn't there," said Peter thoughtfully, "but it was seldom anything of that kind. Rats, cats, and snakes I have heard of and occasionally naked female figures; but delirious lacquer cabinets and hall-tables are new to me."

"As you say, sir," agreed the policeman, "and I see you believe me so far. But here's something else, what you mayn't find quite so easy. There was a man laying in that hall, sir, as sure as I sit here, and he was dead. He was a big man and clean-shaven, and he wore evening dress. Somebody had stuck a knife into his throat. I could see the handle of it—it looked like a carving-knife, and the blood had run out, all shiny, over the marble squares."

The policeman looked at Peter, passed his handkerchief over his forehead, and finished the fourth glass of champagne.

154

"His head was up against the end of the hall table," he went on, "and his feet must have been up against the door, but I couldn't see anything quite close to me, because of the letter-box. You understand, sir, I was looking through the wire cage of the box, and there was something inside—letters, I suppose—that cut off my view downwards. But I see all the rest—in front and a bit of both sides; and it must have been regularly burnt in upon me brain, as they say, for I don't suppose I was looking more than a quarter of a minute or so. Then all the lights went out at once, same as if somebody had turned off the main switch. So I looks round, and I don't mind telling you I felt a bit queer. And *when* I looks round, lo and behold! my bloke in the muffler had hopped it."

"The devil he had," said Peter.

"Hopped it," repeated the policeman, "and there I was. And just there, sir, is where I made my big mistake, for I thought he couldn't a-got far, and I started off up the street after him. But I couldn't see him, and I couldn't see nobody. All the houses was dark, and it come over me what a sight of funny things may go on and nobody take a mite o' notice. The way I'd shouted and banged on the door, you'd a-thought it'd a-brought out every soul in the street, not to mention that awful yelling. But there—you may have noticed it yourself, sir. A man may leave his ground-floor windows open, or have his chimney afire, and you may make noise enough to wake the dead, trying to draw his attention, and nobody give no heed. He's fast asleep, and the neighbors say, 'Blast that row, but it's no business of mine,' and stick their 'eads under the bedclothes."

"Yes," said Peter. "London's like that."

"That's right, sir. A village is different. You can't pick up a pin there without somebody coming up to ask where you got it from—but London keeps itself to itself. . . . Well, something'll have to be done, I thinks to myself, and I blows me whistle. They heard that all right. Windows started to go up all the street. That's London, too."

Peter nodded. "London will sleep through the last trump. Puddley-in-the-Rut and Doddering-in-the-Dumps will look down their noses and put on virtuous airs. But God, Who is never surprised, will say to His angel, 'Whistle 'em up, Michael, whistle 'em up; East and West will rise from the dead at the sound of the policeman's whistle.' "

"Quite so, sir," said P. C. Burt; and wondered for the first time whether there might not be something in this champagne stuff after all. He waited for a moment and then resumed:

"Well, it so happened that just when I sounded my whistle, Withers—that's the man on the other beat—was in Audley Square, coming to meet me. You know, sir, we has times for meeting one another, arranged different-like every night; and twelve o'clock in the square was our rendyvoos tonight. So up he comes in, you might say, no time at all, and finds me there, with everyone a-hollering at me from the windows to know what was up. Well, naturally I didn't want the whole bunch of 'em running out into the street and our man getting away in the crowd, so I just tells 'em there's nothing, only a bit of an accident farther along. And then I see Withers and glad enough I was. We stands there at the top o' the street, and I tells him there's a dead man laying in the hall at Number Thirteen, and it looks to me like murder. 'Number Thirteen' he says, 'you can't mean Number Thirteen. There ain't no Number Thirteen in Merriman's End, you fathead; it's all even numbers.' And so it is, sir, for the houses on the other side were never built, so there's no odd numbers at all.

"Well, that give me a bit of a jolt. I wasn't so much put out at not having remembered about the numbers, for as I tell you, I never was on the beat before this week. No; but I knew I'd seen that there number writ up plain as pie on the fanlight, and I didn't see how I could have been mistaken. But when Withers heard the rest of the story, he thought maybe I'd misread it for Number Twelve. It couldn't be Eighteen, for there's only the eight houses in the road; nor it couldn't be Sixteen neither, for I knew it wasn't the end house. But we thought it might be Twelve or Ten; so away we goes to look.

"We didn't have no difficulty about getting in at Number Twelve. There was a very pleasant old gentleman came down in his dressing-gown, asking what the disturbance was, and could he be of use. I apologized for disturbing him, and said I was afraid there'd been an accident in one of the houses, and had he heard anything. Of course, the minute he opened the door I could see it wasn't Number Twelve we wanted; there was only a little hall with polished boards, and the walls plain paneled—all very bare and neat and no black cabinet nor naked woman nor nothing. The old gentleman said, yes, his son had heard somebody shouting and knocking a few minutes earlier. He'd got up and put his head out of the window, but couldn't see nothing, but they thought from the sound it was Number Fourteen forgotten his latch-key again. So we thanked him very much and went on to Number Fourteen.

"We had a bit of a job to get Number Fourteen downstairs. A fiery sort of gentleman he was, something in the military way, I thought, but he turned out to be a retired Indian Civil Servant. A dark gentleman, with a big voice, and his servant was dark, too. The gentleman wanted to know what the blazes all this row was about, and why a decent citizen wasn't allowed to get his proper sleep. He supposed that young fool at Number Twelve was drunk again. Withers had to speak a bit sharp to him; but at last the servant came down and let us in. Well, we had to apologize once more. The hall was not a bit like—the staircase was on the wrong side, for one thing and though there was a statue at the foot of it, it was some kind of a heathen idol with a lot of heads and arms, and the walls were covered with all sorts of brass stuff and native goods—you know the kind of thing. There was a black-and-white linoleum on the floor and that was about all there was to it. The servant had a soft sort of way with him I didn't half like. He said he slept at the back and had heard nothing till his master rang for him. Then the gentleman came to the top of the stairs and shouted out it was no use disturbing him; the noise came from Number Twelve as usual, and if that young man didn't stop his blanky Bohemian goings-on, he'd have the law on his father. I asked if he'd seen anything, and he said, no, he hadn't. Of course, sir, me and that other chap was inside the porch, and you can't see anything what goes on inside those porches from the other houses, because they're filled in at the sides with colored glass—all the lot of them."

Lord Peter Wimsey looked at the policeman and then looked at the bottle, as though estimating the alcoholic content of each. With deliberation, he filled both glasses again.

"Well, sir," said P. C. Burt, after refreshing himself, "by this time Withers was looking at me in rather an old-fashioned manner. However, he said nothing, and we went back to Number Ten, where there was two maiden ladies and a hall full of stuffed birds and wallpaper like a florist's catalogue. The one who slept in the front was deaf as a post, and the one who slept at the back hadn't heard nothing. But we got hold

157

of their maids, and the cook said she'd heard the voice calling 'Help!' and thought it was in Number Twelve, and she'd hid her head in the pillow and said her prayers. The housemaid was a sensible girl. She'd looked out when she'd heard me knocking. She couldn't see anything at first, owing to us being in the porch, but she thought something must be going on, so, not wishing to catch cold, she went back to put on her bedroom slippers. When she got back to the window, she was just in time to see a man running up the road. He went very quick and very silent, as if he had galoshes on, and she could see the ends of his muffler flying out behind him. She saw him run out of the street and turn to the right, and then she heard me coming along after him. Unfortunately, her eye being on the man, she didn't notice which porch I came out of. Well, that showed I wasn't inventing the whole story at any rate, because there was my bloke in the muffler. The girl didn't recognize him at all, but that wasn't surprising, because she'd only just entered the old ladies' service. Besides, it wasn't likely the man had anything to do with it, because he was outside with me when the yelling started. My belief is, he was the sort as doesn't care to have his pockets examined too close, and the minute my back was turned he thought he'd be better and more comfortable elsewhere.

"Now there ain't no need" (continued the policeman), "for me to trouble you, sir, with all them houses what we went into. We made inquiries at the whole lot, from Number Two to Number Sixteen, and there wasn't one of them had a hall in any ways conformable to what that chap and I saw through the letter-box. Nor there wasn't a soul in 'em could give us any help more than what we'd had already. You see, sir, though it took me a bit o' time telling, it all went very quick. There was the yells; they didn't last beyond a few seconds or so, and before they was finished, we was across the road and inside the porch. Then there was me shouting and knocking; but I hadn't been long at that afore the chap with me looks through the box. Then I has my look inside, for fifteen seconds it might be, and while I'm doing that, my chap's away up the street. Then I runs after him, and then I blows me whistle. The whole thing might take a minute or a minute and a half. Not more.

"Well, sir; by the time we'd been into every house in Merriman's End, I was feeling a bit queer again, I can tell you, and Withers, he was looking queerer. He says to me,

158

'Burt,' he says, 'is this your idea of a joke? Because if so, the 'Olborn Empire's where you ought to be, not the police force.' So I tells him over again, most solemn, what I seen— 'and,' I says, 'if only we could lay hands on that chap in the muffler, he could tell you he seen it, too. And what's more,' I says, 'do you think I'd risk me job, playing a silly trick like that?' He says, 'Well, it beats me,' he says. 'If I didn't know you was a sober kind of chap, I'd say you was seein' things.'

" 'Things?' I says to him. 'I see that there corpse a-layin' there with the knife in his neck, and that was enough for me. 'Orrible, he looked, and the blood all over the floor.' 'Well,' he says, 'maybe he wasn't dead after all, and they've cleared him out of the way.' 'And cleared the house away too, I suppose,' I said to him. So Withers says, in an odd sort o' voice, 'You're sure about the house? You wasn't letting your imagination run away with you over naked females and such?' That was a nice thing to say. I said, 'No, I wasn't. There's been some monkey business going on in this street and I'm going to get to the bottom of it, if we has to comb out London for that chap in the muffler.' 'Yes,' says Withers, nasty like, 'it's a pity he cleared off so sudden.' 'Well,' I says, 'you can't say I imagined *him,* anyhow, because that there girl saw him, and a mercy she did,' I said, 'or you'd be saying next I ought to be in Colney Hatch.' 'Well,' he says, 'I dunno what you think you're going to do about it. You better ring up the station and ask for instructions.'

"Which I did. And Sergeant Jones, he come down himself, and he listens attentive-like to what we both has to say, and then he walks along the street, slow-like, from end to end. And then he comes back and says to me, 'Now, Burt,' he says, 'just you describe that hall to me again, careful.' Which I does, same as I described it to you, sir. And he says, 'You're sure there was the room on the left of the stairs with the glass and silver on the table; and the room on the right with the pictures in it?' And I says, 'Yes, Sergeant, I'm quite sure of that.' And Withers says, 'Ah!' in a kind of got-you-now-voice, if you take my meaning. And the sergeant says, 'Now, Burt,' he says, 'pull yourself together and take a look at these here houses. Don't you see they're all single-fronted? There ain't one of 'em has rooms *both* sides o' the front hall. Look at the windows, you fool,' he says."

Lord Peter squinted at the bottle and poured out the last of the champagne.

"I don't mind telling you, sir" (went on the policeman) "that I was fair knocked silly. To think of me never noticing that! Withers had noticed it all right, and that's what made him think I was drunk or barmy. But I stuck to what I'd seen. I said, there must be two of them houses knocked into one, somewhere; but that didn't work, because we'd been into all of them, and there wasn't no such thing—not without there was one o'them concealed doors like you read about in crook stories. 'Well, anyhow,' I says to the sergeant, 'the yells was real all right, because other people heard 'em. Just you ask, and they'll tell you.' So the sergeant says, 'Well, Burt, I'll give you every chance.'

"So he knocks up Number Twelve again—not wishing to annoy Number Fourteen any more than he was already—and this time the son come down. An agreeable gentleman he was, too; not a bit put out. He says, Oh, yes, he'd heard the yells and his father'd heard them too. 'Number Fourteen,' he says, 'that's where the trouble is. A very old bloke, is Number Fourteen, and I shouldn't be surprised if he beats that unfortunate servant of his. The Englishman abroad, you know! The outposts of Empire and all that kind of thing. They're rough and ready—and then the curry in them parts is bad for the liver.' So I was for inquiring at Number Fourteen again; but the sergeant, he loses patience, and says, 'You know quite well,' he says, 'it ain't Number Fourteen, and, in my opinion, Burt, you're either dotty or drunk. You best go home straight away,' he says, 'and sober up, and I'll see you again when you can give a better account of yourself.' So I argues a bit, but it ain't no use, and away he goes, and Withers goes back to his beat. And I walks up and down a bit till Jessop comes to take over, and then I comes away, and that's when I sees you, sir.

"But I ain't drunk, sir—at least, I wasn't then, though there do seem to be a kind of a swimming in me head at this moment. Maybe that stuff's stronger than it tastes. But I wasn't drunk then, and I'm pretty sure I'm not dotty. I'm haunted, sir, that's what it is—haunted. It might be there was someone killed in one of them houses a many years ago, and that's what I see tonight. Perhaps they changed the numbering of the street on account of it—I've heard tell of such things—and when the same night come round, the house goes back to what it was before. But there I am, with a black mark against me, and it ain't a fair trick for no ghost to go getting a plain man into trouble. And I'm sure, sir, you'll agree with me."

The policeman's narrative had lasted some time, and the hands of the grandfather clock stood at a quarter to five. Peter Wimsey gazed benevolently at his companion, for whom he was beginning to feel a positive affection. He was, if anything, slightly more drunk than the policeman, for he had missed tea and had no appetite for his dinner; but the wine had not clouded his wits; it had only increased excitability and postponed sleep. He said:

"When you looked through the letter-box, could you see any part of the ceiling, or the lights?"

"No, sir; on account, you see, of the flap. I could see right and left and straight forward; but not upwards, and none of the near part of the floor."

"When you looked at the house from outside, there was no light except through the fanlight. But when you looked through the flap, all the rooms were lit, right and left and at the back?"

"That's so, sir."

"Are there back doors to the houses?"

"Yes, sir. Coming out of Merriman's End, you turn to the right, and there's an opening a little way along which takes you to the back doors."

"You seem to have a very distinct visual memory. I wonder if your other kinds of memory are as good. Can you tell me, say, whether any of the houses you went into had any particular smell? Especially Ten, Twelve, and Fourteen?"

"Smell, sir?" The policeman closed his eyes to stimulate recollection. "Why, yes, sir. Number Ten, where the two ladies live, that had a sort of an old-fashioned smell. I can't put me tongue to it. Not lavender—but something as ladies keeps in bowls and such—rose-leaves and what not. Potpourri, that's the stuff. Potpourri. And Number Twelve—well, no, there was nothing particular there, except I remember thinking they must keep pretty good servants, though we didn't see anybody except the family. All that floor and paneling was polished beautiful—you could see your face in it. Beeswax and turpentine, I says to meself. And elbow-grease. What you'd call a clean house with a good, clean smell. But Number Fourteen—that was different. I didn't like the smell of that. Stuffy, like as if the servant had been burning some o' that there incense to his idols, maybe."

161

"Ah!" said Peter. "What you say is very suggestive." **He** placed his fingertips together and shot his last question **over** them:

"Ever been inside the National Gallery?"

"No, sir," said the policeman, astonished. "I can't say as I ever was."

"That's London again," said Peter. "We're the last people in the world to know anything of our great metropolitan institutions. Now, what is the best way to tackle this bunch of toughs, I wonder? It's a little early for a call. Still, there's nothing like doing one's good deed before breakfast, and the sooner you're set right with the sergeant, the better. Let me see. Yes—I think that may do it. Costume pieces are not as a rule in my line, but my routine has been so much upset already, one way and another, that an irregularity more or less will hardly matter. Wait here for me while I have a bath and change. I may be a little time; but it would hardly be decent to get there before six."

The bath had been an attractive thought, but was perhaps ill-advised, for a curious languor stole over him with the touch of the hot water. The champagne was losing its effervescence. It was with an effort that he dragged himself out and reawakened himself with a cold shower.

The matter of dress required a little thought. A pair of gray flannel trousers was easily found, and though they were rather too well creased for the part he meant to play, he thought that with luck they would probably pass unnoticed. The shirt was a difficulty. His collection of shirts was a notable one, but they were mostly of an inconspicuous and gentlemanly sort. He hesitated for some time over a white shirt with an open sports collar, but decided at length upon a blue one, bought as an experiment and held to be not quite successful. A red tie, if he had possessed such a thing, would have been convincing. After some consideration, he remembered that he had seen his wife in a rather wide Liberty tie, whose prevailing color was orange. That, he felt, would do if he could find it. On her it had looked rather well; on him, it would be completely abominable.

He went through into the next room; it was queer to find it empty. A peculiar sensation came over him. Here *he* was, rifling his wife's drawers, and there *she* was, spirited out of reach at the top of the house with a couple of nurses and an entirely new baby, which might turn into goodness knew

162

what. He sat down before the glass and stared at himself. He felt as though he ought to have changed somehow in the night; but he only looked unshaven and, he thought, a trifle intoxicated. Both were quite good things to look at the moment, though hardly suitable for the father of a family. He pulled out all the drawers in the dressing-table; they emitted vaguely familiar smells of face-powder and handkerchief sachet. He tried the big built-in wardrobe: frocks, costumes, and trays full of underwear, which made him feel sentimental. At last he struck a promising vein of gloves and stockings. The next tray held ties, the orange of the desired Liberty creation gleaming in a friendly way among them. He put it on, and observed with pleasure that the effect was Bohemian beyond description.

He wandered out again, leaving all the drawers open behind him as though a burglar had passed through the room. An ancient tweed jacket of his own, of a very countrified pattern, suitable only for fishing in Scotland, was next unearthed, together with a pair of brown canvas shoes. He secured his trousers by a belt, searched for and found an old soft-brimmed felt hat of no recognizable color, and, after removing a few trout-flies from the hat-band and tucking his shirt-sleeves well up inside the coat-sleeve, decided that he would do. As an afterthought, he returned to his wife's room and selected a wide woolen scarf in a shade of greenish blue. Thus equipped, he came downstairs again, to find P. C. Burt fast asleep, with his mouth open and snoring.

Peter was hurt. Here he was, sacrificing himself in the interests of this policeman, and the man hadn't the common decency to appreciate it. However, there was no point in waking him yet. He yawned horribly and sat down. . . .

It was the footman who wakened the sleepers at half-past six. If he was surprised to see his master, very strangely attired, slumbering in the hall in company with a large policeman, he was too well trained to admit the fact even to himself. He merely removed the tray. The faint clink of glass roused Peter, who slept like a cat at all times.

"Hullo, William," he said. "Have I overslept myself? What's the time?"

"Five and twenty to seven, my lord."

"Just about right." He remembered that the footman slept on the top floor. "All quiet on the Western Front, William?"

"Not altogether quiet, my lord." William permitted himself a slight smile. "The young master was lively about five. But all satisfactory, I gather from Nurse Jenkyn."

"Nurse Jenkyn? Is that the young one? Don't let yourself be run away with, William. I say, just give P. C. Burt a light prod in the ribs, would you? He and I have business together."

In Merriman's End, the activities of the morning were beginning. The milkman came jingling out of the cul-de-sac; lights were twinkling in upper rooms; hands were withdrawing curtains; in front of Number Ten, the housemaid was already scrubbing the steps. Peter posted his policeman at the top of the street.

"I don't want to make my first appearance with official accompaniment," he said. "Come along when I beckon. What, by the way, is the name of the agreeable gentleman in Number Twelve? I think he may be of some assistance to us."

"Mr. O'Halloran, sir."

The policeman looked at Peter expectantly. He seemed to have abandoned all initiative and to place implicit confidence in this hospitable and eccentric gentleman. Peter slouched down the street with his hands in his trousers pockets and his shabby hat pulled rakishly over his eyes. At Number Twelve he paused and examined the windows. Those on the ground floor were open; the house was awake. He marched up the steps, took a brief glance through the flap of the letter-box, and rang the bell. A maid in a neat blue dress and white cap and apron opened the door.

"Good morning," said Peter, slightly raising the shabby hat; "is Mr. O'Halloran in?" He gave the *r* a soft continental roll. "Not the old gentleman. I mean young Mr. O'Halloran?"

"He's in," said the maid, doubtfully, "but he isn't up yet."

"Oh!" said Peter. "Well, it is a little early for a visit. But I desire to see him urgently. I am—there is a a little trouble where I live. Could you entreat him—would you be so kind? I have walked all the way," he added, pathetically, and with perfect truth.

"Have you, sir?" said the maid. She added kindly, "You do look tired, sir, and that's a fact."

"It is nothing," said Peter. "It is only that I forgot to have any dinner. But if I can see Mr. O'Halloran it will be all right."

"You'd better come in, sir," said the maid. "I'll see if I

164

can wake him." She conducted the exhausted stranger in and offered him a chair. "What name shall I say, sir?"

"Petrovinsky," said his lordship, hardily. As he had rather expected, neither the unusual name nor the unusual clothes of this unusually early visitor seemed to cause very much surprise. The maid left him in the tidy little paneled hall and went upstairs without so much as a glance at the umbrella stand.

Left to himself, Peter sat still, noticing that the hall was remarkably bare of furniture, and was lit by a single electric pendant almost immediately inside the front door. The letter-box was the usual wire-cage, the bottom of which had been carefully lined with brown paper. From the back of the house came a smell of frying bacon.

Presently there was the sound of somebody running downstairs. A young man appeared in a dressing-gown. He called out as he came: "Is that you, Stefan? Your name came up as Mr. Whiskey. Has Marfa run away again, or— What the hell? Who the devil are you, sir?"

"Wimsey," said Peter, mildly, "not Whiskey; Wimsey the policeman's friend. I just looked in to congratulate you on a mastery of the art of false perspective which I thought had perished with the ingenious Van Hoogstraaten, or at least with Grace and Lambelet."

"Oh!" said the young man. He had a pleasant countenance, with humorous eyes and ears pointed like a faun's. He laughed a little ruefully. "I suppose my beautiful murder is out. It was too good to last. Those bobbies! I hope to God they gave Number Fourteen a bad night. May I ask you how you come to be involved in the matter?"

"I," said Peter, "am the kind of person in whom distressed constables confide—I cannot imagine why. And when I had the picture of that sturdy blue-clad figure, led so persuasively by a Bohemian stranger and invited to peer through a hole, I was irresistibly transported in mind to the National Gallery. Many a time have I squinted sideways through those holes into the little black box, and admired that Dutch interior of many vistas painted so convincingly on the four flat sides of the box. How right you were to preserve your eloquent silence! Your Irish brogue would have given you away. The servants, I gather, were purposely kept out of sight."

"Tell me," said Mr. O'Halloran, seating himself sideways upon the hall table, "do you know by heart the occupation

165

of every resident in this quarter of London? I do not paint under my own name."

"No," said Peter. "Like the good Dr. Watson, the constable could observe, though he could not reason from his observation; it was the smell of turpentine that betrayed you. I gather that at the time of his first call the apparatus was not far off."

"It was folded together and lying under the stairs," replied the painter. "It has since been removed to the studio. My father had only just had time to get it out of the way and hitch down the 'Number Thirteen' from the fanlight before the police reinforcements arrived. He had not even time to put back this table I am sitting on; a brief search would have discovered it in the dining-room. My father is a remarkable sportsman; I cannot too highly recommend the presence of mind he displayed while I was haring round the houses and leaving him to hold the fort. It would have been so simple and so unenterprising to explain; but my father, being an Irishman, enjoys treading on the coattails of authority."

"I should like to meet your father. The only thing I do not thoroughly understand is the reason of this elaborate plot. Were you by any chance executing a burglary round the corner, and keeping the police in play while you did it?"

"I never thought of that," said the young man, with regret in his voice. "No. The bobby was not the predestined victim. He happened to be present at a full-dress rehearsal, and the joke was too good to be lost. The fact is, my uncle is Sir Lucius Preston, the R.A."

"Ah!" said Peter. "The light begins to break."

"My own style of draftsmanship," pursued Mr. O'Halloran, "is modern. My uncle has on several occasions informed me that I draw like that only because I do not know how to draw. The idea was that he should be invited to dinner tomorrow and regaled with a story of the mysterious 'Number Thirteen,' said to appear from time to time in this street and to be haunted by strange noises. Having thus detained him till close upon midnight, I should have set out to see him to the top of the street. As we went along, the cries would have broken out. I should have led him back—"

"Nothing," said Peter, "could be clearer. After the preliminary shock he would have been forced to confess that your draftsmanship was a triumph of academic accuracy."

"I hope," said Mr. O'Halloran, "the performance may still go forward as originally intended." He looked at Peter, who replied:

"I hope so, indeed. I also hope that your uncle's heart is a strong one. But may I, in the meantime, signal to my unfortunate policeman and relieve his mind? He is in danger of losing his promotion, through a suspicion that he was drunk on duty."

"Good God!" said Mr. O'Halloran. "No—I don't want that to happen. Fetch him in."

The difficulty was to make P.C. Burt recognize in the daylight what he had seen by night through the letter-flap. Of the framework of painted canvas, with its forms and figures oddly foreshortened and distorted, he could make little. Only when the thing was set up and lighted in the curtained studio was he at length reluctantly convinced.

"It's wonderful," he said. "It's like Maskelyne and Devant. I wish the sergeant could a-seen it."

"Lure him down here tomorrow night," said Mr. O'Halloran. "Let him come as my uncle's bodyguard. You—" he turned to Peter—"you seem to have a way with policemen. Can't you inveigle the fellow along? Your impersonation of starving and disconsolate Bloomsbury is fully as convincing as mine. How about it?"

"I don't know," said Peter. "The costume gives me pain. Besides, is it kind to a poor policeman? I give you the R.A., but when it comes to the guardian of the law—Blast it all! I'm a family man, and I must have *some* sense of responsibility."

THE WOOD-FOR-THE-TREES

BY PHILIP MacDONALD

Philip MacDonald (b. November 5, 1900) is the grandson of Scottish novelist George MacDonald. He served with the British cavalry in Mesopotamia during World War I. His first detective novel, *The Rasp* (1924), introduced Colonel Anthony Gethryn. In 1931 MacDonald and his wife went to Hollywood, where he has written a number of screenplays. His short stories have won awards from *Ellery Queen's Mystery Magazine* and the Mystery Writers of America. He is dedicated to the principle of fair play. "The ideal detective story," he says, "is a sort of competition between the author and reader."

IT WAS IN THE summer of '36—to be exact upon the fifth of August in that year—that the countryside around the village of Friars' Wick in Downshire, in the southwest of England, was shocked by the discovery of a singularly brutal murder.

The biggest paper in the county, *The Mostyn Courier,* reported the outrage at some length—but since the victim was old, poverty-stricken, female but ill-favored, and with neither friends nor kin, the event passed pracically unnoticed by the London Press, even though the killer was uncaught.

Passed unnoticed, that is, until, exactly twenty-four hours later and within a mile or so of its exact locale, the crime was repeated, the victim being another woman who, except in the matter of age, might have been a replica of the first.

This was a time, if you remember, when there was a plethora of news in the world. There was Spain, for instance. There were Mussolini and Ethiopia. There was Herr Hitler. There was Japan. There was Russia. There was dissension at home as well as abroad. There was so much, in fact, that people were stunned by it all and pretending to be bored . . .

Which is doubtless why the editor of Lord Otterill's biggest paper, *The Daily Despatch,* gave full rein to its leading crime reporter and splashed that ingenious scrivener's account of the MANIAC MURDERS IN DOWNSHIRE all across the front page of the first edition of August 8th.

The writer had spread himself. He described the slayings in gory, horrifying prose, omitting only such details as were unprintable. He drew pathetic (and by no means badly written) word-pictures of the two drab women as they had been before they met this sadistic and unpleasing end. And he devoted the last paragraphs of his outpourings to a piece of theorizing which gave added thrills to his fascinated readers.

". . . *can it be,*" he asked under the sub-heading 'Wake Up, Police!' "*that these two terrible, maniacal, unspeakable crimes —crimes with no motive other than the lust of some depraved and distorted mind, can be but the beginning of a wave of murder such as that which terrorized London in the eighties, when the uncaptured, unknown 'Jack the Ripper' ran his blood-stained gamut of killing?*"

169

You will have noted the date of the *Despatch* article—
August 8th. Which was the day after the *Queen Guinivere*
sailed from New York for England. Which explains how it
came about that Anthony Gethryn, who was a passenger on
the great liner, knew nothing whatsoever of the unpleasant
occurrences near Friars' Wick. Which is odd, because—although he'd never been there before and had no intention
of ever going there again after his simple mission had been
fulfilled—it was to Friars' Wick that he must make his way
immediately the ship arrived at home.

A quirk of fate: one of those odd spins of the Wheel.

He didn't want to break his journey to London and home
by going to Friars' Wick, or, indeed, any other place. He'd
been away—upon a diplomatic task of secrecy, importance,
and inescapable tedium—for three months. And he wanted
to see his wife and his son, and see them with the least possible delay.

But there it was: he had in his charge a letter which a
Personage of Extreme Importance had asked him to deliver
into the hands of another (if lesser known) P.O.E.I. The
request had been made courteously and just after the first
P.O.E.I. had gone out of his way to do a service for A. R.
Gethryn. *Ergo,* A. R. Gethryn must deliver the letter—which,
by the way, has nothing in itself to do with this story.

So, upon the afternoon of August the eleventh, Anthony
was driving from the port of Normouth to the hamlet of
Friars' Wick and the country house of Sir Adrian LeFane.

He pushed the Voisin along at speed, thankful they'd managed to send it down to Normouth for him. The alternatives
would have been a hired car or a train—and on a stifling day
like this the thought of either was insupportable.

The ship had docked late, and it was already after six
when he reached the outskirts of Mostyn and slowed to a
crawl through its narrow streets and came out sweating on
the other side. The low gray arch of the sky seemed lower
still—and the grayness was becoming tinged with black. The
trees which lined the road stood drooping and still, and over
everything was a soft and ominous hush through which the
sound of passing cars and even the singing of his own tires
seemed muted.

He reduced his speed as he drew near the Bastwick cross-
roads. Up to here he had known his way—but now he must
traverse unknown territory.

He stopped the car altogether, **and** peered at a signpost. Its fourth and most easterly arm said, with simple helpfulness, "FRIARS' WICK—8."

He followed the pointing arm and found himself boxed in between high and unkempt hedgerows, driving along a narrow lane which twisted up and across the shoulder of a frowning, sparsely-wooded hill. There were no cars here; no traffic of any kind; no sign of humanity. The sky had grown more black than gray, and the light had a gloom-laden, coppery quality. The air was heavy enough to make it difficult to breathe.

The Voisin breasted the hill—and the road shook itself and straightened out as it coasted down, now steep and straight, between wide and barren stretches of heathland.

The village of Friars' Wick, hidden by the foot of another hill, came upon Anthony suddenly, after rounding the first curve in the winding valley.

Although he was going slowly, for the corner had seemed dangerous, the abrupt emergence of the small township—materializing, it seemed, out of nothingness—was almost a physical shock. He slowed still more, and the big black car rolled silently along the narrow street, between slate-fronted cottages and occasional little shops.

It was a gray place, sullen and resentful and with something about it at once strange and familiar; an air which at the same time fascinated and repelled him; an aura which touched some sixth sense and set up a strange tingling inside him. . . .

He recognized the feeling but wasn't sure if it were genuine; it might have been induced by a combination of the weather and his personal irritation at having to come so far out of his way from London and home.

He reached the end of the main and only street of Friars' Wick, the point where the small church faces the inn across a traditional triangle of emerald grass. Here he stopped the car. He knew he must be within a mile or so of LeFane's house, and the easiest way to find it was to ask.

He looked around for someone to ask. He saw there was no human being in sight—and for the first time realized there had been none at all since he had come around the hill and into the village.

Something hit the leather of the seat beside him with a small, smacking sound. A single florin-sized raindrop.

171

He looked up at the sky. Now it was so close, so lowering, that it seemed almost to brush the tops of the big elms behind the white-fronted inn. A spatter of the big drops hit the dust of the road, each one separated by feet from its fellows. He realized he was waiting for thunder.

But no thunder came—and no relief. The coppery light was greener now, and the hush almost palpable.

And then he saw a man. A man who stood beside the outbuildings of the inn, some twenty yards away.

He was an ordinary-looking man. He fitted his surroundings, yet seemed to stand out from them in sharp relief.

He wore a shapeless hat, and a shapeless coat, and he had a shotgun under his arm.

Anthony felt an increase of the odd tingling. He looked back along the gray street and still saw no one. He looked at the man again. He looked the other way and saw for the first time the cluster of oaks on the rise away to his left; saw too, above the oaks, the chimneys of a big house.

He drove off. He followed his eyes, and sent the car up another twisting lane and came presently to imposing wrought-iron gates.

The gates stood open, and he turned the Voisin into them —and at once was in a different world. Outside, the land had been dead and tired and sterile, but here it was lush and well-groomed and self-conscious. A hundred feet above, and still half a mile away, he could see the chimneys and the rambling Tudor building beneath them.

There came another flurry of the outsized raindrops, and he thought of stopping and closing the car. He slowed and as he did so his attention was attracted by something off the road to his right. A figure which stood under one of the trees and looked at him. A large and square and gauntly powerful figure, as motionless as the man in the deserted village had been.

He stared, and for some reason stopped the car. The figure was clad in nondescript clothes, and it was with something of a shock that he realized it was a woman's.

He went on staring—and it turned abruptly and strode off into the shadows of a copse. . . .

There were no more raindrops and he drove on, toward the lawns and gardens and the house itself. . . .

When the rain came in earnest, it was a solid sheet of water, a deluge. It started almost as soon as Anthony was in the house—while, in fact, he was being greeted by his hostess, who was blondish and handsome and just verging upon the haggard. She was ultra-smart and over-nervous. She laughed a great deal, but her eyes never changed. She was, it appeared, Mrs. Peter Crecy, and she was also the daughter of Sir Adrian LeFane. She swept Anthony away from the butler and took him to a room which was half-library, half-salon, and wholly luxurious. She gave him a drink and sprayed him with staccato, half-finished sentences. He gathered that he couldn't see her father just yet—"the man, as usual, doesn't seem to *be* anywhere . . ." He gathered that he was expected to stay the night—"But you *must*—my parent gave the strictest orders..."

So he murmured politely and resigned himself, helped no little by the sight of the rain beyond the mullioned windows.

He was given eventually into the care of a black-coated discretion named Phillips, who led him up stairs and along corridors to a sybaritic and most un-Tudorlike suite.

He bathed luxuriously and when he had finished, found his trunk unpacked, his dinner clothes laid out. In shirt-sleeves, he walked over to a window and looked out and saw the rain still a heavy, glittering, unbroken veil over the half-dark world. He lit a cigarette, dropped into a chair, stretched out his long legs, and found himself wondering about the village of Friars' Wick and its odd and ominous and indescribable air. But he didn't wonder either long or seriously for, from somewhere below, he heard the booming of a gong.

He put on his coat and slipped LeFane's letter into his breast-pocket and made a leisurely way downstairs.

He had expected a dinner which would at the most have a couple of other guests besides himself. He found instead, when he was directed to the drawing-room, a collection of eight or ten people. They were clustered in the middle of the room, and from the centre of the cluster the voice of Mrs. Peter Crecy rose and fell like a syncopated fountain.

"Well, that's settled!" it was saying. "Not a word about it— too frightfully macabre! . . ."

Anthony made an unobtrusive entrance, but she saw him immediately and surged towards. She was contriving paradoxically to look handsomer and yet more haggard in a black-and-gold evening gown. She led him on a tour of introduction. He met, and idly catalogued in his mind, a Lord and Lady Bracksworth (obvious Master of Fox Hounds—wife knits) ; a Mr. and Mrs. Shelton-Jones (obvious Foreign Office

—wife aspiring Ambassadress); a Professor Martel (possible physicist, Middle-European, bearded, egocentric); a Mr. and Mrs. Geoffrey Dale (newspaper-owner, leader-writing wife) —and then, an oasis in this desert, his old friend Carol Dunning.

She was sitting in an enormous, high-winged chair and he hadn't seen her until Mrs. Crecy led him towards it.

"And—Miss Dunning," said Mrs. Crecy. "The novelist, of course . . . But I believe you know each other—Carol Rushworth Dunning—"

"Hi, there!" said Miss Dunning refreshingly. A wide and impish smile creased her impish and ageless and unmistakably American face.

"What would happen," asked Miss Dunning, "if I said, long time no see?"

"Nothing," Anthony said. "I concur. *Too* long."

He noted with relief that Mrs. Crecy had left them. He saw a servant with a tray of cocktails and got one for Miss Dunning and another for himself.

"Thanks," said Miss Dunning. "Mud in your eye!" She took half the drink at a gulp and looked up at Anthony. "If the answer wasn't so obvious, I'd ask what brought you into this *galère?*"

Anthony said, "Same to you." He reflected on the letter in his pocket. "And what's obvious? Or has the Diplomatic Service—"

He broke off, looking across the room at a man who hadn't merely come into it, but had effected an entrance. A tall, slight, stoop-shouldered person with a velvet dinner jacket, a mane of gray hair, and a certain distinction of which he was entirely aware.

"Enter Right Centre," Anthony said to Miss Dunning. "But who? I've lost my program."

She looked at him in surprise. "Curiouser and curiouser," she said. "So the man doesn't know his own host. That's him —Sir Adrian LeFane in person. Old World, huh?"

"Well, well," said Anthony, and stood up as LeFane, having hovered momentarily over the central group with a courtly smile of general greeting, came straight towards him.

"Colonel Gethryn?" He held out a slim white hand, beautifully shaped. "I trust you'll forgive me for not being here to welcome you. But—" the hand sketched a vague, graceful movement in the air—"I was forced to be elsewhere . . ." The hand came down and offered itself again and Anthony shook it.

"Out, were you?" said Miss Dunning. "Caught in the rain?"

"Not—ah—noticeably, my dear." LeFane gave her an avuncular smile. "I regard myself as fortunate—"

But he never told them why—for at that moment his daughter joined them, words preceding her like fire from a flamethrower. She was worried, it seemed, about someone, or thing, called "Marya"—you could hear the "y"—who, or which, should have put in appearance.

She led her parent away—and again Anthony was relieved. He looked at Miss Dunning and said:

"Who is Marya, what is she? Or it, maybe? Or even he?"

"Dax."

"An impolite sound." Anthony surveyed her. "Unless—oh, shades of Ångelo! Do you mean the sculptress? The Riondetto group at Geneva? The Icarus at Hendon?"

"Right!" Miss Dunning looked at the door and pointed. "And here she is . . ."

Striding from the door towards the advancing LeFane was a gaunt giant of a woman. Despite her size—she must have topped six feet—and her extraordinary appearance—she wore a strange, flowing, monk-like garment of some harsh, dark-green material—she was impressive rather than ludicrous. Her crag-like face gave no answer to the best of LeFane's smiles, but she permitted herself to be steered towards the group around Mrs. Crecy, and in a moment seemed to become its pivot.

"Well?" said Miss Dunning.

"Remarkable," said Anthony. "In fact, I remarked her a couple of hours ago. She was under a tree. Looking."

"Like what?" Miss Dunning wanted to know.

But she wasn't answered. Two more people were entering the room—a well-built, pleasant-faced man of thirty-odd, with a tired look and what used to be called "professional" appearance; a small, angular, weatherbeaten little woman, with no proportions and a face like a happy horse.

Once more Anthony looked at Miss Dunning, and once more she enlightened him.

"Human beings," said Miss Dunning. "Refreshing, isn't it? Local doctor and wife. I like 'em." She looked at her empty glass and handed it to Anthony. "See what you can do," she said.

But he had no chance to do it. Mrs. Crecy swooped, and

he was drawn towards Marya Dax and presented, and surveyed by strange dark eyes which seemed to be all pupil and were almost on a level with his own.

He murmured some politeness, and was ignored. He turned away and was pounced upon again, and found himself meeting Dr. and Mrs. Carmichael. Looking at the woman's freckled, equine face, he was assailed by a flicker of memory.

He shook hands with the husband, but they hadn't said a word to each other when the wife spoke.

"You don't remember me, do you?" She looked up at Anthony with bright, small eyes.

"That's the worst thing you can do to anyone, Min!" her husband chided her affectionately. "You ought to be ashamed of yourself."

"If you'll let me have a moment, I'll tell you," Anthony said—and then, "It's some time ago—and I remember pigtails —of course! You're Henry Martin's daughter."

"There!" Mrs. Carmichael caught hold of her husband's arm. "He did it!"

"And he'd have done it before," said Carmichael, smiling at her, "only he couldn't see Little Miss Moneybags as the wife of a country sawbones." He patted her hand.

"Colonel Gethryn," said Mrs. Carmichael, "I'm going to trade on old acquaintance. I'm going to ask you a—an indiscreet question. I—"

Her husband moved his broad shoulders uncomfortably. "Please, Min, go easy," he said.

"Don't be silly, Jim. You've *got* to try—and Colonel Gethryn won't mind."

She looked up at Anthony like an earnest foal. "Will you?"

Anthony looked down at the appealing face. "I shouldn't think so," he said, and was going to add, "Try me out," when dinner was announced and the party began to split into their pairs and he found, with pleasure, that he was to take in Miss Dunning.

The meal, although heavy and of ceremonious splendor, was excellent, and the wines were beyond reproach. So that Anthony found time passing pleasantly enough until, as he chatted with Miss Dunning beside him, he heard his name emerge from what appeared to be a heated argument lower down the table.

". . . Surely Colonel Gethryn's the one to tell us that!"

176

came the husky voice of Mrs. Carmichael. "After all, he's probably the only person here who knows anything about that sort of thing."

Anthony, as he was obviously meant to, turned his head. He found many eyes upon him, and said to Mrs. Carmichael, "What sort of thing? Or shouldn't I ask?"

"Crime, of course!" Mrs. Carmichael looked as if she were pricking her ears forward. "Crime in general and, of course, one crime in particular. Or two, I should say."

Anthony repressed a sigh. He said, hopefully, "If they're new and British-made, I'm afraid I can't help you. I've been away for months, and only landed this afternoon. I haven't even seen an English paper for a fortnight."

With a smile alarming in its area and determination, Mrs. Crecy cut into the talk. She said:

"How fortunate for you, Mr. Gethryn. So abysmally dull they've been! And I think it's a *shame* the way these people are trying to make you talk shop . . ."

She transferred the ferocious smile to little Mrs. Carmichael, who shriveled and muttered something about being "terribly sorry, Jacqueline," and tried to start a conversation with Lord Bracksworth about hunting.

But she was cut off in mid-sentence by Marya Dax, who was sitting on Adrian LeFane's right, and therefore obliquely across the table from Anthony. Throughout the meal she had sat like a silent, brooding Norn but now she leaned forward, gripping the edge of the table with enormous, blunt-fingered hands, and fixing her dark gaze on Anthony, she said, in a harsh contralto:

"Perhaps you have no need to read the papers. Perhaps you can smell where there is evil."

It was neither question nor statement and Anthony, smiling a smile which might have meant anything, prepared to let it lie.

But the Foreign Office, in the person of Mr. Shelton-Jones, saw opportunity for conversation.

"An interesting thought, Miss Dax," said Mr. Shelton-Jones, turning his horn-rimmed gaze upon the Norn. "Whether or not the trained mind becomes attuned, as it were, to appreciating the *atmosphere*, the *wavelength*—perhaps I should call it the *aura*—which might very well emanate from wrongdoing."

The Norn didn't so much as glance at Mr. Shelton-Jones:

177

she kept her dark gaze fixed upon Anthony's face.

But Mr. Shelton-Jones was undaunted and now he too looked at Anthony.

"What do you say, Mr. Gethryn?" he asked. "*Is there a criminal aura?* Have you ever known of any—ah—'case' in which the investigator was assisted by any such—ah—metaphysical emanation?"

Anthony sighed inwardly; but this was too direct to leave unanswered. He said, "You mean what the Americans might call a super-hunch? I'm no professional, of course, but I have known of such things."

The Press joined in now, in the slender shape of Mrs. Dale. "How *fas*-cinating!" she said. "Could you possibly tell us—"

"Please!" Anthony smiled. "I was going on to say that the super-hunch—the 'emanation'—is utterly untrustworthy. Therefore, it's worse than useless—it's dangerous. It has to be ignored."

Surprisingly, because he had been silent throughout the meal, it was the bearded physicist Martel who chimed in now. He jutted the beard aggressively in Anthony's direction, and demanded, "Unt why iss that?" in a tone notably devoid of courtesy.

Anthony surveyed him. "Because," he said coolly, "one can never be sure the impact of the super-hunch is genuine. The feeling might very well be caused by indigestion."

There were smiles, but not from the Professor, who glared, grunted, and turned back to his plate.

Someone said, "But seriously, Colonel Gethryn—"

Anthony said, "I am serious." The topic couldn't be dropped now, so he might as well deal with it properly. He said:

"I can even give you a recent instance of what I mean . . . I was at the Captain's dinner on the *Guinivere* last night. I drank too much. I didn't get quite enough sleep. And when I landed, the current deluge was brewing. Result, as I drove through Friars' Wick, which I'd never seen before, I had the father and mother of all super-hunches. The countryside— the village itself—the fact that there didn't happen to be anyone about—the black sky—everything combined to produce a definite feeling of—" he shrugged—"well, of evil. Which is patently absurd. And almost certainly, when you think of the Captain's dinner, stomachic in origin."

He was surprised—very much and most unusually surprised

178

—by the absolute silence which fell on the company as he finished speaking. He looked from face to face and saw on every one a ruling astonishment. Except in the case of Professor Martel, who scowled sourly and managed at the same time to twist his mouth into a sardonic smile of disbelief.

Someone said, "That's—*extraordinary*, Colonel Gethryn!"

Martel said, "You ssay you haff not read the paperss. But you haff hear the wireless—perhaps . . ."

Anthony looked at the beard, then at the eyes above it. He said, "I don't know what that means . . . Just as well, no doubt."

Marya Dax looked down the table at Martel, examining him with remote eyes. She said, to no one in particular, "That man should be made to keep quiet!" and there was a moment of raw and uncomfortable tension. Mrs. Crecy bit at her lips as if to restrain them from trembling. Adrian LeFane propped an elbow on the table and put a hand up to his face, half-hiding it.

Miss Dunning saved the day. She turned to Anthony beside her with semi-comic amazement wrinkling her goblin face. She said, on exactly the right note:

"Remarkable, my dear Holmes!" And then she laughed exactly the right laugh. "And the odd thing is—you don't know what you've done. Maybe you'd better find out."

The tension relaxed, and Anthony said, "I seem to have caused a sensation." He looked around the table again. "It could mean there *is* something—" he glanced at the Norn— "evil-smelling in Friars' Wick."

There was a babble of five or six voices then, all talking at once, and through them, quite clearly, came the husky eagerness of Mrs. Carmichael's.

". . . most wonderful thing I ever heard of! Colonel Gethryn, do you realize you've *proved* what Miss Dax was saying."

Anthony looked at Mrs. Carmichael and smiled. "That isn't proof," he said. "Might be coincidence. The Captain's dinner was—lavish."

But Mrs. Carmichael wasn't to be deterred. "You've got to hear," she said. "You've *got* to!" She spoke to her husband across the table. "Jim, tell him all about it."

A worried look came into Doctor Carmichael's tired, nice-looking face. He cast a glance towards his hostess, but she said nothing, and Mrs. Carmichael said, "Go *on*, Jim!" and Mrs. Dale said, "Please, Doctor!" and he capitulated.

He looked across the table at Anthony. "I'm deputed for this," he said, "because I happen to look after the Police work in this part of Downshire. Most of the time the job's a sinecure. But lately—"

He blew out his cheeks in a soundless little whistle and proceeded to tell of the two murders which had so much exercised the Press, particularly the *Despatch*. He was precise and vaguely official. He merely *stated*—but yet, and although it was no news to them, everyone else at the table was absolutely silent. They were, for the most part, watching the face of Anthony Ruthven Gethryn.

Who said, when the statement was over, "H'mm! Sort of Ripper Redivivus." His face had offered no signs of any sort to the watchers. It had, as he listened, been as completely blank as a poker player's, with the lids half-closed over the green eyes.

Doctor Carmichael said slowly, "Yes, I suppose so. If there are any more—which I personally am afraid of—although the Chief Constable doesn't agree with me . . ."

"He doesn't?" Anthony's eyes were fully open now. "Who is he?"

"Major General Sir Rigby Forsythe." Acid had crept into the doctor's tone. "He 'can't see his way' to calling in Scotland Yard. He considers Inspector Fennell and myself 'alarmists.' He—" Doctor Carmichael cut himself off abruptly with a grimace of impatience.

But Anthony finished the sentence for him. "—refuses to realize that two brutal murders, apparently carried out by a sexual maniac, could possibly be the beginning of a series. That it?"

"Precisely!" Dr. Carmichael brightened at this ready understanding. "And he goes on refusing to realize, in spite of the fact that Fennell's tried a hundred times to show him that as the death of either of those poor women couldn't conceivably have benefited anyone, the murders must have been done by a maniac." A faint expression of disgust passed over Dr. Carmichael's face. "A peculiarly revolting maniac! And maniacs who've found a way of gratifying their mania—well, they don't stop . . ."

"For mysself," came the harshly sibilant voice of Professor Martel, "I do not think a maniac." He was sitting back in his chair now, the beard tilted upward. "I think a public benefactor."

He paused and there came the slightly bewildered silence he had obviously expected. He said:

"Thosse women! Thosse creaturess! I haff sseen them both while they were alife. They sserved no purposse and they were hideouss! The worlt is better less them."

Now the silence was shocked. It was broken by Marya Dax. Again she looked down the table towards Martel, and again seemed to examine him. She said:

"There is one hideous thing here with us. It is your mind." She ceased to examine the man, and went on. "No human body," she said, "is completely without beauty."

"Oh, come now, my dear Miss Dax," said Lady Bracksworth surprisingly, in a mild but determined little voice. "Although I have nothing but sympathy—" she darted a look of dislike towards Martel—"for those poor unfortunate women, I must say that at least one of them—Sarah Paddock, I mean—was a truly disgraceful object."

The Norn turned slow and blazing eyes upon this impudence.

"This woman," said the Norn, "this Paddock—I suppose you did not ever look at her hands?" She said, "They were dirty always. They were harsh with work. But they were beautiful."

"An interesting thought indeed!" said Mr. Shelton-Jones. "Can beauty in the—ah—human frame be considered, as it were, in *units*—or must it be, before we recognize it, a totality of such units?"

Mrs. Carmichael said, "I think Miss Dax is right." She looked over at her husband. "Don't you think so?"

He smiled at her, but didn't answer and she said insistently, "Isn't she right, Jim? You think she is, don't you?"

"Of course she is," Carmichael said. He looked around the table. "In my profession I see a great many human bodies. And I see a great many—" he looked at Mr. Shelton-Jones— "beautiful 'units' in otherwise ugly specimens. For instance—" he looked at Marya Dax— "I particularly noticed poor Sarah Paddock's hands."

Mr. Shelton-Jones settled his spectacles more firmly astride his nose. "But, my dear sir—if I may be permitted to support my original contention—what beauty can there be in a 'beauty-unit' if such unit is a mere island, as it were, in an ocean of ugliness?" Obviously prepared for debate, he leaned back in his chair, fixing his gaze upon Dr. Carmichael.

Carmichael said, "Plenty. You can't deny, for instance, that Sarah Paddock's hands weren't beautiful in themselves." He seemed nettled by the Parliamentary manner of Mr. Shelton-Jones. "Suppose Miss Dax had modelled them!"

"Then," Mr. Shelton-Jones blandly observed, "they would have been apart from their hideous surroundings."

"Euclidian," said Anthony. "Some of the parts may or may not be equal to their total."

But Dr. Carmichael went on looking at Mr. Shelton-Jones.

"All right," said Dr. Carmichael. "Suppose you saw magnificent shoulders on a—on an extreme case of *lupus vulgaris*. Would the horrible condition of the face and neck make the shoulders repulsive too?"

"The whole picture would be—ah—definitely unpleasing." Mr. Shelton-Jones was blandness itself and the Norn turned her dark, examining gaze upon him.

Color had risen to Dr. Carmichael's face. He stared hard at Mr. Shelton-Jones and said:

"Let's try again. Do you mean to tell me that if you saw Titian hair on a typical troglodytic head, you'd think it was ugly, because of its setting?"

"I agree with the doctor," said the Norn. "The other killed woman—her name I forget—was worse formed than the first. But the shape of her skull was noble."

"Umpf-chnff!" remarked Lord Bracksworth. "That'd be the fortune-tellin' one, the Stebbins woman. . . . D'ja know, I was talkin' to that Inspector-fellah s'mornin', and he was tellin' me that when they found her, this old gal—"

At the head of the table Adrian LeFane sat suddenly upright. He brought his open hand violently down upon the cloth, so that the glasses beside his plate chimed and jingled.

"*Please!*" His face twisted as if with physical pain. "Let us have no more of this—this—intolerable *ugliness!*"

It was about an hour after dinner—which, thanks mainly to the social genius of Miss Dunning, had ended on a subdued but embarrassing note—that Mrs. Carmichael, her husband in attendance, contrived to corner Anthony in a remote quarter of the vast drawing-room.

He had just come in after a visit to Adrian LeFane's study, where he had at last delivered the letter which has nothing to do with this tale. He allowed himself to be cornered, although he would much rather have talked with Miss Dunning, because there was something desperately appealing in the filly-like gaze of Mrs. Carmichael.

She said, "Oh, please, Colonel Gethryn, *may* we talk to you!" Her long, freckled face was as earnest as her voice.

Anthony said, "Why not?"

Carmichael said, "Oh, Min, why insist on worrying the man?" He gave Anthony a little apologetic smile.

"Because it's worrying *you*, darling!" Mrs. Carmichael laid a hand on her husband's arm, but went on looking at Colonel Gethryn.

"Jim's terribly upset," she said, "about that horrid old Chief Constable. He thinks—I mean, Jim does—that the Downshire police can't possibly catch this dreadful murderer unless they get help from Scotland Yard. And they can't get it unless the Chief Constable asks for it . . ."

Her husband interrupted. "For heaven's sake, dear, Gethryn knows all about that sort of thing!"

She paid no attention to him. She said to Anthony, "And what I was going to ask you: we wondered if there was any way—any way at all—you could use your influence to—"

She left the sentence in midair as she caught sight of a servant approaching her husband.

"Dr. Carmichael," said the man. He lowered his voice, but his words came clearly. "Excuse me, sir, but there's an important message for you." A curious blend of horrified dismay and cassandrine pleasure showed through his servitor's mask. He said:

"Inspector Fennell telephoned. There's been another of these dreadful murders. He wants you to come at once, sir, to Pilligrew Lane, where it comes out by Masham's . . ."

"Just around the next corner," said Dr. Carmichael, and braked hard.

Beside him, Anthony grunted—he never has liked and never will like being driven.

The little car skidded around a sharp turn and into the mouth of a lane which lay dark and narrow between a high hedge and the looming backs of three great barns.

Through the steady, glittering sheet of the rain, a group of men and cars showed ahead, barring the way completely and standing out black in the glare of headlights.

Carmichael stopped his engine and scrambled out. Anthony followed and felt the sweeping of the rain down over him and the seeping of viscous mud through his thin soles. He followed Carmichael towards the group and a figure turned from it, advancing on them and flashing an electric torch—a man in a heavy black storm-coat and the flat, visored cap of a uniformed Police Inspector.

Carmichael said, "Fennell, this is Colonel Gethryn—" and didn't get any further because the man, having darted a look at Anthony, turned back to him in amazement.

"But, Doctor," said Inspector Fennell in a hoarse and confidential whisper, "Sir Rigby's done it already. Did it last night, without saying a word to me. Called London and got the Commissioner, and turned up, after I'd phoned him about this, all complete with a Detective-Inspector who'd just arrived from the Yard!"

Carmichael stared as if he couldn't believe his ears, and Anthony said to Fennell, "Who did they send? Hobday?"

Fennell said, "That's right, sir," and led the way towards the group in the light.

They slithered after him through the mud, and in a moment Hobday was looking at Anthony and saying, "Good Lord, sir, where did *you* drop from?"

And then there was a word with Sir Rigby Forsythe, who seemed somewhat taken aback by Anthony's presence, and a moment or so of waiting while the photographers finished their work over what lay in the ditch against the hedge.

Anthony said, "This new victim? I suppose it's a woman—but what kind? Was she another local character?"

Fennell said, "Yes, she's a woman all right, sir. And it's—it's horrible, worse than the others." He glanced towards the ditch and quickly away again. He seemed to realize he had strayed most unprofessionally from the point, and cleared his throat. "I don't think she's—she was a local, sir. So far nobody's recognized her. Seems to've been one of those gipsy basket-menders. She had an old horse and cart—prob'ly was just passing through on her way to Deyning."

Hobday said, "If it hadn't been for the horse, we wouldn't have known yet. But a farm laborer found it wandering and began to look for its owner."

The photographers finished their work, and one of them came up to the Chief Constable and saluted. "All through, sir," he said, his voice shaky and uncertain.

Sir Rigby Forsythe looked at Anthony, then at Carmichael and the others. His weatherbeaten face was lined and pallid.

184

He said, "You fellahs go ahead. I've seen all I need." He stood where he was while Fennell, visibly conquering reluctance, led the way with Carmichael, and Hobday and Anthony followed.

The headlights of the police cars cut through the water-drenched darkness. They made a nightmare tableau of the thing which lay half in and half out of the ditch. Anthony muttered, "God!" and the usually stolid Hobday drew in his breath with a little hiss. Carmichael, his face set and grim, dropped on his knees in the oozing mud. He made a cursory examination.

Then he stood up. "All right," he said. "We can move her now," and then, helped by Anthony and Hobday, lifted the thing and set it upon clean wet grass and in merciful shadow. He straightened the saturated rags of its clothing, and then suddenly dropped on one knee again and said, "Anyone got a torch?"

Hobday gave him one, and he shone the light on the head, and gently moved the heavy, mud-covered mass of red hair away from the features it was covering.

"Just wondering whether I'd ever seen her," he said. He kept the light of the torch on the face, and it stared up at them, washed cleaner every moment by the flooding rain. It was a brutish, sub-human face, and although it was distorted by death and terror, it could have been little more prepossessing in life.

Carmichael shook his head. "No," he said. "They're right. She's a stranger round here." He switched off the torch, but Anthony said. "Just a minute," and took it from him and knelt beside the body himself and switched the light on again and peered at the throat, where a darkness like a big bruise showed in the hollow below the chin.

But after a moment, he too shook his head. "No. It's a birthmark," he said, and Carmichael peered at it and said, "Yes. Or possibly an old scar."

They stood up, and Hobday took the torch and knelt in his turn and began slow, methodical examination.

Anthony said, "Silly question, I know, but about how long since death?" A little cascade of water tumbled from his hat-brim as he bent his head to button his raincoat, which had come undone.

Carmichael said, "Oh—very loosely, and subject to error— not more than five hours, not less than two."

185

Anthony looked at his watch, whose glowing figures said eleven forty-five, and found himself calculating times. But this didn't get him anywhere, and he was glad when, thirty minutes later, he found himself being driven back to LeFane's house by Carmichael. He said to Carmichael on the way:

"You see, it's definitely not my sort of thing. Mass murders are mad murders, and mad murders, in the ordinary sense of the word, are motiveless. Which makes them a matter for routine policio-military methods. At which I'm worse than useless, while men like Hobday are solid and brilliant at the same time."

Carmichael smiled. "I'm glad you're both here—Hobday and yourself. I'll sleep better tonight than I have for a week."

They reached the house and were no sooner in the big hall than they were surrounded. They were plied with drinks and food, and besieged with questions. Was it really another of the *same* murders? Where had it happened? Was the victim the same *sort* of person? Did they think the murderer would be caught this time? Wasn't there something terribly *wrong* with police methods when things like this were allowed to go on? Wouldn't it be a good idea to have a curfew, or a registration every day of the movements of every man, woman and child in the district?

Mr. Shelton-Jones said, "An interesting point. How far may the liberties of the individual be restricted when such restriction is—ah—for the purpose of protecting the community?"

Miss Dunning said, "Human beings are terrifying, aren't they?" and shuddered a little.

Professor Martel said, "I woult like to know—wass thiss one usseless and hideouss like the otherss?"

Mrs. Carmichael said, "Oh, *had* Sir Rigby sent for Scotland Yard *already?* Oh, thank *goodness!*"

Everyone said something. Except Adrian LeFane and Marya Dax. And they were not present.

Anthony, throwing aside civility, at last forced his way upstairs. It seemed to him that he was even more grateful than the Carmichaels for the advent of Detective-Inspector Hobday.

He made ready for bed and then, smoking a last cigarette and wondering how soon in the morning he could decently leave, strolled over to a window.

The rain had stopped now and a pale moon shone through

clouds onto the sodden earth. By the watery light he saw a figure striding up the steps of a terrace beneath him, making for the house. It was tall and powerful and square-shouldered and unmistakable in spite of its shapeless coat and headgear.

He watched it until it was out of sight beneath him. He heard a door open and close.

He went over to the bed and sat on the edge of it and finished the cigarette. He pondered. He stubbed out the cigarette at last and got into bed. After all, if sculptresses liked to walk at night, why shouldn't they?

But he knew he would stop on his way home tomorrow and have a word with Hobday.

He went to sleep.

It was six o'clock on the next afternoon. He had been in London and at home since one. He sat in the library at Stukely Gardens with his wife and his son.

A violent storm had replaced yesterday's deluge. It had raged intermittently over London and the whole south of England since early morning, and still the hard, heavy rain drove against the windows, while thunder rumbled and great flashes of lightning kept tearing the half-darkness.

Master Alan Gethryn gave his approval to the weather. "It sort of makes it all small and comf'table in here." he said, looking up from the jigsaw puzzle strewn about the floor.

Anthony said, "I know exactly what you mean," and looked at his wife, who sat on the arm of his chair.

Master Alan Gethryn pored over the puzzle—an intricate forest-scene of which he had only one corner done. He sighed and scratched his head, and then suddenly laughed.

"It's like what Mr. Haslam's always saying," he said—and Lucia looked at Anthony and explained *sotto voce,* "Master at the new school." and then said to her son, "What d'you mean, old boy?"

He looked up at her, still smiling. "He's *always* saying, 'You chaps can't see the wood for the trees.'" He chuckled. "Like this puzzle.". . .

Sublimely unconscious of the effect his words had made upon his father, he returned to his labors.

But Lucia, watching her husband's face, was concerned. She had to wait until her son had left them and gone supper-wards, but the moment the door had closed behind him, she stood over Anthony and looked down at him and said:

187

"What's the matter, darling? You've got that look. What did Alan say?"

Anthony reached up a long arm and pulled her down onto his knees. "He gave me an idea—unintentionally, of course." He kissed her. "A damned nasty, uncomfortable idea. I'd like to forget about it."

Lucia said, "You know you won't. So you'd better tell me."

Anthony said, "Suppose I wanted to kill someone—let's say, your Uncle Perceval. And suppose his demise would benefit me to such an extent that I was afraid a nice straight murder would inevitably point at me. And suppose I were that most dangerous of madmen, the secret megalomaniac, and utterly ruthless to boot. So suppose I started a wave of apparently insane slaying, and got well going with three murders of middle-aged clubmen I didn't know at all—and then killed Uncle Perceval in exactly the same way—and then killed three more middle-aged clubmen! The police would be chasing a madman with an extraordinary quirk. They wouldn't dream of chasing me!"

"What loathsome thoughts you do have!" Lucia turned her head to look at his face. "Oh, Anthony—is that just an idea? Or do you think it's what's happening in Downshire?"

"Oh, just an idea." said Anthony slowly. "It doesn't fit . . ."

She dropped a kiss on his forehead and stood up. She said, "I'll get you a drink. And after that, my lad, you've got to change—we're due at the Dufresnes' by eight. White tie."

She started to cross the room, then checked. She said:

"What on earth did Alan say that gave you that dreadful notion?"

Anthony looked at her. "My dear girl!" he said, " 'You can't see the wood for the trees'. . ."

Lucia shivered, went out of the room, came back with his drink, and very soon herded him upstairs.

Forty-five minutes later she walked into his dressing-room. He was tying his tie, and he saw her in the mirror and said, "You know, Americans really develop the possibilities of our language. Baby, you look like a million dollars!"

She said, "I love you. But we're going to be late and then I won't."

He put the finishing touches to the bow. "Get my coat, beldame," he said, and started to distribute keys and money and cigarette case among his pockets.

Lucia crossed towards the big wardrobe. Beside it was

188

Anthony's trunk, and on a nearby chair a neat pile of the clothing with which he had traveled. Something about the pile caught Lucia's eye, and she stopped and looked down at it. She said, "Whatever happened to this dinner jacket?"

"Rain last night," Anthony said. "White'll see to it."

She smiled. Carefully she picked something from the shoulder of the black coat. She said, "He ought to've seen to this, oughtn't he? Before *I* saw it!"

She went towards him, carrying her hands in front of her, one above the other and a good two feet apart.

"Magnificent!" said Anthony. "Most impressive! But what's the role?"

She came close to him. She moved her hands and there was a glint of light between them.

He saw a long hair of glittering reddish-gold.

He said, "Not Guilty, M'lud," and looked at the hair again.

He said, "Nobody at LeFane's had that color. Or length..."

He said, "Good *God!*"

He jumped across the room and snatched at the telephone.

And two minutes later was being informed that, owing to storm-damage, all the trunk lines to Downshire were out of order . . .

He began to tear off the dress clothes.

He said, "Get them to bring round the car! Quick!"

Little Mrs. Carmichael lay on the rather uncomfortable couch in the living-room of Dr. Carmichael's rather uncomfortable house. She was pretending to read but really she was listening to the thunder.

She wished Jim hadn't had to go out on a call, especially on a night like this. She thought about Jim and how wonderful he was. Although it was two years now since they'd been married, she was happier than she had been on her honeymoon. Happy—and proud. Proud of Jim, and proud of herself, too; proud that she didn't mind uncomfortable sofas and cups with chips in them and a gas fire in the bedroom. Proud of her cleverness—her really heaven-inspired cleverness—in realizing right at the start, even before they were married, that a man of Jim's caliber couldn't possibly bear living on his wife's money . . .

The thunder was far away now, and almost casual. Little Mrs. Carmichael dozed . . .

She was awakened by the sound of a key in the front door —Jim's key. She heard Jim's step in the hall and jumped up off the sofa and went to the door to meet him—and then was shocked by his appearance as he threw it open just before she reached it. He had his hat on still, and his raincoat. They were both dark and dripping with water. He was frowning, and his face was very white, there was a look in his eyes she'd never seen before.

She said, "Jim! What is it, dearest? What's *happened?*"

"Accident," he said. "I ran over someone..." He pulled the back of his hand across his forehead so that his hat was pushed back and she noticed, with utter irrelevance, the little red line which the brim had made across the skin.

He said, "Come and help me, will you? Put on a coat and run out to the car. He's in the back seat." He turned away and strode across the hall to the surgery door. "With you in a minute," he said.

She ran to the hall cupboard and dragged out a raincoat. She tugged open the front door and hurried down the path, the uneven brick slippery under her feet.

The gate was open and through the rain she could see the dark shape of Jim's car. She stumbled towards it and pulled open the door and the little light in the roof came on.

There was nothing in the back seat.

Bewildered, she turned—and there was Jim, close to her. She started to say something—and then saw Jim's face—

It *was* Jim's face—but she almost didn't recognize it. And there was something bright in his hand, something bright and sharp and terrifying.

She screamed—and suddenly everything went very fast in front of her eyes, the way things used to go fast in films when she was a child, and there was a shouting of men's voices, and something heavy like a stone swished through the air past her and hit Jim on the head, and he fell down and the bright steel thing dropped out of his hand, and two men ran up, and one of them was Colonel Gethryn and the other knelt over Jim, and Colonel Gethryn put his arm around her as she swayed on her feet, and the black wet world spun dizzily faster and faster ...

"But there isn't anything complex about it," said Anthony. "It started when my son gave me the 'can't-see-the-wood-for-the-trees' idea. And then Lucia found that long, magnificent,

190

red-gold hair on my dinner-jacket. And that's all there was to it . . ."

The others said a lot of things, together and separately.

He waited for them to finish, and then shook his head sadly.

He said, "My dear people, that hair was tantamount to a confession by Dr. James Carmichael, duly signed, attested and registered at Somerset House. I might never have realized it, of course, if Alan hadn't handed me 'wood-for-the-trees.' But as I'd evolved the notion of hiding one murder with a lot of other murders—well, it was completely obvious. Carmichael, whose wife was rich and plain and over-loving, fitted everything. He was a doctor. He could travel about. He—"

"But *why* did the hair necessarily point to him?"

"Because it must have come from the third body. Because no one at LeFane's had hair even remotely red. Of course, it was caked with mud and colorless when it got onto my coat, but by the time it dried—"

"Hold it! Hold it! I *still* don't see how it pointed to the doctor!"

"I'm surprised at you!" Anthony surveyed the speaker with real astonishment.

"After all, you were there at LeFane's. You heard Carmichael arguing with that horn-rimmed intellect from the Foreign Office. Don't you remember him talking about *Titian hair on troglodytes?*"

"Why, yes . . . But—"

"Don't you realize he talked *too soon?* He said that nearly two hours *before* they found the third murderee. And the third murderee was a brute-faced redhead!"

THE MAN WHO SANG
IN CHURCH

BY EDGAR WALLACE

Edgar Wallace was born in Greenwich, England, on April 1, 1875. When he was nine days old he was adopted by a fish porter. When he was 21, stationed in South Africa with the Medical Staff Corps, he became known as the Soldier Poet. He bought himself out of the Army in 1899 and became the South African war correspondent for the London *Daily Mail*. He lived and gambled beyond his means and wrote his first novel, *The Four Just Men*, to recoup his losses. His first marriage failed and in 1918 he married his secretary, "Jim." He died while on a writing assignment in Hollywood in 1932.

To LEON GONSALEZ went most of the cases of blackmail which came the way of the Three Just Men.

And yet, from the views he had so consistently expressed, he was the last man in the world to whom such problems should have gone, for in that famous article of his entitled *Justification*, which put up the sales of a quarterly magazine by some thousand per cent, he offered the following opinion:

". . . as to blackmail, I see no adequate punishment but death in the case of habitual offenders. You cannot parley with the type of criminal who specializes in this loathsome form of livelihood. Obviously, there can be no side of him to which appeal can be made: no system of reformation can affect him. He is dehumanized, and may be classified with the secret poisoner, the baby-farmer, and . . ."

He mentioned a trade as unwholesome.

Leon found less drastic means of dealing with these pests; yet we may suppose that the more violent means which distinguished the case of Miss Brown and the man who sang in church had his heartiest approval.

There are so many types of beauty that even Leon Gonsalez, who had a passion for classification, gave up at the eighteenth subdivision of the thirty-third category of brunettes. By which time he had filled two large notebooks.

If he had not wearied of his task before he met Miss Brown, he would assuredly have recognized its hopelessness, for she fell into no category, nor had he her peculiar attractions catalogued in any of his subsections. She was dark and slim and elegant. Leon hated the word, but he was compelled to admit this characteristic. The impression she left was one of delicate fragrance. Leon called her the Lavender Girl. She called herself Brown, which was obviously not her name; also, in the matter of simulations, she wore one of those closely fitting hats that came down over a woman's eyes and might make subsequent identification extremely difficult.

She timed her visit for the half-light of dusk—the cigarette hour that follows a good dinner, when men are inclined rather to think than to talk, and to doze than either.

Others had come at this hour to the little house in Curzon Street, where the silver triangle on the door marked the habitation of the Three Just Men, and when the bell rang George Manfred looked up at the clock.

"It is too early for the post—see who it is, Raymond: and before you go, I will tell you. It is a young lady in black, rather graceful of carriage, very nervous, and in bad trouble."

Leon grinned as Poiccart rose heavily from his chair and went out.

"Clairvoyance rather than deduction," he said, "and observation rather than either: from where you sit you can see the street. Why mystify our dear friend?"

George Manfred sent a ring of smoke to the ceiling.

"He is not mystified," he said lazily. "He has seen her also. If you hadn't been so absorbed in your newspaper you would have seen her, too. She has passed up and down the street three times on the other side. And on each occasion she has glanced toward this door. She is rather typical, and I have been wondering exactly what variety of blackmail has been practiced on her."

Here Raymond Poiccart came back.

"She wishes to see one of you," he said. "Her name is Miss Brown—but she doesn't look like a Miss Brown!"

Manfred nodded to Leon.

"It had better be you," he said.

Gonsalez went to the little front drawing-room and found the girl standing with her back to the window, her face in shadow.

"I would rather you did not put on the light, please," she said, in a calm, steady voice. "I do not wish to be recognized if you meet me again."

Leon smiled.

"I had no intention of touching the switch," he said. "You see, Miss—" he waited expectantly.

"Brown," she replied, so definitely that he would have known she desired anonymity even if she had not made her request in regard to the light. "I told your friend my name."

"You see, Miss Brown," he went on, "we have quite a number of callers who are particularly anxious not to be recognized when we meet them again. Will you sit down? I know that you have not much time, and that you are anxious to catch a train out of town."

She was puzzled.

"How did you know that?" she asked.

Leon made one of his superb gestures.

"Otherwise you would have waited until it was quite dark before you made your appointment. You have, in point of fact, left it just as late as you could."

She pulled a chair to the table and sat down slowly, turning her back to the window.

"Of course that is so," she nodded—"Yes, I have to cut it fine. Are you Mr. Manfred?"

"Gonsalez," he corrected her.

"I want your advice," she said.

She spoke in an even, unemotional voice, her hands lightly clasped before her on the table. Even in the dark, and unfavorably placed as she was for observation, he could see that she was beautiful. He guessed from her voice that she was about twenty-four.

"I am being blackmailed. I suppose you will tell me I should go to the police, but I am afraid the police would be of no assistance, even if I were willing to risk an appearance in court, which I am not. My father—" she hesitated—"is a government official. It would break his heart if he knew. What a fool I have been!"

"Letters?" asked Leon, sympathetically.

"Letters and other things," she said. "About six years ago I was a medical student at St. John's Hospital. I did not take my final exam for reasons which you will understand. My surgical knowledge has not been of very much use to me, except . . . well, I once saved a man's life, though I doubt if it was worth saving. He seems to think it was, but that has nothing to do with the case. When I was at St. John's I got to know a fellow-student, a man whose name will not interest you, and, as girls of my age sometimes do, I fell desperately in love with him. I did not know that he was married, although he told me this before our friendship reached a climax.

"For all that followed I was to blame. There were the usual letters—"

"And these are the basis of the blackmail?" asked Leon.

She nodded.

"I was worried ill about the . . . affair. I gave up my work and returned home; but that doesn't interest you, either."

"Who is blackmailing you?" asked Leon.

She hesitated. "The man. It is horrible, isn't it? But he has gone down and down. I have money of my own—my mother left me £2,000 a year—and of course I have paid."

"When did you see this man last?"

She was thinking of something else, and she did not answer him. As he repeated the question, she looked up quickly.

"Last Christmas Day—only for a moment. He was not staying with us—I mean it was at the end of . . ."

She had become suddenly panic-stricken, confused, and was almost breathless as she went on: "I saw him by accident. Of course he did not see me, but it was a great shock. . . . It was his voice. He always had a wonderful tenor voice."

"He was singing?" suggested Leon, when she paused, as he guessed, in an effort to recover her self-possession.

"Yes, in church," she said, desperately. "That is where I saw him."

She went on speaking with great rapidity, as though she were anxious not only to dismiss from her mind that chance encounter, but to make Leon also forget.

"It was two months after this that he wrote to me—he wrote to our old address in town. He said he was in desperate need of money, and wanted £500. I had already given him more than £1,000, but I was sane enough to write and tell him I intended to do no more. It was then that he horrified me by sending a photograph of the letter—of one of the letters —I had sent him. Mr. Gonsalez, I have met another man, and . . . well, John had evidently read the news of my engagement."

"Your fiancé knows nothing about the earlier affair?"

She shook her head.

"No, nothing, and he mustn't know. Otherwise everything would be simple. Do you imagine I would allow myself to be blackmailed any further but for that?"

Leon took a slip of paper from one pocket and a pencil from another.

"Will you tell me the name of this man? John——"

"John Letheritt, 27 Lion Row, Whitechurch Street. It is a little room that he has rented, as an office and a sleeping place. I have already had inquiries made."

Leon waited.

"What is the crisis? Why have you come now?" he asked.

She took from her bag a letter, and he noted that it was in a clean envelope; evidently she had no intention that her real name and address should be known.

He read it and found it a typical communication. The letter demanded £3,000 by the third of the month, failing

196

which the writer intended putting "papers" in "certain hands." There was just that little touch of melodrama which for some curious reason the average blackmailer adopts in his communiqués.

"I will see what I can do. How am I to get in touch with you?" asked Leon. "I presume that you do not wish that either your real name or your address should be known even to me."

She did not answer until she had taken from her bag a number of banknotes.

Leon smiled.

"I think we will discuss the question of payment when we have succeeded. What do you want me to do?"

"I want you to get the letters, and, if it is possible, I want you so to frighten this man that he will not trouble me again. As to the money, I shall feel so much happier if you will let me pay you now."

"It is against the rules of the firm," said Leon cheerfully.

She gave him a street and a number which he guessed was an accommodation address.

"Please don't see me to the door," she said, with a half-glance at the watch on her wrist.

He waited till the door closed behind her, and then went upstairs to his companions.

"I know so much about this lady that I could write a monograph on the subject," he said.

"Tell us a little," suggested Manfred. But Leon shook his head.

That evening he called at Whitechurch Street. Lion Row was a tiny, miserable thoroughfare, more like an alley than anything, and hardly deserved its grand designation. In one of those ancient houses which must have seen the decline of Alsatia, at the top of three rickety flights of stairs, he found a door on which had been recently painted:

J. LETHERITT, EXPORTER

His knock produced no response.

He knocked again more heavily, and heard the creaking of a bed, and a harsh voice asking on the other side who was there. It took some time before he could persuade the man to open the door, and then Leon found himself in a very long, narrow room, lighted by a shadeless electric table-lamp. The furniture consisted of a bed, an old washstand, and a dingy desk piled high with unopened circulars.

He guessed the man who confronted him, dressed in a soiled shirt and trousers, to be about thirty-five; he certainly looked older. His face was unshaven and there was in the room an acrid stink of opium.

"What do you want?" growled John Letheritt, glaring suspiciously at the visitor.

With one glance Leon had taken in the man—a weakling, he guessed—one who had found and would always take the easiest way. The little pipe on the table by the bed was a direction post not to be mistaken.

Before he could answer, Letheritt went on:

"If you have come for letters you won't find them here, my friend." He shook a trembling hand in Leon's face. "You can go back to dear Gwenda and tell her that you are no more successful than the last gentleman she sent."

"A blackmailer, eh? You are the dirtiest little blackmailer I ever met," mused Leon. "I suppose you know the young lady intends to prosecute you?"

"Let her prosecute! Let her get a warrant and have me pinched! It won't be the first time I've been inside. Maybe she can get a search warrant, then she will be able to have her letters read in court. I'm saving you a lot of trouble, too! Engaged, eh? You're not the prospective bridegroom?"

"If I were, I should be wringing your neck," said Leon calmly. "If you are a wise man——"

"I am not wise," snarled the other. "Do you think I would be living in this pigsty if I were? I . . . a man with a medical degree?"

Then, with a sudden rage, he pushed his visitor towards the door.

"Get out and stay out!"

Leon was so surprised by this onslaught that he was listening to the door being locked and bolted against him before he realized what had happened.

From the man's manner he was certain that the letters were in that room—there were a dozen places where they might be hidden: he could have overcome Letheritt with the greatest ease, bound him to the bed, and searched the room, but in these days the Three Just Men were very law-abiding people.

Instead he came back to his friends late that night with the story of his partial failure.

"If he left the house occasionally, it would be easy—but he never goes out. I even think that Raymond and I could, without the slightest trouble, make a very thorough search of the place. Letheritt has a bottle of milk left every morning, and it should not be difficult to put him to sleep if we reached the house a little after the milkman."

Manfred shook his head.

"You'll have to find another way; it's hardly worthwhile antagonizing the police," he said.

"Which is putting it mildly," murmured Poiccart. "Who's the lady?"

Leon repeated almost word for word the conversation he had had with Miss Brown.

"There are certain remarkable facts in her statement, and I am pretty sure they *were* facts, and that she was not trying to deceive me," he said. "Curious Item Number One is that the lady heard this man singing in church last Christmas Day. Is Mr. Letheritt the kind of person one would expect to hear exercising his vocal organs on Christmas carols? My brief acquaintance with him leads me to suppose that he isn't. Curious Item Number Two was the words: 'He was not staying with us,' or something of that sort; and he was 'nearing the end'—of what? Those three items are really remarkable!"

"Not particularly remarkable to me," growled Poiccart. "He was obviously a member of a house party somewhere, and she did not know he was staying in the neighborhood, until she saw him in church. It was near the end of his visit."

Leon shook his head.

"Letheritt has been falling for years. He has not reached his present state since last Christmas; therefore he must have been as bad—or nearly as bad—nine months ago. I really have taken a violent dislike to him, and I must get those letters."

Manfred looked at him thoughtfully.

"They would hardly be at his banker's, because he wouldn't have a banker; or at his lawyer's, because I should imagine that he is the kind of person whose acquaintance with law begins and ends in the criminal courts. I think you are right, Leon; the papers are in his room."

Leon lost no time. Early the next morning he was in Whitechurch Street, and watched the milkman ascend to the garret where Letheritt had his foul habitation. He waited

199

till the milkman had come out and disappeared, but, sharp as he was, he was not quick enough. By the time he had reached the top floor, the milk had been taken in, and the little phial of colorless fluid which might have acted as a preservative to the milk was unused.

The next morning he tried again, and again he failed.

On the fourth night, between the hours of one and two, he managed to gain an entry into the house, and crept noiselessly up the stairs. The door was locked from the inside, but he could reach the end of the key with a pair of narrow pliers he carried.

There was no sound from within when he snapped back the lock and turned the handle softly. But he had no way to deal with the bolts.

The next day he came again, and surveyed the house from the outside. It was possible to reach the window of the room, but he would need a very long ladder, and after a brief consultation with Manfred he decided against this method.

Manfred made a suggestion.

"Why not send him a wire, asking him to meet your Miss Brown at Liverpool Street Station? You know her Christian name?"

Leon sighed wearily.

"I tried that on the second day, my dear chap, and had little Lew Leveson on hand to 'whizz' him the moment he came into the street in case he was carrying the letters."

"By 'whizz' you mean to pick his pocket? I can't keep track of modern thief slang," said Manfred. "In the days when I was actively interested, we used to call it 'dip'."

"You are *démodé*, George; 'whizz' is the word. But of course the beggar didn't come out. If he owed rent I could get the brokers put in; but he does not owe rent. He is breaking no laws, and is living a fairly blameless life—except, of course, one could catch him for being in possession of opium. But that would not be much use, because the police are rather chary of allowing us to work with them."

He shook his head.

"I am afraid I shall have to give Miss Brown a very bad report."

It was not until a few days later that he actually wrote to the agreed address, having first discovered that it was, as he suspected, a small stationer's shop where letters could be called for.

A week later Superintendent Meadows, who was friendly with the Three, came down to consult Manfred on a matter of a forged Spanish passport, and since Manfred was an authority on passport forgeries and had a fund of stories about Spanish criminals, it was long after midnight when the conference broke up.

Leon, who needed exercise, walked to Regent Street with Meadows, and the conversation turned to Mr. John Letheritt.

"Oh, yes, I know him well. I took him two years ago on a false pretense charge, and got him eighteen months at the London Assizes. A real bad egg, that fellow, and a bit of a 'squeaker,' too. He's the man who put away Joe Lenthall, the cleverest cat burglar we've had for a generation. Joe got ten years, and I shouldn't like to be the fellow when Joe comes out!"

Suddenly Leon asked a question, and when the other had answered, his companion stood stock-still in the middle of the deserted Hanover Square and doubled up with silent laughter.

"I don't see the joke."

"But I do," chuckled Leon. "What a fool I've been! And I thought I understood the case!"

"Do you want Letheritt for anything? I know where he lives," said Meadows.

Leon shook his head.

"No, I don't want him: but I should very much like to have ten minutes in his room!"

Meadows looked serious.

"He's blackmailing, eh? I wondered where he was getting his money from."

But Leon did not enlighten him. He went back to Curzon Street and began searching certain works of reference, and followed this by an inspection of a large-scale map of the Home Counties. He was the last to go to bed, and the first to waken, for he slept in the front of the house and heard the knocking at the door.

It was raining heavily as he pulled up the window and looked out; and in the dim light of dawn he thought he recognized Superintendent Meadows. A second later he was sure of his visitor's identity.

"Will you come down? I want to see you."

Gonsalez slipped into his dressing gown, ran downstairs, and opened the door to the superintendent.

"You remember we were talking about Letheritt last night?" said Meadows, as Leon ushered him into the little waiting room.

The superintendent's voice was distinctly unfriendly, and he was eyeing Leon keenly.

"Yes, I remember."

"You didn't by any chance go out again last night?"

"No. Why?"

Again that look of suspicion.

"Letheritt was murdered at half-past one this morning, and his room ransacked."

Leon stared at him.

"Murdered? Have you got the murderer?" he asked at last.

"No, but we shall get him all right. He was seen coming down the rainpipe by a City policeman. Evidently he had got into Letheritt's room through the window, and it was this discovery by the constable which led to a search of the house. The City police had to break in the door, and they found Letheritt dead on the bed. He had evidently been hit on the head with a jimmy, and ordinarily that injury would not have killed him, according to the police doctor; but in his state of health it was quite enough to put him out. A policeman went round the house to intercept the burglar, but somehow he must have escaped into one of the little alleys that abound in this part of the city, and he was next seen by a constable in Fleet Street, driving a small car, the number plate of which had been covered with mud."

"Was the man recognized?"

"He hasn't been—yet. What he did was to leave three fingerprints on the window, and he was obviously an old hand at the game, that is as good as a direct identification. The City detective force called us in, but we have not been able to help them except to give them particulars of Letheritt's past life. Incidentally, I supplied them with a copy of your fingerprints. I hope you don't mind."

"Delighted!" Leon said.

After the officer had left, Leon went upstairs to give the news to his two friends.

But the most startling intelligence was to come when they were sitting at breakfast. Meadows arrived. They saw his car draw up at the door, which Poiccart went out to open to him. He strode into the little room, his eyes bulging with excitement.

"Here's a mystery which even you fellows will never be able to solve," he said. "Do you know that this is a day of great tragedy for Scotland Yard and for the identification system? It means the destruction of a method that has been laboriously built up——"

"What are you talking about?" asked Manfred, throwing him a sharp look.

"The fingerprint system," said Meadows, and Poiccart, to whom the fingerprint method was something God-like, gaped at him.

"We've found a duplicate," said Meadows. "The prints on the glass were undoubtedly the prints of Joe Lenthall—and Joe Lenthall is in Wilford County Prison serving the first part of twelve years' penal servitude!"

Something made Manfred turn his head toward his friend. Leon's eyes were blazing, his thin face wreathed in one joyous smile.

"This is the prettiest case that I have ever dealt with," he said softly. "Now, sit down, my dear Meadows, and eat! No, no: sit down. I want to hear about Lenthall—is it possible for me to see him?"

Meadows stared at him.

"What use would that be? I tell you this is the biggest blow we have ever had! And what is more, when we showed the City policeman a photograph of Lenthall, he recognized him as the man he had seen coming down the rainpipe! I thought Lenthall had escaped, and phoned the prison. But he's there all right."

"Can I see Lenthall?"

Meadows hesitated.

"Yes—I think it could be managed. The Home Office is rather friendly with you, isn't it?"

Friendly enough, apparently. By noon Leon Gonsalez was on his way to Wilford Prison, and, to his satisfaction, he went alone.

Wilford Prison is one of the smaller convict establishments, and was brought into use to house long-time convicts of good character and who were acquainted with the book-binding and printing trade. There are several "trade" prisons in England—Maidstone is the "printing" prison, Shepton Mallet the "dyeing" prison—where prisoners may exercise their trades.

The chief warder whom Leon interviewed told him that

Wilford was to be closed soon, and its inmates transferred to Maidstone. He spoke regretfully of this change.

"We've got a good lot of men here—they give us no trouble, and they have an easy time. We've had no cases of indiscipline for years. We only have one officer on night duty—that will give you an idea how quiet we are."

"Who was the officer last night?" asked Leon, and the unexpectedness of the question took the chief warder by surprise.

"Mr. Bennett," he said. "He's sick today, by the way—a bilious attack. Curious thing you should ask the question: I've just been to see him. We had an inquiry about the man you've come to visit. Poor old Bennett is in bed with a terrible headache."

"May I see the governor?" asked Leon.

The chief warder shook his head.

"He has gone to Dover with Miss Folian—his daughter. She's gone off to the Continent."

"Miss Gwenda Folian?" and when the chief warder nodded, Leon continued, "Is she the lady who was training to be a doctor?"

"She *is* a doctor," said the other, emphatically. "Why, when Lenthall nearly died from a heart attack, she saved his life— he works in the governor's house, and I believe he'd cut off his right hand to serve the young lady. There's a lot of good in some of these fellows!"

They were standing in the main prison hall. Leon gazed along the grim vista of steel balconies and little doors.

"This is where the night warder sits, I suppose?" he asked, as he laid his hand on the high desk near where they were standing: "and that door leads——"

"To the governor's quarters."

"And Miss Gwenda often slips through there with a cup of coffee and a sandwich for the night man, I suppose?" he added, carelessly.

The chief warder was evasive.

"It would be against regulations if she did," he said. "Now you want to see Lenthall?"

Leon shook his head.

"I don't think so," he said quietly.

"Where could a blackguard like Letheritt be singing in church on Christmas Day?" asked Leon when he was giving the intimate history of the case to his companions. "In only one place—a prison. Obviously, our Miss Brown was in that prison: the governor and his family invariably attend church. Letheritt was 'not staying with us'—naturally. 'It was at the end of'—his sentence. He had been sent to Wilford for discharge. Poor Meadows! With all his faith in fingerprints gone astray because a released convict was true to his word and went out to get the letters that I missed, while the doped Mr. Bennett slept at his desk and Miss Gwenda Folian took his place!"

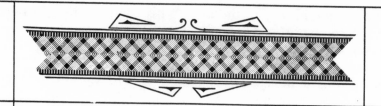

THE DOLLAR CHASERS

BY EARL DERR BIGGERS

Earl Derr Biggers was born in Warren, Ohio, on August 26, 1884, and graduated from Harvard in 1907. He wrote humor and dramatic criticism for the *Boston Traveler* and married Eleanor Ladd in 1912. His mystery novel, *Seven Keys to Baldpate* (1913), was made into a successful stage play by George M. Cohan, who also starred in it. *The House Without a Key* in 1925 was the first of his six novels about Charlie Chan, the affable Chinese-Hawaiian-American detective whose screen investigations are rivaled in number only by those of Sherlock Holmes. Biggers never wrote a short story featuring Charlie Chan. He died in Pasadena in 1933.

IT WAS A LOVELY, CALM evening in San Francisco, and the sun was going down on Simon Porter's wrath. An old habit of the sun's—often it rose to find Simon in an equally turbulent mood, for twenty years of daily newspaper editing had jangled Simon's nerves and wrath sprang eternal in his human breast.

He crossed the city room in his quest of the youngest—and, as it happened, the ablest—of his reporters. The young man he sought was seated before one of the copy-desk telephones, gazing fondly into the transmitter and speaking honeyed words.

"Say, that's mighty kind of you, Sally . . . No, haven't heard about it yet, but I probably will . . . Tomorrow night at six. Pier Ninety-nine. I'll be there. And I may add that in the interval, time will go by on lagging feet. No, I said lagging. It's poetry. See you tomorrow, Sally. Goodby."

He turned to meet the chill eye of his managing editor.

"Ah," Simon Porter said, "so you call her Sally."

"Yes, sir," Bill Hammond answered respectfully. "It saves time."

"Does old Jim Batchelor know how you address his only child?"

"Probably not. He's a busy man."

"He'll be a lot busier when he hears about you. He'll have you boiled in oil. A newspaper reporter at fifty a week!"

"A mere pittance," Bill Hammond agreed.

"All you're worth," added the editor hastily. "I suppose the girl told you. I begin to see now. The whole idea came from her, didn't it?"

"She mentioned a delightful possibility," said the reporter. "However, I take my orders from you."

Simon Porter relapsed into wrath.

"Gives me about enough reporters to get out a good high-school magazine," he cried. "And then sends one of them off on a picnic to please a girl!"

"Yes, sir," put in Bill Hammond brightly.

"I'm speaking of our respected owner. He's just called up—you're to go aboard Jim Batchelor's yacht for a week-end cruise to Monterey. Golf at Del Monte and Pebble Beach;

and if there's anything else you want, ask for it. The launch will be at Pier Ninety-nine tomorrow evening at six. But you know all this."

"It sounds more authentic when you say it, sir."

"Bah! It's an assignment. I don't suppose she told you that."

"No, sir. She didn't mention sordid things."

"There's been an Englishman named Mikklesen afflicting this town for the past week. He's just back from ten years in the Orient and he isn't fond of the Chinese. Neither is Jim Batchelor. Neither is our beloved owner. You're to listen to Mikklesen talk and write up his opinions."

"Sounds easy," commented Bill Hammond.

"It's a cinch. Listening to Mikklesen talk is what those who hang round with him don't do nothing else but. All rot though. With real news breaking every minute—and me short of men!"

He started to move away.

"Er—I presume I don't come in tomorrow," suggested the reporter.

His chief glared at him. "Who says you don't? That line you got off about time going by on lagging feet—you spoke too soon. It won't lag. I'll attend to that—personally. You report tomorrow as usual."

"Yes, sir," answered Bill Hammond meekly. A hard man, he reflected.

"And listen to me." The managing editor retraced his steps. "About this Sally Batchelor—I suppose she's easy to look at?"

"No trouble at all."

"Well, you keep your mind on your work." His expression softened. "Not a chance in the world, my lad. Old Jim Batchelor couldn't see you with the telescope over at Lick Observatory. It's money, money, money with him."

"So I've heard."

"He's still got the first dollar he ever earned. He'll show it to you. Where is the first dollar you earned?"

"Somebody," said Bill Hammond, "got it away from me."

"Precisely. That's where you and old Jim are different. I'm telling you. I don't want to see a good reporter go wrong."

"A good reporter, sir?"

"That's what I said."

Bill Hammond smiled. It brightened the corner where he was.

"Tomorrow," he ventured, "is Friday—the day before the paycheck."

"I'll give you an order on the cashier," said Simon. He wrote on a slip of paper and handed it over.

"Twenty-five dollars!" Bill Hammond read. "And I was thinking of a yachting suit!"

Simon Porter smiled grimly. "You take your other shirt and go aboard. You role is not to dazzle. I've just got through telling you."

And he strode away to the cubbyhole where he did his editing.

His departure left Bill Hammond alone in the city room for this was an evening paper and the last edition was on the street. Jim Batchelor's prospective guest remained seated at the copy desk. He was, to judge from his expression, doing a bit of thinking. Some of his thoughts appeared to be pleasant ones, while others were not. The grave mingled with the gay, and this had been true of his reveries ever since that exciting day when he first met Sally Batchelor.

Sent by his paper to cover a charity fete for the benefit of some orphanage, he had caught his first glimpse of Sally's trim figure. Instantly something had happened to his heart. It had been, up to that moment, a heart that had lain singularly dormant in the presence of the opposite sex. But now it leaped up, threw off its lethargy, and prepared to go into action. It urged him to fight his way at once to this young woman's side.

Arrived in that pleasant neighborhood, he realized that his initial impression, startling and vivid as it had been, had not done the girl justice. She smiled upon him, and his heart seemed to say that this was the smile it had been waiting for. She was selling flowers, her prices were exorbitant; but the soft, lovely voice in which she named them made them sound absurdly reasonable. The somewhat unsteady Bill Hammond became her steady customer. Gladly he handed her all the money he had; and in other ways, too, it would have been evident to an onlooker that he was ready and willing to take her as his life's companion. If not, why not?

The answer was not slow in coming. Some busybody insisted on introducing them, and at the mention of her name Bill Hammond knew that this girl was, alas, not one of the orphans. True, she had at the moment only one parent—but what a parent! Jim Batchelor, president of the Batchelor Construction Company, was the sort of man who never let an obstacle stand in his way; but as an obstacle he himself had stood firmly in the way of a good many other people. And he would certainly make the stand of his life in the path of any practically penniless young man who had the audacity to court his daughter.

This bitter thought clouded the remaining moments Bill Hammond spent in the girl's company, and presently he left the charity fete, resolved never to speak to her again. But as time went on it began to appear that the afternoon had been more eventful for him than for anyone else, the orphans included. He had fallen in love.

Love comes to many as a blessed annoyance, and so it came to Bill Hammond. Up to that moment he had been happy and carefree; which is to say, he had been young in San Francisco. Now he had a great deal on his mind. Should he give up all thought of the girl and go his way a broken man? Or should he get busy and acquire such wealth that his own paper would speak of the subsequent marriage as the union of two great fortunes? Generally, he favored the latter course, though the means to wealth did not appear to be at hand, as anyone who has worked on a newspaper will appreciate.

Meanwhile he was accepting dinner and dance invitations of the sort he had previously eluded. If his plan was to avoid Sally Batchelor, it did not work. She was frequently among those present, and, seemingly unaware of the vast difference in their stations, she continued to smile upon him. A sort of friendship—nothing more, of course—grew up between them. She accepted his escort occasionally, had tea with him at the St. Francis. And now she had arranged for him to go on this yachting trip and meet her famous father. He was to beard the mighty lion in his palatial floating den.

He was, there in the dusk of the city room, a bit appalled at the idea. Ridiculous, of course. Why should he fear Jim Batchelor? As far as family went, he had all the better of it. His ancestors had been professional men and scholars, while Jim Batchelor's were neatly placing one brick in close juxtaposition to another. But money—ah, money. Those few bonds his father had left him, the paltry additional bunch that would be his when Aunt Ella died—chicken feed in the eyes of Batchelor, no doubt. In this cold world only cash counted.

Cynical thoughts, these; he put them aside. The spirit of adventure began to stir in his broad chest. Sally had been kind enough to arrange this party; she would find he was no quitter. He would go and meet this demon father face to face. He would discover what it was all about—the awe with which men spoke of the money king. Probably a human being, like anybody else. Yes, as Simon had suggested, he would take his other shirt.

Suddenly his thoughts took a new and more practical turn. He pictured himself arrayed for dinner on the Batchelor yacht. In what? There was, he recalled, not a single clean dress shirt in his room, and his laundry would not be returned until Saturday. As for buying new linen, the dent in that twenty-five dollars would be serious. What to do?

He pondered. Beyond, in the cubbyhole known—secretly— among the reporters as the kennel, he saw Simon Porter frowning savagely over a rival paper's last edition. Should he ask more money from Simon? The profile was not encouraging. Then into his mind flashed the picture of a Chinese laundry on Kearny Street he had passed many times. It was, according to the sign, the establishment of Honolulu Sam, and a crudely lettered placard in the window bore this promise:

LAUNDRY LEFT BEFORE 8:00 A.M.
BACK SAME DAY

What could be fairer than that? Honolulu Sam solved the problem.

Bill Hammond rose, called a goodnight to the man in the cubbyhole, and was on his way. It was his plan to go somewhere for a brief and lonely dinner, then hurry to his apartment, gather up his laundry, and place it in the hands of the speedy Honolulu Sam. After which he would return home and get a good night's sleep.

But such resolutions are rarely kept in San Francisco. Men hurry to their work in the morning, promising themselves that it will be early to bed that night for them. And then, late in the afternoon, the fog comes rolling in, and vim and vigor take the place of that cold-gray-dawn sensation. As a consequence, another pleasant evening is had by all.

Bill Hammond met some friends at dinner, and when he finally returned to his apartment it was too late to disturb the Chinese from Hawaii. He made a neat bundle of his proposed laundry, set his alarm clock for six, and turned in.

"Get lots of sleep on the yacht," he promised himself.

At 7:30 the next morning, he stood at the counter of Honolulu Sam.

"Back five-thirty this afternoon," Bill ordered loudly.

"Back same day. Maybe seven maybe eight."

"Five-thirty," repeated Bill Hammond firmly.

Sam stared at him with a glassy eye and slowly shook his head.

"Dollar extra for you if you do it," added Bill, and laid the currency on the counter.

Sam appropriated it. "Can do," he admitted.

"All right," said Bill. "I'll depend on you." He had meant the dollar only as an evidence of good faith, to be paid later. But no matter. A Chinese laundryman always kept his word.

He went out into what was practically the dawn, feeling confident of the future. With five clean shirts and other apparel in proportion, let them bring on their yacht. Easy, nonchalant, debonair, he would make himself the pride of the deep—and of Sally. Ah, Sally! At the corner of Post and Kearny the flower vendors were setting out their wares. Bill took a deep breath. Life was a garden of blossoms.

When he reached the office, Simon Porter robbed the garden of its fragrance by sending him on a difficult assignment. All day he was kept hustling, with no time for lunch. It was exactly 5:30 when he grabbed his suitcase and set out for the bounding wave. Simon met him at the door and bowed low.

"Bon voyage, little brother of the rich," he said. "By the way, I've just heard you're to have a very distinguished fellow passenger."

"Of course. The Prince of Wales."

"Nobody so jolly—Henry T. Frost."

"What? Old Henry Frost?"

"Our beloved owner, our dear employer, the good master who has it in his power to sell us all down the river—and would do it without batting an eye. Here's your chance. Make the most of it, win his love and respect, and when I die of overwork, as I certainly shall inside a week, maybe he'll give you my job."

"I can't say I'm yearning to meet him," admitted Bill Hammond.

"You're talking sense. I've met him at least three hundred times, and I've always had cause to regret it. You know, something tells me you'd better stay home. You could develop whooping cough, and I could send one of the other boys."

"Nonsense!"

"Today is Friday."

"What of it?"

"Friday the thirteenth. Does that mean nothing to you?"

"Not a thing, sir. See you later."

"Well, fools rush in—" began Simon, but Bill Hammond had disappeared.

Young Mr. Hammond felt not at all foolish as he hurried down Market Street, bound first for the establishment of Honolulu Sam, and later for Pier 99. The going was slow, for the street was crowded with commuters on their way to the ferries. This little cruise, he thought, might very well prove the turning point in his life. The next few days were as bright with glittering possibilities as a decked-out Christmas tree.

He turned down Kearny Street, that thoroughfare of adventures, and at Post an adventure befell him. The traffic was held up, and he was hurrying to cross in front of a very wealthy-looking automobile, when a familiar voice called, "Whoo-hoo, Bill!"

He looked, and from the window of the car he beheld protruding the head of Sally Batchelor. It was a lovely sight, but one he would gladly have dispensed with at the moment. However, he had gazed straight into her bright eyes, and to pretend not to see her was now out the question. He circled a plebeian taxi and reached her side. She was holding open the door of the car.

"This is luck," she cried gaily. "We're on our way to the pier. Jump in."

Jump in! Without his laundry! A cold shiver ran down his spine. Luck, she called this meeting, but he was not so sure. He noted that there were three other people in the car —an elderly woman and two men. One of the latter was undoubtedly Jim Batchelor, and—yes, the other was Henry Frost. Multimillions sitting there!

"I—I'm sorry," Bill stammered. "I've got a very important errand first. I'll see you later."

"What sort of errand?" inquired Sally.

"It's—it's just around the corner—"

"Get in. We'll take you there."

He shuddered at the thought of this fifteen-thousand-dollar car, with two Japanese servants in front, pulling up before the headquarters of Honolulu Sam, laundry left before 8:00 A.M. back same day.

"Oh, no, no, really—you go along, Sally. I'll follow in a taxi."

The traffic cop had signaled for an advance and a presumptuous flivver was honking indignantly just behind Jim Batchelor's magnificence.

"Go along, Sally," urged Bill Hammond nervously. A passing car flipped his coattail.

"We'll draw up at the curb in the next block and wait for you," she answered, smiling sweetly. Obedience wasn't in her, evidently. "Here, give me your suitcase. I'll keep it for you."

"Ah—er—no—no." He hugged it tight. "I'll keep it. I need it."

Another picture anguished him—the vision of himself rushing back to Jim Batchelor's presence with a large package all too obviously laundry. The clamor in the rear increased; the traffic cop was approaching.

"What's the idea here?" he wanted to know.

"Go along, Sally," Bill pleaded.

Now that he had the law on his side, she obeyed. Sinking back into the car, she closed the door in the policeman's face.

"Don't be long, will you?" she smiled.

The car began to move, and Bill dodged between it and the flivver, holding the precious suitcase close. Leaping for his life, he made the opposite curb, while angry chauffeurs inquired as to his sanity. He hurried on, groaning. Of all the inopportune meetings—

A bell clanged loudly behind him as he entered the steamy precincts of Honolulu Sam. He tossed a red check on the counter, and plumping his suitcase down beside it began to unfasten the clasps.

"Come on," he called. "A little speed here. Give me that wash."

The figure that emerged from the rear was not that of Honolulu Sam, but of a bent and aged Chinese wearing a pair of badly steamed spectacles. Sam, having business over on Grant Avenue, had left the place in charge of his uncle, down from Sacramento on a visit.

"Hurry, man, hurry!" cried Bill Hammond, waiting impatiently above his open suitcase.

But speed was not one of uncle's inborn traits. He deliberately wiped his spectacles on the tail of a handy shirt, took up the red check, and stood helplessly in front of the finished work.

"Please, please!" cried Bill. "It's done—I know it's done. I paid a dollar extra to make sure. Where's Sam? Say, listen, we're keeping all the money in San Francisco waiting. Let me help—oh, I can't read that stuff. But please get a move on."

The old man made a gesture as of one requesting peace. He turned reproving spectacles on the customer. They were steaming up again. Once more he studied the rack, while Bill Hammond chattered wildly at his elbow. Finally the Chinese reached up and captured a fat package. Bill snatched it from, him, tossed it into his suitcase, and began to close it. The Chinese was holding the two pieces of the check close to his eyes.

"One dolla," he announced.

"And very cheap too," said Bill.

He paid with a five-dollar bill, receiving in change four of those heavy silver dollars still in circulation on the coast. As he dashed out the door the bell rang again like an alarm. The old Chinese was once more applying the tail of the shirt to his spectacles.

Making admirable speed, Bill Hammond returned to Post Street and located the splendid equipage that awaited him. One of the Japanese stood ready to take his bag and open the door. A bit breathless, he climbed in and established himself on one of the little collapsible chairs, the other of which was occupied by Sally. He sat sidewise and Sally sat sidewise, and the introductions began.

"Aunt Dora, this is Mr. Hammond." Bill bowed. The large commanding woman on the rear seat, who was mainly responsible for the congestion there, bowed also—sternly. "And do you know Mr. Frost?" Sally continued. "You ought to—you work for him."

Bill looked into the cold, fishy eyes of his employer. Henry Frost had the appearance of a deacon, though such was not by any means his reputation.

"How do you do, sir?" said Bill uncomfortably. "Mr. Frost can't possibly know all those who labor in his cause," he added.

215

"And Father. Father, this is Mr. Hammond."

Father held out a thin small hand. He was, indeed, a thin small man, quite unlike the accepted figure of the great financier. His face was ascetic, his eyes dreamy; there seemed, at first glance, nothing about his personality that would strike terror to an opponent. The aunt, towering like Mont Blanc at his side, was far more impressive.

"I'm glad to meet you, Mr. Hammond," said the multimillionaire. "Sally has spoken of you."

"It's mighty kind of you, sir, to take me along like this, and I'd—"

"An office assignment, I understand," put in Henry Frost in a high, unlovely voice.

"Oh, that's merely incidental," said Batchelor. "You'll find Mikklesen very interesting, Mr. Hammond. Ought to get a good story. But you're not to let work interfere with your outing, even if Henry—Mr. Frost—does happen to be with us." He smiled.

"I'll try not to, sir," Bill answered, smiling too. He felt much better. A human being, after all.

"I'm afraid my party's going to be mostly a stag affair," Jim Batchelor said, as the car swung into the broad expanse of Market Street.

"Well, we're used to that," said Sally. "Aren't we, Aunt Dora?"

"We ought to be by this time," sniffed that lady.

"There'll be Mrs. Keith, however," Batchelor went on.

"Mrs. Keith!" Henry Frost raised his bushy eyebrows.

"A very charming woman, Henry," said Jim Batchelor. "Lived in India a great deal, I believe. I want to have a talk with her about conditions over there. You see, this isn't only a pleasure cruise for me. There are two rather important questions I have to decide before I get back. There's that contract to build a bridge in India. I guess I mentioned it to you. I haven't made up my mind whether to make a bid for the job or not. Talking with Mrs. Keith and Mikklesen may decide me."

"I understand that Blake has already put in his figures," said Frost. "He'll probably underbid you."

"Very likely. But everybody knows Blake is a crook. I imagine I can get the contract away from him if I go after it. They tell me he's waiting anxiously to know what move I'll make. I'll spoil his game if I go in." Batchelor smiled, and

216

it was no dreamer smiling then. "However, I've got several days. The bids don't close until next Thursday."

"And the other question, Jim?" asked Frost.

"Oh, the senatorship. I'm still thinking of entering the primaries."

"Nonsense!" growled his friend. "Why get mixed up in that sort of thing?"

"Just what I tell him," said Aunt Dora. "Still, Washington would be interesting."

"Well, I don't know," mused Batchelor. "Every man has ambitions that way, I guess. At any rate, I'm taking O'Meara, the lawyer, along on this cruise to talk over the situation. When it comes to politics he's one of the wisest."

"O'Meara!" Mr. Frost spoke sourly.

"It's a very mixed crowd, I'm sure," said Aunt Dora, and Bill Hammond felt that the glance she cast at him was a bit personal.

"A lot more interesting than a bunch of society folderols," Batchelor told her. "And when it comes to elegance, that end's taken care of too. I've invited Julian Hill."

"Good news for Sally, I'm sure," remarked Aunt Dora, and again the look she gave Bill Hammond had a meaning all its own.

Bill knew that they were speaking of the third vice-president of the Batchelor concern, a young man of good family and social position whose engagement to Sally Batchelor had more than once been rumored. He glanced at the girl, but she was staring straight ahead, and her charming profile told him nothing.

The car was gliding along the Embarcadero now, that romantic threshold to the Orient. Ships that were destined for far ports waited motionless but ready, and on the piers was abundant evidence of the great business done upon the waters. Suddenly Frost spoke.

"It's a wonder to me you could get anyone to go with you today," he said.

"Why, what do you mean?" asked Batchelor.

"Friday the thirteenth," explained the newspaper owner.

"The thirteenth! Say, I didn't realize that!" Batchelor's tone was serious, and glancing back, Bill Hammond was amazed at the gravity of his face.

"I didn't think you did," smiled Frost, "knowing your weakness as I do."

"What do you mean—weakness? I'm not superstitious." And Jim Batchelor smiled, as though he had just remembered something pleasant. "Besides, no bad luck can happen to us —not while I've got my luck piece in my pocket."

His luck piece? Bill Hammond looked at Sally.

"For goodness' sake," she laughed, "don't ask him to show it to you! That calamity will befall you soon enough, and at a time when I'm elsewhere, I trust."

The car came to a halt before Pier 99, the property of a steamship company in which Jim Batchelor was a heavy stockholder. At the end of the pier, close to where a smart launch was waiting, they found the remaining four guests who had been invited on Jim Batchelor's week-end cruise.

An oddly assorted quartet, Bill Hammond thought, as Sally hastily introduced him. Mike O'Meara he already knew, having more than once sought to pry an interview out of him. A huge, bluff, ruddy man, the lawyer was decidedly out of his element and seemed to know it, but he had a gift of gab to see him through. Julian Hill proved a suave, polished man in his thirties, garbed in just the right apparel; he had no interest whatever in meeting Bill Hammond and didn't pretend any. Mrs. Keith was at that age where a woman knows that youth is going despite her gallant struggle. She had been, Bill sensed, a clinging vine in her day; but now she was a bit too plump and no doubt found the sturdy oaks elusive.

As for Mikklesen, he delighted the eye; he made the senses reel; he was magnificent. Tall, languid, with blue eyes and yellow hair, his slim figure clothed in tweeds, the English-man added an artistic touch to any scene he chose to adorn. Save when he looked at Sally Batchelor, boredom afflicted him, and the indifference he showed in meeting Mr.—er— Hammond made the attitude of Julian Hill seem a bit too eager by comparison.

When the Japanese had got all the luggage aboard the launch, the guests followed. Bill Hammond had intended to sit beside Sally, but Mikklesen and Hill beat him to it, and he reflected that competition was going to be keen in the near future. He sank down beside Mrs. Keith. The launch sputtered and was on its way to where the seagoing yacht *Francesca* waited haughty and aloof, lording it over the more plebeian craft about her.

"Isn't this thrilling!" gushed Mrs. Keith. "You know I haven't been on a yacht for ages."

"Same here," said Bill. "Grand to be rich, don't you think?"

"It must be," sighed the woman. "I never could manage it. You must tell me all about it."

"Me?" Bill Hammond laughed, "You've got the wrong number—excuse it, please. I happen to be one of the humble poor—only a newspaper reporter."

"Oh, indeed!" Her smile faded. "How exciting—a reporter! You have the most wonderful experiences of course. You must tell me all about it."

"Well," said Bill Hammond cautiously, "if I'm not too busy with my work I'll be delighted."

"Work—on the yacht?"

"I'm supposed to interview Mr. Mikklesen on conditions in the Orient."

She laughed. "Oh, really? Mr. Mikklesen is an old—acquaintance of mine. I knew him in India. I'm sure he'll tell you the most interesting things—only you mustn't believe all you hear. He's a dear boy, but—imaginative. Oh, so very imaginative."

She glanced across to where Mikklesen was bending close to Sally Batchelor. The look in her eyes was not friendly.

On the deck of the *Francesca* her captain waited to greet his owner. Japanese in white coats appeared to receive the baggage.

"Dinner's at seven-thirty," Jim Batchelor announced. "After the boys have shown you to your quarters I suggest that you gentlemen join me in the smoking room."

" 'Stag party' is right," smiled his daughter.

"Oh, well, the ladies too, of course," amended the owner of the *Francesca*. "I thought they'd be too busy—"

As a matter of fact, he had forgotten about the ladies. It was his habit; he was a man's man.

One of the Japanese, burdened with luggage, politely requested Bill Hammond to follow, and led the way to the deck below. Mikklesen also was in the procession, and Bill wondered if they were to share the stateroom. It was not a happy prospect, for he knew the Englishman would coolly take seven-eighths of any room assigned them. They entered a passageway off which the cabins opened, and at the third door the Japanese dropped Bill's modest suitcase and, staggering under the load of the Englishman's traps, led Mikklesen inside.

"This is your cabin," Bill heard him say.

219

"Thank heaven," Bill thought. The Japanese emerged, took up the solitary bag, and led the way to the next door.

"So this is mine, eh?" Bill said. "Fine! Got it all to myself, I suppose."

"Yes-s," hissed the Japanese. "*Francesca* sleep fifteen guests."

"Good for the *Francesca.*"

"Bath here," the servant said. He nodded toward an open door, beyond which gleamed spotless plumbing. Even as Bill looked, Mikklesen appeared in the doorway, gave him a haughty glare, then shut the door and locked it.

"Bath for two cabins," the Japanese said. "Yours too." He seemed distressed.

"Well, you'd better explain that to him," suggested Bill. "Otherwise I'll never see the inside of that room again."

The servant disappeared. There was the sound of voices in the next cabin. Then the lock clicked in the bathroom door and the Japanese was again in Bill's room.

"All right now," he smiled.

"Maybe," said Bill. "What's your name?"

"Tatu."

"Well, Tatu—"

He handed him a five-dollar bill. The smile broadened.

"He leave door locked, you go through his room, unlock," said Tatu.

"You got his number, Tatu. Don't worry about me, I'll bathe all right."

The servant disappeared, and Bill stood for a moment staring through the porthole at San Francisco's interesting skyline. This was the life, he reflected, sailing gaily off into the unknown, His heart sank. Had he remembered to bring his shirt studs? Feverishly he opened his suitcase—thank heaven, there they were.

He went out in search of the smoking room. On the upper deck he encountered Jim Batchelor.

"Ah, my boy, come along," said the multimillionaire. "Maybe we can scare up a cocktail."

They found Henry Frost already in the smoking room.

"When do we get to Monterey?" he wanted to know.

"Early tomorrow," said Batchelor. "There'll be plenty of time for me to trim you a round of golf before lunch."

"You hate yourself, don't you?" answered Frost. "Ten dollars a hole is my answer to that."

"Piker!" chided Batchelor. "Play golf, Hammond?"

"In a fashion," Bill said. "Not so expensively as that, however."

"Oh, it wouldn't cost you anything to take him on," Batchelor replied. "He always pays. Henry's golf's a joke to everybody but Henry himself."

O'Meara came in. "Some boat you got here, Mr. Batchelor," he said.

"Yes, it's quite a neat little craft."

"Little! It's the *Leviathan* of the west coast."

"Say, look here, O'Meara," Frost put in, "Jim here's got a crazy idea he's going to enter the senatorial primaries. Now you know the game—I'm relying on you to tell him he hasn't got a chance."

"I can't do that and speak true," O'Meara replied. "He's got as good a chance as any of them. You put up your name, Mr. Batchelor," he added, "and leave the rest to us."

"Well, I haven't decided," Batchelor answered. "We'll talk it over later. Ah, Mr. Mikklesen, come in. Are you comfortably settled?"

"Oh, quite," said the Englishman. "It was most frightfully good of you to invite me."

"Well, my reasons weren't wholly unselfish," Batchelor admitted. "I've sort of lost track of things in India lately—thought you could set me straight."

"Any information I have, my dear sir, is yours. I believe you're thinking of that bridge contract."

"I am—seriously."

Mikklesen nodded. "Of course, it's a bit risky," he said. "The government isn't any too stable, to put it mildly. There are other difficulties—I'll speak of them later. Yes, decidedly risky."

"You bet it is," remarked Julian Hill, who had just come in.

"But I like risks," smiled Batchelor.

"I know, Governor, but this is the limit." Mr. Hill seemed very much in earnest. "I'm strongly opposed."

"You were opposed to that lighthouse job in South America too," Batchelor reminded him.

"I happened to be wrong that time. But something tells me I'm not wrong now. Let's keep out. Don't you say so, Mr. Mikklesen?"

"I will say this"—the Englishman studied the end of his cigarette—"if you do go in, it will be a matter of what you

221

call the breaks. They may be for you; they may be against you. You'll need all the luck in the world."

"Ah, luck," smiled Batchelor. "That's where the Batchelor Construction Company shines. For more than thirty-five years the breaks have been our way. And I've still got my luck piece." He took from his waistcoat a silver dollar.

Frost and Hill smiled at each other and turned away, but the other men regarded the coin with interest.

"Gentlemen," said Jim Batchelor softly, "there it is. The first dollar I ever earned. I was a kid of eleven at the time. My father was a mason and he was working on an apartment building they were putting up on Russian Hill. He heard they wanted a water boy and he got me the job. I had to fetch the water from a well that was a block away—a block down the hill. I carried an empty pail the easy route, but coming back it was filled, and I puffed and sweat and staggered up the grade. It was my first lesson in how hard money comes.

"On the first Saturday night I got my pay—this dollar—and I walked home with my father past shop windows that were one long temptation. 'What you going to spend it for, Jim?' my father asked. 'I'm not going to spend it,' I told him. 'I'm going to keep it—always.' And I have. For thirty-seven years it's been my luck piece and it's made good on the job. I've felt it in my pocket at the big moments of my life, and it's given me confidence and courage. A little silver dollar coined in 1884."

He appeared to be holding it out to Mikklesen, and the Englishman reached out his hand to take it. But Jim Batchelor restored it to his pocket.

"And it's still working for me, gentlemen," he added.

"Poppycock," said Henry Frost.

"Maybe," smiled Batchelor. "But I hear there is a standing offer of one thousand dollars in the office of Blake and Company for that little luck piece. Poppycock, eh?"

"Oh, well, Blake knows what a fool you are," said Frost. "They realize the psychological effect on your mind if you lost that thing, so they're willing to pay for it."

"They'll never get the chance," answered Batchelor, and his eyes flashed. "I think I will go into that India thing. In fact, I know I will. Gentlemen, here are the cocktails."

They stood around a table, each with a glass in his hand. As Bill Hammond looked about him, he saw that the eyes of each man present were on the pocket that held the little silver dollar. Mikklesen lifted his glass.

"Here's to your good luck, sir," he said. "May it continue."

"Thank you," answered Jim Batchelor, and they drank.

At seven o'clock Bill Hammond set out for his stateroom to dress for dinner. At the top of the main companionway he met Sally—Sally in a breathtaking gown and looking her loveliest.

"Hurry up," she said. "I'm eager for someone to help me enjoy the sunset."

"Keep the place open," he begged. "I'm really the best man for the job. Sally, I know who it is I have to thank for this little outing. You're always doing something for the orphans, aren't you?"

"Were you glad to come?"

"Glad? What weak words you use!"

"I thought you would be. The yacht's a lot of fun, really."

"It's not the yacht I'm thinking of. If you'd invited me out in a rowboat my joy would have been the same. You know—"

Henry Frost and Hill came up behind them.

"Dear me," said Sally, "what a long cocktail hour! I'm afraid Dad's been telling you the story of the dollar."

"He did mention it," said Hill.

"And I'm glad he did," Bill Hammond said. "It made him seem mighty human to me. The picture of him struggling up Russian Hill with that water pail—"

"Dear Dad!" Sally smiled "There is something rather appealing about the story. The first time you hear it, I mean. But when you've had it pop up constantly for twenty years, as I have, you're bound to get a little fed up on it. I've been very wicked. There've been times when I wished to heaven he'd lose that dollar."

"Here too," said Julian Hill. "Particularly when it leads Mr. Batchelor into some wild adventure like this India bridge contract."

"Lose it!" cried Henry Frost. His little eyes glittered. "Why, it would ruin him!"

"Yes, I rather think it would," said Hill; and it wasn't so much what he said, Bill Hammond reflected as he hurried off to his cabin. It was the way he said it.

Mikklesen had left the smoking room sometime before, and as Bill Hammond passed the door of the Englishman's cabin, he was glad to hear a voice lifted in song inside. But when he reached his own room and tried to enter the bath, he found himself locked out. As he savagely rattled the knob he was happy to recall that George Washington won his war. Confound this Mikklesen—had he no consideration for anybody?

The answer was that he hadn't; one look at him told that.

As Bill turned angrily back into his room, Tatu entered from the passageway.

"Very late, very busy," said Tatu. "Now I lay you out." And lifted a dinner coat from Bill's suitcase.

"Never mind, I'll attend to that," Bill told him. "You go in and lay that Englishman out. Lay him out cold, and then unlock the bath for me."

Tatu hastened away, and again there was the sound of voices in the next cabin. The lock in the door leading to the bath clicked and Tatu emerged. Bill dashed by him and turned the key in Mikklesen's door.

"You run along, Tatu," he said. "I'm in too much of a hurry to learn how to be valeted tonight. Sometime when we're both free you can give me a lesson."

"You want me, ring bell," suggested Tatu, going.

Bill was hastily peeling off his clothes. If he was to have a few moments alone with Sally and the sunset, speed was the watchword. But he had been known to rise in the morning, bathe, shave, dress, and reach the office in less than twenty minutes, and he was out now to smash the record.

As he was putting the finishing touches on an elaborate shave, Mikklesen began to rattle the door knob. He rattled long and earnestly, and it was music to the reporter's ears.

"Oh, I say, old chap, you're not annoyed, are you?" Bill murmured. "Not really? How beastly!"

"Damn!" said a voice, and the clatter ceased.

Bill hurried from the bathroom, leaving the lock *in statu quo*. By way of preparation he laid out his diamond shirt studs—rich-looking, if old-fashioned—the property of poor Uncle George, handed to Bill by Aunt Ella the day after the funeral.

Humming happily to himself, he lifted the fat package of laundry into the open. Good Honolulu Sam, he had certainly come across as promised. That back-same-day promise was on the level. Must have hurried some. Great people, the Chinese; you could bank on them. If they said they'd do a thing, they did it. He snapped the string with his fingers and

224

gently laid back the wrapping paper. A bright pink shirt stared up at him.

It is astonishing sometimes, in the crises of our lives, how slow we can be in comprehending. Bill's first reaction was to wonder how this sartorial atrocity had got in with his things. He tossed it aside and was confronted by the purplest shirt he had ever met. Next in line of march came a green shirt that would have made excellent adornment on St. Patrick's Day. Then some rather shabby underwear and eloquent socks. A few collars. But no more shirts!

Bill Hammond sat down weakly.

"Good lord," he cried. "It's not my laundry!"

And if comprehension had been slow in coming, it came now with a rush. Alone, all alone on a restless ocean, and without a dress shirt to his name. At least two rivals for Sally's favor present, and each an elegant dresser.

And this was the cruise on which he had hoped to make a dashing impression, to win Sally's family, to say nothing of the girl herself, by his charm. How did one do that without a dress shirt?

Anger overcame him. Nor did he have any trouble locating the object of his wrath. That half blind old Chinese with the steaming spectacles—there was the guilty party.

The old idiot! In one careless moment he had destroyed the priceless reputation of his race for accuracy, built up laboriously through many years of giving back the right shirt to the right customer—destroyed it utterly, doomed his race to extinction. For Bill Hammond would attend to that personally, and he would begin in the establishment of Honolulu Sam.

But time was passing; he mustn't waste any more of it planning the massacre of an aged Chinese. The problem was here and now. What to do? The weather was calm enough, but the *Francesca* was tossing about a bit. He might retire to his berth and plead sickness. And leave Sally to the company of Mikklesen and Julian Hill? Not likely! No, he must have a shirt—robbery—a killing or two, maybe—but he must have a shirt.

Was there anyone aboard who would help him? O'Meara, perhaps; but no, O'Meara's shirt would go round him at least twice. As for the other men, there was not one to whom he would consider revealing his plight. Sally—if he could bring himself to tell her—would be sympathetic, but Sally had no dress shirts to distribute. That left—hold on—that left Tatu. Thank heaven he had given Tatu five dollars.

He rang the bell and almost immediately Tatu appeared. Frankness, it seemed to Bill, was the only course.

"Terrible thing's happened, Tatu," he said. "See"—he indicated the frightful pink shirt—"Chinese laundry returned the wrong wash. I haven't any dress shirt."

"Chinese not reliable people," commented Tatu.

"You said it. Sometime you and I'll have a long talk about that. But now, Tatu, now—dinner coming on. What to do?" An idea flashed into his mind. "You haven't an extra shirt, have you?" he inquired hopefully.

Tatu opened his coat and revealed a fine white bosom—but no shirt went with it.

"Have extra bosom," he said. "Maybe you like—"

"No, no, I couldn't take a chance. Must have an entire shirt. There's five more dollars waiting for you if you can dig one up."

Tatu considered. "Maybe," he said. "I find out."

He went on his momentous errand. Bill, left alone, put on his shoes. Slowly but surely the structure was approaching completion. But the shirt! Would that necessary, that vital bit of facade come to hand? Or must he sit shirtless in his cabin while the gay diners made merry round the festive board?

Something in Tatu's eye made Bill feel that this was a moment for caution. He turned off his light and opened the door leading into the dim passageway. No one in sight. Where was Tatu anyhow? The door of the cabin at the end of the corridor began to open slowly, and a man emerged. He looked warily about him, and then, walking on tiptoe, started down the passageway. Tatu? No, it wasn't Tatu. Bill Hammond, peering from the darkness as the man passed his stateroom, saw clearly who it was. He watched him open the door of a stateroom farther down and disappear.

Nervously Bill sat down on his berth. Would Tatu never come? Why, he'd had time enough to scare up a whole outfit —then Tatu appeared in the doorway. Bill leaped up, closed the door behind him, and snapped on the light.

Rapture! There was a gleaming dress shirt in Tatu's hand. Bill pounced on it avidly.

Tatu hung on to it. "Maybe too big," he said. "I put in studs."

He took up one of Uncle George's diamonds and began to struggle with the shirt. "Very stiff bosom," he announced. "Oh, very stiff."

"What size is it?" demanded Bill, feverishly investigating the collars bequeathed him by the owner of the pink shirt. He had a vision of sending out again for a collar.

"Doesn't tell size," whispered Tatu. "No name of maker, also. That very good."

Bill experienced a momentary qualm.

"Where'd you get this shirt, Tatu?" he demanded sternly.

"I get him," replied Tatu. "Here, try on."

"A little large," said Bill. "But it's a shirt. And say, look—this collar fits. Luck, Tatu, luck. Wow, the bosom is stiff! Got to be proud and unbending tonight." He was silent, working on his tie.

"Everything fine," Tatu hinted.

"Oh, yes, the five dollars. Here you are. Say, listen, Tatu, I'm not sure that we ought to have—er—borrowed this. We'll have to return it."

"I return it," Tatu agreed.

"That's right; of course we'll give it back, along with a dollar to cover depreciation and washing. Honesty, Tatu—the best policy."

"Yes-s, thank you."

"Always be honest and you'll fear no man." The Japanese was at the door. "Say, Tatu, I really ought to know where you got it."

"I got him," smiled Tatu, and went out.

Well, a desperate situation required a desperate remedy. Bill got into his trousers and was slipping on his coat when the first notes of *The Roast Beef of Old England,* played falteringly on a bugle by a pantry boy with ambitions, floated down to him. Mikklesen was once more rattling at the bathroom door, and after extinguishing all the lights, Bill noiselessly unlocked it, then hurried upstairs to find Sally. Her eyes reproached him.

"The sun went down," she said, waving a hand toward where it had been, "and you never came up."

"I know," he answered; "forgive me." He straightened his collar nervously. "I was detained."

"That's not much of an explanation," she told him.

"Thank you," he said absently. He was thinking that the owner of the pink shirt certainly needed some new collars.

This one had a razor edge and seemed to have been recently honed.

"You're perfectly welcome," smiled Sally, "whatever it is you're thanking me for. Pardon me for mentioning it, but are you in your right mind?"

"Of course not," he said. "I knew you were lovely, but somehow tonight—well, as the fellow said, my senses reel."

Sally rose. "We'd better have the next reel in the dining room," she suggested. "Dad hates people to be late."

Bill found he was to sit on Sally's right, and the discovery cheered him, particularly as Henry Frost was on the other side of her—an arrangement that couldn't be improved upon. His spirits rose rapidly. Minutes before plunged in despair, he had emerged triumphant and was all right with the world. What a lot of difference somebody's else's shirt could make!

During the first course Jim Batchelor suggested that Mikklesen tell something of his experiences in the Orient, and from that point the dinner was a monologue. But like most Englishmen of his class, Mikklesen was a charming talker and well worth listening to. He spoke of his adventures as subeditor of an English newspaper in Shanghai, of the time he had typhoid in the General Hospital in Yokohama, of the fight he got into one gory night at the old Danish hotel where the beachcombers hold forth in that lovely port. He took his hearers into the interior of China on a scientific expedition, thrilled them with a holdup by bandits, and brought them back in time for an audience with an ambassador in Peking. Life as he had known it had been glamorous.

It was not until the coffee that he appeared to run down and the conversation became general. Suddenly there was one of those inexplicable lulls in the gentle buzz of talk, and the voice of Jim Batchelor rang out in conversation with Mrs. Keith at his right.

"And I have kept it—all these years. In the big moments of my life I've felt it in my pocket and it has given me courage to go on. A little silver dollar coined in the year—"

"Oh, dear," Sally laughed, "he's telling her about his luck piece."

"Thrilling!" Mrs. Keith said. She smiled encouragingly on the multimillionaire. "You've got it with you still?"

"I certainly have." He removed something from his pocket. "My luck piece." He stared at it, his face paled slightly.

A tense silence fell.

"This—is not—my dollar," he said slowly.

Sally finally spoke: "Not your dollar, Dad? What do you mean?"

"Just what I say. This is a dollar coined in 1903." He threw it down on the table and began to search his pockets. Again the silence. His search was evidently fruitless. "I—I'm very sorry this has happened,." said Batchelor. "It may seem rather trivial to you, but to me it's almighty important. If—if it's a joke of some sort, I—I don't appreciate it. However, I'll overlook it if the joker will own up at once. In heaven's name"—his voice trembled—"is it a joke?"

He looked eagerly into each face around the table. No one spoke. Batchelor's eyes hardened.

"Then there's some more sinister motive back of it," he said.

"Nonsense, Jim!" said Aunt Dora. "You're making a mountain out of nothing."

"I'm the judge of that," Batchelor said, and his voice was like chilled steel. "However"—with an effort he managed to smile—"you're right, in a way. I mustn't spoil the party."

The tension lessened, and Mrs. Keith took that moment to show sympathy.

"What a pity!" she said. "Perhaps one of your crew—"

"No, Mrs. Keith," Jim Batchelor said; "my crew has been with me for years. The servants—I'm not so sure. They will all be examined before leaving the yacht. And before we drop the subject, has anyone else missed anything?"

Bill Hammond's heart stood still. The shirt! Somebody would speak up regarding the mysterious disappearance of a shirt, and where would that lead? Little beads of perspiration stood on his forehead. But no one said anything. Evidently the owner of the shirt was still ignorant of his loss. Bill breathed again.

"Well, that's that," said Batchelor. "We'll let the matter drop."

"One minute!" O'Meara was on his feet. "Before we do that I've got a suggestion to make. Mr. Batchelor here has lost something of value, and until it's found we're all under a cloud. I for one want to be searched, and I guess every honest man here feels the same way."

"Nonsense!" Batchelor cried. "I won't hear of it!"

"But Mr. O'Meara is right," said Mikklesen."I recall a dinner at the British Embassy in Delhi two years ago, when the hostess lost a diamond necklace. It was a most distinguished party, but we were taken one by one into an anteroom and gone over with amazing thoroughness." He, too, stood up. "I also insist," he said.

"Rot! I wouldn't insult my guests," Batchelor was still protesting.

"You'll have nothing to do with it, Governor," Julian Hill told him. "We're going through with this for our own satisfaction. If the ladies will wait in the lounge—"

Reluctantly Aunt Dora, Mrs. Keith, and Sally left. O'Meara promptly removed his coat.

"Now one of you go over me." he said, "and I'll do the job for the rest of you."

Julian Hill stepped forward to oblige. With a none too easy conscience Bill Hammond also removed his coat. That shirt was not a successful fit—suppose someone recognized it? O'Meara, having been pronounced innocent, went at his work with enthusiasm. But the search had no results. Through it Jim Batchelor sat staring at the table as though the matter held no interest for him. O'Meara finished empty-handed.

"Well, if you boys have done with your nonsense," remarked Batchelor, "we'll join the ladies. And as a favor to me we won't speak of this again—tonight."

Aunt Dora was superintending the placing of two tables for bridge in the main lounge. It appeared there were just the right number—with one left over. After she had disposed of the usual impassioned pleas from those desiring to be the one left out, Julian Hill was elected to that position, and shortly disappeared from the room. They cut for partners, and to his horror Bill found himself seated opposite Aunt Dora. She had the air of being the person who had invented bridge, and so she had, practically.

Bill dealt. Majestically Aunt Dora took up her hand and glanced through it.

"Count your cards," she ordered. "That's the first rule. What rules do you play, Mr. Hammond?"

"Rules?" repeated Bill wanly. "I don't know. I just play."

"We'll pivot," said Aunt Dora promptly.

"I'm afraid I don't understand," said Bill meekly.

"I mean to say, we'll change partners frequently."

"Oh," said Bill heartily, "I'm for it."

The glare she turned on him moved him to look the other way, and his eyes met those of the man he had seen creeping

230

along the corridor just before dinner. He became suddenly thoughtful, so that Aunt Dora's voice suggesting that he bid seemed miles away. However, it came rapidly nearer.

As the play progressed, Aunt Dora found that she alone seemed to be giving the matter her best thought. She was a woman of superb endurance, but after a distressing rubber with O'Meara as partner, she called it an evening and rang the gong. The ship's clock had recently struck six bells, and after a careful calculation and a look at his watch, Bill Hammond knew that it was now just after eleven.

Mikklesen and Julian Hill both seemed determined on a bedtime chat with Sally, but after a meaning look at Bill Hammond the girl dissuaded them.

"Wait till I get a wrap," she whispered to Bill. "I want to tell you about that sunset."

When she returned she led the way to a couple of chairs that stood close together in a secluded spot on the afterdeck.

"Wonderful night," Bill murmured. The Pacific was calm, the water was liquid silver in the moonlight, the breeze was not too chill. A great night to be young, and they both were.

"Glad you like it," said Sally. "It's just what I ordered."

They sat silent for a moment.

"How was the sunset anyhow?" Bill inquired.

"Not bad at all," said Sally, "for the sun. I think I prefer the moon myself." A long, long silence. "Bill, say something," the girl protested at length. "What are you thinking?"

"I'm just wishing. I'm wishing your name was Sally Jones and your father was principal of a high school—and paid accordingly. It's what I've been wishing ever since that day at the charity bazaar."

She laughed. "Dad never wasted any time on high schools," she said. "Still, it does no harm to wish."

A cooler breeze arrived from the Pacific. Bill rose, took up a rug from a nearby chair, and tucked it about her. His hand touched hers, and contrary to his intention he seized and held it.

"Sally!" he said ecstatically.

"Bill!" she answered.

He gave up the idea and sat down. Another silence.

"How—how do you like my father?" she asked presently.

"Oh, he's all right. But it doesn't matter what I think of him. He'd be just as interested to get the opinion of one of those goldfish in the lounge."

231

"Well, I don't know," said Sally. "Dad's pretty human. You must remember, he hasn't always traveled on yachts. At one time he was a stonemason, earning a hundred a month."

"How long ago was that?"

"About the time he was—married."

The way she said it, somehow; the night, the moon, the bracing effect of ocean air—whatever the cause—

"Sally," Bill heard himself saying, "I'm in love. With you, I mean. But I guess that isn't news, is it?"

"Not precisely," she answered slowly. "However, I'm glad you said it. We couldn't have got anywhere if you hadn't."

"Sally!" The moon was under a cloud. It was just as well.

"It's no use, Sally," said Bill, coming to. "Your father would never hear of it."

"He'd be bound to."

"You know what I mean. He'd have me—boiled in oil."

"He'd have to boil me too."

"Sally, you're wonderful! Will you—will you take a chance with me?"

"I don't like the way you put it. I'll marry you, if that's what you mean."

"On our own—that's what I'm getting at. I've seen so many men marry rich girls and become lap dogs. I wouldn't take a cent from your father—nor a job either."

"Don't worry, you wouldn't get either."

"Sally, I never intended to tell you this. I was just going to eat my heart out in silence, like the strong, silent man that I am."

"Well, that would have been romantic. But I think I like it better this way. My role is a bit more active."

"Darling! What do you think I'd better do? Should I speak to your father the next time I see him?"

"Of course. Say good night or good morning, as the case may be, and that's all."

"Well, I suppose he would hit the ceiling."

"He wouldn't stamp round and forbid it, if that's what you think. It's not his way—he's too subtle. He'd just quietly queer it; nobody would ever be sure how it was done either. He's fathoms down, Dad is."

"Certainly sounds too deep for a frank, wholesome lad like me."

"I think we'd better—just drift along," Sally said. "Give him a chance to take a liking to you."

"You believe in long engagements, then?"

"Nonsense! I'm fond of you. And Father and I are much alike." She pondered. "If you could only make a hit with him somehow. I'd never be quite happy about marrying anybody—not even you—if he was opposed. He's really wild about me."

"Naturally."

"Poor Dad. He's broken-hearted. That silly little dollar meant so much to him."

It was Bill's turn to ponder.

"You know, Sally," he said, "I've done considerable police reporting, and on more than one occasion a hard-boiled detective has complimented me. I've dug up some rather important evidence."

"Oh, Bill, that's an idea!"

"If I found that dollar for him, do you think he'd give me you as a reward?"

"He wouldn't stop there. He'd throw in Aunt Dora and the yacht."

"You give me pause. I mean—I couldn't afford the yacht."

"Bill!" Her eyes were shining. "Let's work on the case together. What's the first move? We talk over the suspects, don't we?"

"That might be a good idea. We'll start with you. You said yourself there were times when you hoped he'd lose it."

"Yes, I know. I'm sorry I said it now. Do be serious, Bill. Aunt Dora—she wouldn't take it."

"But you can't eliminate anybody that way."

"Yes, you can. A woman's intuition. Mr. Mikklesen—no motive. Mr. O'Meara?"

"He's a politician. Their ways are deep and dark."

"I feel that; and he was so insistent on being searched. That's always suspicious."

"I thought it was rather fine of your father—his courtesy to his guests. He was against the search."

Sally laughed. "Don't be fooled by Dad's courtesy," she warned. "He knew darn well nobody would be fool enough to steal his dollar and then walk in to dinner with the thing in his pocket. Dad's the soul of hospitality and all that, but he wants that dollar back, and before he gives up he'll put all his guests through the third degree, if necessary. Let's see, there's Julian Hill. He seems awfully keen to keep Dad out of that India job."

"Yes, Hill's a possibility. And how about Mrs. Keith? Know anything about her?"

"Not a thing."

"Well, she's poor," said Bill. "She told me so. But then, so am I. By the way, don't let's overlook me."

"Nonsense! You wouldn't take anything that didn't belong to you."

"You think not?" Certainly a stiff bosom on that shirt.

"Oh, Bill, it's all so hopeless," she sighed. "If we only had a shred of evidence to go on!"

"Maybe we have."

"Bill—not really?"

"You've forgotten one guest. What motive would Henry Frost have in stealing that dollar?"

"None whatever, so far as I know."

"That's the way I feel," Bill went on. "Yet as I understand it, your father's cabin is the one at the end of the corridor off which our rooms open." She nodded. "And just before dinner I certainly saw Henry Frost come out of that room, acting very strangely. He tiptoed along the corridor and slipped into his own room very unostentatiously."

"Bill! It seems ridiculous!"

"I know it does. My saintly employer! He'll be awfully pleased with me if I can fasten this thing on him."

"What are you going to do?"

"I don't know. It's a delicate situation. If I go to your father with my story, Frost will probably have some simple explanation that will make me look like a fool. It seems to me it wouldn't be a bad scheme if I put the matter up to Frost and let him explain to me—if he can."

"Goodbye job."

"Probably; but in the interests of justice—and there are other newspapers."

"Well, if you really think it's the best plan—"

"Maybe not, but I'm going to try it. I can't treat old Frost as a criminal, and shadow him. I don't really think he took the dollar anyhow. But I should like to know what he was doing in your father's room. I'd better see if I can find him."

"How thrilling!" Sally said. "We're in this together, remember. Sherlock Holmes and Dr. Watson? Do you think I'll do for Watson?"

"No, you're altogether too intelligent," Bill told her.

"Oh, Bill, do you think I've got brains? I love brains."

"And I love you. You—you really meant all that—about marrying me? It doesn't seem possible."

"It's more than that; it's probable. Good night—and good luck."

"This is my lucky night," he told her. And it was, for she was in his arms.

His luck held even after he left her, for he found Henry Frost sitting alone over a highball in the smoking room. His employer evinced no joy at seeing him, but Bill casually lighted a cigar and seated himself.

"Unusually smooth passage," he remarked.

"Smooth enough," said Mr. Frost.

"Awfully jolly cruise, it seems to me. Nothing to mar it—except, of course, the disappearance of that dollar. Too bad about that."

"A great pity."

The old man drained his glass and seemed about to rise.

"Just a moment, Mr. Frost," Bill said. "You're an older man than I am, and I'd like to ask your advice."

"Yes?"

"If any one of us has any evidence that might prove useful in tracing the—er—thief, it should be passed on to our host. Don't you agree?"

"No question about it."

"I'm in a rather difficult position, sir. I happened to be standing at my door just before dinner—the light was off at my back—and I saw a man come out of Mr. Batchelor's cabin and go down the corridor to his own. His actions were rather peculiar."

"Really?"

"Now what would you do in my position, sir?"

"I'd certainly tell Jim Batchelor all about it."

"But, Mr. Frost—you were the man."

Business rivals sometimes referred to Mr. Frost's countenance as the great stone face. Not without reason, thought Bill as his employer sat grimly regarding him.

"How much," said Frost, "do they pay you at the office?"

"This is not a case of blackmail, sir," he said.

The old man's eyes flashed dangerously.

"Who said anything about blackmail? I was just going to add that whatever you get you're overpaid, for you're the stupidest whippersnapper I've ever met. Why should I take Jim Batchelor's dollar?"

235

"I don't know, sir."

"No, nor does anybody else. I did go to his room, and I did filch something from him; but it was nothing of importance. I'll explain it to you, though I don't know that I'm under any necessity to do so. For years Jim and I have had an argument about valets. He claims I need one, and I claim I'm still competent to dress myself. When I opened my bag tonight I discovered that I had foolishly come aboard without any collars."

"No collars?" repeated Bill. Then multimillionaires had their troubles too.

"Precisely. I wasn't going to tell him—I never would have heard the last of it. I knew we wore the same size, so when he was in his bath I slipped in and took one of his collars. That explains what you saw, and you're at liberty to go to him with your story any time you like."

"You sound fishy, old boy," Bill thought. But then, so would his tale about the shirt. "I'm not going to say anything to Mr. Batchelor," he announced. "Not for the present, at least."

"Just as you please." Frost stood up. "I'll bid you good night."

"One moment, sir. Should I go on with that interview with Mikklesen? I mean—am I still working for you?"

For a long moment they stared into each other's eyes. It was the employer who first looked away.

"Ah, yes, the Mikklesen story. Go on with it by all means."

Bill smiled knowingly as he watched Henry Frost leave the room.

"Who said anything about blackmail?" he murmured.

The decks of the *Francesca* were deserted as Bill hurried to his stateroom. The berth looked good. Hastily he removed his coat, his collar, and then the ill-fitting shirt. Glad to get that off. Still, it had been better than none. He laid it down on the narrow settee and Uncle George's studs seemed to flash up at him reprovingly. A Hammond in a borrowed shirt!

"Get Tatu to return it in the morning," he thought. "I can buy another in Monterey."

Once in the berth he lay for a time reflecting on the great event of the evening. Sally loved him. It had seemed a dream too remote to consider, yet here it was, coming true. Life was certainly kind to him—all this happiness—obstacles in the way, of course—

Ho-Hum. Must find that dollar. Who had it? Funny about old Frost. Explanation didn't sound right somehow. Yet it might be true. How about the others—Hill, O'Meara, Mrs. Keith? So many possibilities. Confusing—sure was confusing—possibilities—He slept.

He awoke with a start. It was still dark; he could see nothing; but he knew instinctively there was someone in the room.

"Whoosh there?" he muttered, still half asleep.

A noise—the opening of a door. Bill leaped from the berth, snapped on the light, and looked out into the corridor. At the far end of that dim passage he saw a dark figure mounting, two at a time, the stairs to the upper deck. He grabbed his dressing gown, shuffled into his slippers, and followed.

His pause to get into slippers was fatal to the pursuit, for when he reached the deck he appeared to be alone in the world. He was fully awake now, but completely at a loss as to his course. He walked along the rail, uncertainly, toward the stern of the boat. Suddenly he stopped.

The sight that arrested him was not on the yacht, but on the calm surface of the moonlit waters. There, floating rapidly away from the *Francesca* on the wet Pacific, was a white shirt —a dress shirt. The thing was unbelievable, yet there it was; and—did he imagine it?—were not those Uncle George's precious diamond studs sparkling in the bosom that lay on the broader bosom of a very large ocean?

Farther and farther away drifted the shirt with Uncle George's legacy aboard, and, fascinated, Bill moved along the rail, his eyes glued on it in fond farewell. A voice spoke suddenly and his heart stood still.

"Hello! Out for a stroll?"

He turned. A dark figure was sitting in the lee of the dining room, and the red light of a cigar burned steadily.

"That you, O'Meara?" Bill asked.

"Sure is. Lovely night, ain't it?"

"Have you been here long?"

"About an hour and a half. Such a fine night that—"

"Never mind the night. Who was it ran up here just before I did?"

"Who was what?"

"Somebody was in my cabin—I followed him up here."

"Say, kid, you'd better take something for your nerves. You're the first human being I've seen for an hour and a half."

237

"Been here all that time, eh?" said Bill. "Yet that cigar's just been lighted."

'It happens to be my third," said O'Meara. "And if I was you, I wouldn't try the detective business. It ain't for kids. There's something doing on this boat—we all know that. But I'm not in on it. I'm just on a little cruise for my health—see? Just out to get a little peace and quiet after a busy week in the city. And that's what I was gettin' until you dashed up like a wild man and made a nasty crack about my cigar."

"Oh, no offense," said Bill "Only—"

"Only what?"

"I suppose you were so taken with the peace and quiet you missed that other fellow completely."

"You go back to bed and rest them nerves."

"That's what I'm going to do," Bill answered, and left hastily.

He was, indeed, in a great hurry to return. He dashed into his stateroom and looked anxiously about. It was as he feared—the shirt was gone! And Uncle George's studs! What would Aunt Ella say?

He sat down on the edge of his berth, trying to grasp this odd turn of events. Somebody had taken a violent dislike to his having that shirt. Who? The owner probably. That was it, the owner had recognized his property at the time of the search, and now—But who was the owner? Well, he could find that out in the morning from Tatu.

He yawned. It was all very confusing. Why should this mysterious stranger come to claim his property in the silent night? Why, having regained it, should he toss it on the chill Pacific's bosom? Had all this any connection with Jim Batchelor's dollar?

Questions—questions. All very confusing. One thing was certain—O'Meara had been lying. Bill yawned again; his berth looked warm and inviting. He rose, turned out the light, left dressing gown and slippers in the middle of the floor, and was soon deep in slumber. . . .

Bill Hammond was awakened the next morning by the noise of Mikklesen singing in the bath. The Englishman had a fair voice, through which at the moment rang a note of triumph natural to one who was securely locked in and had the plumbing all to himself.

"The same old story," Bill muttered, "Britannia rules the

waves." He looked at his watch—8:30—high time to be up and doing.

If he knew Mikklesen, however, it would do him no good to hurry. He lay where he was, watching the fresh salt breeze flutter the curtain at his porthole. Outside was a clean blue world, an empty world. Restful, this cruising on one's yacht.

Something pleasant had happened—ah, yes, Sally. She loved him. Other things had happened, not so pleasant. That little luck piece he had sworn to find. Might be more of a job than it had looked last night in the moonlight with Sally by his side. Somebody had it; somebody who knew only too well its value and was guarding it against the time when it could be traded in for a goodly supply of its little playmates. Somebody—but who?

He thought of Henry Frost, with his foolish story of a collar shortage. He thought of O'Meara, falsifying with the ease that comes from long practice, on the quiet deck at half-past one in the morning. He thought of the man who had invaded his stateroom, fleeing with that dress shirt in his arms. Uncle George's studs were floating far, journeying to some romantic port. A South Sea Islander, no doubt, would wear them next —in his ears, or maybe his nose. What would Aunt Ella say?

Aunt Ella's reactions, however, were unimportant just now. He had agreed to assume the role of detective and his course was clear. He must discover the owner of that vanished shirt.

He rang for Tatu and while he waited, rattled at the door leading to the bath. Not that he expected to gain anything by it, but it relieved his feelings.

Tatu entered, minus his accustomed smile. The boy was worried; there could be no mistake about that.

"Very much trouble today," he announced. "Dollar gone. All Japanese boys catch hell. You want something, please?"

"How about taking back that shirt?" asked Bill, looking at him keenly.

"Yes-s," said Tatu. All expression left his face.

"Well, you can't. It was stolen from me in the night."

"Yes-s," said Tatu.

No surprise; no interest even. Did Tatu know all about the shirt, or was this just his Oriental stoicism? Bill stared at him, and Tatu stared back. And the Occidental felt suddenly hopeless and helpless.

"Look here, Tatu," he said, "this is very important. I want to know where you got that shirt."

Tatu looked at the berth, at the bathroom door, through the porthole, at the ceiling, then back to Bill. "Forget," he said.

"What? Say, don't try that on me!" Bill was annoyed. "Now we'll start all over again. Where did you get the shirt?"

"Forget," said Tatu.

A wonderful people, the Japanese. Bill Hammond managed to control himself.

"You told me a minute ago you would return it. How could you return it if you don't know where you got it?"

"Forget," said Tatu.

East is East and West is West. They stood facing each other, the Occidental glaring, the Oriental staring. Bill Hammond turned away. Never get anywhere by losing his temper. Patience, amiability might do the trick.

"All right, Tatu," said Bill. "You and I won't quarrel. You helped me out of a tight place last night and I appreciate it."

"Most welcome," Tatu assured him, busily brushing Bill's dinner coat.

An idea flashed into Bill's mind.

"I tell you, that fix I was in was no joke. And I understand I wasn't the only one in trouble. I heard that Mr. Frost came aboard with no extra collars." He paused. Tatu brushed industriously. "Yes, sir, I heard that when he came to dress he didn't have any more collars than a bathing suit."

Tatu laid down the coat.

"Mr. Frost have plenty collar," he said.

"Oh, he did?" Bill sought to appear casual. "I guess I didn't get it straight then. Well supplied with collars, was he?"

"Very big box. Maybe ten. Maybe twelve. Plenty."

"You don't say!"

"I lay him out. I know."

Bill turned away lest his face betray him. Here was news! Henry Frost's story disproved already. It certainly began to look as though this Hammond boy was a born detective.

"The morning is okay, Tatu," he remarked, staring out the porthole. "When do we get to Monterey?"

"Maybe not go to Monterey," said Tatu. "Anything else, please?"

"Not go to Monterey? What are you talking about?"

"Things very bad this nice morning," answered Tatu. "Hear bell ringing. Yes-s. Thank you." And he softly bowed out.

Bill turned again to the bathroom, silent now. He rattled the knob, called, but there was no answer. Donning dressing gown and slippers he stepped out into the corridor, warm with honest anger. He knocked at Mikklesen's door.

The Englishman opened it.

"Ah, good morning," he said. "What can I do for you?"

Bill was proud of himself. A grand thing, self-control.

"I believe," he said, "that you and I are supposed to share that bathroom fifty-fifty."

"Certainly, old chap," agreed Mikklesen. "Any time you feel inclined."

The struggle this time was a bit more difficult, but again Bill won.

"Then will you please unlock the door?" he said through his teeth.

"Oh, I'm so sorry. Frightfully careless of me. Just a moment." And Mikklesen closed his door in Bill's face.

The reporter reentered his cabin and managed to spring into the bathroom before Mikklesen had regained his own quarters.

"I'd like to see you today sometime," he said to the Englishman.

"Really? I fancy we'll run into each other. Bound to on a yacht. I mean to say, rather close quarters."

"You never spoke a truer word. You know, I'm supposed to get an interview from you—for my paper."

"Fancy! You're a pressman, then?"

"I work on a newspaper, if that's what you mean."

"Not really? It wouldn't be done in England, you know."

"What wouldn't be done?"

"I mean to say, inviting a pressman as a guest. How extraordinarily confusing!"

"Well, I'll give you time to get a grip on yourself before we start the interview," Bill answered. "And now, if you don't mind, even a pressman prefers to bathe in private."

Bill's resentment was short-lived, and by the time he had finished shaving he had decided that maybe he wouldn't exterminate Mikklesen, after all. Perhaps the fellow served some useful purpose. Who could say? He whistled cheerfully as he dressed, though yesterday's shirt was nothing to whistle about. However, he had it on good authority that clothes don't make the man, and he sincerely trusted that all aboard had heard that one.

In the dining room he found Mrs. Keith and O'Meara breakfasting together. They appeared to be on excellent terms, and not particularly pleased at sight of Mr. Hammond's shining morning face.

"Good morning," said the reporter. "We seem to be rather late."

"Frightfully," admitted Mrs. Keith.

"Natural result of staying up half the night," went on Bill. "Late hours make late breakfasts, eh, O'Meara?"

"Was Mr. O'Meara up late?"

"I ran into him on deck at one-thirty this morning," smiled Bill.

"Yes, and it's lucky you did," growled the lawyer. He turned to Mrs. Keith. "This kid had a funny dream about seeing somebody in his stateroom," he explained. "I had a terrible time quieting him and getting him back to bed."

Mrs. Keith smiled sweetly on Bill.

"So you have queer dreams," she cooed. "How thrilling! You must tell me all about them. By the way, I hope you play golf. I'm looking for someone to take me round the Del Monte links this morning."

"Look no further," Bill said.

"Oh, that's awfully good of you," Mrs. Keith smiled.

"I mean," Bill added hastily, "you're not going to Monterey."

"What's that?" O'Meara cried. "Where are we going?"

"Don't ask me," Bill answered. "All I know is, we'd have been at Monterey long ago if that had been our destination."

"But—I thought it was all settled," O'Meara objected.

Julian Hill came in. He was fresh as the morning in spotless linen. O'Meara at once applied to him for information.

"It's quite true," said Hill. "We're not bound for Monterey—or any other port. We're just cruising."

"Just cruising?" O'Meara repeated.

"Just wandering about the ocean," Hill went on, "playing for time."

"I don't get you," the politician said.

Hill smiled. "You know Jim Batchelor as well as I do. He's lost something—something of great importance—to him. And he's not the sort of man to land his servants and crew—and his guests—until he's been over each and every one with a vacuum cleaner. Yes," added Mr. Hill, looking hard at O'Meara, "I'd advise the man who has that dollar to hand

242

it over. Or it's possible that we may not get back to town this year."

O'Meara stood up.

"It's an outrage!" he cried. "Oh, of course I know how Batchelor feels. But this isn't fair to those of us who happen not to be thieves." And he in turn looked hard at Julian Hill. "I've got to be back in town by Monday morning," he added.

"It's all very exciting, at any rate," purred Mrs. Keith. She, too, rose, and they went out together.

"It begins to look as though there might be an opening here for a first-class detective," Bill Hammond ventured.

"Not at all," Hill answered coldly. "Mr. Batchelor is quite competent to manage his own affairs." The rest was silence.

His breakfast over, Bill went in search of Sally. He found her in the dazzling sunlight on the afterdeck, and not minding it, hers being that sort of complexion.

"Hello," he said. "This is a surprise!"

"What are you talking about?" she wanted to know.

"When I'm away from you I keep thinking how lovely you are. Then I see you, and you're even lovelier than I thought. That's why I say—"

"Yes, but Bill, where in the world have you been?"

"Eating breakfast. Did you miss me?"

"I certainly did."

"Fine!"

"Are we in this detective business together, or are we not? I'm dying to know what you've found out."

He told her of his interview with Henry Frost and of his more recent discovery regarding the collars. A puzzled little frown wrinkled her otherwise perfect brow.

"I can't understand it," she protested. "Henry Frost is father's dearest friend."

"Always dangerous—dearest friends," Bill told her. "How is your father, by the way?"

"Worried to death. He claims he didn't sleep a wink, and I believe him. The first night without his luck piece in thirty-seven years. I told him you were on the job and all about the wonderful evidence you've run down in the course of newspaper work. I was quite eloquent, really."

"Good! I hope you'll always be eloquent when discussing me."

"I always shall, I'm sure."

"You darling! Go on, expand that idea, please."

243

She seemed about to obey, but at that moment Jim Batchelor joined them. He appeared nervous and upset.

"Good morning, Hammond," he said. "Sally's told me that you're willing to help in this unfortunate affair."

"Well, if it's not presumptuous of me—"

"Nonsense! You've had more experience in this sort of thing than I have, and I'll be glad of your assistance. Besides" —he glanced about him—"it's rather a hard thing to say about one's guests; but—well, I trust you, my boy." The emphasis on the "you" was marked.

"That's very kind of you, sir. May I ask what steps you have taken in the matter?"

"The servants and the crew have all been questioned. They've been carefully searched, and their quarters too. I may say that I don't suspect any of them. Sometime during the day guests' cabins and luggage will be—er—examined. I'm hospitality itself, but this is a vital business for me and I'll stop at nothing. I've given orders to the captain not to put in anywhere. There are supplies aboard to carry us for five days, and I'll stay out that long if I have to."

"It's a good idea, sir," Bill agreed.

"I've also just posted a notice offering a reward of three thousand dollars for the immediate return of my luck piece, and no questions asked. 'Immediate' is the important word there. The money's yours if you run down the thief."

"Oh, but I wouldn't take your—money, sir," Bill said. The emphasis on the "money" was not so marked as he had intended.

"Rot! Why not? I'd be getting off cheaply at that. Three thousand is a small price to pay for the peace of mind the return of that dollar would bring me. My boy, I'll never know a happy moment until I get it back."

"Bill, why don't you tell him?" Sally suggested.

"Tell me what?" Jim Batchelor asked quickly.

"Bill's unearthed the most amazing things, Dad. You'll never believe—"

"Good lord, why keep me in the dark?" He was all excitement. "What's up?"

"If you don't mind, sir," Bill said, "I'd like just a little more time before I let you in on it. You see—"

"Well—if you say so. But only a little time. Don't keep me waiting."

"I'll make it snappy, sir," said Bill, and hurried off.

Tatu, making up the berth in Henry Frost's cabin, informed him that Frost had slept late and was now at breakfast.

Bill looked round inquiringly. "How about the collars, Tatu?"

"Him lock collars in suitcase," Tatu explained. "Put key in pocket."

Smiling to himself, Bill went to the dining room, where his employer sat alone at his breakfast.

"Good morning, sir," said Bill.

"Good morning. You breakfast late." Frost's tone implied that it was a bad sign.

"I've had my breakfast, Mr. Frost. I want to speak to you, if you don't mind."

"And if I do mind?"

"I'll have to speak anyhow," said Bill firmly. Henry Frost looked up sourly from his grapefruit.

"I'll say this for you: You're the most offensive man on my payroll."

"I'm sorry, sir. I'm only trying to do the right thing."

"People who are only trying to do the right thing generally make fools of themselves. What is it now?"

"Last night I told you I didn't intend to go to Mr. Batchelor with certain information I had picked up. I've been forced to change my mind."

"Really? What forced you?"

"That story of yours about the collars. I've found out it wasn't true."

"Indeed?"

"Yes, sir. You say you went to Jim Batchelor's room for a collar. I say that's a typographical error. You went there for a dollar."

Henry Frost rose and tossed down his napkin.

"Will you come with me?" he said.

"Certainly, sir." Bill followed his employer on deck. "This is all very painful for me, Mr. Frost."

"Yes, more so than you think. Do you happen to know where Jim Batchelor is?"

"He's on the afterdeck."

Henry Frost turned in that direction.

"Regarding that interview with Mikklesen, you needn't trouble. You're not on the paper any more."

"Just as you say, sir," Bill replied smilingly.

But his heart sank. In love and out of work—a great combination.

Jim Batchelor was waiting with Sally where Bill had left them. He looked up eagerly as the two men approached.

"Jim, I've got something to say to you," began Frost.

"All right. What is it?"

"This young idiot thinks I took your dollar."

"Oh, nonsense!" said Batchelor, disappointed in Bill. "I know you wouldn't take it."

"Well," continued Mr. Frost, "I—I—" His face turned scarlet. "As a matter of fact, Jim—I did."

Jim Batchelor leaped from his chair.

"What's that? Say that again!"

"Now, Jim, don't get excited. I give you my word, it was all a joke."

"A joke! You old simpleton! Getting funny at your age! Well, hand it over!"

"I want you to understand how it was," Frost continued. "I was determined to take you out and trim you at golf today. Last night somebody happened to say something about your losing that dollar, and it came over me all at once that if you did you'd be so upset you'd be easy picking on the golf course. So just for fun, Jim—that was all—I slipped into your room and substituted that other dollar."

"You're a criminal at heart, Henry. I always knew it. But where in Sam Hill—"

"Of course I never dreamed you'd take it so seriously. And I want to talk to you about that. Really, Jim, that dollar's become an obsession with you. No man ought to build his whole life on a thing like that. It's wrong—all wrong. Let this be a lesson to you."

"Will you cut out the sermon and give me the dollar?"

"I'll get it. It's in my room. There's no hard feelings, Jim—"

"There will be if you don't shut up and get that dollar."

Frost departed. Jim Batchelor stalked the deck. He was mad and he showed it.

"The old idiot!" he stormed. "What's got into him? Second childhood, I call it. A joke! You heard him—he said it was a joke!"

"Never mind, Dad, it's all right now," said Sally soothingly. "And you must remember, it was Bill here solved the mystery."

246

"Mighty clever of him too. I'll write him a check in a minute."

"Oh, I couldn't allow that, sir," Bill protested. "Not under the circumstances."

"Rot! Just as serious as a real theft. And for that matter—who knows? The old fox! I never did trust him."

"Dad! Your best friend!" Sally was shocked.

"Well, how do I know what he's up to?"

At that moment Mr. Frost reappeared. For once his famous poker face failed him.

"Jim," he said, "I feel like a fool."

"You're certainly acting like one. Where's my dollar?"

Frost slowly extended his bony hand. Eagerly Jim Batchelor reached out a hand to receive. Into it Henry Frost dropped—a bit of paper, a greenback, the promise of the United States Government to pay the bearer one dollar on demand.

"What the devil's this?" roared Batchelor.

"I found it in the place where I'd hidden your dollar, Jim," said Henry Frost humbly.

Jim Batchelor did not speak. He threw the paper dollar to the deck. His face purpled, so that Bill Hammond wondered what one did first in case of apoplexy.

"What can I say, Jim?" Frost pleaded. "I wouldn't have had this happen for a cool million."

"Apologies!" gurgled Batchelor. "Regrets! What do I care for them? I want my dollar!"

"It was all a joke," said Frost—an unfortunate remark.

"Yeah, a joke! Ha-ha! Fine joke! Somebody else thought so too. Somebody decided to steal your stuff. And now where are we? Just where we started!"

"With this difference," said Frost. "I'm in on this now. You and I will run the thief down together. I've something at stake, too, and my first move will be to add a couple of thousand to that reward you offered."

"A lot of good that will do," shrugged Batchelor. "If three thousand wouldn't bring it, five won't either. I tell you, we're up against it." He turned suddenly to Bill. "You—you haven't any other clue, have you?" he asked. The trustful note in his voice was pathetic. It made two young people very happy.

"Well, I have one," Bill admitted.

"You have?" Batchelor brightened at once.

"Yes; it may not be very important. But I'll work on it. I'd

247

like your permission to do whatever I think necessary—to search other people's staterooms if I think best."

"Go as far as you like." Batchelor turned to Frost. "This boy's promised to help me."

"Oh, he's a wonder!" sneered Frost.

"You bet he is," Batchelor answered. "He ran you down in record time, and I'll back him to get the other thief."

"Dad!" Sally reproved.

"All right, Jim," said Frost. "I've got it coming to me."

"I'll say you have!"

Bill bent over and picked up the greenback from the deck.

"I'll take charge of this, if you don't mind. And by the way, Mr. Frost, did anybody else know you took that dollar?"

"Yes—come to think of it," said Frost. "It seemed best, in case my motives should be misunderstood, to let a second party in on the—er—the joke. So I told Julian Hill."

"When did you tell him?"

"Last evening—before I took it. And afterward I mentioned to him that I had it in my stateroom."

In the silence that followed, Bill had a vision of the night before—two tables of bridge, with Julian Hill wandering alone somewhere outside.

"By the way," said Batchelor, "this may not mean anything; but I heard this morning that Mrs. Keith lunched last Wednesday at the Palace with Blake. The Blakes are old rivals of mine," he explained to Bill, "and they've never made any secret of their interest in that dollar."

"And who told you about Mrs. Keith, sir?"

"Julian Hill."

"Ah, yes," Bill smiled. "Well, I'll do my best."

"I'm sure you will, my boy," said Batchelor. "Don't forget, there's five thousand in it for you now."

"I hope there's more than that," thought Bill.

He smiled at Sally and moved away. Frost called after him.

"By the way, Hammond," he said, "if you get the time you'd better do that Mikklesen story. Simon Porter will be expecting it."

"Thank you, sir," Bill answered. Sally joined him and they went forward along the rail.

"What did he mean, Bill?" she asked.

"Oh, he was just handing me back my job. You see, he fired me a little while ago. Now he loves me again. And speaking of that, where do you stand this morning?"

"Just where I stood last night," she told him.

"The day of miracles arrived last night," he said. "You can sit down now, my dear—if you'll tell me all about it."

"All about what?" They found a couple of deck chairs.

"About how you—like me pretty well."

"Never mind that. You tell me. You love me, don't you, Bill?"

"Sally, words are inadequate! I gave 'em a chance last night, and they fell down on the job."

"When did you start, Bill—being fond, I mean?"

"That day you were helping orphans. The moment I saw you—honest, Sally, I loved you on the spot. And for ten minutes I madly worshiped you. Then somebody told me your name. So I went away and never loved you again."

"Bill!"

"Well, that was the idea. Only it didn't work out very well."

"I'm glad it didn't. But business before pleasure, Bill. What's your other clue?"

His bright look faded.

"It isn't any good," he said. "I thought for a minute there might be something in it. I see now I was wrong."

"But what is it, Bill?"

"It's a shirt."

"A shirt?"

"Yes, we've run the collars to earth, and now we'll get busy on the shirt. I tell you, Sally, this is beginning to look to me like the annual outing of the Laundrymen's Benevolent Society."

"You interest me strangely. What's it all about?"

He told her. The misadventure in the steamy laundry of Honolulu Sam, his agony when he found himself shirtless, Tatu's prompt rescue, the theft in the night, Tatu's reticence on the morning after—all these he detailed at length.

"The trouble with the detective game," said Sally, when he had finished, "is that it's so full of mystery. Whose shirt do you imagine that was?"

"Well, there's Julian Hill. He appears to have an extensive wardrobe."

"Bill, you don't think that Julian—"

"I don't know—just a guess. My job now is to get hold of Tatu and pry the information out of him."

"Japanese are difficult," said Sally.

"You bet they are, and this boy is Gibraltar's little brother. But I'll make him open up."

"I'm sure you will."

"I'll get the facts out of him if I have to strangle him," Bill told her, "just to prove to you how tenderly I love you."

But Bill Hammond's optimistic prediction failed to come true. He did not get the facts from Tatu. After fifteen minutes of the third degree, the little Japanese still stood firm as Gibraltar—maybe firmer. Bill cajoled, pleaded, threatened. Tatu looked at him with all the calm mystery of the Orient in his eyes, and suavely protested that he had forgotten just where he acquired that shirt. The luncheon bugle came as a merciful interruption.

"All right, go along," said Bill. His efforts had wilted him. "But I'm not through with you, my lad."

"Yes-s, thank you," answered Tatu, and had the audacity to smile as he went out.

Near the door of the dining room Sally was eagerly waiting.

"Well?" she asked.

"Salute your hero," said Bill. "He's just been licked by a Japanese."

"Tatu wouldn't tell you?"

"Adamant, that boy. He's never heard the word, but he can act it out."

"Why not set Father on him?"

"No," protested Bill, "let's keep Father out of it. I've got to do this alone. You know why."

"But what are you going to do?"

"Just what a regular detective would do," he told her. "Wait for a lucky break."

"Is that the way they work?" she asked, unbelieving. She was all for action—her father's daughter.

"It certainly is," said Bill. "I read an interview once with a great French detective. I didn't pay much attention to it at the time, as I didn't know then that I was going into the business. But I remember one thing—he said that the detective's chief ally was luck."

"But suppose you're not lucky?"

"Something that happened last night," smiled Bill, "proved I'm the luckiest man in the world."

Jim Batchelor came up.

"What's doing?" he whispered hoarsely.

"I'm working," Bill tried to make it sound businesslike.

"Results—that's what we want," Batchelor reminded him.

"You bet we do," said Bill, and they went in to lunch.

At the table there was little of the cheery animation of the night before. The guests ate in preoccupied silence, and Jim Batchelor's intimation that they might wander about the Pacific for several days added nothing to the general gaiety.

After lunch Bill Hammond saw Mikklesen enter the smoking room and followed. He sat down opposite the Englishman and offered him a cigar.

Mikklesen took it suspiciously and lighted it in the same spirit. Although it was a perfectly good cigar his subsequent expression seemed to indicate that his worst fears were realized.

"If you've no objection," Bill said, "we might as well get that interview over with.",

"As you wish," Mikklesen agreed. "Where's your notebook?"

"My what? Say, it's only in plays that reporters carry those things."

"But I shouldn't care to be misquoted," the Englishman objected.

"Not a chance. I've got a mind like a phonograph record."

"Ah—er—what shall I talk about?" Mikklesen asked.

"Give me something snappy," Bill suggested. "Something they can hang a headline on."

"Oh, but that's hardly my style. Very bad taste, sensationalism. We have practically none of it at home. If you don't mind, I'd like to talk about India."

Mikklesen told his story. Beyond question he had the gift of speech, and Bill Hammond reflected as he listened that he was getting something. By an adroit question now and then, he led the talker on. Some ten minutes had passed when suddenly the second officer of the *Francesca*, who had charge of the yacht's wireless, entered.

"Mr. Hammond," he said. "A message for you."

"Oh, thanks," said Bill. The officer handed it over and departed. "Pardon me just a second."

"Certainly," agreed Mikklesen.

Bill opened the folded paper and read what the second officer had set down. As he read, he smiled happily to himself. The message was from Simon Porter.

"Never mind interview," Simon had wirelessed. "Have in-

251

vestigated by cable. A little black sheep who's gone astray. Kicked out of the English colony in Yokohama because they didn't like his shirts."

His shirts! Oh, lady luck!

"Anything important?" inquired Mikklesen.

"Not at all," said Bill. "Go on, please. You were saying—"

Mikklesen went on, but Bill no longer listened. The interview was cold, but the quest of the dollar was warming up. His shirts! They didn't like his shirts. Well, that might mean much or little; but Mikklesen's shirts certainly must be looked into.

"I fancy that's about all I can give you," said the Englishman finally.

"That's plenty," Bill answered heartily. He stood up. "You know, considering how fond you are of the Orient, I'm surprised you came away."

Mikklesen regarded him with a sudden interest.

"Pater's getting old," he explained. "Cabled me to come home. Couldn't very well refuse—family ties and all that. But sooner or later I shall return to the East."

"I'm sure you will," said Bill. "Thanks a lot."

Eagerly he hurried below. Things were certainly looking brighter. Midway down the passageway he encountered Tatu.

"I want you," he cried, and seizing the Japanese by the arm escorted him energetically into the cabin.

"What now, please?" inquired Tatu.

Bill pointed an accusing finger.

"That was Mikklesen's shirt," he announced.

'Somebody tell," said Tatu, with obvious relief.

"Yes, somebody's told. That lets you out. Now come across with the whole story."

"Nothing to say," Tatu replied. "I see he have two dress shirt. You have no dress shirt. I hear him talk unkind remarks about Japanese people. I take shirt. Why not?"

"It was a noble impulse. But why the dickens wouldn't you tell me this before?"

"Last night, maybe twelve o'clock, Mr. Mikklesen ring," Tatu explained. "Tell me I take shirt, give to you. I say no, indeed. He say very well, but will give me fifty dollar I not tell to you whose shirt you have. I accept with pleasure." His face clouded. "Japanese boy lose fifty dollar," he added.

"Has he given it to you?"

"Give one dollar for a beginning. Very small beginning."

252

Bill's eyes narrowed.

"Let me see the dollar," he demanded. Tatu handed over a crisp new greenback. "You're sure this is the one?"

"Yes-s. Only dollar in pocket," said the Japanese.

Bill took out a silver dollar, glanced at it, and handed it to Tatu.

"I'll trade with you, if you don't mind. Now listen, my lad! From now on you and I are friends."

"Yes-s. Very nice," agreed Tatu.

"You stick to me. I'm helping Mr. Batchelor—he's asked me to. No more secrets with Mikklesen. Otherwise trouble for you—much trouble."

"I know."

"The first thing in order is an examination of Mikklesen's remaining shirt."

"Can't do," Tatu said. "Shirt locked up."

"I suppose so," Bill replied. "However, I'm going to take a look. Go and see if there's anyone in Mikklesen's cabin."

Tatu departed through the bath. In a second he was back.

"Empty," he announced.

"Fine," said Bill. He stationed Tatu in the corridor with orders to signal if the Englishman appeared. Then, with the bath offering a way of escape, he examined the room with care. But Mikklesen had left no dress shirt where eager hands could find it. Undoubtedly it was in the one piece of luggage that was securely locked—a huge battered bag that had a London lock.

"Nothing doing," said Bill finally. He returned to his own cabin, followed by Tatu.

"You want bag open?" inquired Tatu.

"It would be a good idea," Bill admitted.

"Maybe dollar inside," suggested the boy.

"It might be."

"Pretty strong lock," mused Tatu.

"Oh, so you noticed that?" Bill stared at the impassive face. "Well," he continued, thinking aloud. "my chance will come. It's bound to. Mikklesen's got to wear that shirt tonight and perhaps—Oh, good lord—"

"Yes-s," said Tatu.

"Look here, my boy, what do I wear tonight? I'm worse off than I was last night. I haven't even got any studs."

"Excuse, please. Hear bell ringing," lied Tatu, and departed in great haste.

Bill Hammond sat down on his berth to consider developments. So it was Mikklesen's shirt he had worn so jauntily the evening before. Then it must have been Mikklesen who came in the night to reclaim his property. Knowing himself closely pursued, he had not dared turn into his own cabin, once he reached the corridor, and for the same reason he had thrown the shirt overboard. But why all this fuss about a dress shirt? And how, Bill asked himself, was it connected with Jim Batchelor's dollar, as he was sure now it must be? Well, detectives certainly earned their pay.

Bill left the cabin and returned to the upper deck. The *Francesca* appeared to be deserted. He dropped into a chair that stood invitingly in a shady spot and began to consider his problem. The thing was to get into that bag of Mikklesen's. But how?

Heavy footsteps sounded on the deck and O'Meara passed by. He did not speak or turn his head. He appeared worried. Bill Hammond began to worry too. Was he wasting time on a false trail? O'Meara, Julian Hill, Mrs. Keith—all possibilities. Ought to be looking them up a bit too.

But no. For the present he would follow that shirt, see where it led. He'd get into Mikklesen's bag. How would a regular detective go about it? Break open the lock perhaps? No, too crude. Find out where Mikklesen kept his keys? Much better. Find out—how?

It was a rather drowsy afternoon, and a full twenty minutes passed before Bill had an idea. He rose at once to try it out. When he reached the door of the smoking room Mikklesen was just leaving.

"Hello," Bill said. "I've been thinking about that story of ours. We really need a few photographs to dress it up."

"Oh, no, old chap," said Mikklesen hastily. "I shouldn't care for that at all."

"I don't mean pictures of you," Bill explained. "Just some snapshots taken in the Orient. You surely have some of those."

"Well, as a matter of fact, I have," admitted Mikklesen. "I'll give them to you later."

"But if you don't mind"—Bill summoned his most winning smile—"I'm at work on the story now."

For a moment Mikklesen stood regarding him.

"Oh, very well," he said, "come along."

He led the way below and Bill followed close, determined to miss nothing now. When they reached the Englishman's cabin, Mikklesen took a bunch of keys from his pocket. Bill Hammond tried not to look too interested.

"I keep my bag locked," Mikklesen explained. "Things disappearing right and left, you know."

"It's the only safe thing to do," Bill agreed.

The Englishman bent over his bag.

"Look there!" he cried.

Bill looked. The lock on the bag had been smashed open.

"How beastly annoying!" The Englishman's face was crimson with anger. "This is too much, really it is. I understood I was to go on a cruise with gentlefolk, not with a band of thieves." He was hurriedly investigating the contents of the bag.

"Anything missing?" Bill asked.

"There doesn't appear to be," said Mikklesen, cooling off a bit. "But whether there is or not I shall certainly complain to our host." He took out an envelope and glanced into it. "The photos, old chap. Pick out what you want and return the rest, if you will."

"Surely," Bill agreed. He waited hopefully. "If you'd like me to stay here and keep an eye on things while you look up Mr. Batchelor—"

Mikklesen stared at him. Did he imagine it, or was that the ghost of a smile about the Englishman's lips?

"Thank you so much," he said. "But I shall ask Mr. Batchelor to come to me here. I won't leave my cabin again this afternoon—if you're interested."

If you're interested! Now what did he mean by that? Did he know that Bill was on to him, or was it a shot in the dark?

"Oh—er—of course—" said Bill lamely, and departed.

Back in his own room, Bill tried to think things out. What did "if you're interested" mean? And who had broken the lock on that bag? Evidently Mikklesen wasn't the only shady character aboard.

He took out a book and settled down in his berth to read, his ear attuned to eventualities in the next cabin. Would Mikklesen keep his word and remain on guard by his mysterious shirt? An hour passed, and it began to appear that such was the Englishman's intention.

It was, as has been noted, a drowsy afternoon. Bill dropped his book and lay back on the pillow. Ah, this was the life! No harsh call from Simon Porter sending him out on a bit of legwork on the hard pavements. No feverish hurry to make the last edition. Nothing but the soft swish of water, the thump of the engines—sounds that suggested slumber. Bill accepted the suggestion. . . .

He was awakened sometime later by a sharp knock on his door. Leaping up, he opened it. A servant stood outside.

"Mr. Hammond, you're wanted above, sir."

Wanted! What now? Some new development in the matter of the dollar, no doubt. He hastily brushed his hair and went to the upper deck. At the top of the companionway he encountered Aunt Dora, looking extremely competent.

"Ah, Mr. Hammond," she said, "I hope I haven't disturbed you. We've a table for bridge and we lack a fourth."

Trapped! Bill looked wildly to the right and left.

"I—I thought it was something important," he stammered.

"I beg your pardon?"

"I mean—you don't want me. I'm a terrible player—as you have reason to know."

"Practice makes perfect. I'll give you a few pointers."

"It's awfully good of you—I'm very busy and—my eyes aren't in very good shape."

"I noticed your failing eyesight," she answered, "last night when you trumped my ace of spades. However, we'll put the table in a strong light. Come along."

"I—I'll be very happy to," said Bill, surrendering.

Aunt Dora didn't care whether he was happy or not. She had him. He wasn't her ideal bridge player, but he was all she could get. And as Bill followed her into the main lounge he prayed to see Sally there.

But he didn't. Julian Hill and Henry Frost sat glumly at a table, their manner that of captive slaves on Caesar's chariot wheels. Aunt Dora sat down and the game was on. It proved a long and painful session. At the close of each hand Aunt Dora halted the proceedings while she delved into the immediate past, pointing out to one and all the errors of their ways. Bill got a lot of undesirable publicity out of these little talks.

The dinner hour was not far away when Sally came in and released him. When they left the lounge Aunt Dora was going strong. Mr. William Hammond, it seemed, had done something for which he should have been drawn and quartered.

"She'll never forgive me," said Bill. "I got her signals mixed."

"I'm afraid she's rather tiresome at times." Sally smiled.

"Well, she will insist on crossing her bridge after she's got well over it. There are people like that."

"You were good to play, Bill," Sally said.

"Yes, but I didn't play so good, and I wasted a lot of time when I should have been sleuthing."

"Has anything happened?" she inquired.

"I should say it has. It was a big afternoon up to the moment I met your aunt." He told her of Simon's cable and the accident of Mikklesen's bag. "Things are moving," he added.

"They seem to be," she admitted. "What are you going to do now?"

"Ah—er—something very bright, you may be sure. I'm keen-eyed and alert. My brain is hitting on all twelve."

"Yes, but what are you going to do?"

"My dear, don't be so literal. Can it be you don't trust me?"

"Oh, I know you're simply wonderful. Only—"

"Never mind the only. We're on the verge of big things. Watch and wait!"

His manner was confident, but by the time he had reached his cabin his confidence had begun to wane. He stood for a moment wondering just what his preparations for dinner were to be. No evening clothes tonight, that was certain. He would have to make some sort of apology to Jim Batchelor and let it go at that. At any rate, he had appeared properly clad the night before, and the other guests could draw their own conclusions regarding his appearance tonight.

He tried the door into the bath—locked, of course. He rattled and called—there was no sound within. Have to go and open the door again. As he paused outside Mikklesen's cabin something told him not to knock. He entered very quietly.

The cabin was empty and in semidarkness. He moved farther into the room—and his heart stood still. A white blur in the dusk—Mikklesen's dress shirt! It was lying on the settee under the porthole, within easy reach.

He put his hand down and touched it, and as he did so a faint sound in the bath startled him. He drew his hand back from the shirt, but in that brief second he had made an interesting discovery. Mikklesen appeared in the bathroom door.

"Good lord!" he cried. "You gave me a shock! What are you doing here? Confound it all, is there no privacy aboard this yacht?"

"I'm sorry," said Bill. "I didn't know you were in the bath, and I was coming through to unlock it. I thought you'd gone off and left it that way—it wouldn't be the first time, you know."

"Well, I happen to be using it," said Mikklesen testily, and the fact that half his face was lathered and he carried a razor seemed to bear him out. "In the future, I'll thank you to knock before entering my cabin."

Bill considered. He had Mikklesen where he wanted him, but his sense of the dramatic told him to bide his time. Better an unmasking in Jim Batchelor's presence than a scene with only two people in a half-dark cabin.

"I beg your pardon," he said. "Sorry I disturbed you."

"It's rather upsetting," complained Mikklesen. "First my bag broken into and then you popping up like a ghost." He followed Bill to the door and shut it after him in a manner suggesting extreme annoyance.

Out in the corridor Bill gave himself up to a moment of unalloyed joy. It was almost too good to be true. Too easy. A bright lad, this Mikklesen; but not too bright for young Mr. Hammond, the peerless detective. For Bill knew where the dollar was now!

He must have a word with Jim Batchelor before he staged his big scene. He tiptoed down the passage and knocked at the multimillionaire's door. Batchelor called an invitation to enter, and when he did so he was glad to find that Sally also was in the room. She was tying Batchelor's dress tie, for she was a faithful daughter and didn't like Tatu's work as a valet. Her father broke from her ministrations at sight of Bill.

"Something doing?" he inquired, with pathetic eagerness.

"I'll say there is," replied Mr. Hammond cheerily.

"You've got it?"

"I've got it located—same thing."

"Not quite." Batchelor's happy look faded. "However, where is it?"

"That'll be revealed at the proper moment," Bill told him. "I just dropped in to prepare you for a little scene after dinner tonight. Sally, I'm glad you're here. After the coffee you're to take your aunt and Mrs. Keith from the dining room and leave us men alone."

"What—and miss the excitement? Not much!"

"Sally, you heard what Mr. Hammond said," reproved her father. "Obey."

"But, Dad—"

"Sally!"

"Oh, well, if you think Mr. Hammond knows best," smiled Sally.

"I'm sure he does."

"I'm sorry, Sally," Bill said. "But the subsequent events will be such that I don't think it the place for the so-called weaker sex. Mr. Batchelor, I want you to back me up from that point on. Anything I say—and anything I propose to do."

"Of course. But you might give me a little hint—"

"I will, sir." He handed over Simon Porter's wireless message. "Read that, please."

Batchelor read.

"Who's he talking about? Not—Mikklesen!"

"Yes, sir, Mikklesen."

"Good lord! I never thought of him. What about his shirts?"

"You wouldn't believe if I told you, sir. I'll show you after dinner."

"Fine!" Batchelor's spirits rose. "I'll be mighty glad to get this thing solved tonight. The captain's just told me there's something wrong with the engines, and we're circling back to Monterey."

He submitted while Sally put the finishing touch on his tie.

"By the way, Mikklesen called me into his stateroom this afternoon and put up a terrible howl because his bag had been broken into. I was very sympathetic. I didn't tell him the captain was the guilty party."

"Oh, the captain broke that lock."

"Yes; pretty crude work. He swore he could pick it open with a jackknife, but his hand slipped and he ended by smashing it. I didn't approve of his going quite that far."

"Did he find anything?" asked Bill.

"Nothing. He went over the thing carefully—so he claims."

"He didn't have the combination," smiled Bill. "By the way, sir, I won't dress for dinner tonight. I'll come as a plain-clothesman, if you don't mind."

"Come in your pajamas if you want to," said Batchelor. "Only get me that dollar."

"I'll get it." Bill assured him. As he left the cabin he smiled triumphantly at Sally and Sally smiled back.

The conquering hero—that was how he felt.

A tense air hung over the dinner table that evening, as though all present knew that some important development in the dollar chase was close at hand. Only one guest was entirely at ease—Mikklesen. He resumed his tale of far corners and strange adventures, and once more Bill Hammond had to admit that Mikklesen was good.

When the women had left, a pointed silence fell. Jim Batchelor sat for a moment staring at the end of his cigar.

"Gentlemen," he said, "I know you'll pardon my mentioning again the matter of the missing dollar, for I'm sure you're all as interested as I am to see the property recovered. Mr. Hammond has been making an investigation, at my request, and I understand he has something to report."

They turned with interest to Mr. Hammond. Bill smiled cheerily.

"We've made several discoveries," he began. "For instance, we know that the dollar was taken from Mr. Batchelor in the first place as a rather ill-advised joke." Frost squirmed in his chair, but Bill mentioned no names. He told how the unfortunate jokester, on seeking to return the dollar to its owner, had found in the hiding place a greenback of equal value. He took the bank note from his pocket.

"This is a brand-new note," he said, "and its serial number is 2B7654328B. Some of you may have noticed that when you are paid money by a bank, and receive new bills, the serial numbers usually follow in perfect sequence." He removed another bill from his pocket. "I have here," he added, "another new dollar, and the serial number is 2B7654329B. Is it too much to suppose that the two notes came from the same pocket?"

"Good work!" remarked Batchelor, beaming. "Where'd you get that other one?"

"The second note," Bill explained, "was given to Tatu, the valet, in return for some trifling service. It was given to him by one of you gentlemen here present." He paused. No one spoke. "It was given him by Mr. Mikklesen," Bill added.

They all turned and looked at the Englishman. His nonchalance was admirable.

"That may be true," he smiled, "I may have given him that note—I don't recall. What of it?"

"Pretty flimsy, if you ask me," said O'Meara. "I'm a lawyer and I want to tell you, young man—"

"Just a moment, Mr. O'Meara," Bill smiled. "We don't need a lawyer just yet. I recognized that this evidence is rather inconclusive. I mentioned it merely because it makes a good prelude to what will follow. The close relationship of these notes points to Mikklesen. Other things point to Mikklesen. I point to Mikklesen. I ask him to stand up and be searched—that is, of course, if Mr. Batchelor has no objection."

Batchelor nodded. "Go to it," he said heartily.

"Fine!" Bill said. Now, Mr. Mikklesen flushed.

"This is an insult," he protested. "Mr. Batchelor, I appeal to you. The simplest laws of hospitality—"

"You've abused my hospitality, sir," said Batchelor. "I know all about you. Stand up!"

Slowly the Englishman got to his feet.

"The coat, please," Bill Hammond ordered. "Thanks. Now the collar and tie. I'll help you, if you don't mind." He rapidly unfastened the studs in Mikklesen's gleaming bosom. "Our friend here," he explained, "has made a close study of his profession. He has perfected the Mikklesen shirt, for which he was famous in the Orient. The bosom is unusually stiff; it holds its shape well. And at the bottom, on the left side, an extra strip of linen makes a convenient pocket. You wouldn't notice it if the shirt were freshly laundered—I didn't"—he smiled at Mikklesen—"but after prying it open you have a handy receptacle for carrying slender booty—banknotes, or even a silver dollar. And the loot doesn't show, particularly if you are built concavely."

Bill removed from the bosom of the shirt a silver dollar and tossed it to Jim Batchelor. His heart was thumping; this was his big hour. "Your luck piece, I believe, sir," he said.

Batchelor's eyes shone.

"My boy, how can I ever thank you—" he began. With trembling hand he picked up the dollar. A hoarse cry of rage escaped him. He threw the dollar back on to the table and got to his feet. "Damn it," he cried "how long is this thing going to keep up?"

"Wha-what thing, sir?"

"That," roared Batchelor, "is not my dollar! It was coined in the year 1899."

"Good lord!" cried Bill; and glancing at Mikklesen he saw on that gentleman's face a look of undisguised surprise.

The room was in an uproar, everybody talking at once. But above the clamor Batchelor's voice rang out. He was facing Bill, and he was talking to Bill.

"You a detective! You're a defective, that's what you are! You get my hopes up, and then you—you—"

"I'm sorry, sir," poor Bill said. He was a bit dazed.

"Sorry! What kind of talk is that? Sorry! I could—I'd like to—I tell you this, you unearth more dollars for me, and I'll skin you alive!" He turned to Mikklesen, who was tying his necktie as best he could without a mirror. "And you, sir! What have you to say? What explanation have you to offer? Honest men don't go about with trick shirts. I know your reputation in the Orient. How come that dollar was where it was?"

"I'm afraid I've been done, sir," said Mikklesen suavely, putting on his coat.

"Done? How so?"

"Under the circumstances I can't do better than tell you the truth. If you will pause to consider, there has been no real theft. In each case, nothing but substitution—one dollar for another. The value of your luck piece is purely senti-mental. Remember that, if you will."

"Go on," said Batchelor.

"I went to your cabin last night to get that dollar. I'm a bit of a jokester myself. I heard Mr. Frost at the door and had just time to reach the closet. From there I watched him make the substitution. I followed him, and when he left his cabin to go to dinner I slipped in. After locating your dollar I made a little substitution of my own. I had your dollar last night, I had it this morning—right where our young friend here found this other one. I put the shirt with the dollar in it in my bag and securely fastened the lock. Mr. Hammond here will bear me out when I say that sometime in the early after-noon the lock of my bag was broken. That must have been when the dollars were exchanged."

"Nonsense!" answered Batchelor. "You mean to say you haven't made sure of that dollar since?"

"I felt that there was still a dollar in the bosom of the shirt and naturally supposed it was the—er—luck piece."

Jim Batchelor slowly shook his head.

"I don't get you," he said. "You're too deep for me. How-ever, I know one thing—you're not the sort of guest I care to have around. Something has happened to the engines and we're turning back to Monterey. In the morning you will greatly oblige me by taking your luggage and going ashore."

"Oh, naturally," Mikklesen agreed calmly.

"After you've been searched," Batchelor added. "Shall we join the ladies?"

As they left the dining room, Bill Hammond saw O'Meara seize Mikklesen's arm and hold him back. The politician's ruddy face was a study in various emotions, none pleasant.

Entering the main lounge last, Bill encountered Sally just inside the door. Her eyes were shining with excitement as she maneuvered him outside.

"Oh, Bill, I felt dreadfully," she said. "I mean, to miss your big scene of triumph."

"Ha-ha," he remarked mirthlessly.

"Why, what's the matter?"

"Some triumph, Sally! A dud! As a detective I'm a great reporter." And he told her what had happened.

"What did Father say?" she inquired when he had finished.

"Ah," he answered, "you go right to the heart of the matter. Father said plenty, and if a look ever meant poison in the coffee, his look meant that to me. I tell you, Sally, it's all over now. As far as Father goes, I'm out."

"Don't give up," she urged. "Haven't you any more clues?"

"Well," he replied slowly, "a little one."

"I knew it!" she cried. "What is it, Bill?"

"Oh, nothing much. But I happened to pick up that dollar we found on Mikklesen, and—"

Jim Batchelor and Henry Frost emerged from the lounge and came up.

"Ah," said Frost sarcastically, "the young detective."

"Don't kid him, Henry," said Batchelor. "The boy's got a future. He can dig up more dollars than John D. Rockefeller."

"Mr. Batchelor, I certainly regret—" Bill began.

"Never mind that. Where are we now? Things are more confused than ever."

"If you'll take a suggestion from me," Frost began, "how about your captain? He opened Mikklesen's bag. Was he alone at the time?"

"Nonsense!" Batchelor answered, "You're wrong as usual, Henry."

"Well, I don't know. What's all this about the engines and turning back?"

"Rot, I say! The captain's been with me for more than ten years." Batchelor shook his head. "I tell you, I'm up a tree. A lot of things I don't understand. Very strange, for example, that Mikklesen should have made that confession. He could have denied everything and let it go at that."

"Dad," said Sally, "Bill's got another clue."

"I suppose so," her father replied. "He certainly is a marvel for clues. I shouldn't be surprised if he conjured a dollar out of somebody's ear next. But it won't be my dollar. I'm sure of that."

"If you'll give me another chance, sir," suggested Bill.

"Well, you're a broken reed, but you're all I've got to lean on. What is it now?"

"Mikklesen's luggage was broken into about two-thirty. He didn't discover it until after three. The captain couldn't have been in there more than ten or fifteen minutes. What happened in the interval between the time the captain went out and Mikklesen came in?"

"Tell me that and I'll say you're good."

"I can only surmise, sir. But that 1899 dollar we found on Mikklesen—I know who had it last."

"What? You do?"

"Yes. That's the dollar I gave Tatu this morning in exchange for the greenback he got from Mikklesen."

"Tatu! That's an idea! Come into the smoking room and we'll have Tatu on the carpet."

The owner of the *Francesca* led the way, and Frost, Hammond, and Sally followed. Tatu, summoned, appeared a bit lacking in his accustomed calm. He feared his employer, and showed it.

"You've seen this dollar before, Tatu," said Bill, holding it out. "I gave it to you this morning. What did you do with it after that?"

Tatu stared at the silver dollar.

"Give him back," he said.

"Back to whom?"

"Mr. Mikklesen."

"The truth, Tatu," Batchelor demanded.

"So help," answered the Japanese. "Mr. Mikklesen say I do not keep promise. That not true. Make me give dollar back."

That was Tatu's story and he stuck to it. After a few moments of further questioning, Batchelor let him go.

"Well, where does that get us?" he wanted to know.

"Tatu's lying," declared Frost.

"I don't think so," Bill objected. "No, something tells me he speaks true. Mr. Batchelor, that big confession scene of Mikklesen's was staged with a purpose."

"What purpose?"

264

"To lull our suspicions once and for all. I've a hunch he's still got your dollar."

"Where?"

"That's for me to find out, sir." Bill was again the man of action. "Sally, I wish you'd go in and lure Mikklesen into a bridge game. After that's underway, I'll act."

"You sound good," admitted Batchelor. "But then you always do. I wish I could be sure you'd get the right dollar this time."

"I'll get it," said Bill. His heart sank. He'd said that before —with what result? But this time he must make good—he must! However, he wasn't so sure.

When he saw the Englishman uncomfortably settled as Aunt Dora's partner in a game, he hurried below. Without hesitation he turned on the light in Mikklesen's cabin and began to search. He did a thorough job—under the carpet, in the closet, everywhere. But he found no dollar. Nothing at all of interest, in fact, save a little coil of flat wire which lay on the floor almost under the berth. It seemed of no importance, but he put it in his pocketbook.

His heart was heavy as he turned out the light and started to leave via the bath. He had one foot in the bathroom and the other in Mikklesen's cabin when the door into the corridor opened.

"Hello," said a voice—O'Meara's—very softly.

Bill fled. He silently took the key out of the door leading from the bath into his room, and, safe in his cabin, fastened the lock from that side. He laid his hand gently on the knob of the door and waited. Footsteps sounded faintly in the bathroom and then the knob began to turn slowly in his hand. He let it turn. A gentle shake of the knob, and then the footsteps receded. As soon as he dared, Bill unlocked the door and opened it an inch or two. He made out the occasional glimmer of a flashlight in Mikklesen's cabin.

For a time O'Meara searched industriously. Suddenly the flash went dark. Someone else had entered Mikklesen's cabin. Who? In a moment the politician enlightened him.

"Mrs. Keith!" he said in a low voice.

"Mr. O'Meara!" came the woman's answer.

"What can I do for you?" O'Meara inquired sarcastically.

"Is this your cabin. Mr. O'Meara?" she asked, equally sarcastic.

"It is not."

"Then what are you doing here?"

"Just what you're doing. Looking for that dollar."

"Why, Mr. O'Meara—"

"Cut it out. I was on to you early in the game. See here, our interests are the same. Let's work together."

"I don't know what you mean."

"Oh, yes, you do. You're here to get that luck piece for the Blakes; and I—well, I represent other interests; interests that want to keep Jim Batchelor out of the primaries. Let me have that dollar until next Wednesday at six P.M. and you can have it after that."

"But I haven't got it, Mr. O'Meara."

"I know you haven't. I mean, in case we can get hold of it."

"You think it's in this room?"

"I think Mikklesen's got it somewhere. You know, I had my deal all fixed with him. I caught him last night throwing a shirt overboard, and after a little talk he admitted he had the luck piece and agreed to deliver it to me in Monterey for twelve hundred cash."

"I thought of making him an offer myself," said the woman. "I knew his talents of old, and I was sure he had it."

"It's just as well you didn't. This morning, when Batchelor offered that whale of a reward, the dirty crook began to hedge. He'd have double-crossed me then and there, only I threatened to have him arrested before he could get out of the state. So he held off."

"Then that performance tonight was all staged?"

"It sure was," O'Meara said. "I could see it in his eye. It was all for my benefit. I wouldn't be surprised if he led that young fool of a Hammond right into it. He wanted me to think he'd lost the dollar. Probably he's figuring on getting ashore with it, and then sending it to Batchelor by a messenger. But only over my dead body. Let's get busy."

"Where does this door lead?" asked Mrs. Keith.

"Into a bathroom. There's a door into another cabin, but it's locked."

And it was, for Bill Hammond took the hint just in time. He went to the upper deck and left them to search, confident that it would have no results.

The bridge game was just breaking up, with enthusiastic cooperation of everyone save Aunt Dora. Bill took Sally aside, but before he could say anything her father joined them.

"Anything doing?" he inquired.

Bill told them of the conversation in Mikklesen's cabin. Jim Batchelor was indignant.

"Fine business!" he said. "O'Meara, and the woman too! I knew blamed well I couldn't trust anybody on this boat. Well, they'll go ashore, bag and baggage, with Mikklesen in the morning. But not until I've been over all three of them personally."

"Father!"

"Yes, I mean it. Well, Hammond, where are we now? Mikklesen's still got the dollar, you think? But where's he got it?"

"Well—" began Bill.

"You've got a clue, of course."

"Not one," Bill answered sadly.

"What?" Batchelor stood up. "Well, if you've run out of clues, then the skies are dark indeed. Something tells me I'll never see my dollar again. You may be a good newspaperman, my boy, but as a detective—well—oh, what's the use? I'm going to bed. Good night."

Sally and Bill followed him outside. In a shadowy spot on the deck they paused.

"Oh Bill, what are we going to do now?" the girl sighed.

"Well. I have one—one little clue. But it's so silly I didn't have the nerve to tell him about it. Just a little coil of wire I found in Mikklesen's cabin."

"What would that mean, Bill?"

"I don't know. But I'm going to think tonight as I never thought before. I can't lose you, Sally. I won't—that's all."

"Not if I have anything to say about it, Bill, you won't," she answered, and the wisdom of stopping in a shadow became at once apparent. . . .

In his berth Bill settled down to do the promised thinking. He began to go over in his mind, carefully, every point in the possessions of a man like Mikklesen. But somewhere in the neighborhood of the military brushes he fell asleep. . . .

There is a subconscious self that never sleeps, but applies itself to any problem in hand. Which probably explains why Bill awoke the next morning with the hunch of his life. It was very late; and struck by an unaccustomed quiet, he looked out the porthole. The little town of Monterey and the green forest of Del Monte met his gaze, and he knew the *Francesca* had reached port.

The bathroom door was unlocked, and the door leading into Mikklesen's cabin stood open. There was no trace of the

Englishman, nor of his many pieces of luggage. Alarmed, Bill rang for Tatu; but from him he learned that no one had yet gone ashore.

"Hurry," Bill ordered, "and tell Mr. Batchelor not to land anyone until he hears from me." And he prepared himself for a busy morning.

Jim Batchelor arrived just as Bill was putting on his necktie.

"Any news?" inquired the young man.

"Not a glimmer," answered Batchelor. He sat down on the berth, his gloomy face in striking contrast to the sunny morning. "The second officer was in Mikklesen's cabin while he dressed and examined everything he put on. We've been through his luggage again too. But there was nothing doing. Either he hasn't got that dollar or he's too smart for us."

"Where is he now?" Bill asked.

"He's on deck, waiting to go ashore. The launch is ready. O'Meara and Mrs. Keith are there too."

"Did you search them?"

"Well, no. There are limits. Besides, I'm sure they're just as much in the dark as I am. Both of them came to me this morning and said they wanted to leave the cruise here, so I simply told them to go. There seemed no occasion for a row."

"You were quite right, sir," Bill agreed.

"You—you sent me word not to let anybody land until you came up," said Batchelor.

"I did," Bill smiled.

"Are you—are you on a new trail?"

"I think so."

"My boy! No, no, I mustn't let you get my hopes up again."

"You're very wise, sir," Bill admitted. "This isn't much—a fighting chance, that's all."

"Well, let's fight it," said Batchelor as they left the cabin. "I tell you again, you get that dollar back and there'll be nothing too good for you."

"Careful!" said Bill under his breath, and they went on deck.

Sally joined them, as lovely as the California morning, but with a worried look in her eyes. Bill smiled his reassurance. They moved along the deck and came upon Mikklesen, O'Meara, and Mrs. Keith sitting amid their luggage.

"We're losing some of our guests," said Batchelor.

"So I see," Bill answered. "I'd steeled myself to part with

Mikklesen, but these others—I'm awfully sorry—"

O'Meara glared at him. Henry Frost, alert for news, came up.

"Mr. Batchelor," Bill went on, "before Mikklesen goes out of our lives forever, I'd like to ask him one question."

"Certainly. Go to it."

"Mr. Mikklesen"—the Englishman stood up, and he and Bill faced each other—"Mr. Mikklesen," Bill repeated, "what time is it?"

The Englishman's eyes narrowed.

"I don't understand."

"The time—by that watch of yours. I've seen you consult it before. Why not now?"

"My dear fellow"—Mikklesen was quite at ease—"it's a frightfully old thing, really. Belonged to my grandfather. Something has happened to it. It's not running."

"Not running? That's too bad." Bill held out his hand. "Let me have a look at it. I might be able to fix it."

Mikklesen's eyes turned quickly to right and left. He appeared to be measuring the distance between the *Francesca* and the shore.

"Come on," said Bill. "There's no way out. Hand it over."

"Why not?" said Mikklesen. He took from his pocket a large ancient timepiece and unfastened it from the chain. He was smiling. Bill's heart sank—was he wrong, after all?

His strong fingers closed eagerly on Mikklesen's watch. Anxiously he opened the back. The thing was packed with tissue paper. He lifted out the paper—and smiled, for underneath lay a silver dollar.

"I hope it's the right one this time," he said, and handed it to Batchelor.

"By the Lord Harry!" cried Batchelor. "My luck piece! The first dollar I ever earned. Little secret mark and all. My boy—my boy, I take back all I said."

Bill glanced at Sally; her eyes were shining. He handed the watch back to Mikklesen.

"When you took out the works," he said, "you shouldn't have let the mainspring get away from you. Lively little things, mainsprings. Elusive, what?"

"I fancy so." Mikklesen, still smiling, still nonchalant, restored the watch to his pocket. "Mr. Batchelor, I'll toddle along. There's been no actual theft."

"Who says there hasn't?"

O'Meara, purple with rage, was on his feet. "Batchelor, you turn this crook over to me. I'll put him behind bars, where he belongs."

Jim Batchelor shook his head. "Your passion for justice is splendid, O'Meara," he said, "but I prefer it otherwise. Publicity never did appeal to me. Mr. Mikklesen, I congratulate you. You must have been a wonder at hide and seek when you were a kid. You may as well—go along."

"Thanks, awfully," said Mikklesen. "It's been a frightfully jolly cruise, and all that." He glanced at O'Meara, and his smile faded. "I'm going to ask one last favor, if I may."

"Well, you've got your nerve," Batchelor said. "What is it?"

"Will you be so good as to send me ashore alone, and let the launch return for—these others?"

The owner of the *Francesca* was in high good humor. He laughed.

"Of course I will," he replied. "I can't say I blame you either. It isn't always safe for birds of a feather to flock together. Get into the launch. And you, O'Meara"—he put himself in the angry politician's path—"you stay where you are."

Mikklesen indicated his luggage to a sailor and hastily descended the ladder. The launch putt-putted away. O'Meara moved to the rail and shook a heavy fist.

"I'll get you," he cried, "you lowdown crook!"

Mikklesen stood in the stern of the launch and waved a jaunty farewell. He was off in search of new fields and better luck.

"Oh, Mr. Batchelor," purred Mrs. Keith, "it's a woman's privilege to change her mind, you know. If you have no objection I'll stay with the party."

"Oh, no, you won't!" said Batchelor. "I've got my dollar and I intend to hang on to it."

"Why, what do you mean?" she said staring at him with wide innocent eyes.

"I'm on to you—and O'Meara too. I'm sorry you've forced me to say it. Go back to your friends the Blakes, Mrs. Keith, and tell them they've got me to lick on that India contract— if they can. As for you, O'Meara, my name will be entered in the primaries next week. And I'm glad to know where you stand."

"What's it all about?" O'Meara inquired blandly.

"You know very well what it's about. The second officer has some errands in the town, but he'll be back with the launch in an hour or so. When he comes I'll ask you both to leave the *Francesca*." Batchelor turned and his eyes lighted on Bill Hammond. Smiling, he put his arm about Bill's shoulder. "Some detective, if you ask me. Come into the lounge, son. There's a little matter of business between us. Henry, you're in on this. Got your checkbook?"

"I've got it," said Frost, and he and Sally followed the pair into the main lounge.

"Two thousand from you, Henry," Batchelor reminded him.

"I know it." Mr. Frost reluctantly sat down at a desk.

"Wait a minute," Bill interposed. "I don't want any money, Mr. Frost."

"What do you want?" asked Frost.

"A better job."

"And he deserves it too," said Batchelor.

"Well," began Frost, whose first instinct was always to hedge, "I don't like to interfere at the office—" Still, his expression seemed to say two thousand is two thousand.

"The Sunday editor quit last week," Bill went on. "A word from you and the job's mine."

Frost stood up. "All right," he agreed. "We'll consider the matter settled." He patted his checkbook lovingly and departed.

"Now that was sensible," beamed Jim Batchelor. "A job— a chance to make good. Better than money."

"It looks better to me," smiled Bill. "You see, I'm thinking of getting married."

Batchelor got up and seized his hand. "Fine! Fine!" he cried. "My boy, I wish you all the luck in the world."

"Then you approve of it?"

"The best thing that could happen to any young man. A balance wheel, an incentive."

"That's the way I feel, sir," said Bill heartily.

"And it does you credit." Batchelor sat at the desk. "My little check will come in the way of a wedding present." He stopped. "I hope you're getting the right sort of girl?"

"I'm sure of that, sir."

"Of course you feel that way. But these modern girls—not the kind I used to know. Flighty, extravagant—they don't know the value of a dollar."

"This one," said Bill, "knows the value of a dollar. At least, she ought to."

"What's that?" cried Batchelor.

"Put away your checkbook, sir," said Bill. "It isn't your money I want."

Batchelor threw down his pen. "I—I didn't dream—Sally, what about this?"

She came and sat on his knee.

"Dad, you've never refused me anything yet. You're not going to haggle over a little thing like Bill."

"But—but I don't—this young man—why, he hasn't anything!"

"What did you have when you were married?" she asked.

"I had my brains and a strong right arm."

"So has Bill," she told him.

He turned slowly and looked at Bill. "I like you, my boy—I won't deny it. But a girl like Sally—it isn't so much the initial expense—it's the upkeep. Could you manage it?"

"With your permission," said Bill, "I'd like to try."

Batchelor kissed his daughter and stood up.

"You'll have to give me time on this," he said. "All so sudden. I'll think it over."

"Yes, sir," Bill answered. "And in the meantime—"

"In the meantime—" Batchelor stopped at the door. He looked at Bill Hammond long and wistfully. "You know," he said, "I'd give a million dollars to be where you are now." And he left.

"Poor Dad," said Sally. "Isn't he a darling?"

"It runs in your family," Bill told her. "I've noticed that."

"Bill, you'll always love me, won't you?"

"Love you—and keep you close," said Bill. "In the big moments of my life you'll give me courage to go on. The first wife I ever earned."

"Bill, be careful!" she said. "Somebody might come in."

THE GREEN GOODS MAN

BY LESLIE CHARTERIS

Leslie Charteris (Leslie Charles Bowyer Lin) was born in Singapore on May 12, 1907, the son of an English-woman and a Chinese surgeon. He traveled three times around the world with his parents before he was twelve, published his first poem at eleven, and sold his first short story at seventeen. At Cambridge University (for a year) he read every book on criminology and crime fiction he could find and in 1928 the first Simon Templar novel, *Meet the Tiger,* was published. He has worked at a variety of fascinating jobs, but his most phenomenal success is Simon Templar, The Saint, whose stick-figure trademark is Charteris' own sketch.

"THE SECRET OF CONTENTMENT," said Simon Templar oracu-larly, "is to take things as they come. As is the daily office-work of the City hog in his top hat to the moments when he signs his supreme mergers, so are the bread-and-butter exploits of a pirate to his great adventures. After all, one can't always be ploughing through thrilling escapes and captures with guns popping in all directions; but there are always people who'll give you money. You don't even have to look for them. You just put on a monocle and the right expression of half-witted-ness, and they come up and tip their purses into your lap."

He offered this pearl of thought for the approval of his usual audience; and it is a regrettable fact that neither of them disputed his philosophy. Patricia Holm knew him too well; and even Peter Quentin had by that time walked in the ways of Saintly lawlessness long enough to know that such pronouncements inevitably heralded another of the bread-and-butter exploits referred to. It wasn't, of course, strictly true that Simon Templar was in need of bread and butter; but he liked jam with it, and a generous world had always pro-vided him abundantly with both.

Benny Lucek came over from New York on a falling market to try his luck in the Old World. He had half-a-dozen natty suits which fitted him so well that he always looked as if he would have burst open from his wrists to his hips if his blood-pressure had risen two degrees; he had a selection of mauve and pink silk shirts in his wardrobe trunk, pointed and beautifully polished shoes for his feet, a pearl pin for his tie, and no less than three rings for his fingers. His features radiated honesty, candour, and good humour; and as a stock-in-trade those gifts alone were worth several figures of solid cash to him in any state of the market. Also he still had a good deal of capital, without which no Green Goods man can even begin to operate.

Benny Lucek was one of the last great exponents of that gentle graft; and although they had been telling him in New York that the game was played out, he had roseate hopes of finding virgin soil for a new crop of successes among the benighted bourgeoisie of Europe. So far as he knew, the Green Goods ground had scarcely been touched on the eastern side of the Atlantic, and Benny had come across to look it over. He installed himself in a comfortable suite on the third floor of the Park Lane Hotel, changed his capital into English bank-notes, and sent out his feelers into space.

In the most popular Personal Columns appeared temptingly-worded advertisements of which the one that Simon Templar saw was a fair specimen.

> ANY LADY or GENTLEMAN in reduced circumstances, who would be interested in an enterprise showing GREAT PROFITS for a NEGLIGIBLE RISK, should write in STRICT CONFIDENCE, giving some personal information, to Box No. _____

Benny Lucek knew everything there was to know about letters. He was a practical graphologist of great astuteness, and a deductive psychologist of vast experience. Given a two-page letter which on the surface conveyed the vaguest particulars about the writer, he could build up in his mind a character study with a complete background filled in that fitted his subject without a wrinkle ninety-nine times out of a hundred; and if the mental picture he formed of a certain Mr. Tombs, whose reply to that advertisement was included among several scores of others, was one of those hundredth times, it might not have been entirely Benny's fault. Simon Templar was also a specialist in letters, although his art was creative instead of critical.

Patricia came in one morning and found him performing another creative feat at which he was no less adept.

"What on earth are you doing in those clothes?" she asked, when she had looked at him.

Simon glanced over himself in the mirror. His dark blue suit was neat but unassuming, and had a well-worn air as if it were the only one he possessed and had been cared for with desperate pride. His shoes were old and strenuously polished: his socks dark grey and woollen, carefully darned. He wore a cheap pin-striped poplin shirt, and a stiff white collar without one saving grace of line. His tie was dark blue, like his suit, and rather stringy. Across his waistcoat hung an old-fashioned silver watch-chain. Anything less like the Simon Templar of normal times, who always somehow infused into the suits of Savile Row a flamboyant personality of his own, and whose shirts and socks and ties were the envy of the young men who drank with him in the few clubs which he belonged to, it would have been almost impossible to imagine.

"I am a hard-working clerk in an insurance office, earning three hundred a year with the dim prospect of rising to three hundred and fifty in another fifteen years, age about forty, with an anaemic wife and seven children and a semi-detached house at Streatham." He was fingering his face speculatively, staring at it in the glass. "A little too beautiful for the part at present, I think; but we'll soon put that right."

He set to work on his face with the quick unhesitating touches of which he was such an amazing master. His eyebrows, brushed in toward his nose, turned grey and bushy; his hair also turned grey, and was plastered down to his skull so skillfully that it seemed inevitable that any barber he went to would remark that he was running a little thin on top. Under the movements of his swift fingers, cunning shadows appeared at the sides of his forehead, under his eyes, and around his chin—shadows so faint that even at a yard's range their artificiality could not have been detected, and yet so cleverly placed that they seemed to change the whole shape and expression of his face. And while he worked he talked.

"If you have ever read a storybook, Pat, in which anyone disguises himself as someone else so perfectly that the impersonated bloke's own friends and secretaries and servants are taken in, you'll know there's an author who's cheating on you. On the stage it might be done up to a point; but in real life, where everything you put on has got to get by in broad daylight and close-ups, it's impossible. I," said the Saint unblushingly, "am the greatest character actor that never went on the stage, and I know. But when it comes to inventing a new character of your own that mustn't be recognised again— then you can do things."

He turned round suddenly, and she gasped. He was perfect. His shoulders were rounded and stooping; his head was bent slightly forward, as if set in that position by years of poring over ledgers. And he gazed at her with the dumb passionless expression of his part—an under-nourished, under-exercised, middle-aged man without hopes or ambitions, permanently worried, crushed out of pleasure by the wanton taxation which goes to see that the paladins of Whitehall are never deprived of an afternoon's golf, utterly resigned to the sombre purposelessness of his existence, scraping and pinching through fifty weeks in the year in order to let himself be stodgily swindled at the seaside for a fortnight in August, solemnly discussing the antics of politicians as if they really mattered and honestly believing that their cow-like utterances might do something to alleviate his burdens, holding a crumbling country together with his own dour stoicism and the stoicism of millions of his own kind. . . .

"Will I do?" he asked.

From Benny Lucek's point of view he could scarcely have done better. Benny's keen eyes absorbed the whole atmosphere of him in one calculating glance that took in every detail from the grey hair that was running a little thin on top down to the strenuously polished shoes.

"Pleased to meet you, Mr. Tombs. Come along and have a cocktail—I expect you could do with one."

He led his guest into the sumptuous lounge, and Mr. Tombs sat down gingerly on the edge of a chair. It is impossible to refer to that man of the Saint's creation as anything but "Mr. Tombs"—the Simon Templar whom Patricia knew might never have existed inside that stoical stoop-shouldered frame.

"Er—a glass of sherry, perhaps," he said.

Benny ordered Amontillado, and knew that the only sherry Mr. Tombs had ever tasted before came from the nearest grocer. But he was an expert at putting strangers at their ease, and the Simon Templar who stood invisibly behind Mr. Tombs's chair had to admire his technique. He chattered away with a disarming lack of condescension that presently had Mr. Tombs leaning back and chuckling with him, and ordering a return round of Amontillados with the feeling that he had at last met a successful man who really understood and appreciated him. They went in to lunch with Benny roaring with infectious laughter over a vintage Stock Exchange story which Mr. Tombs had dug out of his memory.

"Smoked salmon, Mr. Tombs? Or a spot of caviare? . . . Then we might have *œufs en cocotte Rossini*—done in cream with *foie gras* and truffles. And roast pigeons with mushrooms and red currant jelly. I like a light meal in the middle of the day—it doesn't make you sleepy all the afternoon. And a bottle of Liebfraumilch off the ice to go with it?"

He ran through menu and wine list with an engaging expertness which somehow made Mr. Tombs an equal partner in the exercise of gastronomic virtuosity. And Mr. Tombs, whose imagination had rarely soared above roast beef and Yorkshire pudding and a bottle of Australian burgundy, thawed still further and recalled another story that had provoked howls of laughter in Threadneedle Street when he was in his twenties.

Benny did his work so well that the sordid business aspect of their meeting never had a chance to obtrude itself during the meal; and yet he managed to find out everything he wanted to know about his guest's private life and opinions. Liquefying helplessly in the genial warmth of Benny's hospitality, Mr. Tombs became almost human. And Benny drew him on with unhurried mastery.

"I've always thought that insurance must be an interesting profession, Mr. Tombs. You've got to be pretty wide awake for it too—I expect you always have clients who expect to take more out of you than they put in?"

Mr. Tombs, who had never found his job interesting, and who would never have detected an attempted fraud unless another department had pointed it out to him, smiled non-committally.

"That kind of mixed morality has always interested me," said Benny, as if the point had only just occurred to him. "A man who wouldn't steal a sixpence from a man he met in the street hasn't any objection to stealing half-crowns from the Government by cutting down his income-tax return or smuggling home a bottle of brandy when he comes across from France. If he's looking for a partner in business he wouldn't dream of putting a false value on his assets; but if his house is burgled he doesn't mind what value he puts on his things when he's making out his insurance claim."

Mr. Tombs shrugged.

"I suppose Governments and wealthy public companies are considered fair game," he hazarded.

"Well, probably there's a certain amount of lawlessness in the best of us," admitted Benny. "I've often wondered what I should do myself in certain circumstances. Suppose, for instance, you were going home in a taxi one night, and you found a wallet on the seat with a thousand pounds in it. Small notes that you could easily change. No name inside to show who the owner was. Wouldn't one be tempted to keep it?"

Mr. Tombs twiddled a fork, hesitating only for a second or two. But the Simon Templar who stood behind his chair knew that that was the question on which Benny Lucek's future hung—the point that had been so casually and skillfully led up to, which would finally settle whether "Mr.

278

Tombs" was the kind of man Benny wanted to meet. And yet there was no trace of anxiety or watchfulness in Benny's frank open face. Benny tilted the last of the Liebfraumilch into Mr. Tombs's glass, and Mr. Tombs looked up.

"I suppose I should. It sounds dishonest, but I was trying to put myself in the position of being faced with the temptation, instead of theorising about it. Face to face with a thousand pounds in cash, and needing money to take my wife abroad, I might easily—er—succumb. Not that I mean to imply—"

"My dear fellow, I'm not going to blame you," said Benny heartily. "I'd do the same thing myself. I'd reason it out that a man who carried a thousand pounds in cash about with him had plenty more in the bank. It's the old story of fair game. We may be governed by plenty of laws, but our consciences are still very primitive when we've no fear of being caught."

There was a silence after that, in which Mr. Tombs finished his last angel on horseback, mopped the plate furtively with the last scrap of toast, and accepted a cigarette from Benny's platinum case. The pause gave him his first chance to remember that he was meeting the sympathetic Mr. Lucek in order to hear about a business proposition—as Benny intended that it should. As a waiter approached with the bill, Mr. Tombs said tentatively: "About your—um—advertisement—"

Benny scrawled his signature across the account, and pushed back his chair.

"Come up to my sitting-room and we'll talk about it."

They went up in the lift, with Benny unconcernedly puffing Turkish cigarette-smoke, and down an expensively carpeted corridor. Benny had an instinctive sense of dramatic values. Without saying anything, and yet at the same time without giving the impression that he was being intentionally reticent, he opened the door of his suite and ushered Mr. Tombs in.

The sitting-room was small but cosily furnished. A large, carelessly-opened brown-paper parcel littered the table in the centre, and there was a similar amount of litter in one of the chairs. Benny picked up an armful of it and dumped it on the floor in the corner.

"Know what these things are?" he asked off-handedly.

He took up a handful of the litter that remained on the chair and thrust it under Mr. Tombs's nose. It was generally green in colour; as Mr. Tombs blinked at it, words and patterns took shape on it, and he blinked still harder.

"Pound notes," said Benny. He pointed to the pile he had dumped in the corner. "More of 'em." He flattened the brown paper around the carelessly-opened parcel on the table, revealing neat stacks of treasure packed in thick uniform bundles. "Any amount of it. Help yourself."

Mr. Tombs's blue eyes went wider and wider, with the lids blinking over them rapidly as if to dispel a hallucination.

"Are they—are they really all pound notes?"

"Every one of 'em."

"All yours?"

"I guess so. I made 'em, anyway."

"There must be thousands."

Benny flung himself into the cleared armchair.

"I'm about the richest man in the world, Mr. Tombs," he said. "I guess I must be *the* richest, because I can make money as fast as I can turn a handle. I meant exactly what I said to you just now. I *made* those notes!"

Mr. Tombs touched the pile with his fingertips, as if he half expected them to bite him. His eyes were rounder and wider than ever.

"You don't mean—*forgeries?*" he whispered.

"I don't," said Benny. "Take those notes round to the nearest bank—tell the cashier you have your doubts about them—and ask him to look them over. Take 'em to the Bank of England. There isn't a forgery in the whole lot—but I made 'em! Sit down and I'll tell you."

Mr. Tombs sat down, stiffly. His eyes kept straying back to the heaps of wealth on the floor and the table, as though at each glance he would have been relieved rather than surprised if they had vanished.

"It's like this, Mr. Tombs. I'm taking you into my confidence because I've known you a couple of hours and I've made up my mind about you. I like you. Those notes, Mr. Tombs, were printed from a proof plate that was stolen out of the Bank of England itself by a fellow who worked there. He was in the engraving department, and when they were making the plates they made one more than they needed. It was given to him to destroy—and he didn't destroy it. He was like the man we were talking about—the man in the taxi. He had a genuine plate that would print genuine pound notes, and he could keep it for himself if he wanted to. All he had to do was to make an imitation plate that no one was going to examine closely—you can't tell a lot from a plate, just looking at it—and a couple of lines across it to cancel it. Then that would be locked up in the vaults and probably never looked at again, and he'd have the real one. He didn't even know quite what he'd do with the plate when he had it, but he kept it. And then he got scared about it being found out, and he ran away. He went over to New York, where I come from.

"He stopped in the place I lived at, over in Brooklyn. I got to know him a bit, though he was always very quiet and seemed to have something on his mind. I didn't ask what it was, and I didn't care. Then he got pneumonia.

"Nobody else had ever paid any attention to him, so it seemed to be up to me. I did what I could for him—it didn't amount to much, but he appreciated it. I paid some of the rent he owed. The doctor found he was half starved—he'd landed in New York with just a few pounds, and when those were gone he'd lived on the leavings he could bag from chop houses. He was starving himself to death with a million pounds in his grip! But I didn't know that then. He got worse and worse; and then they had to give him oxygen one night, but the doctor said he wouldn't see the morning anyhow. He'd starved himself till he was too weak to get well again.

"He came round just before the end, and I was with him. He just looked at me and said: 'Thanks, Benny.' And then he told me all about himself and what he'd done. 'You keep the plate,' he said. 'It may be some good to you.'

"Well, he died in the morning, and the landlady told me to hurry up and get his things out of the way as there was another lodger coming in. I took 'em off to my own room. There wasn't much; but I found the plate.

"Maybe you can imagine what it meant to me, after I'd got it all figured out. I was just an odd-job man in a garage then, earning a few dollars a week. I was the man in the taxi again. But I had a few dollars saved up: I'd have to find the right paper, and get the notes printed—I didn't know anything about the technical side of it. It'd cost money; but if it went through all right, that poor fellow's legacy would make me a millionaire. He'd starved to death because he was too scared to try it; had *I* got the guts?"

Benny Lucek closed his eyes momentarily, as if he were reliving the struggle with his conscience.

"You can see for yourself which way I decided," he said. "It took time and patience, but it was still the quickest way of making a million I'd ever heard of. That was six years ago. I don't know how much money I've got in the bank now, but I know it's more than I can ever spend. And it was like that all of three years ago.

"And then I started thinking about the other people who needed money, and I began to square my conscience by helping them. I was working over in the States then, of course, changing this English money in small packets at banks all over the continent. And I started giving it away—charities, down-and-outs, any good thing I could think of. That was all right so far as it went. But then I started thinking, that fellow who gave me the plate was English, and some of the money ought to go back to people in England who needed it. That's why I came across. Did I tell you that fellow left a wife behind when he ran away? It took me two months to find her, with the best agents I could buy; but I located her at last serving in a tea-shop, and now I've set her on her feet for life, though she thinks it was an uncle she never had who died and left her the money. But if I can find any other fellow whose wife needs some money he can't earn for her," said Benny nobly, "I want to help him too."

Mr. Tombs swallowed. Benny Lucek was a master of elocution among his other talents, and the manner of his recital was calculated to bring a lump into the throat of an impressionable listener.

"Would you like some money, Mr. Tombs?" he inquired.

Mr. Tombs coughed.

"I—er—well—I can't quite get over the story you've told me."

He picked up a handful of the notes, peered at them minutely, screwed them in his fingers, and put them down again rather abruptly and experimentally, as if he were trying to discover whether putting temptation from him would bring a glow of conscious virtue that would compensate for the worldly loss. Apparently the experiment was not very satisfactory, for his mouth puckered wistfully.

"You've told me all about yourself," said Benny, "and about your wife being delicate and needing to go away for a long sea voyage. I expect there's trouble about getting your children a proper education that you haven't mentioned at all. You're welcome to put all that right. You can buy just as many of those notes as you like, and twenty pounds per hundred is the price to you. That's exactly what they cost me in

getting the special paper and inks and having them printed—
the man I found to print 'em for me gets a big rake-off, of
course. Four shillings each is the cost price, and you can make
yourself a millionaire if you want to."

Mr. Tombs gulped audibly.

"You're—you're not pulling my leg, are you?" he stammered pathetically.

"Of course I'm not. I'm glad to do it." Benny stood up and
placed one hand affectionately on Mr. Tombs's shoulders.
"Look here, I know all this must have been a shock to you.
It wants a bit of getting used to. Why don't you go away and
think it over? Come and have lunch with me again tomorrow,
if you want some of these notes, and bring the money with
you to pay for them. Call me at seven o'clock and let me
know if I'm to expect you." He picked up a small handful
of money and stuffed it into Mr. Tombs's pocket. "Here—
take some samples with you and try them on a bank, just in
case you still can't believe it."

Mr. Tombs nodded, blinking.

"I'm the man in the taxi again," he said with a weak smile.
"When you really do find the wallet—"

"Who loses by it?" asked Benny, with gently persuasive
rhetoric. "The Bank of England, eventually. I never learnt
any economics, but I suppose they'll have to meet the bill.
But are they going to be any the worse off for the few thousands you'll take out of them? Why, it won't mean any more
to them than a penny does to you now. Think it over."

"I will," said Mr. Tombs, with a last lingering stare at
the littered table.

"There's just one other thing," said Benny. "Not a word
of what I've told you to any living soul—not even to your
wife. I'm trusting you to treat it as confidentially as you'd
treat anything in your insurance business. You can see why,
can't you? A story like I've told you would spread like wild-
fire, and once it got to the Bank of England there'd be no
more money in it. They'd change the design of their notes
and call in all the old ones as quick as I can say it."

"I understand, Mr. Lucek," said Mr. Tombs.

He understood perfectly—so well that the rapturous tale
he told to Patricia Holm when he returned was almost in-
coherent. He told her while he was removing his make-up and
changing back into his ordinary clothes; and when he had
finished he was as immaculate and debonair as she had ever

283

seen him. And finally he smoothed out the notes that Benny had given him at parting, and stowed them carefully in his wallet. He looked at his watch.

"Let's go and look at a non-stop show, darling," he said, "and then we'll buy a pailful of caviare between us and swill it down with a gallon of Cordon Rouge. Brother Benjamin will pay!"

"But are you sure these notes are perfect?" she asked; and the Saint laughed.

"My sweetheart, every one of those notes was printed by the Bank of England itself. The green goods game is nothing like that; though I've often wondered why it hasn't been worked before in this—*Gott in Himmel!*"

Simon Templar suddenly leapt into the air with a yell; and the startled girl stared at him.

"What in the name of—"

"Just an idea," explained the Saint. "They sometimes take me in the seat of the pants like that. This is rather a beauty."

He swept her off boisterously to the promised celebrations without telling her what the idea was that had made him spring like a young ram with loud foreign oaths; but at seven o'clock punctually he found time to telephone the Park Lane Hotel.

"I'm going to do what the man in the taxi would do, Mr. Lucek," he said.

"Well, Mr. Tombs, that's splendid news," responded Benny. "I'll expect you at one. By the way, how much will you be taking?"

"I'm afraid I can only manage to—um—raise three hundred pounds. That will buy fifteen hundred pounds' worth, won't it?"

"I'll make it two thousand pounds' worth to you, Mr. Tombs," said Benny generously. "I'll have it all ready for you when you come."

Mr. Tombs presented himself at five minutes to one, and although he wore the same suit of clothes as he had worn the previous day, there was a festive air about him to which a brand-new pair of white kid gloves and a carnation in his buttonhole colorfully contributed.

"I handed in my resignation at the office this morning," he said. "And I hope I never see the place again."

Benny was congratulatory but apologetic.

"I'm afraid we shall have to postpone our lunch," he said.

"I've been investigating a lady who also answered my advertisement—a poor old widow living up in Derbyshire. Her husband deserted her twenty years ago; and her only son, who's been keeping her ever since, was killed in a motor accident yesterday. It seems as if she needs a fairy godfather quickly, and I'm going to dash up to Derbyshire in a special train and see what I can do."

Mr. Tombs suppressed a perfunctory tear, and accompanied Benny to his suite. A couple of well-worn suitcases and a wardrobe trunk the size of a suburban villa, all ready stacked up and labelled, confirmed Benny's avowed intentions. Only one of the parcels of currency was visible, pushed untidily to one end of the table.

"Did you bring the money, Mr. Tombs?"

Mr. Tombs took out his battered wallet and drew forth a sheaf of crisp new fivers with slightly unsteady hands. Benny took them, glanced over them casually, and dropped them on to the table with the carelessness befitting a millionaire. He waved Mr. Tombs into an armchair with his back to the window, and himself sat down in a chair drawn up to the opposite side of the table.

"Two thousand one-pound notes are quite a lot to put in your pocket." he remarked. "I'll make them up into a parcel for you."

Under Mr. Tombs's yearning eyes he flipped off the four top bundles from the pile and tossed them one by one into his guest's lap. Mr. Tombs grabbed them and examined them hungrily, spraying the edges of each pack off his thumb so that pound notes whirred before his vision like the pictures on a toy cinematograph.

"You can count them if you like—there ought to be five hundred in each pack," said Benny; but Mr. Tombs shook his head.

"I'll take your word for it, Mr. Lucek. I can see they're all one-pound notes, and there must be a lot of them."

Benny smiled and held out his hand with a businesslike air. Mr. Tombs passed the bundles back to him, and Benny sat down again and arranged them in a neat cube on top of a sheet of brown paper. He turned the paper over the top and creased it down at the open ends with a rapid efficiency that would have done credit to any professional shop assistant; and Mr. Tombs's covetous eyes watched every movement with the intentness of a dumb but earnest audience trying to spot how a conjuring trick is done.

"Don't you think it would be a ghastly tragedy for a poor widow who put all her savings into these notes and then found that she had been—um—deceived?" said Mr. Tombs morbidly; and Benny's dark eyes switched up to his face in sudden startlement.

"Eh?" said Benny. "What's that?"

But Mr. Tombs's careworn face had the innocence of a patient sheep's.

"Just something I was thinking, Mr. Lucek," he said.

Benny grinned his expansive display of pearly teeth, and continued with his packing. Mr. Tombs's gaze continued to concentrate on him with an almost mesmeric effect; but Benny was not disturbed. He had spent nearly an hour that morning making and testing his preparations. The upper sashcords of the window behind Mr. Tombs's chair had been cut through all but the last thread, and the weight of the sash was carried on a small steel peg driven into the frame. From the steel peg a thin but very strong dark-colored string ran down to the floor, pulleyed round a nail driven into the base of the wainscoting, and disappeared under the carpet; it pulleyed round another nail driven into the floor under the table, and came up through a hole in the carpet alongside one leg to loop conveniently over the handle of the drawer.

Benny completed the knots around his parcel, and searched around for something to trim off the loose ends.

"There you are, Mr. Tombs," he said; and then, in his fumbling, he caught the convenient loop of string and tugged at it. The window fell with a crash.

And Mr. Tombs did not look round.

It was the most flabbergasting thing that had ever happened in Benny Lucek's experience. It was supernatural—incredible. It was a phenomenon so astounding that Benny's mouth fell open involuntarily, while a balloon of incredulous stupefaction bulged up in the pit of his stomach and cramped his lungs. There came over him the feeling of preposterous injury that would have assailed a practiced bus-jumper who, preparing to board a moving bus as it came by, saw it evade him by rising vertically into the air and soaring away over the house-tops. It was simply one of the things that did not happen.

And on this fantastic occasion it had happened. In the half-opened drawer that pressed against Benny's tummy, just below the level of the table and out of range of Mr. Tombs's glassy stare, was another brown-paper parcel exactly similar in every respect to the one which Benny was finishing off. Outwardly, that is. Inside, there was a difference; for whereas inside the parcel which Benny had prepared before Mr. Tombs's eyes there were undoubtedly two thousand authentic one-pound notes, inside the second parcel there was only a collection of old newspapers and magazines cut to precisely the same size. And never before in Benny's career, once the fish had taken the hook, had those two parcels failed to be successfully exchanged. That was what the providentially falling window was arranged for, and it constituted the whole simple secret of the green goods game. The victim, when he got home and opened the parcel and discovered how he had been swindled, could not make a complaint to the police without admitting that he himself had been ready to aid and abet a fraud; and forty-nine times out of fifty he would decide that it was better to stand his loss and keep quiet about it. Elementary, but effective. And yet the whole structure could be scuppered by the unbelievable apathy of a victim who failed to react to the stimulus of a loud bang as any normal human being should have reacted.

"The—the window seems to have fallen down," Benny pointed out hoarsely; and felt like a hero of a melodrama who has just shot the villain in the appointed place at the end of the third act, and sees him smilingly declining to fall down and die according to the rehearsed script.

"Yes," agreed Mr. Tombs cordially. "I heard it."

"The—the sash cords must have broken."

"Probably that's what it was."

"Funny thing to happen so—so suddenly, wasn't it?"

"Very funny," assented Mr. Tombs, keeping up the conversation politely.

Benny began to sweat. The substitute parcel was within six inches of his hovering hands: given only two seconds with the apt stare of those unblinking eyes diverted from him, he could have rung the changes as easily as unbuttoning his shirt; but the chance was not given. It was an impasse that he had never even dreamed of, and the necessity of thinking up something to cope with it in the spur of the moment stampeded him to the border of panic.

"Have you got a knife?" asked Benny, with perspiring heartiness. "Something to cut off this end of string?"

"Let me break it for you," said Mr. Tombs.

He stood up and moved towards the table; and Benny shied like a horse.

"Don't bother, please, Mr. Tombs," he gulped. "I'll—I'll—"

"No trouble at all," said Mr. Tombs.

Benny grabbed the parcel, and dropped it. He was a very fine strategist and dramatic reciter, but he was not a man of violence—otherwise he might have been tempted to act differently. That grab and drop was the last artifice he could think of to save the day.

He pushed his chair back and bent down, groping for the fallen parcel with one hand and the substitute parcel with the other. In raising the fallen packet past the table the exchange might be made.

His left hand found the parcel on the floor. His right hand went on groping. It ran up and down the drawer, sensitively at first, then frantically. It plunged backwards and forwards. His fingernails scrabbled on the wood. . . . He became aware he couldn't stay in that position indefinitely, and began to straighten up slowly, with a cold sensation closing on his heart. And as his eyes came up to the level of the drawer he saw that the dummy parcel had somehow got pushed right away to the back: for all the use it would have been to him there it might have been in the middle of the Arizona desert.

Mr. Tombs was smiling blandly.

"It's quite easy, really," he said.

He took the parcel from Benny's nerveless hand, put it on the table, twisted the loose end of string round his forefinger, and jerked. It snapped off clean and short.

"A little trick of mine," said Mr. Tombs chattily. He picked up the parcel and held out his hand. "Well, Mr. Lucek, you must know how grateful I am. You mustn't let me keep you any longer from your—um—widow. Good-by, Mr. Lucek."

He wrung Benny Lucek's limp fingers effusively, and retired towards the door. There was something almost sprightly in his gait, a twinkle in his blue eyes that had certainly not been there before, a seraphic benevolence about his smile that made Benny go hot and cold. It didn't belong to Mr. Tombs of the insurance office. . . .

"Hey—just a minute!" gasped Benny; but the door had closed. Benny jumped up, panting. *"Hey,* you—"

He flung open the door, and looked into the cherubic pink full-moon face of a very large gentleman in a superfluous overcoat and a bowler hat who stood on the threshold.

"Morning, Mr. Lucek," said the large gentleman sedately. "May I come in?"

He took the permission for granted, and advanced into the sitting-room. The parcel on the table attracted his attention first, and he took up a couple of bundles from the stack and looked them over. Only the top notes in each bundle were genuine pound notes, as the four whole bundles which departed with Mr. Tombs had been: the rest of the thickness was made up with sheets of paper cut to the same size.

"Very interesting," remarked the large gentleman.

"Who the devil are you?" blustered Benny; and the round rosy face turned to him with a very sudden and authoritative directness.

"I am Chief Inspector Teal, of Scotland Yard, and I have information that you are in possession of quantities of forged banknotes."

Benny drew breath again hesitantly.

"That's absurd, Mr. Teal. You won't find any phoney stuff here," he said; and then the detective's cherubic gaze fell on the sheaf of five-pound notes that Mr. Tombs had left behind in payment.

He picked them up and examined them carefully, one by one.

"H'm—and not very good forgeries, either," he said, and called to the sergeant who was waiting in the corridor outside.

ONE HOUR

BY DASHIELL HAMMETT

When Dashiell Hammett (b. May 27, 1894) was a fresh-
man at Baltimore Polytechnic, his father became ill and
he left school to work for the B & O Railroad. Later he
became an operative for the Pinkerton Detective Agency,
which eventually sent him to San Francisco. The bulk
of his early writing was detective fiction for *Black Mask*,
where his Continental Op was a favorite and his first
four novels were serialized before book publication. In
1934 he published *The Thin Man*, the most financially
successful of his books, and collaborated with artist
Alexander Raymond on the comic strip, *Secret Agent
X-9*. He died in 1961.

"THIS IS MR. CHROSTWAITE," Vance Richmond said.

Chrostwaite, wedged between the arms of one of the attorney's large chairs, grunted what was perhaps meant for an acknowledgment of the introduction. I grunted back at him, and found myself a chair.

He was a big balloon of a man—this Chrostwaite—in a green plaid suit that didn't make him look any smaller than he was. His tie was a gaudy thing, mostly of yellow, with a big diamond set in the center of it, and there were more stones on his pudgy hands. Spongy fat blurred his features, making it impossible for his round purplish face to ever hold any other expression than the discontented hoggishness that was habitual to it. He reeked of gin.

"Mr. Chrostwaite is the Pacific Coast agent for the Mutual Fire Extinguisher Manufacturing Company," Vance Richmond began, as soon as I had got myself seated. "His office is on Kearny Street, near California. Yesterday, at about two-forty-five in the afternoon, he went to his office, leaving his machine—a Hudson touring car—standing in front, with the engine running. Ten minutes later, he came out. The car was gone."

I looked at Chrostwaite. He was looking at his fat knees, showing not the least interest in what his attorney was saying. I looked quickly back at Vance Richmond; his clean grey face and lean figure were downright beautiful beside his bloated client.

"A man named Newhouse," the lawyer was saying, "who was the proprietor of a printing establishment on California Street, just around the corner from Mr. Chrostwaite's office, was run down and killed by Mr. Chrostwaite's car at the corner of Clay and Kearny Streets, five minutes after Mr. Chrostwaite had left the car to go into his office. The police found the car shortly afterward, only a block away from the scene of the accident—on Montgomery near Clay.

"The thing is fairly obvious. Someone stole the car immediately after Mr. Chrostwaite left it; and in driving rapidly away, ran down Newhouse; and then, in fright, abandoned the car. But here is Mr. Chrostwaite's position; three nights ago, while driving perhaps a little recklessly out—"

"Drunk," Chrostwaite said, not looking up from his plaid knees; and though his voice was hoarse, husky—it was the hoarseness of a whisky-burnt throat—there was no emotion in his voice.

"While driving perhaps a little recklessly out Van Ness Avenue," Vance Richmond went on, ignoring the interruption, "Mr. Chrostwaite knocked a pedestrian down. The man wasn't badly hurt, and he is being compensated very generously for his injuries. But we are to appear in court next Monday to face a charge of reckless driving, and I am afraid that this accident of yesterday, in which the printer was killed, may hurt us.

"No one thinks that Mr. Chrostwaite was in his car when it killed the printer—we have a world of evidence that he wasn't. But I am afraid that the printer's death may be made a weapon against us when we appear on the Van Ness Avenue charge. Being an attorney, I know just how much capital the prosecuting attorney—if he so chooses—can make out of the really insignificant fact that the same car that knocked down the man on Van Ness Avenue killed another man yesterday. And, being an attorney, I know how likely the prosecuting attorney is to so choose. And he can handle it in such a way that we will be given little or no opportunity to tell our side.

"The worst that can happen, of course, is that, instead of the usual fine, Mr. Chrostwaite will be sent to the city jail for thirty or sixty days. That is bad enough, however, and that is what we wish to—"

Chrostwaite spoke again, still regarding his knees.

"Damned nuisance!" he said.

"That is what we wish to avoid," the attorney continued. "We are willing to pay a stiff fine, and expect to, for the accident on Van Ness Avenue was clearly Mr. Chrostwaite's fault. But we—"

"Drunk as a lord!" Chrostwaite said.

"But we don't want to have this other accident, with which we had nothing to do, given a false weight in connection with the slighter accident. What we want, then, is to find the man or men who stole the car and ran down John Newhouse. If they are apprehended before we go to court, we won't be in danger of suffering for their act. Think you can find them before Monday?"

"I'll try," I promised; "though it isn't—"

The human balloon interrupted me by heaving himself

to his feet, fumbling with his fat jeweled fingers for his watch.

"Three o'clock," he said. "Got a game of golf for three-thirty." He picked up his hat and gloves from the desk. "Find 'em, will you? Damned nuisance going to jail!"

And he waddled out.

From the attorney's office, I went down to the Hall of Justice, and, after hunting around a few minutes, found a policeman who had arrived at the corner of Clay and Kearny Street a few seconds after Newhouse had been knocked down.

"I was just leaving the Hall when I seen a bus scoot around the corner at Clay Street," this patrolman—a big sandy-haired man named Coffee—told me. "Then I seen people gathering around, so I went up there and found this John Newhouse stretched out. He was already dead. Half a dozen people had seen him hit, and one of 'em had got the license number of the car that done it. We found the car standing empty just around the corner on Montgomery Street, pointing north. They was two fellows in the car when it hit Newhouse, but nobody saw what they looked like. Nobody was in it when we found it."

"In what direction was Newhouse walking?"

"North along Kearny Street, and he was about three-quarters across Clay when he was knocked. The car was coming north on Kearny, too, and turned east on Clay. It mightn't have been all the fault of the fellows in the car—according to them that seen the accident. Newhouse was walking across the street looking at a piece of paper in his hand. I found a piece of foreign money—paper money—in his hand, and I guess that's what he was looking at. The lieutenant tells me it was Dutch money—a hundred florin note, he says."

"Found out anything about the men in the car?"

"Nothing! We lined up everybody we could find in the neighborhood of California and Kearny Streets—where the car was stolen from—and around Clay and Montgomery Streets—where it was left at. But nobody remembered seeing the fellows getting in it or getting out of it. The man that owns the car wasn't driving it—it was stole all right, I guess. At first I thought maybe they was something shady about the accident. This John Newhouse had a two- or three-day-old black eye on him. But we run that out and found that he had an attack of heart trouble or something a couple days ago, and fell, fetching his eye up against a chair. He'd been home sick for three days—just left his house half an hour or so before the accident."

"Where'd he live?"

"On Sacramento Street—way out. I got his address here somewhere."

He turned over the pages of a grimy memoranda book, and I got the dead man's house number, and the names and addresses of the witnesses to the accident that Coffee had questioned.

That exhausted the policeman's information, so I left him.

My next play was to canvass the vicinity of where the car had been stolen and where it had been deserted, and then interview the witnesses. The fact that the police had fruitlessly gone over this ground made it unlikely that I would find anything of value; but I couldn't skip these things on that account. Ninety-nine per cent of detective work is a patient collecting of details—and your details must be got as nearly first-hand as possible, regardless of who else has worked the territory before you.

Before starting on this angle, however, I decided to run around to the dead man's printing establishment—only three blocks from the Hall of Justice—and see if any of his employees had heard anything that might help me.

Newhouse's establishment occupied the ground floor of a small building on California, between Kearny and Montgomery. A small office was partitioned off in front, with a connecting doorway leading to the press-room in the rear.

The only occupant of the small office, when I came in from the street, was a short, stocky, worried-looking blond man of forty or thereabouts, who sat at the desk in his shirtsleeves, checking off figures in a ledger, against others on a batch of papers before him.

I introduced myself, telling him that I was a Continental Detective Agency operative, interested in Newhouse's death. He told me his name was Ben Soules, and that he was Newhouse's foreman. We shook hands, and then he waved me to a chair across the desk, pushed back the papers and book upon which he had been working, and scratched his head disgustedly with the pencil in his hand.

"This is awful!" he said. "What with one thing and another, we're heels over head in work, and I got to fool with these

294

books that I don't know anything at all about, and—"

He broke off to pick up the telephone, which had jingled.

"Yes. . . . This is Soules. . . . We're working on them now
. . . I'll give 'em to you by Monday noon at the least. . . . I know
we promised them for yesterday, but . . . I know! I know!
But the boss's death set us back. Explain that to Mr. Chrostwaite. And . . . And I'll promise you that we'll give them to
you Monday morning, sure!"

Soules slapped the receiver irritably on its hook and looked
at me.

"You'd think that since it was his own car that killed the
boss, he'd have decency enough not to squawk over the
delay!"

"Chrostwaite?"

"Yes—that was one of his clerks. We're printing some leaflets
for him—promised to have 'em ready yesterday—but between
the boss's death and having a couple new hands to break in,
we're behind with everything. I been here eight years, and
this is the first time we ever fell down on an order—and every
damned customer is yelling his head off. If we were like most
printers they'd be used to waiting; but we've been too good
to them. But this Chrostwaite! You'd think he'd have some
decency, seeing that his car killed the boss!"

I nodded sympathetically, slid a cigar across the desk, and
waited 'til it was burning in Soules' mouth before I asked:

"You said something about having a couple new hands to
break in. How come?"

"Yes. Mr. Newhouse fired two of our printers last week—
Fincher and Key. He found that they belonged to the I. W.
W., so he gave them their time."

"Any trouble with them, or anything against them except
that they were Wobblies?"

"No—they were pretty good workers."

"Any trouble with them after he fired them?" I asked.

"No real trouble, though they were pretty hot. They made
speeches all over the place before they left."

"Remember what day that was?"

"Wednesday of last week, I think. Yes, Wednesday, because I hired two new men on Thursday."

"How many men do you work?"

"Three, besides myself."

"Was Mr. Newhouse sick very often?"

"Not sick enough to stay away very often, though every

295

now and then his heart would go back on him, and he'd have to stay in bed for a week or ten days. He wasn't what you could call real well at any time. He never did anything but the office work—I run the shop."

"When was he taken sick this last time?"

"Mrs. Newhouse called up Tuesday morning and said he had another spell, and wouldn't be down for a few days. He came in yesterday—which was Thursday—for about ten minutes in the afternoon, and said he would be back on the job this morning. He was killed just after he left."

"How did he look—very sick?"

"Not so bad. He never looked well, of course, but I couldn't see much difference from usual yesterday. This last spell hadn't been as bad as most, I reckon—he was usually laid up for a week or more."

"Did he say where he was going when he left? The reason I ask is that, living out on Sacramento Street, he would naturally have taken a car at that street if he had been going home, whereas he was run down on Clay Street."

"He said he was going up to Portsmouth Square to sit in the sun for half an hour or so. He had been cooped up indoors for two or three days, he said, and he wanted some sunshine before he went back home."

"He had a piece of foreign money in his hand when he was hit. Know anything about it?"

"Yes. He got it here. One of our customers—a man named Van Pelt—came in to pay for some work we had done yesterday afternoon while the boss was here. When Van Pelt pulled out his wallet to pay his bill, this piece of Holland money—I don't know what you call it—was among the bills. I think he said it was worth something like thirty-eight dollars. Anyway, the boss took it, giving Van Pelt his change. The boss said he wanted to show the Holland money to his boys—and he could have it changed back into American money later."

"Who is this Van Pelt?"

"He's a Hollander—is planning to open a tobacco importing business here in a month or two. I don't know much about him outside of that."

"Where's his home, or office?"

"His office is on Bush Street, near Sansome."

"Did he know that Newhouse had been sick?"

"I don't think so. The boss didn't look much different from usual."

"What's this Van Pelt's full name?"

"Hendrik Van Pelt."

"What does he look like?"

Before Soules could answer, three evenly spaced buzzes sounded above the rattle and whirring of the presses in the back of the shop.

I slid the muzzle of my gun—I had been holding it in my lap for five minutes—far enough over the edge of the desk for Ben Soules to see it.

"Put both of your hands on top the desk," I said.

He put them there.

The press-room door was directly behind him, so that, facing him across the desk, I could look over his shoulder at it. His stocky body served to screen my gun from the view of whoever came through the door, in response to Soules' signal.

I didn't have long to wait.

Three men—black with ink—came to the door, and through it into the little office. They strolled in careless and casual, laughing and joking to one another.

But one of them licked his lips as he stepped through the door. Another's eyes showed white circles all around the irises. The third was the best actor—but he held his shoulders a trifle too stiffly to fit his otherwise careless carriage.

"Stop right there!" I barked at them when the last one was inside the office—and I brought my gun up where they could see it.

They stopped as if they had been mounted on the same pair of legs.

I kicked my chair back, and stood up.

I didn't like my position at all. The office was entirely too small for me. I had a gun, true enough, and whatever weapons may have been distributed among these other men were out of sight. But these four men were too close to me; and a gun isn't a thing of miracles. It's a mechanical contraption that is capable of just so much and no more.

If these men decided to jump me, I could down just one of them before the other three were upon me. I knew it, and they knew it.

"Put your hands up," I ordered, "and turn around!"

None of them moved to obey. One of the inked men grinned wickedly; Soules shook his head slowly; the other two stood and looked at me.

I was more or less stumped. You can't shoot a man just because he refuses to obey an order—even if he is a criminal. If they had turned around for me, I could have lined them up against the wall, and, being behind them, have held them safe while I used the telephone.

But that hadn't worked.

My next thought was to back across the office to the street door, keeping them covered, and then either stand in the door and yell for help, or take them into the street, where I could handle them. But I put that thought away as quickly as it came to me.

These four men were going to jump me—there was no doubt of that. All that was needed was a spark of any sort to explode them into action. They were standing stiff-legged and tense, waiting for some move on my part. If I took a step backward—the battle would be on.

We were close enough for any of the four to have reached out and touched me. One of them I could shoot before I was smothered—one out of four. That meant that each of them had only one chance out of four of being the victim—low enough odds for any but the most cowardly of men.

I grinned what was supposed to be a confident grin—because I was up against it hard—and reached for the telephone: I had to do something! Then I cursed myself! I had merely changed the signal for the onslaught. It would come now when I picked up the receiver.

But I couldn't back down again—that, too, would be a signal—I had to go through with it.

The perspiration trickled across my temples from under my hat as I drew the phone closer with my left hand.

The street door opened! An exclamation of surprise came from behind me.

I spoke rapidly, without taking my eyes from the four men in front of me.

"Quick! The phone! The police!"

With the arrival of this unknown person—one of New-house's customers, probably—I figured I had the edge again. Even if he took no active part beyond calling the police in, the enemy would have to split to take care of him—and that would give me a chance to pot at least two of them before I was knocked over. Two out of four—each of them had an even chance of being dropped—which *is* enough to give even a nervy man cause for thinking a bit before he jumps.

"Hurry" I urged the newcomer.

"Yes! Yes!" he said—and in the blurred sound of the "s" there was evidence of foreign birth.

Keyed up as I was, I didn't need any more warning than that.

I threw myself sidewise—a blind tumbling away from the spot where I stood. But I didn't move quite quickly enough.

The blow that came from behind didn't hit me fairly, but I got enough of it to fold up my legs as if the knees were hinged with paper—and I slammed into a heap on the floor. . . .

Something dark crashed toward me. I caught it with both hands. It may have been a foot kicking at my face. I wrung it as a washerwoman wrings a towel.

Down my spine ran jar after jar. Perhaps somebody was beating me over the head. I don't know. My head wasn't alive. The blow that had knocked me down had numbed me all over. My eyes were no good. Shadows swam to and fro in front of them—that was all. I struck, gouged, tore at the shadows. Sometimes I found nothing. Sometimes I found things that felt like parts of bodies. Then I would hammer at them, tear at them. My gun was gone.

My hearing was no better than my sight—or not so good. There wasn't a sound in the world. I moved in a silence that was more complete than any silence I had ever known. I was a ghost fighting ghosts.

I found presently that my feet were under me again, though some squirming thing was on my back, and kept me from standing upright. A hot, damp thing like a hand was across my face.

I put my teeth into it. I snapped my head back as far as it would go. Maybe it smashed into the face it was meant for. I don't know. Anyhow the squirming thing was no longer on my back.

Dimly I realized that I was being buffeted about by blows that I was too numb to feel. Ceaselessly, with head and shoulders and elbows and fists and knees and feet, I struck at the shadows that were around me. . . .

Suddenly I could see again—not clearly—but the shadows were taking on colors; and my ears came back a little, so that grunts and growls and curses and the impact of blows sounded in them. My straining gaze rested upon a brass cuspidor six inches or so in front of my eyes. I knew then that I was down on the floor again.

As I twisted about to hurl a foot into a soft body above me, something that was like a burn, but wasn't a burn, ran down one leg—a knife. The sting of it brought consciousness back into me with a rush.

I grabbed the brass cuspidor and used it to club a way to my feet—to club a clear space in front of me. Men were hurling themselves upon me. I swung the cuspidor high and flung it over their heads, through the frosted glass door into California Street.

Then we fought some more.

But you can't throw a brass cuspidor through a glass door into California Street between Montgomery and Kearny without attracting attention—it's too near the heart of daytime San Francisco. So presently—when I was on the floor again with six or eight hundred pounds of flesh hammering my face into the boards—we were pulled apart, and I was dug out of the bottom of the pile by a squad of policemen.

Big sandy-haired Coffee was one of them, but it took a lot of arguing to convince him that I was the Continental operative who had talked to him a little while before.

"Man! Man!" he said, when I finally convinced him. "Them lads sure—God! have worked you over! You got a face on you like a wet geranium!"

I didn't laugh. It wasn't funny.

I looked out of the one eye, which was working just now, at the five men lined up across the office—Soules, the three inky printers, and the man with the blurred "s," who had started the slaughter by tapping me on the back of the head.

He was a rather tall man of thirty or so, with a round ruddy face that wore a few bruises now. He had been, apparently, rather well-dressed in expensive black clothing, but he was torn and ragged now. I knew who he was without asking—Hendrik Van Pelt.

"Well, man, what's the answer?" Coffee was asking me.

By holding one side of my jaw firmly with one hand I found that I could talk without too much pain.

"This is the crowd that ran down Newhouse," I said, "and it wasn't an accident. I wouldn't mind having a few more of the details myself, but I was jumped before I got around to all of them. Newhouse had a hundred-florin note in his hand when he was run down, and he was walking in the direc-

300

tion of police headquarters—was only half a block away from the Hall of Justice.

"Soules tells me that Newhouse said he was going up to Portsmouth Square to sit in the sun. But Soules didn't seem to know that Newhouse was wearing a black eye—the one you told me you had investigated. If Soules didn't see the shiner, then it's a good bet that Soules didn't see Newhouse's face that day!

"Newhouse was walking from his printing shop toward police headquarters with a piece of foreign paper money in his hand—remember that!

"He had frequent spells of sickness, which, according to friend Soules, always before kept him at home for a week or ten days at a time. This time he was laid up for only two and a half days.

"Soules tells me that the shop is three days behind with its orders, and he says that's the first time in eight years they've ever been behind. He blames Newhouse's death—which only happened yesterday. Apparently, Newhouse's previous sick spells never delayed things—why should this last spell?

"Two printers were fired last week, and two new ones hired the very next day—pretty quick work. The car with which Newhouse was run down was taken from just around the corner, and was deserted within quick walking distance of the shop. It was left facing north, which is pretty good evidence that its occupants went south after they got out. Ordinary car thieves wouldn't have circled back in the direction from which they came.

"Here's my guess: This Van Pelt is a Dutchman, and he had some plates for phony hundred-florin notes. He hunted around until he found a printer who would go in with him. He found Soules, the foreman of a shop whose proprietor was now and then at home for a week or more at a time with a bad heart. One of the printers under Soules was willing to go in with them. Maybe the other two turned the offer down. Maybe Soules didn't ask them at all. Anyhow, they were discharged, and two friends of Soules were given their places.

"Our friends then got everything ready, and waited for Newhouse's heart to flop again. It did—Monday night. As soon as his wife called up next morning and said he was sick, these birds started running off their counterfeits. That's why they fell behind with their regular work. But this spell of Newhouse's was lighter than usual. He was up and moving around within two days, and yesterday afternoon he came down here for a few minutes.

"He must have walked in while all of our friends were extremely busy in some far corner. He must have spotted some of the phony money, immediately sized up the situation, grabbed one bill to show the police, and started out for police headquarters—no doubt thinking he hadn't been seen.

"They must have got a glimpse of him as he was leaving, however. Two of them followed him out. They couldn't, afoot, safely knock him over within a block or two of the Hall of Justice. But, turning the corner, they found Chrostwaite's car standing there with idling engine. That solved their getaway problem. They got in the car and went on after Newhouse. I suppose the original plan was to shoot him—but he crossed Clay Street with his eyes fastened upon the phony money in his hand. That gave them a golden chance. They piled the car into him. It was sure death, they knew—his bum heart would finish the job if the actual collision didn't kill him. Then they deserted the car and came back here.

"There are a lot of loose ends to be gathered in—but this pipe-dream I've just told you fits in with all the facts we know—and I'll bet a month's salary I'm not far off anywhere.

"There ought to be a three-day crop of Dutch notes cached somewhere! You people—"

I suppose I'd have gone on talking forever—in the giddy, head-swimming intoxication of utter exhaustion that filled me—if the big sandy-haired patrolman hadn't shut me off by putting a big hand across my mouth.

"Be quiet, man," he said, lifting me out of the chair, and spreading me flat on my back on the desk. "I'll have an ambulance here in a second for you."

The office was swirling around in front of my one open eye—the yellow ceiling swung down toward me, rose again, disappeared, came back in odd shapes. I turned my head to one side to avoid it, and my glance rested upon the white dial of a spinning clock.

Presently the dial came to rest, and I read it—four o'clock.

I remembered that Chrostwaite had broken up our conference in Vance Richmond's office at three, and I had started to work.

"One full hour!" I tried to tell Coffee before I went to sleep.

The police wound up the job while I was lying on my back in bed. In Van Pelt's office on Bush Street they found a great bale of hundred-florin notes. Van Pelt, they learned, had considerable reputation in Europe as a high-class counterfeiter. One of the printers came through, stating that Van Pelt and Soules were the two who followed Newhouse out of the shop, and killed him.

THE DEATH OF DON JUAN

BY ELLERY QUEEN

Ellery Queen is the pseudonym of Frederic Dannay (b. October 20, 1905) and Manfred B. Lee (b. January 11, 1905; d. April 3, 1971)—the Brooklyn-born cousins, whose first novel, *The Roman Hat Mystery,* featuring writer-detective Ellery Queen, helped bridge the two decades of the Golden Age in 1929. (Not until late 1936 did Dannay and Lee reveal the identities behind Ellery Queen and their other pseudonym, Barnaby Ross.) Ellery Queen has won five Edgars from the Mystery Writers of America and *The Adventures of Ellery Queen* won *TV Guide*'s award for best mystery show on television. Frederic Dannay is editor-in-chief of *Ellery Queen's Mystery Magazine,* now in its 37th year of publication.

ACT I. Scene 1.

AN EARLY ACCOUNT OF THE death of Don Juan Tenorio, 14th-century Spanish libertine—who, according to his valet, enjoyed the embraces of no fewer than 2,954 mistresses during his lifetime—relates that the great lover was murdered in a monastery by Franciscan monks enraged by his virility. For four hundred years poets and dramatists have passed up this ending to Don Juan's mighty career as too unimaginative. No such charge can be brought against *their* versions.

Don Juan, they tell us, planted the seeds of his own destruction when he harrowed the virtue of a certain noble young lady, daughter of the commander of Sevilla. While this sort of thing was no novelty to the famous gallant, it was to the young lady; and Don Juan found himself fighting a duel with her father, the commander, whom he killed.

Here the poetic imagination soars. Don Juan visits the tomb of the late victim of his sword. A marble statue of the grandee decorates the tomb. Don Juan invites the statue to a feast, an inexplicable gesture under the circumstances. Having failed in the flesh, the ensculptured nobleman leaps at this second chance to avenge his daughter's ruptured honor. The marble guest shows up at the feast, grasps the roué in his stony clutch, and drags him off to hell. Curtain.

This Don Juan changeling counts among its affectionate foster-parents Molière, Mozart's librettist Da Ponte, Dumas *père,* Balzac, Byron, and Shaw. Now to the roster must be added the modest name of Ellery Queen, who has fathered his own. According to Ellery, Don Juan was really murdered in a New England town named Wrightsville, and this is how it came about.

From the days of William S. Hart and Wallace Reid, Wrightsville's dramatic appetite was catered to by the Bijou Theater in High Village. When in the course of human events the movies' fat years turned lean, the Bijou's owner bought up the old scrap-iron dump on Route 478 and on the site built Wright County's first alfresco movie theater, a drive-in that supplanted Pine Grove in the Junction as the favorite smooching place of the young in heart.

This left the two-by-fours nailed over the doors of the

abandoned Bijou; and the chairman of the Wrightsville Realty Board, whose office faced the empty building from the other side of Lower Main, vowed at a Board lunch over his fourth old-fashioned that one dark night he was going to sneak over to that eyesore on the fair face of High Village and blow the damn thing up, he was so sick of looking at it.

When, suddenly, Stanley Bluefield bought it.

Stanley Bluefield was a rare specimen in the Wrightsville zoo. Where the young of the first families grew up to work with their money, Stanley played with it. Seven generations of Bluefields had labored and schemed so that Stanley's life might be one grand game.

As Stanley often said, his vocation was hobbies. He collected such unexpected things as chastity belts, Minié balls, and shrunken heads. He financed one expedition to prove the historicity of Atlantis and another to unearth the bones of Homer. He flitted from Yoga to Zen to voodoo, and then came back to the Congregational church. And the old Bluefield mansion on the Hill was usually infested with freeloaders no one in Wrightsville had ever laid eyes on—"my people collection," he called them.

Stanley Bluefield looked like a rabbit about to drop its first litter. But there was a sweet, stubborn innocence in the portly little bachelor that some weedy souls of the region found appealing.

Stanley bought the Bijou because he discovered The Theater. To prepare himself, he lived for two years in New York studying drama, after which he financed a play and watched the professionals spend his money in a lost but educational cause. He hurried home to organize an amateur company.

"No, indeed, no red barns surrounded by hollyhocks for me," he told the *Wrightsville Record* reporter. "My plan is to establish a permanent repertory theater, a year-round project to be staffed by local talent."

"This area hasn't supported professional companies in years, Mr. Bluefield," the reporter said. "What makes you think it will support an amateur one?"

One of the little man's pinkish eyes winked. "You wait and see."

Stanley's secret weapon was Joan Truslow. Joanie was what the boys at the Lions and the Red Men luncheons called "a real stacked little gopher," with natural ash-blonde hair and enormous spring-violet eyes. She had been majoring in drama at Merrimac U. when the arthritis got her father and 'Aphas was forced to resign as town clerk. Joan had had to come home and take a job as receptionist at The Eternal Rest Mortuary on Upper Whistling. She was the first to answer Stanley's call, and her audition awed him.

"*Wonderful,*" he had confided to Roger Fowler. "That girl will make us all *proud.*"

Rodge was not comforted. A chemical engineer, he had used his cut of Great-uncle Fowler's pie to buy one of the blackened brick plants standing idle along the Willow River in Low Village and convert it to Fowler Chemicals, Inc. His interest in Stanley Bluefield's Playhouse was strictly hormonal; he had been chasing Joan Truslow since their high-school days.

To keep an eye on her, young Fowler had offered his services to Stanley, who was not one to look a gift horse under the crupper. The Playhouse needed a technician-in-charge to be responsible for carpentry, props, lights, and other dreary indispensables. So long as the backstage crew functioned, Stanley did not care how many opportunities Roger seized to corner the stage-struck Miss Truslow and, *sotto voce, con amore,* try to sell her a bill of household goods.

Stanley did the Bijou over, inside and out, and renamed it The Playhouse. It cost him a fortune, and of course Emmeline DuPré's was the first voice of doom. (Miss DuPré, known to the cruder element as the Town Crier, taught Dancing and Dramatics to the children of the already *haut monde* of Wrightsville.)

"Stanley will never see a penny of his unearned lucre," Miss DuPré announced.

For once the Town Crier seemed to cry true. The Playhouse was a resounding flop, Joanie Truslow notwithstanding. Stanley tried Shaw, Kaufman and Hart, Tennessee Williams, even (these were conceived in desperation and born calamities) Ionesco and Anouilh; comedy, farce, melodrama, tragedy; the square and the off-beat. They continued to play to dwindling houses.

"Of course, we're not very *good* yet," Stanley reflected aloud after a lethal week.

"Joan's colossal, and you know it," Rodge Fowler said in spite of himself.

"Thank you, sir." Joan's dimple drove him crazy. "I

thought you were against careers for females."

"Who's against careers for females? I'm just against a career for you," Roger said, hating himself for driving the dimple to cover. "Look, Stan, how much more of your ancestral dough are you prepared to drop into this cultural tomb we call home?"

Stanley said in his precise, immovable way, "I am *not* giving up yet, Roger."

A *Record* editorial said: "Is local taste so low that our favorite amusements must be TV Westerns and dramatized deodorant commercials, and movies that give our children the willies? At a time when Wrightsville is reflecting the nation-wide jump in juvenile delinquency, alcoholism, dope addiction, gambling, and what have you, the community should be supporting Mr. Bluefield's efforts to bring us worthwhile dramatic fare. Why not attend The Playhouse regularly, and bring along your teen-agers?"

The empty seats kept spreading like a rash.

A letter to the *Record* signed Cassandra, in a literary style indistinguishable from Emmeline DuPré's, suggested that the Wrightsville Playhouse be renamed The Haunted Playhouse.

When the town's snickers reached the Hill, Stanley's pink eyes turned a murderous red. Very few people in Wrightsville were aware of the paper thinness of Stanley Bluefield's skin.

He flung himself onto the Viking throne in his catchall study, and he thought and he thought.

All at once the name of Archer Dullman flew into his head.

Ten minutes later Wrightsville's patron of the performing arts was driving lickety-hop for the airport and the next plane connection to New York.

ACT I. Scene 2.

Ellery checked in at the Hollis, showered and changed, cased the lobby, toured the Square (which was round), and returned to the hotel without having seen a single familiar face.

He was waiting for the maitre d' (also new to him) in a queue of strangers at the entrance to the main dining room, thinking that time was being its usual unkind self, when a voice behind him said, "Mr. Queen, I presume?"

"Roger!" Ellery wrung young Fowler's hand like Dr. Livingstone at Ujiji. The truth was, he had met Rodge Fowler less than half a dozen times during his various visits to Wrightsville. "How are you? What's happened to this town?"

"I'm fine, and it's still here with certain modifications," Roger said, blowing on his hand. "What brings you this-a-way?"

"I'm bound for the Mahoganies—vacation. I hear you're Wrightsville's latest outbreak of industrial genius."

"That's what they tell me, but who told you?"

"I'm a *Record* mail-subscriber from 'way back. How come you've joined a drama group, Rodge? I thought you got your kicks in a chem lab."

"Love," Roger said hollowly. "Or whatever they're calling it these days."

"Of course. Joan Truslow. But isn't the company folding? That ought to drop Joanie back into your lap."

Roger looked glum. *"The Death of Don Juan."*

"That old stand of corn? Even Wrightsville—"

"You're not getting the message, man. Starring Mark Manson. Complete with doublet, hose, and codpiece. We open tomorrow night."

"Manson." Ellery stared. "Who dug him up?"

"Stanley Bluefield, via some Times Square undertaker named Archer Dullman. Manson's a pretty lively corpse, Ellery. We're sold out for the run."

"So the old boy still packs them in in Squedunk," Ellery said admiringly. *"The Death of Don Juan . . .* This I've got to see."

"There's Stanley at that corner table, with Manson and Dullman. I'm meeting them for dinner. Why not join us?"

Ellery had forgotten how much like a happy rabbit Stanley Bluefield looked. "I'm *delighted* you're here for the opening," Stanley cried. "You will be, Ellery, won't you?"

"If I have to hang from a rafter. I haven't had the pleasure of attending one of Mr. Manson's performances in—" Ellery had been about to say "in a great many years," but he changed it to "in some time."

"How are things at the Embassy, Mr. Green?" the actor asked sadly, tilting his cocktail glass, finding it empty, running his forefinger around the inside of the glass, and licking the finger. "You should have seen me with Booth, sir.

John Wilkes, that is. Those were the days. *Garçonne,* may I trouble you for an encore?"

The wavering finger pushed the empty glass into alignment with nine others, whereupon Manson smiled at Ellery and fell asleep. Head thrown back, he resembled a mummy; his gentle, fine-boned face was overlaid with a mesh of wrinkles.

The waitress took their orders. Manson woke up, courteously ordered *Chaud-Froid de Cailles en Belle Vue,* and fell asleep again.

"What's that?" the waitress demanded.

"Never mind, honey. Bring him a rare T-bone."

Stanley looked peevish. "I do hope—"

"Don't worry, Bluefield. He never misses a curtain."

Ellery turned, surprised. The speaker was the man introduced to him as Archer Dullman. He had immediately forgotten Dullman was there. He now saw why. Dullman was not large and not small, neither fat nor thin, ruddy nor pale. Hair, eyes, voice were neutral. It was hard to imagine him excited, angry, amorous, or drunk. Ellery paid close attention to him after that.

"Are you Mr. Manson's manager, Mr. Dullman?"

"It's a buck."

Even so, it was some time before he realized that Dullman had not actually answered his question.

Ellery buttered a roll. "By the way, isn't it an Actors' Equity rule that its members may not perform with amateurs?"

It was Stanley who answered; in rather a hurry, Ellery thought. "Oh, but you can almost always get Equity's permission in special cases. Where no Equity company is playing the area, and provided the amateur group initiates the request, deposits the full amount of the member's salary with them, and so forth. Ah, the soup!" He greeted the return of their waitress with manifest relief. "Best chowder in town. Right, Minnie?"

Ellery wondered what was bugging the little man. Then he remembered.

The "Archer" had fooled him. Around Broadway, Dullman was always called "The Dull Man." It was a typical Broadway quip; Dullman was supposed to be sharper than a columnist's tooth. If Stanley Bluefield had allowed himself to be sucked into a typical Dullman deal . . .

"They've been calling us The Haunted Playhouse and

laughing their heads off," Stanley was chortling. "Who's laughing now?"

"Not me," Rodge Fowler growled. "That scene on the couch between Manson and Joan in the first act is an absolute disgrace."

"How would you expect Don Juan to act on a couch?" Dullman asked with a smile.

"You didn't have to direct it that way, Dullman!"

"Oh, you're directing?" Ellery murmured. But nobody heard him.

"Think of the dear old ladies, Fowler."

"I'm thinking of Joan!"

"Now, Rodge," Stanley said.

Manson chose that moment to wake up. He peered around the crowded dining room and staggered to his feet. His hairpiece had come loose and slipped to one side, exposing a hemisphere of dead-white scalp. He stood there like some aged Caesar in his cups, bowing to his people.

"My dear, dear friends," the actor said; and then, with simple confidence, he slid into Dullman's arms.

Stanley and Roger were half out of their chairs. But Ellery was already supporting the actor's other side.

"Manson can walk, Dullman. Just give him some support."

Between them they dragged Manson, graciously smiling, from the dining room. The lobby seethed with people attending a Ladies' Aid ball; a great many were waiting for the elevators.

"We can't maneuver him through that mob, Dullman. What floor is he on?"

"Second."

"Then let's walk him up. Manson, lift your feet. That's it. You're doing nobly."

Ellery and Dullman hustled him up the staircase toward the mezzanine. Dullman was crooning in the actor's ear, "No more martinis, huh, Mark? So tomorrow night you can step out on that stage in those sexy tights of yours and give these Yokelsville ladies a thrill. You're the great Mark Manson, remember?" Manson made small pleased noises.

Stanley and Roger came running up behind them.

"How is he?" Stanley panted.

"Beginning to feel pain, I think," Ellery said. "How about it, Manson?"

"My dear sir," the actor said indulgently. "Anyone would

311

think I am intoxicated. Really, this is undignified and un-necessary."

He achieved the mezzanine landing and paused there to recuperate. Ellery glanced at Dullman, and Dullman nodded. They released him.

Ellery grabbed in vain. *"Catch him!"*

But both Stanley and Roger stood there, stunned. Manson, still smiling, toppled backward between them.

Fascinated, they watched the star of *The Death of Don Juan* bounce his way step after step down the long marble staircase until he landed on the lobby floor and lay still.

ACT I. Scene 3.

They went straight from the hospital to Dullman's room at the Hollis. Dullman sat down at the telephone.

"Long distance? New York City. I want to speak to Phil Stone, theatrical agent, Forty-fourth Street. I'll hold on."

"Stone." Stanley was hopping about the room. "I don't know him, Archer."

"So you don't know him," the New Yorker grunted. "Phil? Arch Dullman."

"So what do you want?" Ellery could hear Stone's bass rasp distinctly.

"Philly boy," Dullman said.

"Please, Archie, no routines. It's been an itch of a day, and I was just going home. What's on your mind?"

"Phil, I'm on a spot up here—"

"Up where?"

"Wrightsville. New England."

"Never heard. Can't be a show town. What are you, in a new racket?"

"There's a stock company here just getting started. I made a deal for Mark Manson with this producer to do *The Death of Don Juan*."

"What producer?"

"Stanley Bluefield. Opening's tomorrow night. Tonight Manson falls down a staircase in the hotel and breaks the wrist and a couple fingers on his right hand, besides cracking two ribs."

"Old lushes never die. That's all?"

"It's plenty. There might even be concussion. They're

keeping him in the hospital twenty-four hours just in case."

"So what?" The agent sounded remote.

"The thing is, they've taped his ribs and put a cast on his forearm and hand. He won't be able to work for weeks." A drop of perspiration coursed down Dullman's nose and landed on the butt of his cigar. "Phil—how about Foster Benedict?"

Stone's guffaw rattled the telephone.

"Foster Benedict?" Stanley Bluefield looked astounded. He leaped to Dullman's free ear. "You get him, Archer!"

But Ellery was watching Rodge Fowler. At the sound of Benedict's name Roger had gripped the arms of his chair as if a nerve had been jabbed.

Dullman paid no attention to Stanley. "Well, you hyena?"

Stone's voice said dryly, "Might I be so stupid as to ask if this Bluefield and his company are pros?"

Arch Dullman spat his cigar butt, a thing of shining shreds, onto the carpet. "It's an amateur group."

"Look, crook," the agent boomed. "This backwoods Sam Harris wants a replacement for Manson, he's got to contact me, not you. He's got to satisfy Equity, not you. You still there, Archie?"

"I'm still here," Dullman sighed. "Here's Bluefield."

Stanley was at the phone in a flash. Dullman picked up the butt and put it back in his mouth. He remained near the phone.

"Stanley Bluefield here," Stanley said nervously. "Do I understand, Mr. Stone, that Foster Benedict is available for a two-week engagement in *The Death of Don Juan,* to start tomorrow night?"

"Mr. Benedict's resting between engagements. I don't know if I could talk him into going right back to work."

"How well does he know the part?"

"Foster's done that turkey so many times he quacks. That's another reason it might not interest him. He's sick of it."

"How much," Stanley asked, not without humor, "will it take to cure him?"

Stone said carelessly, "Fifteen hundred a week might do it."

"Give me that phone," Dullman said. "Who do you think you're dealing with, Phil? Benedict's washed up in Hollywood, dead on Broadway, and TV's had a bellyful of him. I happen to know he's flat on his tokus. I wouldn't let Mr. Bluefield touch him with a skunk pole if Manson's accident hadn't left us over this barrel. Seven fifty, Phil, take it or leave it. You taking or leaving?"

After ten seconds the agent said, "I'll call you back." Dullman gave him the numbers of the Hollis phone and his extension and hung up.

"He'll take." Dullman lay down on the bed and stared at the ceiling.

Stanley began to hop around the room again.

"You're asking for it," Roger Fowler said tightly. "Benedict's a bad actor, Stan. And I'm not referring to his professional competence."

"*Please,* Roger," the little man said testily. "Don't I have enough on my mind?"

Twelve minutes later the telephone rang. From the bed Dullman said, "You can take it."

"Yes?" Stanley cried.

"We're taking," Stone's bass said. "But you understand, Mr. Bluefield, you got to clear this deal with Equity yourself before we lift a hoof."

"Yes, yes. First thing in the morning."

"I'll be waiting for Equity's go-ahead. Soon as I get it, Benedict's on his way."

"Hold it," Dullman said.

"Hold it," Stanley said.

Dullman got wearily off the bed, whispered something, and returned to the bed.

Stanley pursed his lips. "According to my information, Mr. Stone, Benedict might start out tomorrow for Wrightsville and wind up in a Montreal hotel room with some girl he picked up en route. Can you guarantee delivery?"

"What's that sucker Dullman want, my blood? I'll put him on the plane. That's the best I can do."

Stanley glanced anxiously at Dullman. Dullman shrugged.

"Well, all right, but please impress on Mr. Benedict . . ."

"Yeah, yeah."

"He'll have to change planes in Boston, by the way. There's no through flight. I'll have a car waiting at Wrightsville Airport. If he makes an early enough connection we ought to be able to get in a quick run-through."

"That's up to Equity. Like I said, he ain't moving a muscle—"

"Leave Equity to me. You just get Benedict here."

"Up in his lines," Dullman said.

314

"Up in his lines," Stanley said, and he hung up. "Archer, that was an inspiration!" Dullman grunted. "Roger, would you run across the Square and ask the *Record* to hold the press? I'll phone them the new copy for tomorrow's ad in a few minutes."

"You're dead set on going ahead with this?" Roger said, not moving.

"Now, Rodge," Stanley said.

Dullman began to snore.

Ellery thought the whole performance extraordinary.

ACT I. Scene 4.

Ellery made his way around the Square and into Lower Main under a filthy sky.

It had been an exasperating day for Stanley Bluefield. The little man had been on the long distance phone with Equity since early morning. By the time the details were straightened out to Equity's satisfaction, and Foster Benedict was airborne to Boston, the actor was on a schedule so tight that he could not hope to set down in Wrightsville before 7:55 P.M. This would give Benedict barely enough time to make up, get into costume, and dash onstage for the 8:30 curtain.

Ellery walked into the lobby of the rejuvenated Bijou, pushed through one of the new black patent-leatherette doors, and entered Stanley Bluefield's Playhouse.

The elegantly done-over interior lay under a heavy hush. The cast, already made up and in costume, were sitting about the nakedly lit first-act set either sipping from coffee containers that might have been poisoned or staring into the gloom of the theater in emotional rapport. A pretty blonde girl he recognized as Joan Truslow was stretched out tensely on the set couch where, Ellery surmised, Don Juan Benedict was shortly to seduce her in the service of art. Roger Fowler, in coveralls, was stroking her temples.

Ellery slipped down the last aisle on his right and through the stage door. He found himself in a cramped triangle of space, the stage to his left. To his right a single door displayed a painted star and a placard hastily lettered *MR. BENEDICT*. A narrow iron ladder led to a tiny railed landing above and to another dressing room.

Curious, Ellery opened the starred door and looked in. Stanley had outdone himself here. Brilliant lighting switched on in the windowless room at the opening of the door. Air conditioning hummed softly. The driftwood-paneled walls were hung with theatrical prints. Costumes lay thrown about and the handsome tri-mirrored dressing table was a clutter of wigs, hand props, and pots and boxes of theatrical make-up, evidently as Manson had left them before his accident.

Impressed, Ellery backed out. He edged around an open metal chest marked *Tools* and made his way behind the upstage flat to the other side of the theater. Here there was ample space for the property room, the stage entrance, the lighting board, and a spiral of iron steps leading up to half a dozen additional dressing rooms. Beneath them, at stage level, a door announced *Mr. Bluefield. Keep Out.*

Ellery knocked.

Stanley's voice screamed, "I said *nobody!*"

"It's Ellery Queen."

"Oh. Come in."

The office was a little symphony in stainless steel. Stanley sat at his desk, left elbow anchored to the blotter, left fist supporting his cheek, eyes fixed on the telephone. All Ellery could think of was Napoleon after the Battle of Waterloo contemplating what might have been.

Arch Dullman stood at the one window, chewing on a dead cigar. He did not turn around.

Ellery dropped into a chair. "Storm trouble?"

The bunny-nose twitched. "Benedict phoned from the airfield in Boston. All planes grounded."

The window lit up as if an atom bomb had gone off. Dullman jumped back and Stanley shot to his feet. A crash jarred the theatrical photographs on the walls out of alignment. Immediately the heavens opened and the alley below the window became a river.

"This whole damn production is jinxed," Dullman said, glancing at his watch. "They'll be starting to come in soon, Bluefield. We'll have to postpone."

"And give them another chance to laugh at me?" The little Bluefield jaw enlarged. "We're holding that curtain."

"How long do you think we can hold it? Benedict's plane mightn't be able to take off for hours."

"The storm is traveling north-westward, Archer. Boston should clear any minute. It's only a half-hour's flight."

Dullman went out. Ellery heard him order the house lights switched on and the curtain closed. He did not come back.

The phone came to life at 8:25. Stanley pounced on it. "What did I tell you? He's taking off!"

Foster Benedict got to the The Playhouse at eighteen minutes past nine. The rain had stopped, but the alley leading to the stage entrance was dotted with puddles and the actor had to hop and sidestep to avoid them. From his scowl, he took the puddles as a personal affront. Stanley and Dullman hopped and sidestepped along with him, both talking at once.

The company waiting expectantly in the stage entrance pressed back as Benedict approached. He strode past them without a glance, leaving an aroma of whiskey and eau de cologne behind him. If he was drunk, Ellery could detect no evidence of it.

Rodge Fowler was stern-jawed. And Joan Truslow, Ellery noticed, looked as if she had just been struck in the face.

Foster Benedict glanced about. "You—Mr. Bluefish, is it? Where's my dressing room?"

"At the other side of the stage, Mr. Benedict," Stanley puffed. "But there's no time—"

"They've been sitting out there for over an hour," Dullman said. The booing and stamping of the audience had been audible in the alley.

"Ah." The actor seated himself in the stage doorman's chair. "The voice of Wrightsburg."

"Wrights*ville*," Stanley said. "Mr. Benedict, really—"

"And these, I gather," Benedict said, inspecting the silent cast, "are the so-called actors in this misbegotten exercise in theatrical folly?"

"Mr. Benedict," Stanley said again, *"please!"*

Ellery had not seen Benedict for a long time. The face that had once been called the handsomest in the American theater looked like overhandled dough. Sacs bulged under the malicious eyes. The once taut throat was beginning to string. Only the rich and supple voice was the same.

"The little lady there," the actor said, his stare settling on Joan, an orchid in the vegetable patch. What does she play, Dullman? The heroine, I hope."

"Yes, yes," Dullman said. "But there's no time for introductions or anything, Benedict. You'll have to go on as you are for the first act—"

"My make-up box, Phil." Benedict extended his arm and

317

snapped his fingers, his eyes still on Joan. Her face was chalky. Ellery glanced at Roger's hands. They were fists.

"Phil Stone isn't here," Dullman said. "Remember?"

"Oh, hell, I forgot my make-up. But does it really matter?"

"There's no time to make up, either! Manson's stuff is still in the star dressing room and you can use his when you dress between acts. Look, are you going on or aren't you?"

"Mr. Benedict." Stanley was trembling. "I give you precisely thirty seconds to get out on that stage and take your position for the curtain. Or I prefer charges to Equity."

The actor rose, smiling. "If I recall the stage business, dear heart, and believe me I do," he said to Joan, "we'll have an enchanting opportunity to become better acquainted during the first act. Then perhaps a little champagne supper after the performance? All *right*, Bluefish!" he said crossly. "Just as I am, eh?" He shrugged. "Well, I've played the idiotic role every other way. It may be amusing at that."

He stalked onstage.

"Places!" Dullman bellowed. Joan drifted away like a ghost in shock. The rest of the cast scurried. "Fowler, Fowler?"

Roger came to life.

"Where's that lights man of yours? Get with it, will you?" As Roger walked away, Dullman froze. "Is that Benedict out there making a *speech?*"

"In the too, too solid flesh," Ellery said with awe, peeping from the wings. Benedict had stepped out on the apron and he was explaining with comical gestures and facial contortions why "this distinguished Wrongsville audience" was about to see the great Foster Benedict perform Act One of *The Death of Don Juan*—"the biggest egg ever laid by a turkey"—in street clothes and *sans* make-up. The audience was beginning to titter and clap.

Ellery turned at a gurgle behind him. Stanley's nose was twitching again.

"What is he *doing?* Who does he think he *is?*"

"Barrymore in *My Dear Children*, I guess." Dullman was chewing away on his cigar. He seemed fascinated.

They could only watch helplessly while Benedict played the buffoon. His exit was a triumph of extemporization. He bowed gravely, assumed a ballet stance, and then, like Nijinsky in *The Spectre of the Rose*, he took off in a mighty leap for the wings.

318

ACT I. Scene 5.

Ellery, jammed in with Stanley Bluefield among the stand-ees at the rear of the theater, watched the first act in total disbelief.

Benedict deliberately paraphrased speech after speech. The bewildered amateurs waiting for their cues forgot their lines. Then he would throw the correct cue, winking over the footlights. He capered, struck attitudes, invented business, addressed broad asides to the hilarious audience. He transformed the old melodrama into a slapstick farce.

Ellery glanced down at Stanley. What he saw made him murmur hastily, "He's doing far more damage to himself than to you."

But Stanley said, "It's me they're howling at," in a pink-eyed fury, and he groped his way through the lobby doors and disappeared.

The seduction scene was an interminable embarrassment. Once during the scene, in sheer self-defense, Joan did something that made Benedict yelp. But he immediately tossed an ad lib to the audience that Ellery did not catch, and in the ensuing shriek of laughter returned to the attack.

At the scene's conclusion Joan stumbled off the stage like a sleepwalker.

Ellery found that he was grinding his teeth.

The curtain came down at last. Ushers opened the fire exit doors at both sides of the theater. People, wiping their eyes, pushed into the alleys. Ellery wriggled through the lobby to the street and lit a bitter-tasting cigarette. Long after the warning buzzer sounded, he lingered on the sidewalk.

Finally, he went back in.

The house lights were still on. Surprised, Ellery glanced at his watch. Probably Benedict needed extra time to get into costume and make up for the second act. Or perhaps—the thought pleased him—Roger had punched him in the nose.

The house lights remained on. The audience began to shuffle, murmur, cough.

Ellery edged through the standees to the extreme left aisle and made for the stage door. It was deathly quiet backstage.

Stanley Bluefield's door was open, and Arch Dullman was stamping up and down the office in a cloud of angry smoke. He seized Ellery.

"Seen Bluefield anywhere?"

319

"No," Ellery said. "What's wrong?"

"I don't give a damn who Benedict thinks he is," Dullman said. "Even a sucker like Bluefield deserves a better shake. First that moldy hunk of ham turns the first act into a low-comedy vaudeville bit, now he won't answer his call! Queen, do me a favor and get him out of there."

"Why me?"

"I don't trust myself. What's more, you tell him for me that if he doesn't play the rest of this show straight I'll personally bust that balloon he calls a head!"

Ellery's built-in alarm was jangling for all it was worth. "You'd better come with me."

They hurried behind the upstage flat to the other side of the theater. Ellery rapped on the starred door. He rapped again. "Mr. Benedict?"

There was no answer.

"Mr. Benedict, you're holding up the curtain."

Silence.

"Benedict?"

Ellery opened the door.

Foster Benedict, his back to the door, was in the chair at the dressing table, half lying among the wigs and make-up boxes.

He was partly dressed in a Don Juan costume. The shirt was of flowing white silk and just below the left shoulder blade, from the apex of a wet red ragged stain, the handle of a knife protruded.

ACT II. Scene 1.

"This character is clean off his chump," Dullman said, jamming a fresh cigar between his teeth. "Imagine playing around with the trick knife and the goo at a time like this. How about acting your age, Benedict? In fact, how about acting?" He brushed past Ellery. "Come on, snap out of it."

"Don't touch him," Ellery said.

Dullman stared at him. "You're kidding."

"No."

Dullman's mouth opened and the cigar fell out. He stooped and fumbled for it.

Ellery leaned over the dressing table, keeping his hands to himself. The skin was a mud-yellow and the lips were already cyanotic. Benedict's eyes were open. As Ellery's face came within their focus they fluttered and rolled.

He saw now that the stain was spreading.

"Bluefield," Dullman said. "My God, where's Bluefield? I've got to find Bluefield."

"Never mind Bluefield. I saw a doctor I know in the audience—Dr. Farnham. Hurry, Dullman."

Dullman turned blindly to the doorway. It was blocked by the cast and the stagehands. None of them appeared to understand what had happened. Joan Truslow had her hand to her mouth childishly, looking at the blood and the knife. As Dullman broke through he collided with Roger Fowler, coming fast.

"What's going on? Where's Joan?"

"Out of my way, damn you," Dullman said. He stumbled toward the stage.

Ellery shut the door and went quickly back to the dressing table. "Benedict, can you talk?"

The lips trembled a little. The jaws opened and closed and opened again, and a thick sound came out. It was just a sound, meaningless.

"Who knifed you?"

The jaws moved again. They were like the jaws of a fish newly yanked from the water. This time not even the thick sound came out.

"Benedict, do you hear me?" The eyes remained fixed. "If you understand what I'm saying, blink."

The eyelids came down and went up.

"Rest a moment. You're going to be all right." You're going to be dead, Ellery thought. Where the devil was Dr. Farnham? He won't be able to touch the knife, he thought.

The door burst open. Dr. Conklin Farnham hurried in. Dullman ran in after him and shut the door and leaned against it, breathing hard.

"Hello, Conk," Ellery said. "All I want from him is a name."

Dr. Farnham glanced at the knife wound and his mouth thinned out. He took Benedict's dangling arm without raising it and placed his fingertips on the artery. Then he felt the artery in the temple, examined the staring eyes.

"Call an ambulance."

"And the police," Ellery said.

Arch Dullman opened the door once more. The cast and

321

the stagehands were still standing outside, all except Joan and Roger. Dullman said something to someone and shut the door again.

"Can't you at least stop the bleeding, Conk?"

"It's pretty much stopped by itself."

And Ellery saw that the stain was no longer spreading. "I've got to talk to him. Is it all right?"

The doctor nodded. His lips formed the words, *Any minute now.*

"Benedict," Ellery said. "Use the eye signal again. Do you still hear me?"

Benedict blinked.

"Listen. You were sitting here making up. Someone opened your door and crossed the room. You could see who it was in the mirror. Who was it came at you with the knife?"

The bluing lips parted. The tongue fluttered; its sound was like a small bird's wings. Finally a grudging gurgle emerged. Dr. Farnham was feeling for the pulse again.

"He's going, Ellery." This time he said the words aloud.

"You're dying, man," Ellery cried. *"Who knifed you?"*

The struggle was an admirable thing. He was really trying to communicate. But then over the eyes slipped a substance through which they looked far and away. Without warning the dying man raised his head a full inch from the dressing table, and he held it there quite steadily. He made the fish mouth again.

But from it now, in a confiding whisper, came two words.

Then the head fell back to the table with a noise like wood. The actor seemed to clear his throat. His body stiffened in some last instinctive stubbornness and his breath emptied long and gently and he was altogether empty.

"He's dead," Dr. Farnham said after a moment.

Dullman said in a queer voice, "What did he say?"

"He's dead," Ellery said.

"I mean *him.* I didn't hear what he said from here."

"You heard him, Conk."

"Yes," the doctor said. " 'The heroine.' "

"That's what he said." Ellery turned away. He felt as empty as Benedict looked.

"The heroine." Dullman laughed. "Get what you wanted, Queen? Feel like a big man now?"

"He didn't know her name," Ellery said, as if this explained something important.

"I don't understand," Dr. Farnham said.

"Benedict arrived so late tonight there wasn't time for introductions. He could only identify her by her role in the play. The heroine."

Ellery turned away.

"But I took Joan's appendix out when she was fifteen," Dr. Farnham muttered. "My father delivered her."

Someone rapped on the door. Dullman opened it.

"I'm told something's happened to Mr. Benedict—"

"Well, look who's here," Dullman said. "Come on in, Bluefield."

ACT II. Scene 2.

Stanley Bluefield's shoes, the cuffs of his trousers, were soaked.

"I've been walking and walking. You see, I couldn't stand what he was doing to the play. I felt that if I stayed one minute longer . . ."

"Stanley," Ellery said.

"And how dreadful," Stanley went on, still looking at the occupied chair. "I mean, he doesn't look human any more, does he? I've never seen this kind of death."

"Stanley—"

"But he brought it on himself, wouldn't you say? You can't go about humiliating people that way. People who've never done you any harm. Who killed him?"

Ellery swung the little man around. "You'll have to talk to the audience, Stanley. I think you'd better use the word 'accident.' And tell your ushers privately not to allow anyone to leave the theater until the police get here."

"Who killed him?"

"Will you do that?"

"Yes, of course," Stanley said. He squished out, leaving a damp trail.

Ellery wandered back to the dressing table. All at once he stooped for a closer look at the knife handle.

Dr. Farnham stirred.

"It's a fact they're taking their sweet time," Dullman said. "You want out, Doctor?"

"I left my wife in the audience," Farnham said stiffly.

"Don't worry about Molly, Conk." Ellery dug a small

323

leather case out of his pocket. "And you're my corroborating witness to Benedict's statement."

"That's right," Dullman said. "I didn't hear a thing. I don't have the stomach that goes with ears like yours."

The leather case produced a powerful little lens, and through it Ellery examined the handle of the knife on both sides.

"What," Dullman jeered, "no deerstalker hat?"

Ellery ignored him. The heavy haft had been recently wound in black plastic friction tape. An eighth of an inch from the edge, the tape showed a straight line of thin, ir- regular indentations some five-eighths of an inch long. In a corresponding position on the underside there was a line of indentations similar in character and length.

Ellery stowed away his lens. "By the way, Dullman, have you seen this knife before?"

"Any particular reason why I should tell you?"

"Any particular reason why you shouldn't?"

"It's not mine. I don't know whose it is."

"But you have seen it before." When Dullman did not answer, Ellery added, "Believe me, I know how much you wish you were out of this." The way Dullman's glance shifted made Ellery smile faintly. "But you can't wish away Bene- dict's murder, and in any case you'll have to submit to police questioning. Where have you seen this knife before?"

Dullman said reluctantly, "I don't even know if it's the same one."

"Granted. But where did you see one like it?"

"In the metal tool chest just outside. It was a big-bladed knife with a black-taped handle. From the look of this one I'd say they're the same—but I can't swear to it."

"When did you see it last?"

"I didn't see it 'last.' I saw it once. It was after the first act curtain. Benedict had weakened one of the legs of the set couch with his damfool gymnastics during that scene with the Truslow girl, and even the stage crew was demoral- ized. So I decided to fix the leg myself. I went for tools, and that's when I spotted the knife. It was lying on the top tray of the chest in plain sight."

"Did you notice any peculiar-looking indentations in the tape?"

"Indentations?"

"Impressions. Come here, Dullman. But don't touch it."

Dullman looked and shook his head. "I didn't see anything like that. I'm sure I'd have noticed. I remember thinking how shiny and new-looking the tape was."

"How soon after the curtain came down was this?"

"Was what?"

"When you saw the knife in the chest."

"Right after. Benedict was just coming offstage. He went into the dressing room here while I was poking around in the tools."

"He was alone?"

"He was alone."

"Did you talk to him?"

Dullman examined the pulpy end of his cigar. "You might say he talked to me."

"What did he say?"

"Why, he explained—with one of those famous stage leers of his—exactly what his plans were for after the performance. Spelled it out," Dullman said, jamming the cigar back in his mouth.

"And you said to him—?"

"Nothing. Look, Queen, if I went after every bum and slob I've had to deal with in show business I'd have more notches to my account than Dan'l Boone." Dullman grinned. "Anyway, you and the doctor here say you heard who Benedict put the finger on. So why cross-examine me?"

"Who occupies the dressing room just above this one?"

"Joan Truslow."

Ellery went out.

The lid of the chest marked *Tools* was open, as he had seen it on his backstage tour early in the evening. There was no knife in the tray, or anywhere else in the chest. If Dullman was telling the truth, the knife in Foster Benedict's back almost certainly had come from this tool chest.

Ellery heard two sirens coming on fast outside.

He glanced up at the narrow landing. The upper dressing room door was halfway open.

He sprang to the iron ladder.

ACT II. Scene 3.

He knocked and stepped into Joan Truslow's tiny dressing room at once, shutting the door behind him.

Joan and Roger jumped apart. Tears had left a clownish design in the girl's make-up.

Ellery set his back against the door.

"Do you make a habit of barging into ladies' dressing rooms?" Roger said truculently.

"No one seems to approve of me tonight," Ellery complained. "Rodge, there's not much time."

"For what?"

But Joan put her hand on Roger's arm. "How is he, Mr. Queen?"

"Benedict? Oh, he died."

Ellery studied her reaction carefully. It told him nothing.

"I'm sorry," she said. "Even though he was beastly."

"I saw his lips moving during your speeches in that couch scene. What was he saying to you, Joan?"

"Vile things. I can't repeat them."

"The police just got here."

She betrayed herself by the manner in which she turned away and sat down at her dressing table to begin repairing her make-up. The trivial routine was like a skillful bit of stage business, in which the effect of naturalness was produced by the most carefully thought-out artifice.

"Anyway, what are people supposed to do, go into mourning?" Roger sounded as if he had been following a separate train of thought. "He was a dirty old goat. If ever anyone asked for it, he did."

Ellery kept watching Joan's reflection in the mirror. "You know, Rodge, that's very much like a remark Stanley made a few minutes ago. It rather surprises me. Granted Benedict's outrageous behavior tonight, it was hardly sufficient reason to stick a knife in his back. Wouldn't you say?" The lipstick in Joan's fingers kept flying. "Or—on second thought —does either of you know of a sufficient reason? On the part of anyone?"

"How could we know a thing like that?"

"Speak for yourself, Rodge," Ellery smiled. "How about you, Joan?"

She murmured, "Me?" and shook her head at herself.

"Well." Ellery pushed away from the door. "Oh, Roger, last night in Arch Dullman's room, when Benedict was first mentioned as a substitute for Manson, I got the impression you knew Benedict from somewhere. Was I imagining things?"

"I can't help your impressions."

"Then you never met him before tonight?"

"I knew his smelly reputation."

"That's not what the lawyers call a responsive answer," Ellery said coldly.

Roger glared. "Are you accusing me of Benedict's murder?"

"Are you afraid I may have cause to?"

"You'd better get out of here!"

"Unfortunately, you won't be able to take this attitude with the police."

"Get out!"

Ellery shrugged as part of his own act. He had baited Roger to catch Joan off-guard. And he had caught her. She had continued her elaborate toilet at the mirror as if they were discussing the weather. His hostile exchange with Roger should have made her show some sign of alarm, or anxiety, or at least interest.

He left gloomily.

He was not prepared for the police officer he found in charge below, despite a forewarning of long standing. On the retirement of Wrightsville's perennial Chief of Police, Dakin, the old Yankee had written Ellery about his successor.

"Selectmen brought in this Anselm Newby from Connhaven," Dakin had written, "where he was a police captain with a mighty good record. Newby's young and he's tough and as far as I know he's honest and he does know modern police methods. But he's maybe not quite as smart as he thinks.

"If you ever get to Wrightsville again, Ellery, better steer clear of him. I once told him about you and he gives me a codfish look and says no New York wiseacre is ever going to mix into *his* department. It's a fact there ain't much to like about Anse."

Ellery had visualized Chief of Police Newby as a large man with muscles, a prominent jaw, and a Marine sergeant's voice. Instead, the man in the Chief's cap who turned to look him over when he was admitted to the dressing room was short and slight, almost delicately built.

"I was just going to send a man for you, Mr. Queen." Chief Newby's quiet voice was another surprise. "Where've you been?"

The quiet voice covered a sting; it was like the swish of a lazily brandished whip. But it was Newby's eyes that brought old Dakin's characterization into focus. They were of an inorganic blue, unfeeling as mineral.

"Talking to members of the company."

"Like Joan Truslow?"

Ellery thought very quickly. "Joan was one of them, Chief. I didn't mention Benedict's talking before he died, of course. But as long as we had to wait for you—"

"Mr. Queen," Newby said. "Let's understand each other right off. In Wrightsville a police investigation is run by one man. Me."

"To my knowledge it's never been run any other way."

"I've heard tell different."

"You've been misinformed. However, I've known and liked this town and its people for a long time. You can't stop me from keeping my eyes open in their interest and reaching my own conclusions. Broadcasting them, if necessary."

Anselm Newby stared at him. Ellery stared back.

"I've already talked to Dr. Farnham and Mr. Dullman," Newby said suddenly, and Ellery knew he had won a small victory. "You tell me your version."

Ellery gave him an unembroidered account. Newby listened without comment, interrupting only to acknowledge the arrival of the Coroner and issue orders to uniformed men coming in to report. Throughout Ellery's recital the Chief of Police kept an eye on a young technician who had been going over the room for fingerprints and was now taking photographs. Times had certainly changed in Wrightsville.

"Those words Benedict said, you heard them yourself?" the Chief asked when Ellery stopped. "This wasn't something Farnham heard and repeated to you?"

"We both heard them. I'm positive Dullman did, too, although he pretended he hadn't."

"Why would he do that?"

Ellery could not resist saying, "You want my *opinion*, Chief?"

The blue eyes sparked. But he merely said, "Please."

"Dullman is walking on eggs. This thing is the worst possible break for him. He wants no part of it."

"Why not?"

"Because to admit he heard Benedict's accusation would mean becoming an important witness in a sensational murder case. I don't think Dullman can stand the publicity."

"I thought show people live on publicity."

328

"Not Dullman. For an Actor's Equity member like Benedict or Manson to work in an amateur company, it has to be a legitimately amateur operation from start to finish. Arch Dullman is an 'operator.' He makes an undercover deal with someone like Stanley Bluefield—desperate to run a successfull amateur playhouse—in a set-up that otherwise satisfies Equity's strict specifications. Dullman delivers a name actor —one who's passé in the big time and who'll do anything for eating money—in return for taking over behind the scenes, with Bluefield fronting for him."

"What's Dullman get out of it?"

"He pockets most—or all—of the box office take," Ellery said. "If this deal with Bluefield became a matter of public record, Dullman might never represent a professional actor again."

"I see." Newby was watching his technician, "Well, that's very interesting, Mr. Queen. Now if you'll excuse me—"

Take that, Ellery thought, Aloud, he said, "Mind if I hang around?"

Newby said politely, "Suit yourself," and turned away.

The knife had been removed from Benedict's back and it was lying on the dressing table. It was a long, hefty hunting knife, its bloodstained blade honed to a wicked edge.

The Coroner grunted, "I'm through for now," and opened the door. Two ambulance men came in at his nod and took the body out. "I'll do the post mortem first thing in the morning."

"Could a woman have sunk the knife to the hilt?" Newby asked.

"Far's I can tell without an autopsy, it went into the heart without striking bone. If that's so, a kid could have done it." The Coroner left.

Newby walked over to the table. The technician was packing his gear. "Find any prints on the knife?"

"No, sir. It was either handled with a handkerchief or gloves or wiped off afterward. This plastic tape is pretty slick, Chief, anyway."

"What about prints elsewhere?"

"Some of Benedict's on the dressing table and on the make-up stuff, and a lot of someone else's, a man's."

"Those would be Manson's. No woman's prints?"

"No, sir. But about this knife. There are some queer marks on the handle."

329

"Marks?" Newby picked up the knife by the tip of the blade and scrutinized the haft. He seemed puzzled.

"There's some on the other side, too."

The Chief turned the knife over. "Any notion what made these, Bill?"

"Well, no, sir."

Newby studied the marks again. Without looking around he said, "Mr. Queen, did you happen to notice these marks?"

"Yes," Ellery said.

The Chief waited, as if for Ellery to go on. But Ellery did not go on. Newby's ears slowly reddened.

"We could send the knife up to the big lab in Connhaven," the young technician suggested.

"I know that, Bill! But suppose first we try to identify them on our own. Right?"

"Yes, sir."

Newby stalked out to the stage. Meekly, Ellery followed.

The little police chief's interrogation of the company was surgical. In short order he established that, between the lowering of the curtain on Act One and the discovery of the dying man, every member of the cast except Joan Truslow had either been in view of someone else or could otherwise prove an alibi. With equal economy he disposed of the stage-hands.

He had long since released the audience. Now he sent the cast and the crew home.

On the emptying of the theater the curtain had been raised and the house lights turned off. Stanley Bluefield and Archer Dullman sat in gloom and silence, too. Each man an island, Ellery thought; and he wondered how good an explorer Anselm Newby really was. For the first time he sensed an impatience, almost an eagerness, in Newby.

"Well, gentlemen, it's getting late—"

"Chief." Stanley was lying back on the set couch, his lips parted, gazing up into the flies and managing to resemble an old lady after an exhausting day. "Are you intending to close me down?"

"No call for that, Mr. Bluefield. We'll just seal off that dressing room."

"Then I can go ahead with, say, rehearsals?"

"Better figure on the day after tomorrow. The Prosecutor's office will be all over the place till then."

Stanley struggled off the couch.

"Oh, one thing before you go, Mr. Bluefield. Did you see or hear anything tonight that might help us out?"

Stanley said, "I wasn't here," and trudged off the stage.

"You, Mr. Dullman?"

"I told you all I know, Chief." Dullman shifted the remains of his cigar to the other side of his mouth. "Is it all right with you if I go see what's with my client before somebody does a carving job on him?"

"Just don't leave town. And Mr. Dullman."

"What?"

"Don't talk about what Benedict said."

When Dullman was gone, Newby said, "Well." He got up and made for the stage steps.

"Chief," Ellery said.

Newby paused.

"You don't have much of a case, you know."

The little policeman trotted down into the orchestra. He selected the aisle seat in the third row center and settled himself. Like a critic, Ellery thought. A critic who's already made up his mind.

"Gotch," Chief Newby called.

"Yes, sir."

"Get Miss Truslow."

ACT II. Scene 4.

Joan sailed out of the wings chin up. But all she saw was Ellery straddling a chair far upstage, and she began to look around uncertainly.

Roger yelled, "You down there—Newby!" and ran over to the footlights. "What's the idea keeping Miss Truslow a prisoner in her dressing room all this time?"

"Roger," Joan said.

"If you think you've got something on her, spit it out and I'll have a lawyer down here before it hits the floor!"

"Sit down, Miss Truslow," Newby's soft voice said from below. "You, too, Fowler."

Joan sat down immediately.

Whatever it was that Roger glimpsed in her violet eyes, it silenced him. He joined her on the couch, reached for her hand. She withdrew it.

Newby said, "Miss Truslow, when did you make your last stage exit?"

331

"At the end of my scene with Foster Benedict on the—on this couch."

"How long before the act ended was that?"

"About ten minutes."

"Did you go right to your dressing room?"

"Yes."

"In doing that, you had to pass by the tool chest. Was it open?"

"The chest? I can't say. I didn't notice much of anything." Joan caught her hands in the act of twisting in her lap, and she stilled them. "I was badly upset. They must have told you what he—the way he carried on during our big scene."

"Yes, I hear he gave you a rough time." The little Chief sounded sympathetic. "But you did notice the tool chest later, Miss Truslow, didn't you?"

She looked up. "Later?"

"During intermission. After Benedict got to his dressing room."

Joan blinked into the lights. "But you don't understand, Chief Newby. I went straight to my dressing room and I stayed there. I was . . . frozen, I suppose is the word. I just sat asking myself how I was going to get through the rest of the play. It was all I could think of."

"While you were up there, did you hear anything going on in the room below? In Benedict's dressing room?"

"I don't remember hearing anything."

"When did you leave your dressing room, Miss Truslow?"

"When I heard all the commotion downstairs. After he was found."

"That was the first time, you say?"

"Yes."

Newby said suddenly, "Fowler, Queen found you with this girl. How come?"

"How come?" Roger snapped. "Why, somebody ran into the prop room to tell me something had happened to Benedict. I ran back with him and spotted Joan in the crowd around Benedict's doorway. I hauled her out of there and up to her dressing room so I could put my arms around her in privacy when she broke down, which she promptly did. Wasn't that sneaky of me?"

"Then that was the first time you saw her after she left the stage?"

"I couldn't get to her before, though God knows I wanted

332

to. I was too tied up backstage—" Roger halted. "That was sneaky of *you*, Newby. And damn nasty, too! What are you trying to prove, anyway?"

"Miss Truslow, how well did you know Foster Benedict?"

Ellery saw Joan go stiff. "Know him?"

"Were you two acquainted? Ever see him before tonight?"

She said something.

"What? I couldn't hear that."

Joan cleared her throat. "No."

"Logan." A police officer jumped off the apron and darted to his Chief. Newby said something behind his hand. The man hurried up the aisle and out of the theater. "Miss Truslow, a witness says that when Benedict went into his dressing room the tool chest was open and a big knife with a taped handle was lying in the tray. I'll ask you again. Did you or didn't you leave your dressing room, climb down, go to the tool chest—"

"I didn't," Joan cried.

"—go to the tool chest, pick up the knife—"

"Hold it." Roger was on his feet. "You really want to know about that knife, Newby?"

"You have some information about it?"

"Definitely."

"What?"

"It's mine."

"Oh?" Newby sat waiting.

"I can prove it," Roger said quickly. "If you'll strip the tape off you'll find my initials machine-stamped into the haft. I've used it on hunting trips for years. I brought it to the theater just today. We'd bought some new guy-rope yesterday and I needed a sharp knife—"

"I know all about your ownership of the knife," Newby smiled. "The question isn't who owned the knife, or even who put it in the tool chest. It's who took it out of the chest and used it on Benedict. Now, Miss Truslow—"

"Excuse me," Ellery said. The Chief was startled into silence. "Roger, when did you tape the handle?"

"Tonight, after the play started. I'd used it in replacing a frayed guy-rope and I hadn't been able to keep a good grip on it because my hands were sweaty from the heat backstage. So I wound some electrician's tape around the haft in case I had to use it again in an emergency during the performance."

"When did you drop it into the chest?"

"Near the end of the act."

"I thought I'd made it clear, Mr. Queen!" The whiplash in the policeman's voice was no longer lazy. "Interrupt once more and out you go. And I mean it."

"Yes, Chief," Ellery murmured. "Sorry."

Newby was quiet. Then he said, "Now I want to be sure I've got this right, Miss Truslow. You claim you went from the stage straight to your dressing room, you stayed there all the time Benedict was being knifed in the room right under yours, you didn't hear a sound, you didn't come down till after Benedict was found dying, and at no time did you touch the knife. Is that it?"

"That's it." Joan jumped up. "No, Roger!" She walked steadily over to the footlights. "Now let me ask you a question, Chief Newby. Why are you treating me as if you've decided I killed Foster Benedict?"

"Didn't you?" Newby asked.

"I did *not* kill him!"

"Somebody said you did."

Joan peered and blinked through the glare in her eyes. "But that's not possible. It isn't true. I can't imagine anyone making up a story like that about me. Who said it?"

"Benedict, in the presence of witnesses, a few seconds before he died."

Joan said something unintelligible. Newby and Ellery sprang to their feet. But Roger was closest, and he caught her just as her legs gave way.

ACT III. Scene 1.

Ellery awoke at noon. He leaped for the door and took in the *Record,* with its familiar yellow label conveying the compliments of the Hotel Hollis. For the first time in years the *Record's* front page ran a two-line banner:

MURDER HITS WRIGHTSVILLE!
FAMOUS STAGE STAR SLAIN!

The account of the crime was wordy and inaccurate. There were publicity photos of Foster Benedict and the cast. The front page was salted with statements by Dr. Farnham, members of the audience, cast, stage crew, even police. Chief Anselm Newby's contribution was boxed but uninformative.

The *Record* quoted Stanley Bluefield ("The Playhouse must go on"), Archer Dullman ("No comment"), and Ellery Queen ("Any statement I might make about Benedict's death would encroach on the authority of your excellent Chief of Police").

There was a story on Mark Manson under a one-column cut showing him at a bar, uninjured arm holding aloft a cocktail glass ("Mr. Manson was found at the Hollis bar at a late hour last night on his discharge from Wrightsville General Hospital, in company of his manager, Archer Dullman. Asked to comment on the tragedy, Mr. Manson said, 'Words truly fail me, sir, which is why you discover me saying it with martinis.' With the help of this reporter, Mr. Dullman was finally able to persuade Mr. Manson to retire to his hotel room.")

A choppy review of the first act of *The Death of Don Juan* showed evidences of hasty editing. What the original copy had said Ellery could only imagine.

The sole reference in print to Joan was a cryptic "Miss Joan Truslow and Mr. Roger Fowler of The Playhouse staff could not be located for a statement as we went to press."

Of Foster Benedict's dying words no mention was made.

Ellery ordered breakfast and then hurried his shower.

He was finishing his second cup of coffee when the telephone rang. It was Roger.

"Where the devil did you hide Joan last night?"

"In my Aunt Carrie's house." Roger sounded harassed. "She's in Europe, left me a key. Joan was in no condition to face reporters or yak with the likes of Emmeline DuPré. Her father knows where we are, but that's all."

"Didn't you tell Newby?"

"Tell Newby? It's Newby who smuggled us over to Aunt Carrie's. Considerate guy, Newby. He has a cop staked out in the back yard and another in plain clothes parked across the street in an unmarked car."

Ellery said nothing.

Roger continued grimly, "I gave Joanie a sleeping pill and stayed up most of the night biting my nails. Far as I know, Newby has no direct evidence against Joan—just those last words of a dying man whose mind, if you ask me, was already in outer space. Just the same, I'll feel better with a lawyer around. Before I call one in, though . . ." Roger hesitated. "What I mean is, I'm sorry I blew my stack last night. Would you come over here right away?"

"Where is it?" Ellery almost chuckled.

Roger gave him an address on State Street, in the oldest residential quarter of town.

It was an immaculately preserved 18th-century mansion under the protection of the great elms that were the pride of State Street. The black shades were drawn, and from the street the clapboard house looked shut down.

Ellery strolled around to the rear and knocked on the back door, pretending not to notice the policeman lurking inside a latticed sumerhouse. Roger admitted him and led the way through a huge kitchen and pantry and along a cool hall to a stately parlor whose furniture was under dust covers.

Joan was waiting in an armchair. She looked tired and withdrawn.

"This is all Roger's idea," she said, managing a smile. "From the way he's been carrying on—"

"Do you want my help, Joan?"

"Well, if Roger's right—"

"I'm afraid he is."

"But it's so stupid, Mr. Queen. Why would Foster Benedict accuse *me*? And even if he had some mysterious reason, how can anyone believe it? I didn't go near him . . . I've always hated knives," she cried. "I couldn't use a knife on a trout."

"It isn't a trout that was knifed. Joan, look at me."

She raised her head.

"Did you kill Benedict?"

"No! How many times do I have to say it?"

He lit a cigarette while he weighed her anger. She was an actress of talent—her performance the night before in the face of Benedict's coarse horseplay had proved that. It was a difficult decision.

"All right, Rodge," Ellery said suddenly. "Speak your piece."

"It's not mine. It's Joan's."

"I'm all ears, Joan."

Her chest rose and fell. "I lied to Chief Newby when I said I'd never known Foster Benedict before last night. I met Foster six years ago here in Wrightsville. I was still in high school. Roger was home from college for the summer."

336

"In *Wrightsville?*"

"I know, he acted as if he'd never heard of Wrightsville. But then I realized it wasn't an act at all. He'd simply forgotten, Mr. Queen. He was one of Stanley Bluefield's house guests for a few weeks that summer."

"He didn't even remember Stanley," Roger said bitterly. "Let's face it, the great lover was one step ahead of the butterfly net."

"Then it was a practical lunacy," Ellery remarked. "Every six months out of the past ten or twelve years Benedict practiced house-guesting as a sort of unemployment insurance. Dullman claims he averaged fifteen hosts a year. He must have had a hard time keeping track. Go on, Joan."

"I was sixteen, and Foster Benedict had been my secret crush for years," Joan said in a low voice. "When I read in the *Record* that he was staying at Mr. Bluefield's I did a very silly thing. I phoned him."

She flushed. "You can imagine the conversation—how much I admired his work, my stage ambitions . . . He must have been having a dull time, because he said he'd like to meet me. I was in seventh heaven. He began to take me out. Drives up to the lake. Moonlight readings . . . I certainly asked for it."

She sat forward nervously. "I guess it was like one of those old-time melodramas—the handsome roué, the foolish young girl—the only thing missing was the mortgage. Would you believe that when he promised me a part in his next play I actually fell for it?" Joan laughed. "And then he went away, and I wrote him some desperate love letters he didn't bother to answer, and I didn't see or hear from him again until last night.

"And then when he made his royal entrance into The Playhouse, he not only didn't remember Wrightsville, or Mr. Bluefield, he'd forgotten me, too."

She was staring into the mirror of the time-polished floor. "I was a stranger to him. Just another scalp to add to his collection. I'd meant so little to him that not even my features had registered, let alone my name."

"I warned you six years ago that Benedict was pure poison," Roger shouted, "but would you listen? Ellery, if you knew how many times I've begged her to get off this acting kick and marry me—"

"Let's get to you, Rodge. I take it your evasions last night

337

also covered up a prior acquaintance with Benedict?"

"How could I explain without dragging Joan into it?"

"Then you met him at the same time, six years ago?"

"I knew she was dating him—a high school kid!—and I'd read of his weakness for the young ones. I was fit to be tied. I collared him one night after he took Joan home and I warned him to lay off. I said I'd kill him, or some such juvenile big talk. He laughed in my face and I knocked him cold. He was sore as hell about it—I'd mussed up his precious profile—and he banged right down to headquarters to prefer charges of assault. That was when Dakin was Chief of Police. But then I guess Benedict had second thoughts—bad publicity, or something. Anyway, he dropped the charges and left town."

"Did the brawl get into the *Record?*"

Roger shrugged. "It was a one-day wonder."

"And was Joan named in the story?"

"Well, yes. Some oaf at headquarters shot his mouth off. Dakin fired him."

Ellery shook his head. "You two are beyond belief. How did you expect to keep all that from Newby? Last night when you denied having known Benedict, Joan, didn't you notice Newby send one of his men on an errand? He's a city-trained policeman—he wouldn't take your word. He'd check the *Record* morgue and his own headquarters files. He may even have phoned the New York City police to search Benedict's apartment—Benedict's bragged often enough in print about his collection of feminine love letters.

"So Newby either knows already, or he'll learn very soon, that you both lied to him on a crucial question, and exactly what happened six years ago, and exactly why. Don't you see what you've handed him?—On a silver platter?"

Joan was mute.

"From Newby's viewpoint there's a strong circumstantial case against you, Joan. Situated in the only other dressing room on that side of the theater, you had the best opportunity to kill Benedict without being seen. The weapon? You wouldn't have had to move a step out of your way en route to Benedict's dressing room to take the knife from the tool chest. What's been holding Newby up is motive."

Joan's lips moved, but nothing came out.

"Newby knows perfectly well that Benedict's conduct on stage last night, rotten as it was, toward a girl who'd never laid eyes on him before would hardly pass muster as a reason for her to run for the nearest knife. But with the background of that romance between you six years ago in this very town, Joan, and your lie about it, and especially if the New York police dig up your letters, Benedict's humiliation of you in public last night takes on an entirely different meaning. It becomes a motive that would convince anybody. And any jury.

"Add to opportunity, weapon, and motive Benedict's dying declaration, and you see how near you are to being formally charged with the murder."

"You're a help," Roger flared. "I thought you'd be on Joan's side."

"And on yours, Roger?"

"Mine?"

"Don't you know you're Newby's ace in the hole? You threatened six years ago to kill Benedict—"

"Are you serious? That was just talk!"

"—and you beat him up. You've admitted the knife that killed Benedict is yours, and you brought it to the theater the day of the murder. You probably can't account for your whereabouts every minute of the short murder period. If not for Benedict's statement, Newby would have a stronger case against you than against Joan. As it is, Rodge, you may be facing an accessory charge."

For once Roger found nothing to say. Joan's hand stole into his.

"However," Ellery said briskly. "Joan, do you still say you didn't kill Benedict?"

"Of course. Because I didn't."

"Would you be willing to take a test that might prove you didn't?"

"You mean a lie detector test?"

"Something far more direct. On the other hand, I've got to point out that if you did kill Benedict, this test might constitute evidence against you as damning as a fingerprint."

Joan rose. "What do I do, Mr. Queen?"

"Rodge, ask the police officer in the car parked across the street to drive Joan and you to Newby's office. I'll meet you there." He took Joan's hand in both of his. "This is beginning to shape up as quite a girl."

"Never mind her shape," Roger said. "Can't you go with us?"

"I have something to pick up," Ellery said, "at a hardware store."

Ellery walked into Anselm Newby's office with a small package under his arm to find Joan and Roger seated close together under Newby's mineral eye. A tall thin man in a business suit turned from the window as Ellery came in.

"Fowler's been telling me about some test or other you want to make, Queen," the little police chief said acidly. "I thought we'd agreed you were to keep your nose out of this case."

"That was a unilateral agreement, you'll recall," Ellery said, smiling. "However, I'm sure you wouldn't want to make a false arrest, and the Prosecutor of Wright County wouldn't want to try a hopeless case. Isn't that so, Mr. Odham?" he asked the man at the window.

"So you know who I am." The tall man came forward with a grin.

"The *Record* runs your photo with flattering regularity."

Prosecutor Odham pumped Ellery's hand. "Art Chalanski, my predecessor, has told me some fantastic stories about you."

"Apparently Chief Newby doesn't share your enthusiasm for fantasy," Ellery murmured, "By the way, Mr. Odham, you *were* about to charge Joan Truslow with the Benedict murder, weren't you? I haven't dared ask the Chief."

Newby glared and Prosecutor Odham chuckled. But there was no humor in the Prosecutor's frosty gray eyes.

"What have you got, Mr. Queen?"

Ellery said politely to the police chief, "May I see the knife?"

"What for?"

"In a moment. Don't worry, Chief. I won't so much as breathe on it."

Newby opened the safe behind his desk and brought out a shallow box padded with surgical cotton. The bloodstained knife lay on the cotton. He held on to the box pointedly.

"This thin short line of indentations in the tape of the handle." Ellery made no attempt to touch the knife. "Have you determined yet what made them, Chief?"

"Why?"

"Because they may either blow up your case against Joan or nail it down."

Newby flushed. "You'll have to show me."

"I intend to. But you haven't answered my question. Have you decided what kind of marks these are?"

340

"I suppose you know!"

"Anse," Odham said. "No, Mr. Queen, we haven't. I take it you have?"

"Yes."

"Well?" Newby said. "What are they marks of?"

"Teeth."

"Teeth?" The Prosecutor looked startled. So did Joan and Roger.

"Maybe they're teeth marks and maybe they're not," Newby said slowly, "though I admit we didn't think of teeth. But even if they are. Only two teeth could be involved—"

"Four," Ellery said. "Two upper and two lower—there are corresponding impressions on the other side of the haft. What's more, I'm positive they're front teeth."

"Suppose they are. These could only be edge impressions, and they're certainly not distinctive enough for a positive identification."

"You may be right," Ellery said soberly. "They may not prove to be positive evidence. But they may well prove to be negative evidence."

"What's that supposed to mean?"

"Suppose I can demonstrate that Joan Truslow's front teeth couldn't possibly have left these marks? Or any pairs of her contiguous teeth upper and lower, for that matter? Mind you, I don't know whether they demonstrate any such thing. The only teeth I've experimented with so far are my own. I've explained to Joan the risk she's running. Nevertheless, she's agreed to the test."

"Is that so, Miss Truslow?" the Prosecutor demanded.

Joan nodded. She had a death grip on the sides of her chair seat. As for Roger, he had entangled himself in an impossible combination of arms and legs.

Odham said, "Then Mr. Queen, you go right ahead."

Ellery's package remained intact. "Before I do, let's be sure we agree on the significance of the teeth marks. Last night Roger told us he didn't put the freshly taped knife in the tool chest backstage until Act One was nearly over. Rodge, were those marks in the tape when you dropped the knife in the chest?"

"You've forgotten," Roger said shortly. "I've never seen them."

"My error. Take a look."

Roger untangled himself and took a look. "I don't see

341

how they could have been. The knife wasn't out of my possession until I put it in the chest, and I'm certainly not in the habit of gnawing on knife handles." He went back to Joan's side and entangled himself again.

"What would you expect Fowler to say?" Newby said.

Joan's hand checked Roger just in time.

"Well, if you won't accept Roger's testimony," Ellery said, "consider Arch Dullman's. Last night Dullman said he saw the knife in the chest directly after the curtain came down— as Benedict came offstage, in fact—and he was positive there were no indentations in the tape at that time. Didn't Dullman tell you that, Chief?"

Newby bit his lip.

"By the testimony, then, someone bit into the tape *after* Benedict entered his dressing room and *before* we found him. In other words, *during the murder period.*" Ellery began to unwrap his package. "The one person who we know beyond dispute handled the knife during the murder period was the murderer. It's a reasonable conclusion that the impressions were made by the murderer's teeth."

Chief Newby's teeth were locked. But Odham said, "Go on, Mr. Queen."

Out of the wrappings Ellery took a roll of new black plastic friction tape and a large hunting knife. He stripped the cellophane from the roll and handed roll and knife to Roger. "You taped the original knife, Rodge. Do a repeat on this one." Roger set to work. "Meanwhile, Joan, I'd like you to take a close look at the original."

Joan got up and walked over to Newby. She seemed calmer than the Chief.

She really has talent, Ellery thought. "Notice the exact position of the marks relative to the edge of the handle."

"About an eighth of an inch from the edge."

"Yes. Oh, thanks." Ellery took the test knife from Roger and gave it to Joan. "I want you to take two bites. First with your front teeth about an eighth of an inch from the edge, as in the other one." He looked at her. "Go ahead, Joan."

But Joan stood painfully still.

"The moment of truth, Joan?" Ellery said with a smile. "Then try the Method. You're a pirate and you're boarding the fat Spanish galleon with a knife in your teeth, like any self-respecting buccaneer." He said sharply, "Do it."

Joan placed the haft to her mouth, and bit into it firmly.

Ellery took it from her at once and examined the marks. "Good! Now I want you to take a second bite—well clear of the first, Joan, so the two bites don't overlap. This time, though, make it a full bite."

When she returned the knife Ellery ran to the window. "May I have the other one, Chief?" He was already studying the test impressions through his lens. Newby, quite pale, brought the murder weapon, Odham at his heels.

Joan and Roger remained where they were, in a dreadful quiet.

"See for yourselves."

The police chief peered, squinted, compared. He went back to his desk for a transparent ruler. He made a great many deliberate measurements. When he was through examining the upper surfaces of the hafts he turned the knives over and did it all again.

Finally he looked up. "I guess, Mr. Odham," he said in a rather hollow voice, "you'd best check these yourself."

The Prosecutor seized knives and lens. Afterward there was a glint of anger in his eyes. "No impressions of any two adjoining teeth, either in the matching bite or the full set, are identical with the impressions on the murder knife. Same sort of marks, all right, but entirely different in detail—not as wide, not the same spacing—there can't be any doubt about it. You have a lot to thank Mr. Queen for, Miss Truslow. And so do we, Anse. I'll be talking to you later."

Not until Odham was gone did Joan's defenses crumble. She sank into Roger's arms, sobbing.

Ellery turned to the window, waiting for Newby's explosion. To his surprise nothing happened, and he turned back. There was the slender little chief, slumped on his tail, feet on desk, looking human.

"I sure had it coming, Queen," he said ruefully. "What really gripes me most is having put all my eggs in one basket. Boom."

Ellery grinned. "I've laid my quota of omelets, Chief. Do you know anyone in this business who hasn't?"

Newby got to his feet. "Well, now what? Between Benedict's putting the finger on this girl and your removing it, I'm worse off than when I started. Can you make any sense out of this, Queen?"

"To a certain point."

"What point's that?"

Ellery tucked his lens away. "I know now who killed Benedict and why, if that's any help."

"Thanks, buddy."

"No, I mean it."

"I wish I could appreciate the rib," Newby sighed, "but somehow I'm not in the mood."

"But it's not a rib, Chief. The only thing is, I haven't a particle of proof." Ellery rubbed his nose as Newby gaped. "Though there *is* a notion stirring . . . and if it should work . . ."

ACT III. Scene 3.

The following morning's *Record* shouted:

Local Girl Cleared in Killing!

The lead story was earmarked "Exclusive" and began:

"Joan Truslow of the Wrightsville Playhouse company was proved innocent yesterday of the Foster Benedict murder by Ellery Queen, the *Record* learned last night from an unusually reliable source.

"Miss Truslow, allegedly Chief Anselm Newby's main suspect in the Broadway star's sensational killing, was cleared by the New York detective in a dramatic session at police headquarters. A secret demonstration took place in the presence of Chief Newby and Prosecutor Loren Odham of Wright County. The exact nature of the test was not disclosed, but it is said to have involved the knife that slew Benedict.

"Chief Newby would neither affirm nor deny the *Record's* information.

" 'I'll say that Miss Truslow is no longer a suspect,' Newby told the *Record*. 'However, we are not satisfied with some of her testimony. She will be questioned further soon.'

"Asked whether he was referring to strong rumors around headquarters last night, Chief Newby admitted that Miss Truslow is believed to be withholding testimony vital to the solution of the murder.

"By press time last night, Miss Truslow had not been located by newsmen. She is said to be hiding out somewhere in town.

"Prosecutor Odham could not be reached," *etc., etc.*

The *Record* story's "Exclusive" tag was an understandable brag. Wire service and metropolitan newspaper reporters had invaded Wrightsville at the first flash of Foster Benedict's slaying, and the war for news raged through the town. The *Record* disclosure almost wrecked Stanley Bluefield's plans to take up his personal war with Wrightsville's Philistines where mere murder had broken it off.

Stanley had sent out a call for his entire company. They converged on The Playhouse on the morning the *Record* story broke to find the forces of the press drawn up in battle array. In a moment the surrounded locals were under full-scale attack; and Stanley, purple from shouting, sent to police headquarters for reinforcements.

A wild fifteen minutes later Chief Newby laid down the terms of a truce.

"You people have one hour out here for interviews with Mr. Bluefield's company," the Chief snapped. "Nobody gets into the theater after that without a signed pass from me."

As it turned out, the newsmen retired from the field in less than half their allotted time. One of their two main objectives was not present: Ellery had slipped out of the Hollis early in the morning and disappeared.

Their other target, Joan, who showed up at The Playhouse with Roger, had refused to parley. To every question fired at her about "the testimony vital to the solution" that she was reported to be withholding, Joan looked more frightened and shook her head violently. "I have nothing to say, nothing," she kept repeating. Nor would she reveal where she was staying.

On being attacked in his turn, Roger became totally deaf. In the end he had charged into the theater with her, and the press beat a disgusted retreat shortly after, to bivouac at various High Village bars.

Chief Newby stationed police at the stage entrance, fire exits, and in the lobby, and left for an undisclosed destination.

So it was with slightly hysterical laughter that the company greeted Stanley Bluefield's opening words: "Alone at last."

They were assembled onstage under the working lights. Stanley had hopped up on a set chair.

"You'll all be happy to hear that we're going right ahead with *The Death of Don Juan.*" He raised his little paw for silence. "With due respect to the late Foster Benedict, he saw fit to make a farcical joke out of our production. We're going to do it *properly*."

Someone called out, "But Mr. Bluefield, we don't have a Don Juan."

Stanley showed his teeth. "Ah, but we will have, and a good one, too. I can't disclose his name because I haven't completed the business arrangements. He should be joining us the day after tomorrow.

"I spent most of yesterday making cuts and line changes and revising some of the business, especially in Act One, where I think we've been in danger of wrong audience reactions. Today and tomorrow we'll go over the changes, so we ought to be in good shape when our new Don Juan gets here. Meanwhile, as a favor to me, Mr. Manson has kindly consented to walk through the part for us. Does anyone need a pencil . . . ?"

They plunged into the work with relief.

The day passed quickly. Sandwiches and coffee were brought in twice. There was only one interruption, when a tabloid photographer tried to get into the theater by stretching a ladder across the alley between a window in the next building and The Playhouse roof. But he was intercepted, and an extra policeman was assigned to the roof.

It was almost ten o'clock when Stanley called a halt.

The company began to disperse.

"Not you, Miss Truslow!"

Joan stopped in her tracks. It was Chief Newby.

"I haven't wanted to interfere with Mr. Bluefield's working day. But now, Miss Truslow, you and I are going to have a real old-fashioned heart-to-heart talk. Whether it takes five minutes or all night is up to you. I think you know what I'm talking about."

Joan groped for one of the set chairs. "I have nothing to tell you! Why won't you let me alone?"

"She's out on her feet, Chief," Roger protested. "Can't this wait?"

"Not any more," Newby said quietly. "You stay where you are, Miss Truslow, while I get rid of those newspaper men outside. I don't want the papers in on this just yet. I'll come back for you when the street's clear."

The theater emptied. Lights began winking out. One harsh spotlight remained onstage. Joan cowered in its glare.

"Roger, what am I going to do? I don't know what to do."

"You know what to do, Joanie," Roger said gently.

"He won't let go of me till . . . ."

"Till what? Till you tell him what you're hiding?" Roger pushed a curl of damp blonde hair back from her forehead. "I know you've been hiding something, darling. I've known it longer than Newby. What is it? Can't you tell even me?"

Joan's hands quivered in her lap.

"He's bound to get it out of you tonight."

"Rodge—I'm afraid."

"That's why I want you to share it with me, baby. Look, Joan, I love you. What good would I be if I didn't share your troubles?"

"Rodge . . ."

She swallowed twice, hard, looked around nervously. The deep silence of the theater seemed to reassure her.

"All right. All right, Rodge . . . The other night—during the intermission—when I was in my dressing room feeling so hurt by Foster's not remembering me . . . ."

"Yes?"

"I decided to go down to his dressing room and—and . . . Oh, Rodge, I don't know why I wanted to! Maybe to tell him what I thought of him . . . ."

"Hurry it up," Roger urged her. "The reason doesn't matter! What happened?"

"I was about to step onto the ladder from the landing when I heard Foster's dressing room door open below, and . . . *I saw him.*"

"The murderer?" Roger cried.

Joan nodded, shuddering. "I saw him sneak out . . . and away."

"Did you recognize him?"

"Yes."

"But my God, Joan, why didn't you tell Newby?"

"Because he'd accuse me of making it up. At that time the Chief was sure I'd done it."

"But now he knows you didn't!"

"Now I'm just plain scared, Roger."

"That Benedict's killer will come after you? He's not getting the chance!" Roger cupped her chin fiercely. "You're ending this nightmare right now, young lady. Let me get out of these work clothes, and then you're going outside to tell Newby who murdered Benedict—and the more reporters that hear it the better. Don't move from here, Joanie. I'm only going as far as the prop room—I'll be right back."

The darkness swallowed him. His rapid footsteps died away.

Joan found herself alone on the stage.

She was perched stiff-backed on the edge of the big Spanish chair at the base of the light cone formed by the spot. There was no other light anywhere. The dark surrounded and held her fast, like walls.

The dark and the silence. The silence that had reassured her before, now made her uneasy.

Joan began to move her head. They were small, jerky movements. She kept probing here and there with furtive glances, over her shoulder, toward the invisible wings, out into the crouching blackness beyond the dead footlights.

"Rodge?" she called.

The quaver of her own voice only brought the silence closer.

"*Roger?*"

Joan curled up in the chair suddenly, shut her eyes tight.

And as if drawn to the place of her imprisonment by her fear, a bulky blob of something detached itself from the murky upstage formlessness and crept toward the light.

It began to take stealthy shape.

The shape of a man.

Of a man with something gripped at chest level.

A knife.

"*Now!*" Ellery's roar dropped from the catwalk far over the stage like a bomb.

Quick as Chief Newby and his men were, Roger was quicker. He hurtled out of the wings and launched himself at the man with the knife like a swimmer at the start of a race. He hit the man at the knees and the man went over with a crash that rattled the stage. The knife went skittering off somewhere. The man kicked out viciously, and Roger fell on him and there was a sickening *crack!* and the man screamed, once. Then he was still.

As soon as he could, Chief Newby hurried to the set chair. "That was as good an act as Broadway ever saw! And it took guts, Miss Truslow." He bent over the chair, puzzled. "Miss Truslow?"

But Miss Truslow was no longer acting. Miss Truslow had peacefully passed out.

One of the waitresses in the Hollis private dining room was clearing the table as the other poured their coffee.

"I hope you didn't mind my choice of menu, Joan," Ellery was saying.

Under the cloth her fingers were interwoven with Roger's. "How could I mind such a lovely steak?"

"I was commemorating the steak knife he lifted from the Hollis in your honor."

"In case I forgot?" Joan laughed. "That was the longest dream of my life, Ellery. But I'm awake now, and that's even lovelier."

"Queen, where's the dessert you promised?" Chief Newby asked. "I've got a lot to do at headquarters."

"No dessert for me," Joan said dreamily.

"Likewise," Roger said likewise.

"You don't eat this dessert," the Chief explained, "you listen to it. Anway, *I'm* listening."

"Well, it goes like this," Ellery began. "I kept urging Benedict, as he was dying, to tell me who stabbed him. When he was able to get some words out, seconds before he died, Conk Farnham and I were sure we heard him say, 'The heroine'—an unmistakable accusation of you, Joan. You were heroine of the play, and Benedict didn't know—or, as it turned out, didn't remember—your name.

"But then the toothmark test proved Joan's innocence. Dying men may accuse innocent persons falsely in mystery stories, but in life they show a simple respect for the truth. So Benedict couldn't have meant the heroine of the play. He must have meant a word that sounded like heroine but meant something else. There's only one word that sounds like heroine-with-an-e, and that's heroin-without-an-e.

"The fact was," Ellery continued, "at the very last Benedict wasn't answering my who-did-it question at all. His dying mind had rambled off to another element of the crime. Heroin. The narcotic."

He emptied his coffee cup, and Chief Newby hastily refilled it.

"But no drug was found," Joan protested. "How did drugs come into it?"

"Just what I asked myself. To answer it called for reconstructing the situation.

349

"When Act One ended, Benedict entered the star dressing room for the first time. He had forgotten to bring along his make-up kit and Arch Dullman had told him to use the make-up in the dressing room. In view of Benedict's dying statement, it is now clear that he must have opened one of the boxes, perhaps labeled make-up powder, and instead of finding powder in it he found heroin."

"Benedict's finding of the drug just pointed to the killer," Newby objected. "You claimed to be dead certain."

"I was. I had another line to him that tied him to the killing hand and foot," Ellery said. "Thusly:

"The killer obviously didn't get to the dressing room until Benedict was already there—if he'd been able to beat Benedict to the room no murder would have been necessary. He'd simply have taken the heroin and walked out.

"So now I had him standing outside the dressing room, with Benedict inside exploring the unfamiliar make-up materials, one box of which contained the heroin.

"Let's take a good look at this killer. He's in a panic. He has to shut Benedict's mouth about the drug before, as it were, Benedict can open it. And there's the tool chest a step or two from the door, the tape-handled knife lying temptingly in the tray.

"Killer therefore grabs knife.

"Now he has the knife clutched in one hand and all he has to do is open the dressing room door with the other—"

"Which he can't do!" Newby exclaimed.

"Exactly. The haft of the knife showed his teeth marks—he had held the knife in his mouth. A man with two normal hands who must grip a knife in one and open a door with the other has no need to put the knife in his mouth. Plainly, then, he didn't have the use of *both* hands. One must have been incapacitated.

"And that could mean only Mark Manson, one of whose hands was in a cast that extended to the elbow."

Joan made a face. "Really, Roger, was it necessary to break his wrist all over again last night?"

"It was him or me—or you." Roger leaned over and kissed her. Joan blushed.

"Don't mind these two," Newby said. "You sure make it sound easy, Queen!"

"I shouldn't have explained," Ellery sighed. "Well, the rest followed easily. The hospital said they would keep Manson under observation for twenty-four hours. So he must have been discharged too late on opening night to get to the theater before the play started. He must have arrived during intermission.

"With the audience in the alleys and the fire exit doors open, all Manson had to do was drape his jacket over his injured arm to conceal the cast, mingle with the crowd in the alley, stroll into the theater, and make his way to the backstage door on the side where the star dressing room is. He simply wasn't noticed then or afterward, when he slipped out and parked in the Hollis bar—where Dullman and the *Record* reporter found him."

"But Mark Manson and *dope*," Joan said.

Ellery shrugged. "Manson's an old man, Joan, with no theatrical future except an actors' home and his scrapbooks. But he's still traveling in stock, hitting small towns and big-city suburbs. It's the perfect cover for a narcotics distributor. No glory, but loot galore."

"He did a keen Wrightsville business before he took that tumble. We've already picked up the two local pushers he supplied." Chief Newby folded his napkin grimly. "Middlemen in the dope racket are usually too scared to talk, but I guess the pain of that wrist you broke for him all over again, Fowler, was kind of frazzling. Or maybe he figures it'll help when he comes up on the murder rap. Anyway, Manson got real chatty last night. The Feds are pulling in the big fish now."

Ellery pushed his chair back. "And that, dear hearts, as the late Mr. Benedict might have said, is my cue to go on—on to that vacation waiting for me in the Mahoganies."

"And for yours truly it's back to work," Newby said, pushing his chair back too.

"Wait! Please?" Joan was tugging at Roger's sleeve. "Rodge . . . haven't you always said—?"

"Yes?" Roger said alertly.

"I mean, who wants to be an actress?"

That was how it came about that young Roger Fowler was seen streaking across the Square that afternoon with young Joan Truslow in breathless tow, taking the short cut to the Town Clerk's office, while far behind puffed the Chief of Police and the visiting Mr. Queen, their two witnesses required by law.